ghost writing

DANIELLE SMYTH

ASTRALUMEN
PRESS

Copyright © 2025 by Danielle Smyth. All rights reserved.

No part of this publication may be reproduced, distributed, or transmitted in any form or by any means, including photocopying, recording, or other electronic or mechanical methods, without the prior written permission of the publisher, except as permitted by U.S. copyright law. For permission requests, contact the author at info@daniellesmythbooks.com.

This is a work of fiction. Names, characters, businesses, places, events, and incidents are either the products of the author's imagination or used in a fictitious manner. Any resemblance to actual persons, living or dead, or actual events is purely coincidental.

Book cover design and cover illustrations by Danielle Smyth.

Editing by Dan Smyth.

ISBN 979-8-9933163-2-1 (paperback); ISBN 979-8-9933163-1-4 (hardcover); ISBN 979-8-9933163-0-7 (Kindle eBook)

Library of Congress Control Number: 2025947760

Publisher's Cataloging-in-Publication data

Smyth, Danielle, author.

Ghost Writing / Danielle Smyth. — First edition. — Burnt Hills, NY: Astralumen Press, 2025.

Edited by Dan Smyth; cover design and illustration by Danielle Smyth.

LCCN: 2025947760

ISBN (Paperback): 979-8-9933163-2-1 | ISBN (Hardcover): 979-8-9933163-1-4 | ISBN (Kindle eBook): 979-8-9933163-0-7

LCSH: Ghostwriters—Fiction | Women—Fiction | Family life—Fiction | Romance fiction

Classification: LCC: PS3619.M66 G46 2025 | DDC: 813/.6–dc23

Visit the author's website at www.daniellesmythbooks.com

Printed in the U.S.A.

Published by Astralumen Press: www.astralumenpress.com

This book is dedicated to the real-life Esperanza, who was larger than life in every conceivable way, and to my husband, who taught me a thing or two about falling in love in a library.

one

A blast of cold air invades my lungs as I open the library's double doors, leaving the humid mid-Atlantic summer behind. Shouldering my laptop bag, I push past the circulation desk and find an open table near the back window.

I let the bag drop and start to take out my MacBook, but my phone buzzes in my pocket. Sighing, I pull it out. It's Thomas. I'm not ready to talk to him.

"No phone calls in the library," I mumble wryly. I silence the phone and toss it into the depths of my bag.

Taking a deep breath, I finish setting up my workstation: laptop, notebook, pencil. Pile of boring finance books. I slide into my chair and stare at the cursor blinking expectantly on my screen. I probably should be more excited to be ghostwriting my first book, but it's a marketing piece for Thomas's boss. Not exactly my dream job.

I scan the room for some sort of distraction, noting first the mom wrangling three kids and a veritable mountain of books at the checkout. She looks beyond overwhelmed as her youngest daughter attempts to climb her leg while the older two kids play tug-of-war with a DVD.

"Freya and Max! Stop that right now! Josie, get off me." The woman shoves her library card at the clerk and apologizes for their chaos, then haphazardly adjusts her blonde topknot.

The clerk, a late-twenty-something in a green plaid shirt, just chuckles. "You'd be surprised at the sorts of chaos we deal with in here," he says, scanning her card and sliding it back across the counter.

The frazzled mom gives him a wan smile, as if doubting anything could possibly be more ridiculous than the game of duck, duck, goose her children are now playing in the middle of the floor.

"Just last week, we had to call the police to remove a flasher," the clerk says conspiratorially.

I laugh before I can stop myself, and they quickly turn in my direction, the illusion of a private conversation shattered.

"I know everyone says you shouldn't judge a book by its cover, but I would've been okay with him keeping his dust jacket on, if you catch my drift," the clerk continues, grinning at me while he says it.

I snicker, then look down. I should stop eavesdropping.

A man who looks like he might have witnessed the formation of the universe coughs loudly from behind his newspaper. I guess all the flasher talk is too much for his antiquated sensibilities.

"Thanks, Will," the woman at the desk grunts as she pulls a pile of what must be 20 books toward herself and shoves them into an enormous tote bag.

"Have a good day, Susan," he says. "Bye, ducks!" He waves to the kids. They troop out of the library in a cacophony of youthful energy that I wished I'd enjoyed more when I had it.

Let's be real, I think to myself. *I've never had that much energy, either at their age or now that I'm nearing 2 times 10 plus 6.* It's easier to turn my age and my associated lack of accomplishments into an equation than to face them.

Grumpily, I turn my attention back to my laptop and the mind-numbing task at hand.

. . .

WHEN I LEAVE the library three hours later, I decide I'm ready to deal with Thomas. I dig my phone out of my bag and see I have three new missed calls, none of which are from my boyfriend. In fact, all three of them are from my Aunt Esperanza.

I chuckle to myself. Esperanza is notorious for worrying that maybe one of her calls didn't go through, and perhaps that's why you didn't answer. Just in case, she typically dials repeatedly.

She's also left me three voicemails. I hit play on the first one as I unlock my car.

"Oh, hello, Callie," it begins, as if she's surprised to find herself in my inbox. "I was just thinking, do you need any chairs for your little apartment? Because I have two chairs that I'm not using, and a dining table. A nice dining table. Last time I was over, I thought things looked a little bare at your place, and maybe you'd want these. I really don't need them. Anyway, call me up!"

I smile. So like Esperanza, to try to give away all of her earthly possessions. She only has one table. But I believe her that she isn't using it. I don't think she eats in her kitchen very often. In fact, she often keeps her refrigerator unplugged, because she's never home and can barely afford groceries.

I'm pretty sure the last time that table saw action was whenever I last visited her. I make a mental note to grocery shop for her this week, then I play message number two.

"Oh, Callie? Hi, it's Esperanza again. I just called you, and there was a clicking noise when I hung up, so I thought maybe you were trying to call me. I have a table. It's a nice table for your little apartment. Maybe you want it? Call me back!"

I slide my bag onto the passenger seat of the car and hit play on the last voicemail. "Callie!" It starts with an excited shout. "It's me! Listen, I have to go out. I'm walking to your grandmother Josephine's. So if you try to call me back, I won't be home. Call me at Josephine's. I'll call you when I get home! Love you, kid!"

I laugh out loud without really meaning to. Esperanza is so quirky. She's actually my great-aunt, but I've always just called her

Esperanza. She's like a second mother to my mom, so she's been around most of my life.

Every concert, every soccer game, every birthday party—there was Esperanza, fashionably early by at least an hour (but usually more), carrying a bag of doughnuts or some random treasure she'd collected that she thought someone might want.

Once, she showed up at my parents' house on Christmas two hours before we'd asked guests to come. She had a half-empty container of walnut cream cheese in her hand. "Hey, kid!" She grinned when I answered the door. "I bought you a bagel, but I ate it. Can you use this cream cheese?"

I told her I couldn't, so she parked herself on the couch and ate the rest of it with a spoon.

Then, she was upset with herself because cream cheese is "too fattening," so she walked on our treadmill in her socks until the rest of the family showed up. This was a pretty typical visit with Esperanza.

I roll my window down and breathe a sigh of relief as the breeze hits my face, offering momentary respite from the stifling July heat. I dial Esperanza's number. No answer. She must still be at my grandmother's house. I call Josephine's landline instead.

The phone rings just once, and then a chipper voice greets me. "Hello! Callie?"

I laugh. "Hi, Esperanza. How did you know it was me?" *Of course* she would be answering someone else's phone.

Esperanza explains like it should have been obvious. "I told you to call me here."

"Too true. Hey, thanks for the offer about the table. You're right that I don't have one, but I really don't want to take yours."

"But I want you to have it! I don't need it!"

Esperanza gets agitated when she feels like someone isn't understanding her, so I want to proceed gently. "Yeah, but what about when you have guests? Or when you eat your dinner?" I ask.

"You know I'm never home," she retorts. "I'm just going to bring it by your place tomorrow. Tell your roommate I'm coming over."

At the thought of this 83-year-old woman (who, ostensibly, looks and acts about 70) dragging a dining table down the stairs from her second-story apartment, loading it *into* her car, driving for over an hour, and pulling it back *out of* her car, I blanch a little. "No, no. Please don't. I'll come by tomorrow after work and take a look. I'm also going to take you grocery shopping. Plug in your fridge."

She chuckles. "Okay, C. We'll talk about it then. Bye, kid!"

"Have a good night," I say, hanging up as I start the car. I breathe a sigh of relief. The engine doesn't always want to turn over, especially on stifling hot days like this one. But what can you expect from a 15-year-old hand-me-down?

As I drive away, my thoughts flow back to the call I ignored from Thomas. We don't ever fight, thankfully, but I'd been pretty upset before I escaped to the library earlier.

It was mostly my fault. He'd offered that I could work on my book at his apartment today. He was going golfing with a client and planned to be away until late in the evening.

My roommate, Scarlett, on the other hand, would be *extremely* present and her usual bubbly, distracting self if I stayed at home. I really needed to get some solid writing in, so I took Thomas up on his offer.

Unfortunately, when he got back from golfing several hours early, he caught me in the middle of my first break. What he saw when he walked in was me, sprawled out on the couch with a seltzer, hand on my head. I was exhausted and feeling like this book was going to be the death of me.

In his measured way, so in line with his crisply ironed polo shirt and khakis, he'd immediately let me know he was disappointed I wasn't working.

"Callie," he'd said like he was talking to a messy corgi, "what're you doing?"

"Taking a break. I have a headache."

He'd looked concerned, offered me medicine, and then moved to the desk to read what I'd written.

"Stop!" I'd yelled without thinking.

He had been surprised, because the two of us never really exhibited intense emotions. Our lives together these days were like a lazy river of structure and sameness. There were no ups and downs, no explosions of passion or anger.

I loved him, but we just weren't *that* couple. We'd moved directly from the flirtation phase to the old-married-folks-sitting-in-matching-armchairs era, and I appreciated the reliability and safety of the relationship.

Usually, I kept my more animated emotions to myself, subconsciously trying to match his uncanny ability to always stay even. I didn't want to become one of those couples that fought all the time. I guessed it was just my headache making me testier than usual today.

"Why can't I look at it?" he'd asked. "You're writing this for my boss. I know him, and I know the material. I can help you."

I looked down uncomfortably. I didn't want his help. I was doing meticulous research, so I knew I'd get all the right information included eventually. Even more than that, I wanted to live alone in the world of my draft until I decided it was ready to be shared.

Scarlett's a writer, too (a *real* writer with an actual agent), and she's the same way—protective of her creation until she's finessed it within an inch of its life. If he'd tried to read her manuscript, she would have yelled a *lot* louder.

Not to mention, this is my first book. I'm fairly ashamed that my first published book won't have my byline, since I've dreamed of being a novelist my whole life, but still. I'm writing something that will see the light of day in paperback. I want to experience the whole journey for myself. I don't want a coauthor.

But I couldn't tell Thomas any of that. He definitely wouldn't understand. For him, the ends would justify the means; the logic of finishing better and sooner would trump any of the fluffy, emotional reasons surrounding my writing dreams.

"Okay, sure," I had agreed before I could stop myself. "Give it a read." I lay back on the couch and put my hand over my eyes again.

The apartment had hummed with nervous energy (me) and unsettling calm (him) while he took seemingly forever to make it through my draft. Then the real trouble began.

"You're off to a great start," he'd broken the silence.

"Like I said, I'm nowhere near done. I've only got 30 pages completed so far." I'd sat up and sipped my seltzer.

"Oh, I don't mean length-wise," Thomas had said, reaching for his economics book near my laptop. "You have a fairly solid understanding of the subject matter, but there's a lot missing here, even in what you've written so far. Let me help you fill in some of the blanks."

Warmth had crept up my cheeks, edging into my scalp and growing so hot I worried my hair might catch fire. I wasn't done, and I hadn't wanted him to read it. This was exactly why.

I didn't need to be humiliated by him. I knew deep down I should tell him to shove it, to leave and go work somewhere else, but instead I pretended there was ice cream behind my eyes to freeze the tears forming there. That's a trick I'd learned from Esperanza, and it worked wonders.

Then, I let him point out all of my draft's inadequacies.

When I couldn't take it anymore, I'd made up an excuse about running home to turn on the slow cooker.

I hadn't gone home. Instead, I'd driven right to the library down the street and ignored his phone call.

two

I go to the library again the next day. It had been so easy to focus there yesterday, and Scarlett is planning to write at the apartment all afternoon. Often, this means she blasts The Beatles and dances around wildly, waiting for inspiration to strike. I know I won't be able to focus while she's twisting and/or shouting, so I head out as soon as I'm dressed.

I want to get a solid chunk of writing done if I can. Tomorrow's Friday, and I have to meet Thomas right at five o'clock so we can drive to the lake for a much-anticipated weekend away. I'm looking forward to it, because it's been so long since we've had a chance to spend quality time together. I miss the steady rhythm of our past, and I'm hoping it makes an appearance this weekend.

In any case, his parents' camp doesn't have Wi-Fi, so I won't be able to work at all while I'm there. I really need to buckle down today.

Every table is empty, but I sit down at the same one and arrange my things the same way I did yesterday. *Let it never be said that Callie Sheffield hates order,* I think to myself smugly.

I'd hit a bit of a wall the day prior, struggling to get through a section on the history of supply-side economics that was particularly dry. Thomas probably would have loved to help me add the relevant details, but we hadn't made it that far before my feigned crockpot disaster sent me running for the hills.

I flip through Thomas's college textbooks, checking my post-it notes and trying to find something, anything, I can use to finish this godforsaken section. I'm coming up woefully short of ideas. This is the project from hell.

Suddenly, I have the sense that I'm being watched. I look up and see the clerk from the day before giving me a quizzical glance.

Since no one else is around, I chance a normal, non-library volume. "Is everything okay?"

"Are you a student at the college?" he asks. I assume he's referring to Briarford University, the institution that controls most aspects of our town, from tourism to traffic.

I wrinkle my nose at him. "No, why?" This small talk is getting in the way of my nonexistent progress.

He stands up and comes out from behind the desk. "That looks like a textbook. But you seem...a bit older than most of the college students who study here."

As he's walking toward me, I remember overhearing that the clerk's name is Will. "I'm flattered that I look so old to you," I say snarkily.

He's not wrong, though. I graduated from Briarford four years ago and just never left. What kind of loser washes up in the city where they go to college, clinging to dreams of a maybe-career while waitressing and riding their upwardly mobile boyfriend's coattails? I guess me, that's who.

I'm only an hour and a half away from home, but still I stayed here and split rent with a roommate rather than do the practical thing and move back in with my parents until I found a real job. Leaving just felt like giving in, throwing in the towel on becoming an author, and I wasn't ready to do that yet. Plus, Thomas was here, and he couldn't relocate because of his job.

Will grins, clearly pleased that his snarky subtext isn't lost on me.

"So what are you working on that requires a pile of annotated textbooks?"

He's standing right in front of me now. I notice he's wearing another plaid shirt. Blue this time. It's fully unbuttoned in the front to display a black T-shirt from a Rolling Stones concert.

I'm not really in the mood to explain myself to a virtual stranger, so I just say, "I'm working. For my geriatric grown-up job." I start typing something about lowering taxes without really knowing where my sentence is heading, just to seem busy.

He is either very persistent or extremely bored, because he slides one of the books to the edge of the table and tips it on its side far enough that he can see the title. "*Intro to Economics?* Riveting material. I see why you'd want to come here two days in a row to read this."

"Aren't you at work?" I ask drily.

Will smiles. "Thanks for noticing. Since no one else is here right now, I am completely at your disposal. Can I help you find any mind-numbing books about Reaganomics?"

A grin escapes my lips despite my attempts to feign annoyance. "I'm good, thanks."

He's still standing there, so I decide to explain. "I'm a writer."

Will raises an eyebrow, so I hurriedly continue, lest he be actually impressed. "Well, I'm just a ghostwriter, actually. I'm working on a book for my boyfriend's boss, who runs a financial advisory firm. Benderson Partners?"

He stares blankly, clearly not familiar with the name.

I shake my head. "Doesn't matter. Anyway, the textbooks are just to help me brush up on my economics."

Will does seem impressed, I think at first.

At least until he opens his mouth.

"That's pretty cool. Most little kids don't grow up dreaming to ghostwrite thought leadership books about fiscal policy. I'm glad you found your niche." He's smiling kindly despite the sarcasm, so I don't think he's trying to be a total jerk. Probably.

"I guess I did get pretty lucky," I quip. "I'll be looking for beta readers when I'm done, if you'd be down."

"Why don't I just read it right now?"

I consider trying to stop him, but before I can say anything, Will steps around my desk and leans over my shoulder.

I get a strong whiff of ocean breeze, which I assume must be his cologne. I'm not one of those women who goes nuts over a guy's cologne, but it does smell pretty good.

I feel fairly confident he's not going to correct my knowledge of retirement planning strategies, so I decide to let him forge ahead.

He makes a big show of scrolling through my Word document and skimming what I've written so far. "Compelling start. You know, if you added a chart or two, I might actually understand tax-loss harvesting."

"I thought you were supposed to shelve the books, not critique them," I return.

He smirks. "Fair. But let me tell you, I do alphabetize them very well."

I can't help but laugh out loud. "Well, Will, was it? It's been a pleasure. I'll be sure to thank you in my acknowledgements section."

His brow furrows. "I thought this was being ghostwritten?"

"Oh, yeah," I say. It's easy to forget that this isn't my book, and that I won't get credit for it. "I guess not, then."

"Speaking of that, though," he says, rubbing his unruly dark hair as if to somehow mash it back into place, "if it *weren't* being ghost-written, who would I see on the byline?"

If it weren't being ghostwritten, I wanted to say, it wouldn't be written at all, because it's boring junk that no one would ever want to write, or, for that matter, read. Least of all me.

But I don't say any of that. "Callie Sheffield." I stick my hand out to shake his.

"Will Pearson," he replies, offering a warm handshake. "I feel like I'm in the presence of greatness. Do you think we could book you for an author's night sometime? We always need writers to come in and read about back-door IRAs to keep the old folks busy."

I glare at him. "I'll have to check with my agent."

His lips twitch, but he fights the smile. Just then, a patron stumbles out of the stacks with several books, brandishing their library card. They must be in a hurry, because they clear their throat upon seeing the empty desk.

"That's my cue," he says. "It was nice to meet you, Callie. Remember, always be closing!"

I roll my eyes, but I wave as he turns back toward the circulation desk. When I tell him it was nice to meet him, too, I'm surprised to find I really mean it.

I GET PRETTY ABSORBED in my writing today. Something about the slightly chaotic quiet of the library helps me to focus. People stream in and out; books get checked out with a pleasant beep; parents shush their excited children; patrons make strange requests, and Will offers to help with a smile in his voice. There's a lot going on, and I'm totally content for the clickity-clacking of my keyboard to be a part of the library's rhythm.

At one point, I reach down to check my phone and realize it's five o'clock. Swearing (mostly) silently, I close my laptop and start packing up. If I'm going to visit Esperanza to convince her I don't want her table, I need to get going.

I should've left by 4:15 to avoid rush hour traffic, but it's too late for that. On a good day, I can manage the drive in 55 minutes. I've never done it in less than that at this time of day, though.

I hastily wave goodbye to Will and run out the door. Suddenly, my phone rings. It's Scarlett.

"Hello?" I hold the phone between my ear and shoulder while I get in the car.

"Hey, Cal. Did you order some furniture?" Scarlett has a musical voice that is often very loud. Right now, she sounds both lyrical and amused.

"You know I didn't," I say. The engine turns over. "What's going on?"

"I've gotta be honest, the delivery person isn't as jacked as I would've hoped. But I guess it's okay, since you didn't alert me to your purchase, so I didn't have time to put on a cute outfit anyway." Scarlett clanks some glasses together in the background. I hope she's putting away the dishes. She usually forgets when it's her turn.

"I have no idea what you're talking about, but I have to go. I'm heading to Mayville to see Esperanza." I want to get off the phone. Every second I waste, the worse the traffic will be.

Scarlett laughs. "There's no need. She's here. And she brought three friends—a table and two chairs."

I groan. "Stall her, please. Don't let her carry those by herself. I'll be right there."

"Oh, she already had them on the landing before she even rang the bell," Scarlett says. "You know Esperanza. She will not be denied."

I put the car in reverse. "Okay, I'm on my way," I grumble.

WHEN I GET to the second-story apartment I share with Scarlett, I see Esperanza's car in the parking lot. There's no sign of Esperanza or the furniture, though. Hopefully Scarlett helped her with it.

As I get inside, I hear an utter cacophony of voices. It sounds like there are 20 people over, but I realize it's just Scarlett and Esperanza both talking at once.

They've set the table up in the breakfast nook, leaning the TV trays we'd been using for meals up against the wall. Scarlett has made tea and is in the process of pouring some for Esperanza. They seem to be having a spirited discussion about women's basketball, which I'm more than confident neither of them knows anything about.

"Oh, hi, C!" Esperanza grins when she notices me. "I brought you the table! What do you think?"

I smile at her. "It's beautiful. But I thought *I* was coming to see *you* today? Remember, I was going to take you grocery shopping?"

She waves her hand in the air like there is nothing in the world she needs less than food. If she were the type to say, "Aw, pshaw," I'm pretty sure she would have done so then.

Scarlett shoots me a secret smile. My roommate loves Esperanza as much as I do, and we both think she's funny as hell. We aren't totally sure if she's always trying to be hilarious, but we suspect she knows we like her quirks and amps up her eccentricities to get a laugh.

"This is good tea." Esperanza takes a long sip. "It reminds me of the kind Mama used to make."

She loves to talk about her mother, who died of cancer after many torturous months of being nursed at home by my grandmother and Esperanza when they were in their late twenties. Neither of them has ever really moved past the loss.

I never met my great-grandmother, but she sounds like she had a huge heart. She took care of eight kids while dealing with an abusive husband who also happened to be an alcoholic. Two of her children didn't reach adulthood, and most of the other kids didn't even go to high school. My grandmother, the third-youngest, was the first one who graduated.

Sometimes I wonder if their circumstances were why my great-grandmother gave Esperanza a name that means "hope." Like some desperate part of herself dared to dream that things would get better someday. It breaks my heart a little to think that, for her, they never really did.

IT'S ALMOST 6:45 now, and Esperanza is still happily chatting away, regaling us with tales from her youth. We've now heard about the time she went to the town hall to sign up for the Women's Army

Corps, but the skeevy officer in charge wouldn't let her unless she gave him a key to her apartment. Never one to conform, she punched him in the nose.

She's shared how her very Italian mother used to make pasta, leaving long, narrow bits of dough out to dry all over every available surface in the house. Including, she explained proudly, the very table we're sitting at now.

When she says it, I look down at the rough surface under my teacup. *What stories this table must have to tell*, I muse.

She tells us about her older brother, Michael, who went for a walk one day and never came back, his life cut short by a drunk driver. And she talks wistfully, somewhat regretfully, about the night she married a man she never really loved. Their union ended badly several years later, and she didn't ever so much as date again.

Her life has been filled with so much pain, so much wanting. She's a fantastic storyteller, and it's fun to see my family's history through her eyes, but it makes me sad nevertheless for all that she's lost; all that she's missed.

I know Esperanza doesn't like to drive after dark, so I gently nudge her shoulder. "It's getting a little late. Do you want another cup of tea before you head out?"

She nods. "Sure, C. Thanks."

I pour it for her. "Hey, tell Scarlett the story about the fire." I've heard it before, but it's one of my favorites.

A shadow crosses her face, but she nods. "Okay. Well, it was really nothing, though."

I stare at her, incredulous. "It wasn't nothing. You saved someone's life."

Scarlett gasps dramatically. "You what now?"

"Right?" I say. "This lady is a hero, right here."

Esperanza laughs a little and says, "I just did what anybody would do."

"I can assure you," I push the tea cup toward her, "that most people would *not* do what you did."

I think, deep down, she knows that.

"Well, I was sitting outside with my mother. It was back when we lived in Prospect Heights. It was a really nice day. Anyway, all of a sudden, we noticed smoke coming out of the house next door. And then there were flames." She pauses to take a sip of her tea.

I look at Scarlett, whose attention is rapt. Her eyes are wide when she asks, "And you did what, exactly? Ran straight into the flames like some sort of superwoman?"

Esperanza smiles at her softly. "The woman ran out of the house with her older son screaming, 'My baby! My baby!' She'd left her little one inside. My mother said, 'E, you go in there and get that baby!' And so I got up, and that's what I did."

I somewhat regret asking her to tell this story, because I see something a lot like sadness reflected in her eyes now. But she continues.

"When I got into the baby's room, there were flames everywhere, all around the crib. And the baby was just in the middle of it all, staring up at me. So I picked her up and ran out." She pantomimes picking up a child and cradling it in her arms. "And that was it."

Scarlett's jaw might as well be on the floor. "I can't believe you ran into a burning building and rescued an infant from certain death. This is the stuff movies are made about, you know. You could have saved a kid who grew up to be a doctor and, in turn, saved thousands of people. You could have saved the life of the man who turned out to be George Bailey. Without you, he wouldn't have saved Harry, and then that whole transport ship of soldiers would have died, too."

I roll my eyes. Scarlett does have a flair for the dramatic. Esperanza is looking at her a bit blankly.

"She's talking about *It's a Wonderful Life*," I explain.

"Oh yeah, yeah. I love that movie." She hurries to pick up her mug and bring it to the kitchen. "I'm going to use your bathroom, and then I have to get home before it gets dark."

It's funny, in a way, that she likes that film so much, because she's always reminded me of Clarence the guardian angel, for some reason. The generosity, maybe, or the childlike innocence?

While she's in the bathroom, I put together three bags of cereals, crackers, canned fruit, and soups from our pantry. When she gets out, I pretend that I bought them for her, carry them to her car, and hug her good night.

She beeps about 45 times as she drives away, waving like she's the queen of England and I'm her congregated public.

"She's really something," Scarlett remarks when I get back inside.

"She sure is," I say, closing the door.

three

Will, who is once again dressed like Paul Rudd in *Clueless*, gives me a goofy smile when I get to the library on Friday.

"Ready to make some finance magic?" he quips, pushing a packed book trolley near the copier.

"Oh, absolutely." I smile wryly. "Are you meeting Tai Frasier at a Mighty Mighty Bosstones party later?"

He pauses for a moment, and then enlightenment hits. "Big Josh and Cher fan, are you?"

"I mean, who isn't? People of a *certain age*," I emphasize those words since he thinks I'm ancient, "need to be true to their roots."

"So you're saying...you don't want to be a traitor to your generation?" Will grins at me, clearly pleased with himself.

I can't believe I missed the chance to quote *Clueless*; it's one of my favorite movies. "You got it! As if, and whatnot."

His mouth starts to tip up, and then his face falls a bit. "In all seriousness, I'm sorry if I offended you the other day. I'm sure you're younger than I am." He pauses, then speaks quickly. "Not that it's a contest, or anything."

I study the faint band of freckles that sprinkles his cheeks, popping out like an absurdity against his suddenly somber demeanor.

His lashes are dark against his skin as he lowers his eyes in apology, and he has the general aura of a little boy who broke his mom's favorite vase and knows he's about to get in trouble.

"No worries," I say gently. "I'm only 2 times 10 plus 6."

A smile starts, crinkling his eyes first.

"And anyway," I continue, "we ladies of a *certain age* have to learn to stop caring what other people think. Age is just a number, after all."

He chuckles. "Well, you're living proof that with age comes wisdom."

I think of Esperanza, the dining table, and her overall vibe. "Age doesn't have to change you too much, I don't think."

"No, I suppose that's true," he agrees.

I wonder if I should explain Esperanza to him. It's usually hard to get people to understand until they meet her, since describing her behavior seems like it must be some fictionalized version of reality.

I should probably get to work. But something in his face suggests he's actually interested in continuing to talk to me. I decide to go for it.

"Along those lines, I actually had a pretty crazy encounter this week with my great-aunt."

"Oh?" He raises an eyebrow.

"Yeah," I continue. "She lives alone and gets bored really easily. So, she walks for miles every day and spends the rest of her time casually dropping in on relatives. And this week, I guess it was my turn."

"And what happened when she came over?" He pulls out a chair from the nearest table and gestures for me to take it, then sits across from me, leaning on his elbows. "I'm intrigued."

I look back at the circulation desk. "Don't you need to get back to work?"

"Nah." He nods his head toward the staff area. "Marian is working today. She's covering for me while I reshelve these books."

As if on cue, a portly woman with gray hair takes up her position behind the front desk. He nods, satisfied that whatever magical library spell he'd cast had been successful.

I gesture toward the book cart. "I hate to be the one to tell you this, but it doesn't look like you're reshelving those right now."

"Huh, you're right," he says in mock surprise. "Okay, Sheffield. Get alphabetizing." He pulls the cart up next to our table and starts putting books in order.

I laugh and grab a few novels, moving them to the table so I can make organized stacks.

"We'll put these away later," he gestures to my growing pile, a silly little thrill going through me that he's including me in his plans. "Now, tell me your story."

TALKING about Esperanza with Will eats up the better part of an hour, until he's called away to help run a children's program. He invites me to join them in making Very Hungry Caterpillars out of pom-poms, but I politely decline. I very much need to get some writing done.

By 4:30, I've really hit my stride, blazing through a chapter on irrevocable trusts in record time. When I realize I need to head out to meet Thomas, I close my laptop and pack up my bag, sighing. I'd love more of this productive flow state.

Once I get to the car, I wedge my laptop bag and textbooks between a few duffels in the trunk. I'm a little worried my computer might overheat if I leave it in the hot car all weekend, but Thomas wants to meet his parents at the lake house by seven o'clock for dinner, so I don't have time to go home.

It only takes me ten minutes to get to Benderson Partners. The building is made of reflective tiles, so today it looks like it's constructed of fluffy clouds. The illusion is shattered by the rows of luxury vehicles mirrored along the base of the building, including Thomas's new BMW. And by my 2002 Honda Civic, which certainly doesn't fit in here.

"This doesn't mean I'm a snob," he'd joked when he bought the car. "I just need something with a little more wow factor to impress my clients." He'd traded in his mom's old Subaru Forester, which had taken us on many an enjoyable road trip, to get the 3 Series.

I think I'd laughed along with him, but I remember feeling a "Yeah, but..." forming in my mind. I don't know if I was more bothered that he didn't see the problem with his statement, or that he was leaving me behind.

Things used to be different, with Thomas and me. He didn't come from money, exactly, though his parents were certainly better off than mine. But he'd been quiet and witty when I'd met him; studious and ready to change the world. We got along well, going through life smoothly and without incident. And I enjoyed feeling like I was with someone who had it all together.

It's only been lately, since he started working for Benderson Partners and spending all his time with the upper crust, that I've begun to notice a change in him. A change in how I feel when I'm around him, like I don't know him anymore. Like maybe I don't belong.

I'm about to call Thomas to let him know I'm out front when I see him breeze through the front door. His jacket is slung over his shoulder, and his French-cuffed sleeves are rolled up to the elbows like he's in some sort of cologne ad. *He really is a perfect specimen,*" Scarlett liked to quip.

"Hey, sweetheart," he says when he gets to the car. He adds his suitcase to the pile of bags in the trunk, hangs his jacket on the hook in the back, and hops in through the passenger-side door.

We're taking my car to the lake because he doesn't want to risk scratching his BMW on the gravel drive at his parents' camp. And, honestly, I prefer my beater. The seats are worn into just my shape, and I know all the radio presets like the back of my hand.

"Hi," I greet him, putting the car in reverse. "How was work?"

Thomas goes on to tell me a long-winded story about winning a new client whose portfolio was just *so wild*, and all the advising he'd needed to do to get things back on track. He loses me a bit in the details, but I nod along politely until he's done.

"How was the library?" he asks me.

"Oh, it was good," I say noncommittally. "I got a lot done."

For some reason, I don't feel like talking about my Esperanza story hour with Will. I also don't bother mentioning how Susan and I exchanged phone numbers after she finished up in the Very Hungry Caterpillar class and we got to talking about our favorite books, or how her daughter, Freya, gave me a hug when they left.

Instead, I tell him about the chapter I wrote today, and how I should talk to my grandparents about putting their assets in a trust in case only one of them needs a nursing home someday. It might protect their house.

"Absolutely," he nods sagely. "Have them come into the office sometime. I can help them set something up."

I smile wryly. It would give Thomas the thrill of his life to be able to financial-plan my grandparents' future, which I'm pretty sure consists solely of social security checks and meager savings withdrawals for the rest of their lives.

"For sure," I agree. I'm distracted by the rise and fall of the road, navigating its way up through the mountains. The lake house is almost two hours north, nestled between peaks and valleys, perched on the eastern shore of Lake Manacqua. It's been in Thomas's family for two generations, and his parents and his dad's siblings take turns using it for vacations or entertaining.

The highway is narrow here, with very little traffic. It's mostly switchback turns, and it's covered by a canopy of lush green trees and dappled sunlight. It's a beautiful drive, and I get lost in my thoughts.

Thomas and I ride in silence the rest of the way to the lake house. I feel a little guilty, but I just don't have anything to say.

THE BOAT SWAYS GENTLY BACK and forth, moving with the whims of the waves on the lake. I sit on a vinyl bench with

Thomas's mother, staring at my boyfriend and his brother, Matthew. They're deep in conversation about the stock market. I'm pretty sure I couldn't be less interested. Apparently, Thomas's dad feels the same way—he's asleep in the captain's chair.

My thoughts start to drift in time with the boat. I wonder if Susan, the mom with the three energetic kids, will be back at the library on Monday. When she and I had started talking near the New Fiction display today, I feel like we really hit it off. Turns out we have the same taste in novels. I make a mental note to tell her about the latest Sarah Miller book that I read. I think Susan will like it, too.

Plus, I need to return the favor. When we'd talked, she'd recommended several new books that I couldn't wait to borrow.

Conveniently, they were sitting right on the shelf behind us. Less conveniently, I'd accidentally left my library card at home.

But Will, who was eavesdropping on our conversation from behind his Ken Jennings memoir, offered to hide the books behind the circulation desk so no one else would check them out. At first, I said no, because apparently I'm conditioned to reject my own desires at every turn, but...

He'd looked so earnest, and somehow very charismatic despite the harsh lighting of the library, so I'd agreed to let him break the law for me. Okay, not the law. But the probably-very-strict-library-rules.

And seriously, what is with him? Is he an agent for Big Plaid, or something? I swear, he has to be keeping the entire plaid button-down industry in business.

And also, what is with me? Why am I spending so much time thinking about this snarky public servant instead of my actual boyfriend, who checks every box on the mental list I (and probably most women) keep of ideal partner material?

I'm brought back to the present by a splash. I look to the rear of the pontoon and see that Thomas's mom has jumped into the lake. Maybe both physically, and in a more symbolic sense, to escape the incessant, clichéd man talk of her sons.

I can't say I blame her. It's sweltering in the sun, and the benches on the boat don't have much shade. If I try to shift on them at all, I know my legs are going to resist, sticking to the vinyl and painfully peeling away with a squelch. This whole summer has been so unbearably hot and humid. *The lake would feel so refreshing*, I'm thinking, when I hear my name.

I look up and meet Thomas's expectant gaze. "Did you want some wine?" He holds up a bottle of white zin.

"No, thanks. I could go for some water, though."

He flips open the cooler top and tosses a bottle my way. I snatch it midair, feeling pretty pleased with myself. Sports were never my forté. Thomas had been big into lacrosse, because of course he was. And now business dictated that he be big into golf.

Once upon a time, I would have expected him to praise my catch, or call me "so cute," because that's the sort of thing that impresses him—casual athleticism on display in social situations. Today, he says nothing.

"So what else is new?" he asks, pouring himself a glass of wine.

"Well, Esperanza brought me a table this week," I begin, excited to tell him this story that borders on absurdist comedy.

"That's so sweet of her," he says, sipping his wine. "She's really something, isn't she?"

I don't know how to respond. Yes, she is, of course. But also, how is that all he has to say? She's an octogenarian-turned-furniture-mover. How does he not have any questions? Like, why she did this, or how?

I just nod.

He turns to Matthew. "How was your week?" he addresses his younger brother.

"Eh," Matthew shrugs. "A little frustrating. I'm working on a big campaign, and we had to push all the assets back to creative several times. They're just really missing the mark."

Matthew is 24, fresh off his MBA. He's a bit of a snob, but we generally get along. He works for a sports marketing agency and acts like his job is the most stressful one on earth.

Thomas assesses his brother, offering a measured nod. "That would be frustrating," he agrees calmly.

I zone out of their conversation, tracing the lines of Thomas's face from across the boat. Even here, in the violent humidity I'm pretty sure came from the Seventh Circle of Hell itself, he looks put together, with pin-straight hair and a bathing suit that cuts all the right lines. His perfect masculinity used to make my heart palpitate on sight.

I can't believe the nothing I feel right now.

I guess that's normal, I reason with myself. *Relationships change over time. I can't expect the butterflies to last forever.*

But would it be too much to ask, really, to feel *something*?

I settle back against the bench, legs squelching a little as I shift, wishing I were just about anywhere else. Tears prick the backs of my closed eyelids, and I wrap my arms around my chest. I must just be having an off day.

Thomas is good, he's kind, and he's willing to put his reputation at risk to help boost my career. He's smart and successful. And he looks so freaking good in a suit. It's been a long week. I just need some sleep. I think.

Between the sense that my heart has a hole in it and the gentle rocking of the boat, I have very little will to be present. It doesn't take long before I'm lulled off to sleep.

I have a bizarre dream in which I write my first novel and have a launch party at the library. Thomas is there, stoically watching me do a book reading. Afterward, he shakes my hand to congratulate me.

Esperanza, Scarlett, and Will are in the audience too, cheering my name and clapping loudly. Susan and my parents are eating cake together at the refreshments table, where she tells them about her kids. They invite me over for a glass of punch. When I look back to find Thomas, to bring him with me to join the party, he's gone.

four

The rest of the weekend at the lake passes uneventfully, in that nothing really happens, and I have no choice but to admit to myself I'm bored. Bored with nature, bored with myself, and bored with Thomas.

It's hard to come to terms with the truth—that maybe I've outgrown our relationship. I'm torn about what to say or do. I've been dealing with a lot lately, and the book is putting a lot of stress on us as a couple.

I don't want to throw away almost four years of stability for what might be a temporary discomfort. I figure I'll wait for the book to be done, then I'll decide how I feel.

WHEN I GET BACK to civilization on Sunday night, my phone blows up with voicemails and texts. As it turns out, the lake not only has no Wi-Fi, but it also has no cell service. The last time I was there, I'd dropped my phone in the lake, so I'd never had the chance to find out.

I'd missed six calls and four voicemails from Esperanza, and Scarlett had sent me basically a novel's worth of text messages about a guy she met at a book reading. To my surprise, I also saw a text from Susan, inviting me to go out to a trivia night with her on Monday evening.

And there was one text from a number I didn't have in my contact list. *Hi, Callie. It's Will. I hope you don't mind; I got your number from Susan. She mentioned you might be coming to our trivia night this week. I just wanted to let you know it's Monday night, but it's all the way in Rockledge, so if you're coming by the library during the day, I can give you a ride to the bar when I clock out at six. Just let me know. Have a nice weekend!*

So Susan and Will do trivia together, I muse. I'm fairly surprised, as they seem more like casual acquaintances than friends, but Susan certainly does bring her kids to the library a lot. I guess being seen at your messiest, surrounded by your unruly spawn, might make it easy to forge a genuine connection with someone.

It's been ages since I went out for trivia, I think, as I pull into the parking lot. Scarlett and I used to go all the time in college. We'd clean up in a big way during any literature or film rounds. It's also a matter of personal pride, the degree to which I decimate any questions about show tunes.

It might be fun to go with them, albeit a little weird, because we're such new friends. But I could use a night out that doesn't involve a book reading and my boisterous best friend. Or a too-quiet evening in, watching Thomas read *The Financial Times* over the top of my book.

I unlock the apartment door, shoving my duffel bags inside and dropping my keys in the bowl by the door. When she'd brought it home from the thrift store, Scarlett had said the bowl was meant for keys, but it now also contains about 25 tubes of Chapstick (hers), several pairs of sunglasses (also hers), and various receipts she's fished out of the bottom of her parade of purses. Her attempts at organization often end this way—creating more ADHD-style catchalls of junk.

"Lucy, I'm home!" I yell.

"Ricky!" Scarlett calls back, running down the hallway and into my arms. She almost knocks me over.

"Hi, friend," I say, straightening up. "How was your weekend? Sounds like you had an *awful* lot of fun."

"Oh my God, Cal. You have no idea. This guy is so hot. And he's really interesting, too."

I laugh as I walk past her to grab a glass of water. "Wow, hot *and* interesting. What a rare combination. You should snatch him up right away."

She wrinkles her nose at me in feigned annoyance, following me into our cramped kitchen. "Well, whatever. You'll have to meet him next weekend. I invited him over for game night."

I'd totally forgotten about game night. We try to have our college friends over once a month or so for drinks and board games, just to keep the connections alive. It gets a little lonely sometimes as a washed-up late-twenty-something in a university town. We joke that game night keeps us young.

"Can't wait!" I say, wondering if this "relationship" will run its course before game night even arrives. Scarlett doesn't have the best track record with men. She jokes it's because she's the namesake of *the* Scarlett O'Hara.

"I'll find my Rhett someday," she always promises. I love to remind her that Scarlett and Rhett end the novel very much *not* together. Typically, that's when she playfully hits me.

"Speaking of gentlemen callers, how was your weekend with Thomas?" Scarlett asks, stirring a pot of pasta on the stove.

"It was fine," I say in what I hope is a voice devoid of any revealing emotion. "You know, lake stuff. It was hot. His brother talked about work a lot. There was a stock-market-themed game of charades, but I managed to escape with a feigned migraine."

Scarlett whips around to face me. "No. Please tell me you're joking."

I shake my head. "Sadly, I am not. At least his mom is friendly."

"Janice is very sweet," Scarlett acknowledges. "You had fun, though?"

I swallow. I don't really want to lie to Scarlett. And, loud and boisterous though she is, she does tend to keep secrets well.

"I don't know." I pull sauce out of the cabinet. "To be honest, I found myself feeling...nothing."

I sense her eyes on my back as I empty the jar into a pan. It takes her a minute to respond.

"You mean, like, *feeling* feelings?" She grabs the pan from me and sets it on the stove. "Honey, come talk to me."

I flip the burner on as she grabs my arm and pulls me over to our new dining table. She commands me to sit. I do.

Then, she puts her hand gently on my arm. "Okay, tell me everything."

I fill Scarlett in on what's been going on in my head lately, from the anger at Thomas reading my unfinished manuscript (she squirms uncomfortably) to the dream about my book launch (she raises a knowing brow). She's very understanding, just sits and listens. She knows better than to try to tell me what to do.

When I'm done talking, she's quiet for a minute, then replies, "You already know what I think."

I do, and I'm glad she doesn't say it. Once it's out there, hovering in the air between us, I'll have to acknowledge its reality. I take a deep breath. "I'm just going to wait and see if things get better once the book is done."

"Okay," she nods. "But Callie, my love, you deserve the butterflies."

AFTER SCARLETT LEAVES to take a shower, I listen to the voicemails from Esperanza. She was first calling to see how I was doing, then she remembered that I was away for the weekend. Then, she wanted to know how I liked the table. Then, she wanted to let me know she was going out, so if I called her back, she wouldn't be home.

With a laugh, I call her back. She answers on the first ring.

"Hello? Who is it?" she asks, loaded with nervous energy.

"Hi, Esperanza. It's Callie. I'm sorry I missed your calls. I went away this weekend to the lake with Thomas."

"Oh, I know, I know. I called your mother, and that's what she said, too. Then I remembered you told me about it. How is young Tom?"

I stifle a giggle. He's never been Tom, to me or anyone else. Anyone but Esperanza, that is.

Thomas, not Tom, and his brother is Matthew, not Matt. There's no room for informality in that family. But Esperanza has a way of just saying whatever eccentric thing she wants, and somehow, she gets away with it.

"He's doing well," I say evenly. "He's busy with work, so it was nice to get away."

"Oh, I bet. You kids work too hard."

"Well, I don't know about that. But it was a great weekend to be at the lake. It was so hot here."

"You're telling me," she says. "Well, I should let you go. You probably just got home."

"I did a bit ago. But I need to get unpacked and head to bed. I have a busy day tomorrow." My mind races through all of the things I need to get done in the morning. "But hey, I'll be seeing you next week for your birthday, right? At the diner?"

There's a loud noise like she's suddenly turned the television on in the background. "Yep, I'll see you then! Have a good night, C!"

"Good night, Esperanza!" I hang up. I hope I'm this adorable when I'm old. Hell, I hope to simply *be* that old someday.

Stretching my legs, I pull the blanket off my lap and start to stand up. Then I remember the texts from Susan. And Will.

I reply to Susan first. *That would be so much fun. Thanks for thinking of me! I'll see you there.*

I'm not sure what to say to Will. It doesn't make sense to take two cars all the way to Rockledge, especially when I only live ten minutes from the library. In terms of the environment, my time, and my gas money, it's logical to take him up on his offer. Plus, he's funny, and it might be a good time.

I have the vague notion that I should say no, but I'm not really sure why. Maybe I don't quite trust myself, or my feelings, with a guy like Will. Maybe it's because of how messy his black hair is. Maybe it's because some small part of me knows that, if I go with him and have fun, it will make it impossible to ignore what I'm no longer feeling with Thomas.

I think about Esperanza, who just does what feels right to her and forges her own path, come what may. I think about Scarlett, who certainly wouldn't give this a second thought. Even as every fiber of my being tells me to stop, to conform, to take the safe route, I start to type.

Hey, Will! Sorry for the delay; I was out of town for the weekend. I'd love a ride; thanks so much! I'll be at the library by two tomorrow to write, so I'll hang around until you're off at six. See you then!

Taking a deep breath, I hit send before I can change my mind. Then, I head to the bathroom to take a shower.

five

I spend the last hour of my writing time on Monday playing *Jeopardy!* games online to brush up on my trivia. I don't know Will and Susan well enough yet to ruin our burgeoning friendship by seeming like a dunce.

When six o'clock rolls around, Will grabs his messenger bag and meets me at my usual table. "Ready to go?" he asks.

"I've been practicing," I admit, pointing to my computer screen.

"Jack Nicholson," says Will.

"What?" I'm confused.

"The answer to that one," he gestures. "It was Jack Nicholson."

I read the question again. He's right, of course. "Good one." I high-five him, then start to pack up.

"Thanks for taking this so seriously, by the way. But I should warn you, we don't typically make our teammates study. It's not that kind of bar." His eyes twinkle.

It dawns on me it's a play on words, and he means bar *exam*, like for lawyers. I grin, which is obviously the reaction he was hoping for, because then he does, too.

I swing my bag over my shoulder and push in my chair. "Yeah, well, you spend all of your time around books, and Susan has a doctorate. I'm sure the rest of your team is equally brainy. I don't want to fall short." I'm only partially joking.

"You're not nervous, are you?" he teases. "I promise, we're all really nice." He leads the way to the exit. "And anyway, studying trivia when you should be working proves you're just as much of a nerd as the rest of us."

I laugh. He holds the door for me. When I pass him, my left arm accidentally brushes his right. I feel a little tremor of something rising in my chest, but I shove it back down. *I'm just lonely*, I tell myself.

Will heads toward a gray Toyota Camry that looks even older than my own ancient clunker and opens both doors. He stands outside the passenger side, waiting.

"Thanks," I blush, sliding past him and taking a seat. Thomas doesn't hold the door for me. He typically goes right to the back seat to hang up his suit jacket.

I don't mind fending for myself, or anything. I'm a modern woman, and all. But it isn't the worst thing in the world to feel like chivalry is alive and well.

I position my bag in my lap and take a quick peek at my hair in the sunshade mirror. It's looking a little frizzy, thanks to the ever-present humidity. My roots are also coming in, revealing more of the chocolate brown I've tried to cover with deep auburn highlights. I gather it all into a chignon, my go-to for taming unruly locks.

Will gets into the car on the other side and turns the engine over. The radio comes on fully blasting Tom Petty. He quickly shoves the dial most of the way down. "Sorry about that."

"No worries," I say. "I like to rage in my car when I'm by myself, too." I'm only half joking. I do tend to turn the music up really loudly when I know Thomas won't be anywhere near my Honda. He's a bit of a buzzkill and likes to remind me about ear health. Things get even louder when Scarlett and I are together. We treat any moving vehicle like it's our own personal concert hall.

Will seems surprised. "Really, now? You strike me more as a

Prokofiev and NPR kind of girl." He runs a hand absently through his hair, which looks even messier than usual today.

"Aw, come on, Will." I offer a faux pout. "Just because I spend my days slaving away for elitists doesn't mean the heart of rock and roll is lost on me."

He snickers. "I'm glad to hear it."

"Glad to tell it." *Why am I so nervous?* "And for what it's worth, I absolutely love Tom Petty."

He smiles, as if he's surprised again, like I'm impressing him. Like he's happy. It's incredibly cute, and I have to take a deep breath to remind myself of who I'm with. *Get it together,* I berate myself. *This is not happening.*

As if sensing that I don't know what to say, Will offers, "So, you already know Susan." He pulls out of the parking lot and eases the car down the road. "You're also going to get to meet Jenna, Jax, and Priya this week. Jenna's a pro when it comes to all things movies. Jax is our sports guy, and Priya is a bit of a generalist, but don't discount her—she's the biggest nerd of all."

"I'm surprised that isn't you," I tease.

He chuckles, a warm sound that emanates from somewhere deep in his throat. "I am pretty nerdy myself. I just think she's smarter than I am, that's all."

My eyes crinkle a bit over my nose, not believing him for a second. "I don't know, Will. You seem pretty smart."

He smiles softly. "Thanks for the vote of confidence, Cal."

Suddenly, my chest is filled with a warm fizz, gently flowing up toward my heart. The familiarity in his use of my nickname makes me feel...things. Things I probably shouldn't be feeling.

I clear my throat delicately. "So, which category do *you* dominate?"

His eyes twinkle in the rearview. "Oh, you know. Putting things in alphabetical order. Dewey decimal stuff. How to scan a barcode. All the skills I've perfected in my years as a library clerk."

Without thinking, I respond like an idiot. "Well, you're definitely the most impressive library clerk I've ever met."

This somehow sounds like a come-on, even though I don't really know what it means. I blush. A quick dart of my eyes reveals a pink flush creeping up his cheeks, as well. *Damn it, Callie. What even was that?*

"And I've met my fair share of library clerks," I playfully bluster, making myself both sound like an incredible loser and a very specific type of woman-about-town.

I realize I actually have no idea how long he's worked at the library, so I try to save the conversation with something a normal human might say. "How long have you worked at the library, anyway? And what did you do before that?"

Will shakes his head a little, as if trying to reset his brain from my momentary lack of coherence. "I started there seven years ago," he explains. "Got a part-time job while I was in school."

"Oh, nice! Did you go to the university, too?" I ask, glad to have moved away from the awkward train wreck I'd created of our conversation. I wonder if he and I had ever unknowingly crossed paths in college.

"Yeah, for a while." He stops the car at a traffic light. He seems uncharacteristically quiet, but I don't know whether to push for more details or if I've gone unintentionally too far somehow.

I decide to be light-hearted in an attempt to resuscitate things. "Not enough flashers there for your liking?"

He snorts, eyes snapping out of a sad sort of trance. "Yeah. Something like that."

We ride in comfortable silence for a minute, then I ask, "So, what's the best drink at this place?"

"Oh, definitely the frozen strawberry daiquiri. Extra whip."

I think he's being quippy again, because I can't picture him drinking anything so vivacious.

"Not that I can order one tonight, of course. I have to drive you back to your car later. But you should totally indulge."

His pointer finger slides to the radio and skips to a different station preset. "Sorry," he says. "Not in the mood for REM right now."

"Interesting. "Nightswimming" is actually the only REM song I like," I admit. "It's kind of melancholy, but beautiful."

"Yeah, well, for me, it's basically just melancholy." He settles on "Free Will" by Rush instead and darts an apologetic look my way. "I hope you don't mind."

"No, not at all." I'm wondering what woman broke his heart to the dulcet tones of Michael Stipe when I feel my phone vibrate. Fishing it out of my jeans pocket, I see it's Thomas.

What color is your dress for the gala? I want to make sure my tie matches.

I groan louder than I mean to. I'd forgotten about the Chapters for Change Gala, which is in a couple of weeks. It's a fundraising event for a local children's literacy organization, held at the university. Thomas gets free tickets through work. Even though it's about helping kids, it's treated as a big see-and-be-seen thing for local businesses, and Benderson Partners is huge on networking.

We've had a good time in the past, though the food is nothing to write home about. Still, they do a decent job keeping the drinks flowing, and the DJ is typically solid. Normally it's something I look forward to, but I'm a little behind the eight ball this year. I haven't had the time (or funds) to shop for a new dress. And to be honest, with everything going on with the book, I'd kind of forgotten about the gala.

I'm just going to wear the same dress as last year, I type quickly.

What color was it? he texts back.

I suddenly feel like I've swallowed a lead balloon. He doesn't remember introducing me to his boss, his hand firmly on the small of my back in my delicate blue satin gown? The one I agonized over with him at the mall, both because I wanted to choose the perfect outfit so I looked like I belonged there, and because I knew I shouldn't spend $250 on a dress?

Slow dancing to Frank Sinatra's "My Way," which Thomas (somewhat ironically) thinks is the pinnacle of all music ever written? Eating crudité until it felt like our stomachs might burst? Me having a few too many cocktails and spilling one right down the front of said blue dress, necessitating a hasty trip to the restroom for paper towels, and my borrowing his jacket for the rest of the night to cover up the stain?

Hell, I have a picture of us there, smiling together in the photo booth, hanging right at eye-level on my refrigerator. There's that blue dress, peeking out at him every time he goes to get himself a drink when he's visiting, which is to say at least twice a week.

Honestly, it was one of the best nights we ever had. And he doesn't even remember it.

I put my phone back in my pocket. Will's eyebrows are raised, but he doesn't say anything.

"Sorry," I mumble. "My boyfriend had a question about the gala we're going to later this month."

He visibly brightens. "Oh, is it Chapters for Change?"

I'm surprised he's familiar, but then again, he does work for a library. "One and the same."

"I guess I'll see you guys there!" He seems excited. "I'll be introducing some of the bigger donors. The library always helps manage the event."

His excitement is contagious, so I smile at him, even though my insides are still feeling out of sorts from the realization that my boyfriend doesn't remember our time together. Not even our best moments. The stuff that makes us who we are as a couple. And I'm angry, but I find that, somehow, I'm not surprised. I think that realization is most surprising of all.

"Can't wait," I say, and a small part of me means it. The same part of me that notices how Will's hair is falling over his forehead in the twilight, and wondering what it would feel like to run my fingers through it. I'm starting to realize that part of me may not be going away anytime soon.

. . .

WHEN WE GET to the bar, I feel nervous again. I hide behind Will like a toddler clinging to her mother's leg in the supermarket, following him to a high-top table. I see Susan's blonde ponytail right away, and she grins at me. "Callie!" She holds up an overly foamy beer in greeting.

I wave, genuinely glad to see her. She's a really interesting person, and I'm looking forward to getting to know her better, away from her (admittedly adorable) children. I love that her husband, Doug, is cool with her taking a night off to just be Susan.

I shove down the reminder that Thomas is fine with me being here without him, too. It's different, in so many ways, and I'm not in the mood to be happy with him right now.

Will reaches his arm back and fishes me out of his shadow. He rests it on my shoulders and pushes me gently forward as he introduces me to the rest of the group. "This is Jax," he indicates a cheerful blonde man with piercing blue eyes and a Manchester United shirt.

Jax salutes. "The pleasure is mine," he says.

I nod in greeting.

"Callie, meet Jenna," he gestures to a sweepingly tall woman perched on the stool next to Jax, "our movie maven." She grins and waves.

"And this is Priya," he points to the brunette next to Jenna, who is appraising me quietly. She's strikingly beautiful, with deep-set eyes and a cupid's bow that most women would kill for.

"Nice to meet you," she murmurs, pushing her pin-straight hair behind her ear with a perfectly pink-manicured finger.

Something feels a little strange about her reaction, but I shake it off. "Nice to meet you all," I say, as Will's hand drops to my low back. He gently guides me to an empty stool. "Thanks for letting me crash your trivia team! I only hope I'm worthy of your greatness."

Will takes the stool next to mine, leaning forward to intimate to his friends, "She studied for most of the afternoon. She really wants to impress you guys."

I roll my eyes and say teasingly as I look at Will, "This one gives me such a hard time when I work at the library. I just figured his friends would be equally difficult."

They all laugh, and Susan starts telling a story about a ridiculous assignment one of her PhD students turned in last week. In addition to being an extremely hands-on mother, she's somehow also an associate biology professor.

The conversation slides away from me, bouncing amicably back and forth between the friends. I slip into the background, trying to internalize their rhythm so I can join in when I'm ready.

As I glance around the table with what I hope is a pleasant expression on my face, I can't help but notice Priya isn't smiling. In fact, she's giving me a look like I've just told her that her puppy is dead.

I quickly lower my eyes, but I think Will notices the sudden chill. I can feel him tense up beside me. *Something is definitely going on here,* I think to myself.

The waiter comes by to take our drink order. "I'm telling you," Will leans close to my ear so I can hear him over the noise of the restaurant. "The frozen strawberry daiquiri is the way to go."

What the hell, I think. I order one. And I ask for extra whipped cream, because he put the idea in my head, and, frankly, it sounds like a delicious escape from the hellhole that my life has been recently.

He asks for a Coke with no ice.

I look at him in confusion. "Why no ice?"

"I don't like how the ice rushes my face when I tip the glass," he says, looking a little embarrassed.

It strikes me as somehow beyond adorable that he's afraid of the ice touching his face. "Don't they have straws in this establishment?" I wonder, feeling like that's the obvious solution.

"Sometimes," he explains, then lowers his voice. "Service can be a little hit or miss here, especially on trivia nights because it's so busy. Everybody's really friendly, but it's just easier to assume you might not get exactly what you order. Some nights, they don't even bring napkins."

He slowly appraises my outfit, and I feel more than a little frisson as he surveys me and then raises his eyes back up to meet mine. "I hope you're not too fond of that white shirt," he says, shaking his head seriously. "The dark jeans are a solid choice, but chances are good you're going home with a conspicuous stain on that shirt."

I look at him dubiously. "Because of no straws?"

He nods in mock sincerity. "Because of no straws."

I snort. "Well, fortunately, I'm not a very messy eater." I shift on the stool to try to get comfortable. High-top tables have never been my favorite, and my stool is both very hard and a little wobbly.

As I tip to the right, I accidentally brush against his leg. He doesn't react, just stares straight ahead like nothing happened. There's no way he didn't notice. *Maybe he just doesn't care, because we're not 13 and this is a ridiculous thing to be worried about,* I tell myself. I shift back the way I'd been sitting before. *Too much. Too close.*

Susan catches my eye. "So, Callie, how's your book coming?"

I eagerly grab the opportunity to escape the tension, which it's increasingly seeming might be both one-sided and all in my head. "Not bad," I admit. "It's not going to win any awards, or anything. But I'm more than halfway done now. I'm looking forward to turning in my draft. And getting paid."

I laugh, a little uncomfortably. For some reason, talking about being a ghostwriter always makes me feel like I'm endorsing my being one. And I really can't do that, because it would be a lie.

I so desperately wish I were Scarlett in this moment. Both because then I'd be a novelist, and because I'd know exactly what to say. I make a mental note to drag her with me if they invite me back.

Susan gives me an appraising look. "Are you enjoying writing the book? Because I'll be honest, you sound about as excited as Freya does when I tell her she needs to pick up her toys."

I'm taken aback, but I smile at her and try to sound flippant. "Oh, well, you know. Not exactly where I pictured myself, but such is life."

Just then, the waiter brings our drinks. Neither one has a straw. Will gives me a knowing look. "Goodbye, pristine white shirt," he says solemnly.

I roll my eyes at him.

We order our food, and the trivia game begins. "So, it's structured in five 20-point rounds," explains Susan from my left. "Each round has a theme. Most have ten questions that are two points each. We hand in our score sheets between each round. If you win the whole thing, you get a $25 gift card to the bar. But there are other prizes, like rounds of shots and a pitcher of margaritas." She takes a swig of her beer. "We usually win at least something, but with you here, we're angling to win the whole shebang." She smiles. "No pressure, or anything, though."

I chuckle, then nod. Priya is writing answers for our team, looking down at her paper with all the unsettling austerity of an undertaker. She's barely spoken since we arrived. Jax and Jenna have carried on a lively conversation about soccer, something I know very little about, and Susan and Will and I have been chatting. But Priya hasn't joined in.

I take a big sip of my daiquiri. Whipped cream gets all over my mouth. Some of the pink below dribbles onto my shirt. *Damn it.* I look around for a napkin, but of course, there isn't one. I wipe my face with the side of my hand, looking hopelessly down at the strawberry blotch on my chest. I'll have to remember to bring some purse tissues next time. And a Tide pen.

When I look over, I can see Will laughing.

THREE ROUNDS IN, and we've won both the shots and the margaritas. Will is driving, and Jax says he has an early morning workout, so they're not imbibing. But Doug's picking Susan up, and Priya and Jenna apparently live within walking distance, so the four of us are indulging in a big way.

I was feeling a little tipsy after my daiquiri, but with that under my belt, the addition of two shots and half a margarita has really sent me over the edge toward just plain drunk. I decide to skip the rest of my margarita and switch to water.

Susan and I are having a hilarious conversation we've christened Drunk Book Club, in which we rip apart the New Releases we've both been reading and mercilessly mock the protagonists.

"Let's actually bring the books next week," she suggests. "Then we can do shots every time the main character does something dumb."

"I think that's a great idea," I say.

I'm thrilled when the fourth round is announced and the theme is Broadway songs. I know I can contribute here.

The MC plays "Surrey with the Fringe on Top."

"That's from *Oklahoma!*" I say to Priya. She barely lifts her eyes, but she writes the answer down.

Next, we hear "One Night in Bangkok" (*Chess*), "The Heather on the Hill" (*Brigadoon*), and "At the Ballet" (*A Chorus Line*). Priya looks increasingly annoyed with every answer I give her. I don't know what her problem is, but I'm pretty drunk, and I'm dangerously close to asking.

I catch Will staring at me, open-mouthed.

I shrug sheepishly. "My parents took me to a lot of plays when I was a kid."

"Geez, apparently," he says. "We've never won a theater round before. I'm glad you're here!" He claps me on the back. "Nice job, Cal!"

My stomach flip-flops. There he goes again with the "Cal" business. I catch Priya's eye. She does not look amused. I think I'm starting to understand something about her problem with me.

"I knew we were smart to bring you here," Susan jokes.

"I think you are to theater what I am to soccer," says Jax. "And by that, I mean, a straight-up genius."

I blush. I don't think all this praise is helping my case with Priya, who abruptly excuses herself to go to the bathroom and shoves the scorecard at Jenna.

I glance sidelong at Will. His eyes are following Priya as she leaves the room. He looks concerned, and maybe a little frustrated. I so want to know what the story is there.

The room is spinning now. The lights are a little too bright, the music a little too loud. I definitely overdid it with the drinks. "Excuse me," I flag our waiter. "Could I get some more water?"

He nods and dashes away, not at all in the direction of the kitchen.

"You okay?" Will asks me as I lean my forehead on my hand.

"Yeah," I nod. "I just need a second. So many drinks."

Now he definitely seems concerned. "If you need me to take you home, please just let me know."

I shake my head. "I'm okay for now. Thank you."

The rest of the night is a bit of a blur. Priya comes back after a while, still looking upset. The room keeps spinning for me, though I manage to pull out a perfect score for the team on the Broadway round.

Ultimately, we don't win the night—that honor goes to a very loud group in the corner that calls itself "My Couch Pulls Out, But I Don't," which feels like a very long-winded way of letting us know they're douchebags.

When the game is over, everyone says their goodbyes.

"I picked up our tickets for the gala. I'll bring them next week," says Priya quickly, stepping closer to Will.

I look sharply at him. She's going with him to the gala? Are they *together*? I don't understand what's going on. *Why am I even upset about this?*

"Awesome, thanks! See you next week," he waves, either missing or ignoring the expression on my face. "Ready?" he asks, helping me off the stool and offering an elbow as I teeter a bit unsteadily out of the bar.

He laughs. "You're so not going to be able to drive home from the library."

I'd sort of forgotten about that. "Oh, that's okay. I can walk."

His brows go up. "Alone? Drunk? In the dark?" He shakes his head vehemently. "I don't think so. I'll just drop you off at home."

I can't let him do that. I can't be alone with him any longer than I have to, because what's happening in my brain right now is very much not okay.

My mind is racing. I could call Scarlett. Although she may be asleep by now; she has a big meeting tomorrow morning with her editor. I shake my head. That won't work.

Maybe I can call Thomas. I'm sure that would go over well toward reinforcing his vision of me as a lazy failure.

Will touches my arm. "Callie? What's wrong?"

I shake my head. "Nothing. It's fine. Thank you; a ride would be great."

WE DRIVE in silence for a few minutes, then my curiosity gets the best of me. I'm sure the drunkenness isn't helping, either.

"So, what's the deal with you and Priya?" I ask, perhaps more abruptly than I would have under normal circumstances.

His fingers tighten on the steering wheel, and he pauses for a moment before responding. "Ah. You picked up on that, did you?"

"Will," I say teasingly, "I think a deaf, dumb, and blind kid could pick up on that. And play a mean pinball."

He laughs so loudly, so suddenly, it's like it burst straight out of his chest. "And now you're quoting The Who to me? Who are you, Callie Sheffield?"

"Who who, who who, indeed?" I joke. If he likes it when I quote song lyrics, why not keep it going?

He's still laughing. I really like it when he laughs. I know it's wrong. I know I'm taken, and I'm the worst kind of person for feeling this way about another person who isn't Thomas. I try to stuff my feelings down, so far into my chest that I might just forget that they're there.

He clears his throat, mirth still in his eyes. "So, Priya is actually my ex-girlfriend," he begins slowly. "And she's having sort of a hard time moving past it."

I nod. Her behavior makes a lot of sense. Being territorial over her ex is understandable, although I'm not sure why she sees me, specifically, as a threat.

"When did you two break up?" I wonder aloud, realizing as soon as it's slipped out that it might be an insensitive question. "Sorry," I tack on, as if that will fix what I've said.

"It's okay," he reassures me. "It's been about eight months. But we have a lot of the same friends, as you saw tonight. Jenna, Jax, Priya, and I were pretty inseparable in college. Susan was our TA, and we got to know her really well, too."

"Nothing like a teacher who will party with her students," I joke.

He cracks a smile. "We've been doing things as a group for years now. It's been pretty challenging to separate our failed relationship from our friends. I don't want to box her out. Plus, Jenna was her roommate in school, so they're really close. It's just...awkward."

"How long were you guys together?" I ask, figuring if he shared all that, he's probably willing to answer one more question.

"Just over two years," he says quietly.

"Wow," I say, not sure how else to respond. "That seems hard."

"Yeah," he nods. "It has been."

A lingering question hangs in the air, one that I'm not entirely sure I want to ask. But I'm drunk, so I go for it before I can wrestle enough self-control to stop myself.

"So, why did I get the distinct feeling that Priya really didn't like me?" I toy with a hole in the knee of my jeans, looking at Will out of the corner of my eye to gauge his reaction.

His eyes shift uncomfortably. "She's pretty territorial," he says quietly. "I think she might have seen you and gotten the wrong idea about us."

My heart sinks. It *is* the wrong idea. But it still makes me sad to hear him say it.

"That's what I figured. Well, hopefully I can patch things up with her next week." *Shit*, I think. I don't even know if they're going to invite me back. "Assuming you want me to come back," I say hurriedly.

He grins. "You definitely need to come back. And bring your roommate, if you want. She sounds like a lot of fun."

I'd been telling him about Scarlett last week during one of his many breaks to unjam the copier, which happens to be situated very near the table I use at the library.

"She'd love it," I tell him.

"Oh, and bring your boyfriend, too," he adds. My heart sinks even further. I hate the reminder of Thomas. And I hate that I feel that way.

I hate that I'm this kind of person, who is having very rom-com-y feelings about someone who isn't my boyfriend. I hate this stupid Benderson book, which is keeping me distracted from what makes Thomas and me great. I hate the ultimatum I've given myself about waiting until the book is done to decide on the future of my relationship.

And I *really* hate how badly I want to reach out and touch Will's messy hair, which is so shiny it's practically glinting in the moonlight, like some sort of enticement for horrible skanks, which I apparently am.

But of course, I don't say any of that. Instead, I mumble, "Yeah, sounds great." And then I let Will tell me about the new project he's working on at the library, a literary scavenger hunt party for teenagers, as if my insides aren't swirling with lust and confusion and anger and booze; as if I'm not about to implode from the weight of it all.

But his voice is soothing, and I realize I'd rather be here, drunk and confused and probably a horrible person, than at home writing my stupid book.

I TELL WILL my address when we get back into town, and he delivers me safely to the apartment complex. My poor car will have to survive without me for the night at the library.

"Can I walk you to your door?" he asks. "Please say yes; I'm a little concerned about your ability to get up those stairs on your own, to be honest."

I smile ruefully. "I share your concerns. I'll gladly accept your offer of assistance."

He helps me out of the car, and I stumble a little unsteadily into the parking lot. I cannot drink this much, perhaps ever again. He reaches out his arm for me, and I hook my elbow through his.

I'm tired, and drunk, and my brain feels so addled that it's harder to ignore my feelings now than it was earlier when I had my wits about me. His arm is so warm. His ocean scent wafts across the breeze and hits my nose. I'm caught up in all kinds of wanting, but mostly it's just a wanting to feel something. Tears start in my eyes when I realize it's been ages since I've had any sort of feeling like this.

Like butterflies.

We get to my apartment, and I dig my keys out of my purse. "Well, thank you so much for bringing me along. I had a lot of fun," I say, unlocking the door. I start to push it open and turn to face him, my back to the entryway.

His eyes are bright in the moonlight, brighter than the library fluorescents at midday. His arm is still outstretched; he'd been helping me stumble up the stairs until just a moment ago.

He reaches out and squeezes my hand. I look at him in surprise, and my breath catches in my throat. He immediately lets go, as if he acted on impulse and then thought better of it. "It was a lot of fun," he says hurriedly. His smile shoots all the way up to his eyes. "Good night, Cal."

"Good night," I respond as he waves and heads down the stairs.

I'm still standing in the open doorway when he drives away.

six

"Lucyyyy, I'm hoooome! And I'm sad!"

Scarlett gets back from her editor meeting at ten the next morning and kicks off her black pumps by the door. She runs straight to the couch and throws herself upon it dramatically.

I shoot her an amused look from the kitchen, where I'm stirring a bowl of oatmeal, nursing the world's worst hangover. A glass of water, a mug of steaming coffee, and two ibuprofen sit beside me on the counter.

"Well, how was it?" I touch the oatmeal to my lips. Way too hot. Also fairly disgusting. Oatmeal is not my favorite, but I'm hoping it will soak up some of the booze from last night.

"Ugh, Cal," she tips her head back dramatically. "They want me to revise so much of the book. They don't like the lake house plot. They think it's 'too rustic,'" she says with very sarcastic air quotes. "I'm just tired. I threw everything I had into this book, and I'm so ready to be done."

I nod sympathetically, but inside, I'm not sure I really understand. I would give anything to be upset about a meeting with my editor. Hell, I'd give anything to *have* an editor in the first place.

"So what are you going to do?" I sink into one of the Esperanza chairs in the dining nook, but I can still see Scarlett, since our apartment subscribes wholeheartedly to the open floor plan philosophy.

She closes her eyes tightly. "I guess I'm going to take a day off," she begins, "and then I'm going to get back into it tomorrow. Want to do something mindless today? We could go shopping and buy a bunch of useless mall junk."

A mall day sounds awfully good to me, too. I can take one day off from my book. I'm not eager to face Will today anyway, even though nothing actually happened last night. It's more what's in my head when he's around that makes me feel like I need some distance.

I nod, slowly at first, then with more conviction. "A day of useless mall junk sounds like the perfect thing."

SCARLETT and I wander the shopping center aimlessly, popping in and out of stores whenever inspiration strikes. We try on hats in Nordstrom like we're in some sort of chick flick makeover montage, then we grab pretzels in the food court.

After about an hour of walking and chatting, she remembers that she needs a new sports bra. She just signed up for hot yoga and seems to think that this latest attempt at organized exercise is going to stick.

We head to Victoria's Secret, the only store in the mall that specializes in expensive underthings, and find the small section devoted to workout clothing.

"If I wanted something that looks like my grandmother would wear it, I would've just gone to Boscov's," Scarlett mumbles to herself, flipping through the racks.

I attack the search from the next aisle, moving from garment to garment, trying to find something to meet her criteria of both comfort and, apparently, style.

"Do looks really matter, here, Scarlett? You're going to be hiding this under your shirt." I've seen about 35 navy blue bras with ugly foam cups at this point, but nothing particularly youthful.

She grins mischievously at me. "Well, I might meet up with Jonathan after hot yoga."

I raise an eyebrow. Jonathan is her new "super hot but very interesting" gentleman friend. Scarlett had managed to turn her book-reading meet-cute into a string of several apparently successful dates.

As far as I know, she hasn't slept over at his house yet, but the more innocent phase of their budding relationship sounds like it might be coming to an end.

"That sounds like fun," I reply, trying not to seem judgmental. Or jealous. Things have been a little dry in the physical realm of my relationship with Thomas lately.

Scarlett surveys me over a strappy yellow sports bra that looks like it would offer no support whatsoever. "Are you going to shop for anything while we're here?"

I shoot her a pointed look. "I don't think I should be spending my limited funds on lacy unmentionables."

"I bet Thomas would looooove this one." She holds up some obnoxious red lingerie that would probably make Victoria herself feel like a trollop.

"I'm not wearing that," I mumble, flushing and shoving it back on the rack. "And I don't want to talk about this."

Concern settles over her face. "Is everything okay?"

I nod, but I'm not sure it's the truth.

"If you say so." She goes back to looking at bras.

I feel my phone buzz in my pocket. Wanting to escape the awkward silence Scarlett and I now find ourselves trapped in, I grab it.

It's Will. *Hey! How are you feeling today?*

I shift further behind a garment rack so Scarlett won't notice that I'm on my phone. Or that I'm blushing.

I'll admit to a bit of a hangover, if that's why you're asking.

I suspected that might be the case. I'm sorry; I pushed you toward that daiquiri. I feel responsible, he texts back.

I snort. *I'm a full-grown adult. It's on me, not you.*

Well, I'm sorry anyway.

My heart somersaulting in my chest because he cared enough to text is *so* not the distance I needed from Will today.

No worries, I reply.

He answers before I can put my phone away. *I was surprised you didn't come to the library to write this afternoon. Was the hangover that severe?*

Sorry, I answer. *Got caught up with some roommate stuff.*

I look up over a sea of pink lace and see Scarlett eyeing me quizzically.

"Who are you texting?" She grins mischievously. "Something about the way you're blushing makes me think it's not Thomas."

Damn it. "Why wouldn't I be blushing if I were talking to Thomas?"

She rolls her eyes. "Please. There's no mystery left there. He's about as scintillating as the book you're writing for him."

I don't bother to correct her, that the book isn't for *him*, specifically. Nor do I refute her assessment of Thomas's lack of scintillation.

Instead, I clear my throat, hoping to sound casual. "It's just someone who works at the library."

Her brows shoot up. "A guy, right?"

There's no hiding things from Scarlett, that's for sure. "Yes, a guy." At the eager expression she's now wearing, I quickly add, "His name is Will, and he works at the circulation desk. I got to know him and his friend, Susan, and they invited me out to trivia last night in Rockledge. It was very much a group thing."

Scarlett laughs. "A group thing you came home drunk from?" She pauses, then gasps and reaches for my shoulders. "Oh my God, Callie! Was he the one who gave you a ride home?"

I shove my phone back into my pocket, furious at its betrayal of my confidence. "It's honestly nothing." Turning around, I head toward the perfume aisle. I just need to get away from this conversation.

"But he's texting you today?" Scarlett follows me to where I'm sniffing a bottle of Secret Bombshell Summer.

I clink the bottle back onto the shelf and fix her with what I hope is a firm glare. "He just wanted to see how I'm feeling. He's a nice guy." My head twinges, and I realize my hangover hasn't left the building. I don't have the energy to deal with an interrogation on top of everything else. "You're making too big a thing out of this."

"Callie, please," she says condescendingly. "Men don't just take you out, get you drunk, and then text you the next day to see how you're doing if they're not interested in you." She sprays a perfume called Very Sexy Now into the air and walks through its cloud. "And you, my friend, don't go out, get drunk, and let men drive you home. Or text them. Like, ever."

"Look," I mutter under my breath, hoping to evade further notice from the bored sales clerk who seems to have perked up upon hearing our drama, "Will's just a friend, he did *not* get me drunk, and I don't want to talk about this anymore, okay?"

Scarlett gives me a very frustrating, obnoxiously *knowing* look, but she walks back toward the bras, leaving me in peace. "I'll finish up, then we can go," she yells over her shoulder.

SCARLETT FINALLY PICKS out a pink floral sports bra that promises extra support and moisture-wicking, and then we head out.

As soon as we get to the escalator, she pounces.

"I think there's something wrong between you and Thomas, and I think there has been for a long time." Never one to bury the lede, that Scarlett.

I start to object, but she cuts me off. "It's okay," she says quickly. "You don't have to say anything."

"Well, that's good." I give her a wry grin. "Because I'm not sure you're going to let me."

Her shrill cackle catches the attention of an elderly woman passing us on the up escalator. "Callie, Callie, Callie," Scarlett pats me on the arm, waving reassuringly at the woman she startled like she's the mayor of the mall. "Your actions say more than your words ever could."

"What exactly is that supposed to mean?" I know she's trying to help, but now I'm kind of annoyed.

Scarlett investigates what may be a split end, frowns, and then says, "Look, I've known you a long time. I've known Thomas almost as long. He's a good guy, and it is certainly helpful that he's *beyond* dreamy. But things have always been a little stilted there, especially lately. You know what I mean." She purses her lips. "Like, you've been together for four years, and you don't live together?"

"Because I live with *you*," I cut her off.

She shakes her head vigorously, reddish waves flouncing across her shoulders. "Yeah, but you could live with *him*. And you don't even seem to want to. Have you guys even talked about it, ever? About your future together? Are you going to get married someday? What's your plan?"

"Whoa, Scarlett," I hold up my hands. "Let's not get ahead of ourselves."

Her mouth tightens into a line. "Callie, you're 26." Clearly, she doesn't remember my equation method of age calculation. "You see him once or twice a week. That's it. He rarely spends the night. You vacation with his family. You work for his boss." She frowns. "You're fitting yourself into his world, but I don't see much of that coming back the other way. And when you talk about him, I don't know. I just don't think you seem happy."

I feel my eyes flash. "This is so not your business."

"It isn't, but you're my best friend, and I'm worried about you." She steps off the escalator.

"Well, don't be." I don't usually get angry with Scarlett, but right now, I'm fuming. I pick up the pace, getting a little bit ahead of her.

"Honestly, you seemed happier texting Will just now than you have any time I've seen you with Thomas, maybe ever."

"That's so not true," I shout over my shoulder, not bothering to stop and wait for her.

"Callie, I just don't want to see you looking back someday and realizing you weren't happy. That you were wasting your time, living in something that was way too safe just because you're afraid to be alone." She rushes to catch up.

I whirl to face her, almost knocking into her with my purse in the process. "Screw you, Scarlett. Why don't you focus on your own pathetic attempts at finding love and leave me to enjoy my mature, stable relationship in peace?"

Her mouth hangs open, and I wonder if I've gone too far. But how often I see Thomas, or how often he spends the night, are *so* not things I should have to justify to my roommate. Even if she also happens to be my best friend.

"You know what?" she snaps. I've never seen her face this shade of pink before. "I'm not going to apologize for caring about you. You can continue to live in your own myopic little world and ignore reality for as long as you want, but I'm telling you, it's going to come home to roost eventually. And when it does, you're going to be sorry you wasted so much time."

I want to be furious with her, but she just said "come home to roost," so I can't take her quite as seriously. Still, this is not her business, and I'm done discussing it.

"Thanks for your concern," I manage. I don't look at her, because I'm not sure I can without saying something I'll regret. "I'd like to go home now."

THINGS ARE tense on the ride back from the mall, as well as at the apartment when we get home. I'm struggling to deal with the silence, which is so atypical with Scarlett around. I consider calling Susan to see if she wants to talk about a book we're both reading, but then I realize it's dinnertime, and she's probably busy feeding her kids.

On an impulse, I grab my keys and head to the door. "Going for a walk," I yell over my shoulder.

"Fine," Scarlett replies, not looking up from her phone.

The evening is sticky when I get outside, the kind of languid summer night that suggests the promise of Ferris wheels and fireworks. I think about Thomas, wondering what he's doing now.

As Scarlett so aggressively reminded me earlier, he and I usually get together once or twice a week for dinner and talk on the phone most nights. We try for a weekend date night whenever we can swing it, too.

We'd probably go out more often, but it hasn't been so long since my waitressing career ended, and I'm still getting used to having evenings free.

I haven't seen him much on our regular days lately, anyway. He's been busy with a project at work, and I've been nursing some frustration because he attempted to interfere with the Benderson book.

I feel a twinge of regret because, for how angry I'd been with Scarlett earlier, I know she was at least a little bit right. Things *are* weird with Thomas right now. I can't even remember the last time I wanted to do something romantic like buy lingerie to surprise him. Or even just show up at his apartment unannounced to spend time together. *This stupid book*, I think to myself. *It's ruining everything*.

I check my phone. It's 6:30. He might be home by now. Impulsively, I turn around and start walking in the direction of Thomas's apartment. It's only a 15-minute trip on foot. *I'll head over and surprise him*, I decide. Maybe the spontaneity will help me *feel* something again.

I STAND EXPECTANTLY on the generic black welcome mat outside Thomas's door, waiting for him to answer the bell. He lives in a building with a doorman (Steve, a kindly older guy who always remembers my name), so he can do cool things like have door mats in the hallway without worrying they'll get destroyed by the elements.

I try to paste on my most cheerful smile, but for some reason, I'm feeling nervous. Like I need tonight to go well, to prove to Scarlett, and myself, that this relationship is still worth fighting for.

After three minutes of waiting and as many rings of the doorbell, Thomas comes to the door with a puzzled look on his face.

"Callie?" he asks, like he isn't quite sure it's me.

"One and the same!" I stick out my hand in mock introduction.

He smiles slightly but doesn't take my hand. "Is everything okay?"

I put my arm back at my side, feeling suddenly as self-conscious as if I were wearing the lacy red babydoll from the mall. "I was just out for a walk and thought I would stop by to see how you were doing. Maybe come in and visit for a few minutes."

His brows furrow. "My apartment isn't on your usual walking route."

My heart warms a little, cheered by the knowledge that he remembers where I like to walk. "No, silly," I say, stepping closer to him. "But I wanted to see you."

"Well, thank you," he replies.

Thank you? I'm not sure that's the reaction you're supposed to get when you do something romantic like drop by your boyfriend's apartment unannounced to revive your ailing relationship.

He stands back from the door. "Come on in."

I follow him inside, kicking off my shoes in the entryway. I bend over and straighten them so they don't stand out quite so much from the row of pin-straight Cole Haans and Sperrys on his shoe rack.

"I was just reading *The Financial Times*," Thomas says over his shoulder as we go to the living room. "I thought about making some risotto. Do you want any?"

"I'd love some." I catch up to him and squeeze his hand. "I'm so glad to see you."

He smiles, and it hits me that I feel nothing.

. . .

DANIELLE SMYTH

I HEAD HOME AT EIGHT. Thomas says he has an early meeting, and I'm honestly pretty bored watching him read the paper. I try to clean up the dishes, but he tells me not to worry about it and shoos me away.

I wade through the humidity, a deep ache thrumming in my chest. The evening was pleasant enough, but it wasn't really anything to write home about. I'd been sure this would be the salve he and I needed—spontaneity, some flirtation, a night just for us.

I didn't count on freezer meals dumped onto white Fiestaware and solo reading hour from different sides of the couch. I don't keep any books at Thomas's apartment, so I had to borrow a Sinclair Lewis novel he'd been bothering me to read. I wanted to like it, but it felt like a slog so far.

I mean, who even buys *frozen risotto*?

I don't want to think about my colossally bland evening, and I'm not ready to go home and face Scarlett, especially now that I'd have to hide the events of my night from her. I don't need to give her even more fodder for her argument that I'm wasting my time with Thomas.

I sink onto a bench outside the pool area of our apartment complex and pull out my phone. I stare at it blankly for a minute, willing it to give me an excuse not to go inside.

It's been a couple of days since I've talked to Esperanza, so I dial her number. There's a good chance she's still up and watching old Westerns on VHS.

It rings only once. "Hello!" she exclaims, sounding as surprised as ever to be answering her own phone.

"Hi, Esperanza," I say. "I was just out for a walk and thought I'd see how you were doing."

"Oh, I'm good, kid. I was just here watching *The Man Who Shot Liberty Valance*. It has that James Stewart. He's a good-looking man, Jim Stewart. Have you seen that one?"

I smile. Leave it to Esperanza to use Jimmy Stewart's name slightly differently not once but twice in one thought.

"I haven't, but I do love Jimmy Stewart." I pause and inspect my chipped nail polish. I really need to give myself another manicure. "Maybe we can watch it together sometime."

She laughs. "Okay, C. That would be nice." There's a pause, and I can tell she's gone back to her movie.

"Anything else new with you?" I ask, desperate to keep the conversation going so I can avoid Scarlett a little longer.

"You know, I was thinking I might give up my car," she says suddenly.

I'm surprised by this. Esperanza is so incredibly *busy*, constantly driving to visit friends and relatives. Because she doesn't work and has no husband or kids, she has very few actual responsibilities. But she more than makes up for that with self-imposed trips all over the place just to "check in" on people.

She'll drive an hour to see me, 40 minutes in the other direction to visit my parents, a half hour east to call on her brother and his wife. All over, to see everyone she knows.

She's like a little celebrity within her circle, deigning to grace people with her presence whenever she's bored. Just, of course, never after dark, when driving turns her into a combat veteran with PTSD. And also only when she's done with her daily 5k's worth of walking.

"What makes you want to do that?" I ask. I hear the TV turn off.

"Eh, I don't know," she begins. "I'm getting older, and I don't know if I want to keep driving. The car is expensive. I can just walk everywhere. Walk everywhere, or take the bus."

I grin to myself. *Getting* older? She's 83. A young 83, but still. "Yeah, but what would you do with yourself without your car?"

She sighs. "Oh, I guess you're right. You're right, C. I don't know." She sounds resigned to her fate. "I just don't know."

Now I feel bad, because it's obviously her choice. I tell her as much. "You should do whatever feels right to you, Esperanza. Take some time to think about it, okay?"

I can see her impulsively selling the car for cash this week and changing her mind a few days later. And if *I* can't afford the down payment for a new ride, she certainly wouldn't be able to. I don't think you're allowed to use Section 8 money for transportation costs, since it goes directly to your landlord, and that's about all she has.

"I will, I will," she says. The TV turns back on.

I clear my throat. I should probably let her go. "Hey, so I'll see you on Friday for your birthday dinner, right?"

"You got it! The shiny diner, yes?" I hear her open a drawer and rummage around. "I'm just going to get a pencil and write that down on my calendar. The shiny diner, Friday. This Friday."

It's a little ridiculous, since nearly all diners are shiny, at least historically. But we've called the little place where we typically have dinner with Esperanza "the shiny diner" for about 20 years, and I don't see it changing anytime soon.

"Yes indeed," I confirm. "Five o'clock?"

"I'll be there," she agrees. "But hey, don't bring me any presents, okay? I don't want you to get me anything."

I'd already gotten her a gift card to the grocery store and a bottle of the perfume she likes. I'd invited Scarlett to the dinner, too, before I knew we were going to be having a super awkward fight about my nonexistent sex life. I knew Scarlett had bought Esperanza a few large-print books that she thought would go over well. I'm pretty sure my parents won't show up empty-handed, either.

I'd also invited Thomas to join us, but he hasn't confirmed yet if he's coming or if he'll have to work late.

"I'll see what I can do, but some presents might have fallen into my cart at the store," I tease.

"Well, all right. Just nothing expensive! You need to save your money so you can buy a nice house for you and Tom."

This is a recurring fixation of hers; she likes to talk about Thomas and me settling down and buying a place, ideally closer to her. I usually go along with it, but given the day's events, I'm not really in the mood.

I force a small laugh so I don't seem rude. "I guess that's true."

I finish up the call and wish her a good night, then walk slowly back to the apartment. When I get inside, the lights are off. I see a note from Scarlett in the key bowl. *Went out with Jonathan*, it says in curly pink script. I breathe a sigh of relief and head right to my room.

Collapsing on the bed in the dark, alone with my thoughts, I feel the truth pushing roughly against my mind, vying for an opening. I try to resist, but I'm no match for the refrain that swirls through me, tearing me apart with a ferocity I'm not ready for.

It's over it's over it's over.

I see Thomas's face as clearly as if he's standing before me. The tears fall with a vengeance then.

It's over.

seven

The sky is turning to twilight by the time I leave the library on Wednesday. I'm making so much progress in the Benderson book that I'm starting to worry I'll miss it when it's gone. I also don't know what I'm going to do next, income-wise.

Shoving the thought from my mind, I start the car.

Or at least, I try to. I turn the key in the ignition once, twice. A third time.

The engine won't turn over.

"Come on!" I plead, trying it again. Silence rings through the air.

I guess this is the car's way of letting me know it didn't appreciate being left alone in the library parking lot since Monday morning.

"Damn it!" I stand up and slam the door, as if that will convince the car to cooperate. Rifling through the trunk, I finally find some jumper cables that my dad gave me for Christmas when I'd first bought the car. *What undergrad doesn't love auto accessories*, I'd thought sarcastically at the time. Suddenly, I'm very glad to have them.

I look around desperately for someone who can help me. "Damn it!" I swear again. The library is about to close. A blue minivan just pulled away, leaving the parking lot depressingly empty.

Scarlett is at her book club, and I know she never checks her phone while she's there. Plus, we haven't spoken more than a few words to each other since yesterday afternoon. I asked her to pass the milk this morning while I was making my coffee, but that was about it. I don't want our first foray back into friendship to be me begging for her help.

I'll have to call Thomas. Dialing him, I drum my fingers against the phone anxiously. Ring. Ring. Ring. Voicemail.

Shaking my head, I try again. Still nothing.

Sighing, I decide leaving a message is better than nothing. "Hi, Thomas. I'm at the library, and my car won't start. Call when you can, please."

Just then, the door to the library swings open and Will emerges. I'd forgotten he was still inside. He locks the door, gives it an extra tug to be sure it's secure, and heads toward the rear of the building. *Of course.* I'd also forgotten that the staff park around back.

It looks like it's going to rain, or maybe even storm. The wind is picking up, and the sky is starting to look a little green. I remind myself to start checking the weather.

I need to get out of here.

"Will!" I yell to him.

He turns around. "Callie? What are you still doing here?" He crosses the distance between us, taking in my concerned face and the jumper cables. "Ah," he says. "Car won't start?"

"Nope. Can you help me?"

He's already lifting the hood of my car and lining up the first red cable clip. "Let me move my car closer." He jogs away. I hear an engine start up behind the library, and moments later, Will pulls up beside me in his Camry.

"I really appreciate it," I manage, practically wringing my hands with nerves as he gets out of the car.

"Don't worry about it," he says, working quickly to pop his hood. I hand him the other end of the cables, my hand brushing his as he takes them and gets the next red clip set up, then the black one.

My heart jumps a bit at the surprise touch. Like I'm the car whose battery needs to be recharged. I feel like I'm living in some sort of cheesy romance novel. Stuck in a parking lot, boyfriend unavailable (emotionally and otherwise), with a dark, handsome stranger the only one available to help.

He *is* really cute, I admit to myself as I watch him work. It's more noticeable today, in the outdoor light, than it was in the dimly lit bar on trivia night. And because I'm stone-cold sober, it's a lot harder to pretend I don't notice how his unruly hair keeps falling into his eyes, and slipping again the minute he shoves it back. He's like a really earnest, messy puppy.

I can't honestly say I hate the plaid, either. And how does he even know how jumper cables work? No one else ever gets it right without reading the instructions first. He might actually be a genius.

"Okay," he says, moving back to my Honda. "Time to hook up the black one." He clips it to a spare metal part of my engine. "I'm going to turn my car on. Then, you should do the same."

I nod, walking to the driver's side of my car and putting the key back in the ignition. I issue a silent plea to the universe that it will work.

Nothing.

"We can let it go for five minutes or so," he offers, taking in my worried face.

I nod, swallowing hard. My budget doesn't have a lot of wiggle room for major car repairs. We stand in silence for a moment, staring at the car as it glares back in defiance.

"How was writing today?" Will asks, wiping his brow with the side of his arm. It *is* extremely humid. I wish I had a bottle of water or something to offer him.

I tear my gaze away from the silent car. "It was pretty good. I'm making a lot of progress."

I feel awkward that I basically ignored him all day today; that I avoided the library yesterday simply because I can't control my thoughts around him. Especially after he brought me to trivia with him and dragged me home in my drunken stupor. It isn't his fault that I've let my imagination get away from me. He's just being a good friend.

"That's awesome." Will peels off his plaid button-down, revealing surprisingly muscular forearms and...a tattoo? I try to ignore the overwhelming urge to get closer to investigate.

His Tom Petty t-shirt looks relieved to no longer have to share the spotlight with its long-sleeved cousin. My mouth falls open in feigned shock. "I'm sorry, I don't think you're allowed to *not* be plaid."

Will laughs loudly. "I guess I deserve that."

"I'm only kidding," I offer, suddenly regretting my choice to insult his fashion sense. "I just don't think I've ever seen you without a plaid shirt."

"What can I say? I'm a man of surprising depth." Will tosses his shirt through the open window of his car. It drops down next to the seat.

I'd just told him two nights ago that I really like Tom Petty. Is that why he picked this outfit?

Stop it, Callie, I reprimand myself silently. I'm probably reading too much into things.

I feel a drop of water. "Oh, no." Tears well up in my eyes. "It's starting to rain." A distant roll of thunder makes my heart sink even further.

I'm pretty sure Will notices that I'm about to cry, because he reaches out and touches my arm reassuringly. His hand is warm, and he lingers maybe a moment longer than he should, which he seems to realize all of a sudden. He pulls away and busies himself with brushing his hair off his forehead, which is a bit of a lost cause.

Warmth swirls to the surface of my skin where his fingers made contact. I feel like a teenager with her first crush. This is turning into the worst kind of life imitating bad rom-com art.

Will clears his throat. "It's going to be okay. Here, let's go." He reaches in and turns off his car, then he starts unclipping the jumper cables.

"Go where? I can't leave. I need to get my car towed." My brain is mush, overwhelmed by the heat and the car, and *why the hell do I care so much that he touched my arm?*

"We'll call them from the road." Will slams my trunk shut and opens the passenger door to his car. "Hop in."

Without any other options in mind, I accept his offer, sliding into the Camry. "I really appreciate your help," I say, feeling flustered and a little embarrassed that he's saved me twice in one week.

And why can't I have a car made in this decade? Scarlett managed to put a down payment on a brand-new Subaru with the advance from her first novel. I love her (less so today than usual), but damn, am I jealous of her.

"Well, I can't very well leave you standing outside the library in what's about to be a thunderstorm." He puts the car in reverse and looks over his shoulder with a grin. "That wouldn't be very good customer service."

I crack a little smile. "Well, thank you for your chivalry."

He feigns a bow, stilted somewhat by the steering wheel. We ride in silence for a moment, and then he asks, "So, did you always know you wanted to be a ghostwriter?"

I go cold. No one has ever asked me that, and I feel like Will and I are past the point of getting-to-know-you small talk. I don't know what to say so I don't sound like a complete moron.

I swallow harder than usual, and I think he notices.

He sneaks a glance in my direction. "I'm sorry; did I say something wrong?"

"No, no." I look down at my lap. "It's just that I don't know how to answer. I didn't really ever want to be a ghostwriter." I frown. "I actually don't want to be one now."

"Oh," he muses slowly, as if mulling over my words in his head, trying to shape them into something resembling sense. "Then why are you?"

I start to answer, to explain my pathetic existence and lack of trajectory or prospects. I start to explain how I can't hack it as a novelist, so this is the next best thing. I start to tell him how I have to get my successful boyfriend to catch breaks for me.

But all of those answers sound hollow in my mind, so I just shake my head. "I really don't know."

It's the most honest I've been in a long time. Even though Will and I are just becoming friends, something about the concern in his eyes makes me feel more secure telling him the truth.

Before I realize what's happening, everything is spilling out. My dream of being a novelist, how I submitted my first manuscript to 27 agents, all of whom rejected me. How I graduated with no job and no prospects, like a modern-day, vocationally challenged Jane Austen heroine.

How I waitressed my way around town like some kind of hospitality tramp, and how I couldn't bear to move home and accept defeat, even though I could barely afford my half of the rent with Scarlett. How Thomas had gotten me this lucrative contract, and how I owed him big time and couldn't afford to mess it up.

Will listens to everything I have to say, and then he grins. "Sounds like it's time for a letter to agent number 28."

I smile in spite of myself. "I appreciate your faith in me, but I need to focus on finishing this finance book so I get the other half of my retainer. And I think the firm 'no' from the first 27 agents should tell me something."

"Maybe," he says. "Or maybe they were just wrong." He throws on his directional to turn down my street.

The rhythmic dance of the windshield wipers is the only thing making a sound. I don't know what to say. Obviously, it would be lovely if Agent 28 wanted to publish my book. But I don't even know if I have the motivation to keep going anymore.

Could I make it through the rewrite process? The edits? The beta readers, the discussions about marketing and cover designs? The energy for that sort of thing feels like it's been swallowed up by descriptions of investment horizons and index funds. And by the taste of failure, which I've let linger a little bit too long to clear it now.

Will speaks softly. "I mean, let's be real, Callie. You're an amazing storyteller."

I blush, all the way up to my temples. "I don't think the Benderson book is a great reflection of my writing style."

He chuckles. "I'm not talking about that. When you just talked about your journey, how you got here? Or when you told me about your aunt the other day? You have a way with words. It's captivating to listen to you."

I'm pretty sure my blush is visible to other drivers on the road now, even through the torrents of rain. "Thanks, Will. That's really sweet of you." I'm still confused about where his line of questioning came from, but I appreciate that he cares enough to ask.

"I have to come clean," he says, as if he read my mind. "I only asked about ghostwriting because I heard what you said to Susan about your book on Monday. Something about it struck me as profoundly sad. You seemed...I don't know. You seemed like you weren't okay. It's not my business at all. I just couldn't let it go."

I just stare at him. He's right, of course. It *is* sad. *I* am sad. The whole situation is depressing as hell, and I feel like I'm living in an alternate reality where I control nothing, choose nothing. Become nothing. This isn't how I thought my life was going to turn out.

But no one else seems to see that. They think ghostwriting someone else's book is enough. They think writing is writing, and that paying the bills is all that matters. That it's too great a risk to follow your dreams like some sort of '90s movie heroine who moves to New York City to become a journalist, only to find her real life is waiting for her back home in Podunk Valley, Arkansas, and it was all a waste of time.

No one has ever seen through me like this before.

"I don't know what to say," I admit when my mind finally catches back up.

He pulls into the parking lot of my apartment complex and turns off the engine. "You don't have to say anything," he replies gently. "But I'm here if you need to talk."

I nod my thanks, unable to form words. I feel like I'm going to cry. I don't even think I can articulate why. It's like him telling me that it's okay to feel my life isn't enough for me, letting those words hit air for the first time, makes them real. Even though in my heart they've been real for a very long time.

He squeezes my hand. "I mean it, Callie. I'm here."

A tear slips down, so I grab my hand back and wipe it away. I turn toward the window, hoping he didn't notice.

The rain is coming down even harder now. I don't have an umbrella.

We turn toward each other and both start to talk at once. I laugh uncomfortably. "Sorry," I say. "Go ahead."

"I was just going to ask if you want to borrow my button-down. It's certainly no umbrella, but you could wear it over your head if you wanted." He wrestles the shirt from between the seat and the center console, where it had gotten stuck when he tossed it through the window earlier.

"Oh." I'm taken aback. I don't know why, but it feels like borrowing his shirt is somehow too intimate? Even though it's just a shirt. *It's just a shirt*, I tell myself. A kind gesture from a friend.

"Sure, that would be nice. Thanks, Will." I take the shirt from him and hold it over my head, ready to hop out of the car. At least I can walk myself in this time without having to be held upright.

"Anytime." He smiles at me, and my heart makes that flip-flop again. *Oh no. I can't do this.*

"Hey, what were you going to say?" he asks as I push the door open.

I say it before I can think, before I let reason stop me from taking the leap of faith. "Oh. I was just going to say, maybe I'll dust off my old manuscript and bring it to the library sometime. Would you want to read it?" I look at him expectantly. Suddenly, I care very much about not being rejected by Will.

"I'm going to require that you do just that," he replies with a grin.

"We'll have a beta reader session after my shift sometime next week. Tuesday? As payment for the ride."

"Deal!" I agree. "It's a date."

Realizing what I said, I blush, yet again, and shake my head. "You know what I mean. Sorry. Anyway, thank you!"

Disgusted at how awkward I am, I close the door as quickly as possible. Jogging toward the building, I hold Will's shirt over my head to shield me from the rain. It smells like the ocean. *Damn it.*

It's not until I'm inside and have closed the door behind me that I realize I forgot to call a tow truck. Sighing deeply, I pull out my phone to dial one.

I see that I've missed a call from Thomas. He also sent a text. *I'm at the library. Where are you?*

Shit! *So sorry,* I type quickly. *I got a ride home from a friend. I hope you weren't waiting long.*

His reply comes immediately. *No problem. I'll call you later.*

Talk to you then, I say.

Then, I go to my room and throw Will's shirt in my laundry basket. It looks so strange, lying there on top of my pink sweatshirt and yoga pants. *It's probably going to get his stupid cologne smell all over my clothes,* I think to myself. I smile a little before I can stop myself. *Oh, God.*

I shake it off and go to my desk. Opening the top drawer, I dig out a thick manila envelope. My manuscript. I haven't looked at it in two years.

I hesitate. I know that, inside, I'll find all 27 rejection letters neatly piled atop the title page.

"I'm not ready for this," I say into the darkness. I put the envelope back in the drawer and shove it closed. Will is going to have to wait.

eight

When I arrive at the library on Thursday, I'm soaked in sweat from the excruciating walk through what felt like the inside of a dryer vent. The building is cool, though; so crisp, in fact, that I'm glad I have a cardigan in my bag. If I sit in here all day, I might actually need it.

As I stride toward my usual table, I see Will hanging a flyer on the community bulletin board over by the copier.

"What have you got there?" I circle him to get a better glimpse of the board, maybe a little too close. His ocean scent makes my insides hum a bit, in a way that suddenly makes me want to be even closer.

Get a grip, I tell myself.

"Writing class starting next month," he says, shoving a tack into the top of the sign. "You should sign up!"

"Tuesday *and* Thursday nights, from 6:30 to 8? Wow. I don't know if I have time for that," I reply. But something like excitement flickers inside my chest.

"I feel like your Nerd of Wall Street opus can wait," Will teases. His mouth twitches up on one side.

My stomach lurches with something like wanting. I try to shake it off.

I smile ruefully. "I'm not sure it can, but maybe," I say.

"Well, anyway, this is right up your alley," he continues. "The university is sending one of its professors to teach the class. I know her; she's really great. She was my advisor, actually."

When I don't react, he pretends to pout. "Calllllie."

"Willlllll," I mimic his tone.

"This is, in your own words, your one and only lifelong goal. The thing that keeps you up at night. Your dream deferred." His eyes are bright. It's hard not to fall into them.

I flash him a grin. "I'm pretty sure those were *not* my words."

"Okay, fine. But why not come see what it's all about?" He looks at me expectantly.

Why does he care so much?

It's kind of sweet, in a way. But he clearly doesn't understand how little time I have, what with the Benderson deadline looming large. And then there's the trauma of the 27 rejection letters filling my desk drawer.

"I don't know," I say, trying to let him down easy. "I really need to focus on this project. Thomas would never forgive me if I made him look bad at work."

Will surveys my face, and I feel like he's looking right through me. I know we're both remembering our conversation last night. "And what about what *you* want? When does that come into play?"

I shift my bag on my shoulder, where it's digging in. Thoughts race through my mind. This book is how I'm making my living right now. It's already a big leap, not having something steadier. I'm lucky to have this opportunity.

Being a novelist is a pipe dream, anyway. And if I don't do this for Thomas after he stuck his neck out for me, I don't know that we'll even have anything left. Our relationship feels so tenuous and distant these days as it is.

But Will is standing there, his thick hair looking mussed, his brown eyes still locked on mine. He's exuding some combination of hope and the bitter anticipation that he's about to be disappointed.

I don't know why, but I really don't want to disappoint Will.

My stomach dances again. I can't be having these thoughts about him.

"You know what, I'll look into it," I say, grabbing my phone and snapping a picture of the flyer. "Maybe I can make it work."

Okay, he's definitely surprised. Knowing that he expected me to reject his idea makes me feel more embarrassed than I'm ready to admit.

A smile spreads across his face, one that makes my face feel hot. "That's awesome!" He gently grabs my shoulders in excitement, and warmth spreads down my arms, through my chest, all the way into my toes. "I promise you won't regret it. This is your ticket to fame; mark my words."

I roll my eyes at him. "If you say so."

His hands slide down my arms, dropping from my shoulders to my fingers. They leave a trail of heat in their wake. The motion is so casual and chummy, like all he's doing is letting go. Like this was just the tail-end of an exuberant response to a friend's good news.

The motion is also very much something else, for me, whether Will intended it that way or not.

I feel like I'm holding my breath, skin still swirling with warmth from where he made contact.

When he takes a step back, I exhale.

"And anyway," Will busies himself with tacking up a flyer about a learn-to-knit workshop. "If you have time for trivia night, you can definitely make time for this."

"Thanks for letting me know about the class," I manage shakily.

Clearly, Will isn't aware of the effect he's having on me, or he'd have known better than to touch my shoulders like that.

I pause, wanting to say more, like how there's really no way I'll be able to swing it, or how Thomas is going to be pissed if I even bring it up when I haven't finished the finance book.

But he looks so happy that I just can't. *Nothing like a public servant, overeager to change lives*, I tell myself. That's all this is.

DANIELLE SMYTH

I excuse myself to go to work. He grins and waves goodbye, going back to his desk. But for the rest of the afternoon, I find myself sneaking looks at him and his stupid tousled hair, wondering why I care so much what he thinks.

I MENTION the writing class over dinner at Thomas's apartment that night. I don't even know why I bring it up, because I've already spent all afternoon convincing myself it's a bad idea right now. But I just have that feeling again, the flickering in my chest, like a pilot light that's been lying in wait has finally been given a little more gas.

"So the library's offering a 12-week creative fiction class," I slip in during a silent moment.

Thomas barely looks up from his steak. "Huh," he says, talking with food in his mouth even though he knows I hate it. "That's cool. I like knowing that our tax dollars are supporting the arts."

I slowly finish chewing and watch him bent over his plate. His straight brown hair is perfectly groomed, even in the relaxed hours of the day when it should be longing to kick back and get a little unruly.

Part of what made me fall in love with him was his commitment to the greater good. His comment about supporting the arts was classic Thomas, whose idea of a perfect afternoon was a spirited discussion of how FDR's New Deal paved the way for responsible government spending in the modern day. I used to think it was adorable how buttoned up he was, sitting on the couch in his argyle socks and reading *The Financial Times.*

He loved to talk about economic policy and social welfare programs. It only occasionally gave off us-and-them vibes, like he was content to do the right thing simply by sitting in a high-rise and signing off on charity programs for the masses like they were only a *little* less-than.

But as I sit here, watching him cut the pre-portioned steak he ordered from some mail-order grocery service that wouldn't fit into my budget, I can't help but feel a disconnect. I didn't come from money. I'm exactly the type of person a free writing class is created for, the amorphous "arts" he's so glad to support.

I clear my throat. "I was thinking I might sign up."

He looks up in surprise, blue eyes bright across the table. "Oh. Are you sure that's a good idea?"

I expected this. I hold my face steady so I don't react. "You know I've always wanted to write."

He smiles at me. "You do write. That's your job. In fact, last I checked, you have a pretty big ghostwriting project on your plate that you haven't finished. Maybe you should focus on that first before running off to do something fun?"

Okay, I expected this, but his words still sting. "I think I can do both. I spent hours at the library today writing the book, as I've been doing for two weeks now. I'm making good headway. In fact, I expect to be done within the next month. Well before the deadline."

I'd committed to Mr. Benderson that I'd have my full first draft to the firm by August 15th. Thanks to the flow state the library's gentle chaos has been helping me to achieve, I'm pretty sure I'll be done by the 1st instead.

Thomas goes back to cutting his steak. "Of course, do whatever you want. But I really went out on a limb for you at the office. Please don't make me look bad."

Anger simmers in my belly, and I struggle to keep the edge from my voice. "Why would I make you look bad, exactly?"

He shrugs. "If you get caught up writing for your class and don't finish the book, it'll be really embarrassing for me."

I take in his nonchalant air of superiority, and my frustration reaches a boil. "When have I ever not finished an assignment?" I jab my fork into the steak and leave it standing upright. "I'm incredibly reliable."

He gently lays his silverware to the side of his plate. "I didn't say you weren't," he replies slowly, as if explaining something to a very simple child. "But I've watched you struggle to find your footing ever since we graduated, and now you finally have a major project. One that you couldn't have gotten without me. And I don't want to see you throw it all away over some pipe dream." His empty eyes sweep over my face. "Especially when it isn't going to go anywhere. We've been there before."

I blink, not quite believing he went there. He is obviously talking about my novel and the 27 agents. And the deep depression I'd fallen into after I shoved the entire pile of rejection letters into my drawer.

For a while after that, it was all I could do to brush my hair and plaster on a smile for my shift at The Blue Parrot, the restaurant where I'd been waitressing. I stopped coming out of my room when Scarlett and I had game nights, instead binging my way through the entirety of *Gilmore Girls* in my bedroom by myself. I didn't even want to sit down and read in my spare time, because the cheerful author bios at the backs of my novels reminded me far too much of my failure.

And it had been hard for me to deal with Scarlett's excited squeal when she got her first book contract, just two months after I gave up. We'd started the process of applying to agents together, and she was fortunate to find someone who not only believed in her book but was able to sell it to a Big Five publisher within a matter of weeks. I desperately wanted to be there for her, but I was so incredibly jealous.

Every time I went out with Thomas during that period of darkness, I just sat there, as if inhabiting a shell of my former self. Sometimes, it felt like he didn't even notice. Other times, he'd reach out and squeeze my hand, then try to distract me by suggesting we go for a walk. But I wanted to rage, to cry, to crawl up in bed and never come out.

Walking was fine; I'm sure it was good for me. It did nothing to actually fix the hurt inside, though. It just covered the wound for a while, until eventually it was buried so deep, I could sort of forget it was there. But honestly, I don't think I ever really *dealt* with the feelings. Even now.

While my brain is doing a double-take, Thomas gently picks up his utensils and resumes eating.

"What exactly are you suggesting?" I ask quietly. "That I'm bound to fail just because I haven't had meteoric successes so far? That me working odd jobs after college means I'm lost? That you somehow *saved me* from myself?" I emphasize the last accusation with an extra ounce of bite.

"Callie," Thomas says quietly. "Please don't get upset."

"Too late."

"You're not being realistic," he tries again. "You know you need steady work. Writing is virtually guaranteed to come in waves. That's irresponsible. I think you've worked in every café in town at this point."

I glare at him, but he presses on. "Do you really want to keep doing that for the rest of your life? I'm here to help you pick up the pieces when your next big dream falls through, but we can't fail this time, since my reputation at work is what got you the project in the first place."

What started as frustration is now boiling over inside me, burning my insides with full, violent rage. But I don't know what to say. He's right. Isn't he?

I studied English in college and graduated into a bad market. Found work in a restaurant, then started juggling two jobs at a time to make ends meet. I tried to write in the edges of the day, but there never seemed to be enough time to get much done.

By the time the September after graduation rolled around, Scarlett and I were sick of minimum wage jobs and decided we were ready to make our mark. So we struck a deal: we'd each complete a novel by the end of the year. It was a huge push. I waited tables, came home exhausted, and wrote into the wee hours of the night. And I finished. And then we started querying agents. She got one; I didn't.

I started freelancing and managed to earn enough to drop down to one waitressing job, but it was exhausting. Since we lived in a college town, summers were slow, and I was forever trying to find a restaurant that would give me better hours. I was a good worker, and I didn't burn any bridges, but I kept trading up, always trying to nudge my pathetic finances to a better place.

With every new freelance project, I'd get excited, feeling like this was finally the client or contract that would free me from delivering buffalo wings to drunk college kids at one o'clock in the morning for paltry tips.

Thomas clearly just tolerated my hope, rarely saying much when I'd burst through the door for a date night with the news of my latest big break. He'd smile at me kindly and say he was happy for me, then quickly change the subject. I should have been more upset, I suppose, but I just *knew* I was going to succeed one of these times.

It wasn't until his boss had mentioned wanting to find a ghostwriter for a thought leadership book that I landed a serious writing gig. Serious enough that I could quit waitressing and live on a few one-off freelance projects and the book for the better part of a year.

It was a big deal and offered a lot of opportunities for the future. Thomas's boss was really well-connected, and both he and Thomas had made it seem like they'd bring me along for the ride to meet other business owners who might need my services. I couldn't afford to fail.

Still, in this moment, I'm furious.

Slowly, I stand up from the table. "Maybe you're right," I say in a measured way, eyes down.

Thomas has gone back to his steak, clearly not understanding how big a deal this is to me. I'm not even sure why I care so much this time. He's probably right. But something about the way hope is still flickering in my chest, the way Will's excitement for me reignited that flame, makes me feel like I can't let this go.

"See?" he says without looking up. "It's going to be okay. The book will be great, and it'll open up other doors for you down the road. Just focus on that."

"Mmhmm," I nod, seething behind my calm façade. "I think I'd like to go home to get some work done. I can walk." I still don't have my car, but I don't care. It's only a few blocks, and I need to get out of here.

"Sounds good, sweetheart." Thomas decimates a green bean.

As I walk out the door, I think I surprise us both when I say, "By the way, I hated that steak."

ON THE WAY HOME, I call Esperanza. She doesn't answer, but I figure she's at my grandparents' house, so I try her there. I exchange brief pleasantries with my grandmother, then she puts Esperanza on.

"Hey, kid!" Esperanza seems excited to hear from me. "I came over to Josephine's for supper."

"Nice," I say, walking up a hill and trying not to breathe so loudly into the phone that it's distracting.

It's been ages since I've seen my grandparents. We get along well enough, but Esperanza is the one I've always felt closer to. Probably because she never has anything to do. She invited herself over to my house all the time when I was a kid.

And since she's basically a big kid herself, she liked to play games with me, even when my parents were busy. Checkers, War, Go Fish. None of my friends had a really goofy playmate who was almost 60 years their senior, so they liked to come over and hang out with her, too. Everybody loved Esperanza.

"Yep, we had ziti," she says. "Yeah, that's right. I just came over to say hello. I told her, 'Josephine, I don't want anything!' But then she said she had too much pasta, and so I had some. I probably ate too much, to be honest. I didn't go for my walk today. I'll go tomorrow."

This is a classic Esperanza play: going visiting, insisting she isn't hungry, then basically binge eating all of the food that's set in front of her. I'm sure it comes from some combination of deep-rooted food insecurity and hatred of her short, curvy stature. I guess even the elderly aren't immune to body image woes.

"Well, that sounds good." I round the corner to my street. "Did I tell you that my car broke down?" I ask.

"Oh dear!" I hear her yell for her sister. "Josephine, did you know that Callie's car stopped working?" My grandmother yells something unintelligible back, and then Esperanza redirects to me. "Oh dear. That's not good. Not good at all. Did you get it fixed?"

I tell her about the repairs, for which the mechanic quoted $350. That's about $350 more than I was hoping to spend, but I don't have much choice. It's cheaper than buying a new car.

I'm back at the apartment now, and it's almost seven o'clock. Esperanza is only 15 minutes from home when she's at my grandparents', but I should let her go so she doesn't have to drive in the dark.

I want to do the right thing, even though I *really* don't want to go inside. I see the light on in the living room, so I know Scarlett's home. Things are still tense on the home front.

"I should probably get going. I'll see you tomorrow for your birthday dinner, right?" I remind her. Not that she's going to forget. For all her idiosyncrasies, the woman has a mind like a steel trap. Plus, we just talked about it on Tuesday night.

"Yep, yep, you'll see me then! Bye, C!"

I smile in the twilight, struck by how amusing she is, and how lucky I am to know this very unique human. "Have a good night, Esperanza."

SCARLETT and I don't talk at all tonight, other than a few necessary exchanges when I first get home (yes, she picked up soap; no, I don't need a ride to the mechanic tomorrow).

I grab a shower to wash away the day's humidity, then I head to the kitchen to make myself some ramen noodles. I feel Scarlett's eyes on my back from her vantage on the couch, where she's working on edits to her book. I don't turn around.

Balancing the bowl in my arms, I head to my room to watch *Gilmore Girls* on my laptop. I don't want to sit in the living room with

Scarlett, even though under normal circumstances, I know she'd love to visit Stars Hollow with me. Watching shows on a grainy 13-inch computer screen feels better to me, in this moment, than suffering through an evening of awkward silence in front of the television with my roommate.

I set the bowl on my desk and flip on the light. While I wait for my laptop to power up, I feel my phone buzz. It's Will.

Callllie.

I smile. *Willlll.*

Just wanted to see if you're famous yet.

What a loser. *Not yet. I think I need a Wikipedia page first.*

Want me to make one for you? he returns. And then: *I'll only mention that I pushed you toward meteoric success once or twice.*

My laugh echoes through the silence of my bedroom. *I promise I'll dedicate my first novel to you. Just as thanks for the Wikipedia page.*

That feels fair.

It's almost eight o'clock at night. Doesn't he have anything better to do right now?

I decide to ask. *Don't you have other, more exciting things to be doing right now?*

Oh, most definitely. I'm actually in the middle of restoring an antique car and saving a bunch of orphaned kittens.

Wow, I'm honored that you took time out of your evening to check in on my rise to fame. I toss the first disc of *Gilmore Girls* season three into my DVD drawer and push it closed.

Hey, I'm planning to ride your coattails all the way to a Pulitzer, he shoots back. *I need to ingratiate myself as much as possible.*

I snort. *I don't really do coattails. Not sure they're my style.*

His reply comes immediately. *Oh, you could definitely rock some formalwear.*

I feel a blush creep all the way up to my hairline. I type out, *Well, you'll have to see for yourself at the gala.*

My finger hovers over the delete button. This feels too far, like we're openly flirting in a way that maybe isn't okay. Because of Thomas. Because Will and I are just friends. Because I think maybe this is only in my head, and Will is probably just a really nice, admittedly very cute guy, who doesn't realize the impact he's having on my heart rate.

Before I can stop myself, I hit send.

A couple of minutes pass. I cringe. I definitely went too far.

My episode starts, and I settle in to watch Lorelai have the weirdest dream of all time just as my phone goes off again.

Can't wait to prove my point.

My heart skips a beat. He wants to see me rock some formalwear? God, he is *so* flirting. *So competitive*, I text back.

Like I'm the only one. I saw your face during that Broadway round at trivia. You were basically hyperventilating at the thrill of being better than everyone else at something.

He's right, of course. Especially since one of those people was Priya.

Operating on pure adrenaline because of how he's making me feel, I type another message and hit send before I even have time to think about it. *By the way, I decided I'm going to take that writing class.*

I don't think I'd actually decided that before this very moment, at least not consciously. My heart is beating so fast, I think it might burst out of my chest.

He responds only seconds later. I definitely have his undivided attention. *Yay! It's going to be so good for you.* I imagine his deep brown eyes, pupils wide, crinkling at the edges while he grins at me.

I definitely would not have done this without his...excitement? His blind faith in me, however undeserved.

I feel a sudden rush of gratitude, tears forming behind my eyes. I can't think of the last time I felt like someone believed in me this much.

Truly, Will, thank you for pushing me. I really needed that.

Believe me, Callie, I understand what it's like. Here to help anytime you need.

I'm not sure what he means about understanding, exactly, but the sentiment, and his offer of help, is so sweet. Shaking my head, I try to push away the warmth that's seeping through my chest.

I have to stop before I fall headlong into this—the push and pull, the teasing, the earnestness. It's so intense, and I know I'm going to lose myself completely if I give in, even a little bit. *I can't do this*, I tell myself, shaking my head.

Have a good night, Will.

His reply comes just as I redirect my attention to *Gilmore Girls*, where Rory's looking like she's about to cry because Jess has moved on, even as she ignores her actual boyfriend, whom she hasn't seen all summer.

Night, Cal.

nine

I stay home on Friday. I don't trust myself to be around Will right now, and my work day has to wrap up earlier than usual, anyway, thanks to the dinner for Esperanza tonight.

Scarlett is spending the day with Jonathan, so I'll have the apartment to myself. I get a solid four hours of writing done before the mechanic calls, letting me know my car's ready.

I should go pick it up now. It looks like it's going to storm again, and my list of people to call for help if I get stuck in the rain is growing shorter by the day.

I've barely spoken to Thomas since our steak dinner, and Scarlett and I are just getting by with the bare minimum right now. And Will...well, he's at work, anyway, and I think it's safer if I put some distance there.

I can't get back into my writing zone after I come home with the car, so I decide to wrap Esperanza's presents. While I'm digging around in my desk for tape, my hand brushes the manila envelope containing my manuscript.

I hesitate. My instinct is to shove it back into the drawer, as far as it will go, as if doing so will erase this failure from my history. But something gets the better of me, and I find myself opening it and pulling out the stack of papers inside.

I quickly set the pile of rejections to the side and turn them upside down. I don't need that right now.

A lump the size of Alaska forms in my throat as I look down at my manuscript.

The sunset was pink the night we met.

The words swim before me. I wipe a tear from my right eye and keep going.

He was wearing blue.

I'd let my mother convince me to curl my hair, even though I didn't expect to be making a first impression on anyone new tonight. I assumed it would be business as usual; just me and Janie, dancing, laughing, coming alive to the music.

The dance hall was packed to the brim, mostly with couples eager to get out from under their parents' critical gaze so they could cozy up a bit. With each swell of the band, I caught a glimpse of another girl, falling, doe-eyed, onto another jacketed guy's shoulder while they swayed gently to the music.

I was used to this; these weekend outings with my sister. It was comforting, if not a little bit depressing, to be here, on the outside, looking in. I was accustomed to getting all dolled up and pushing aside my own loneliness, watching other people fall in love.

I can't honestly say I ever expected to be one of them.

I set the paper down on my desk. This world I built, here on the page, feels so real to me, even now, years after I first dreamed it up.

That flicker of hope in my chest comes to life again. I still want this. I want other people to experience the daydream I've put into words here. I so badly want to share this story, any story. My story.

I shuffle the pages, tapping them against the desk so they fall into a neat pile of my hopes and dreams. I lay them gingerly on top of the manila envelope.

Then, I grab a roll of tape and close the drawer. When I turn off the light to head out for dinner a while later, the pages are still sitting on my desk, teasing the promise that there's still time.

SCARLETT MEETS me at the diner promptly at five.

"Well, it certainly is shiny," she quips, barely making eye contact with me as we hover near the host stand.

Even though we still haven't worked things out from Tuesday's fight, I know she loves Esperanza and wouldn't miss her birthday party for anything. That fact makes my heart swell a little. I can feel forgiveness brewing.

I sneak a look at Scarlett. She's staring at the floor, like if she makes eye contact with it hard enough, it might just swallow her whole, letting her slip away from me and this tension.

"Thank you for coming, Scarlett," I say quietly. "I really appreciate it. Esperanza will love that you're here."

A smile starts then, but I notice it doesn't reach her eyes. "I'm always going to be here for Esperanza." She pauses and inspects her nails, painted a neon pink to match her beaded tank top. "And for you."

I feel a lump forming in my throat. "I know that. Thank you."

Before I can apologize for the other day, tell her she was right, that I love her and know she's just trying to help, the hostess calls us to our table. I follow behind Scarlett, watching her wavy auburn hair bounce against her shoulders. *I'm sorry I'm sorry I'm sorry.*

We sit down and open our menus.

"What's good here?" Scarlett muses, running her index finger up and down the list of breakfast options. "Do I want an omelet?" She flips to the back of the menu. "Or should we just skip right to the ice cream?"

I snort. There have been many (many) nights of ice cream for dinner in our apartment, spearheaded by my roommate, with me happily along for the ride.

Just then, my parents come around the corner. My mom waves,

and I nod in greeting. She sits down next to me, sliding her purse onto the table beside her.

I look down to hide a silent chuckle. *"Never put your purse on the floor, Callie,"* she'd always told me. *"You'd be appalled by how many germs there are in a restaurant."*

Dad takes the seat on her other side, leaving an empty chair between himself and Scarlett. "I'm surprised Esperanza isn't already here," he says, pulling his readers out of his pocket and picking up the menu.

"I talked to her this morning, and she definitely remembered that we were going out." Mom picks up her menu, then closes it almost immediately.

Scarlett and I exchange an amused look. Mom orders a salad about 95 percent of the time when we go out to dinner. Usually Cobb, but when she's feeling more "exotic" (her words), she'll go Tex-Mex.

It feels good to even be on looking-at-each-other terms with Scarlett again.

"What'll it be tonight, Mom?" I ask, deciding on the veggie burger and laying down my menu. "Cobb salad?"

"You know me too well, Callie." She rolls her eyes at me, then pulls her phone out of her purse and checks the screen. "Nothing from Esperanza. It's 5:15. This is really weird."

She's right. In most scenarios, Esperanza would have gotten to the diner at four, stood in the entryway, talked to everyone who came in and out, and told them she was waiting for someone. Paced around the parking lot, called her home phone several times to check her messages, and been anxiously shifting from one foot to the other near the door when we rolled up at five.

"I'm going to call her." Mom dials and waits nervously through several rings. She leaves a voicemail, then lays her phone next to her purse, worriedly eyeing it every few seconds as if it's about to hop up off the table and dance.

"This *is* weird," I say, standing and looking around the restaurant.

"I'm just going to do a lap and see if she's sitting at another table. I'll ask the hostess if they've seen her."

"I'll come with you," Scarlett offers.

A few minutes later, we've checked the entire restaurant, the bathrooms, and the parking lot. There's no sign of her. No one on staff has seen Esperanza.

I pull out my cell and call her, too, but I get her answering machine.

The sky is still foreboding, but it hasn't rained yet. I can't imagine she went out for a walk, but maybe. Esperanza had been pretty upset yesterday about her apparent ziti overindulgence. Maybe she took a longer-than-usual stroll and lost track of the time? She doesn't have a cell phone.

It's possible, I reassure myself.

"Something's wrong," Scarlett breaks the silence with a worried look on her face.

I meet her gaze and purse my lips, wordlessly agreeing with her. She's right. Deep down, I know she is.

We go back inside and find my parents standing at our table, engaged in a serious conversation with the manager.

"We're just trying to find out if anyone here saw her earlier today, maybe before this shift started," explains my dad as we walk over. "Mom already called your grandmother and a bunch of other relatives. We even tried the diners down the road to see if she went there by mistake. No one has seen her."

My stomach sinks even further. A thought pops into my head, bringing a chill that settles over me, dousing my entire body in foreboding. "You don't think," I say slowly, "that she went for a walk and..." I swallow hard. I can't bring the words to the surface. I'm afraid it will make them real.

Scarlett looks about as upset as I feel. She reaches out and touches my arm.

Bolstered by her strength, I'm able to get it out. "You don't think she got hit by a car, do you?"

My mom's face blanches. Dad doesn't look surprised. I can tell he's already wondered the same thing.

Mom grabs her phone. "I'm going to call the police."

WE'RE STANDING outside the diner when the rain starts. The police just left, having taken our statement. They haven't gotten any reports of an accident. They say they'll send a patrol car to Esperanza's apartment to do a wellness check.

Dad, always prepared, opens an umbrella with a flourish. "Shall we?" He holds the umbrella out to Mom, Scarlett, and me. We're going to follow the squad car over to Esperanza's.

Just then, through the rain, I see a small gray sedan pull up. The driver starts beeping at us hysterically.

"Oh my God." I take off at a run.

Before I get there, the car has parked and Esperanza is getting out, shrugging on a hooded rain jacket.

"Callie! I'm so sorry, I'm so sorry, kid! I just got your mother's message."

I wrap her in a hug, not caring that I'm getting soaked and that we're standing in the middle of a parking lot. "Where were you? What happened? We were so worried!"

"Oh my God, Callie," she says, distressed. "I went to the wrong diner. I did. I went to the one over in Easton."

My mind races. What is she talking about? Then, suddenly, I see it in my mind: a small building, shiny in the sun, sitting out on Route 33. A big red sign out front: Easton Diner.

Esperanza and I, saying goodbye in the parking lot after having coffee together on Christmas Eve morning last year. I wasn't going to see her for the holidays because I was going to Scarlett's parents' house for dinner the next day, and I wanted to make time to celebrate with Esperanza, too.

"The Easton Diner," I breathe. "It certainly is shiny." I laugh in spite of myself, all the tension of the last two hours bubbling up in my chest. "Oh my God," I try to catch my breath and find that I can't.

Esperanza is looking at me like I'm insane. At this point, I think I might be.

"Come on," I finally gasp. "Let's go tell the others."

I grab her arm and pull her through the parking lot to the entrance of the diner. Mom, Dad, and Scarlett are watching from just under the overhang, unable to tell who I'm with, thanks to the torrential downpour.

When we get close enough and they realize it's Esperanza, they all break out in huge grins. My mom gives her a tight squeeze. "Thank God. We were in a panic!"

"I'm sorry, I'm so sorry. I'm such a stupido. I'm such a jamoke." Esperanza is beside herself.

"Don't worry about it, Esperanza. This is going to make for quite the story." I throw my arm around her shoulders. "Let's go inside and get you some dinner."

"And also," Scarlett adds from my other side. "You're not a jamoke." She pauses. "At least, I don't think so. I'm not actually all that familiar with old-timey insults."

"I'll call the police and let them know they can call off their search," I hear my mom say behind us.

"Cancel the APB!" Dad jokes as we get back to our table. The busboy hasn't cleared it yet and says it's okay for us to sit back down.

Esperanza laughs, shaking her head. "Happy birthday to me."

"Happy birthday to you!" I raise a plastic cup of water, sloshing it onto my already very soaked arm. Everyone cheers.

"WELL, THAT WAS QUITE THE PARTY," Scarlett remarks when we get home later.

"You're telling me. Talk about the full spectrum of human emotions. I'm pretty sure I felt them all tonight."

"Speaking of which," she says, digging in the freezer for the ice cream she never ordered at the diner, "I think we need a night of melodrama."

My mouth quirks into an amused expression. "You haven't had enough of that today?"

She shoots me a huge grin. "I hereby declare it a *Dawson's Creek* night."

When we first got to Briarford as scared freshmen (okay, so it was mostly just me who was scared), we had enacted a rule: anytime one of us was having a tough day, dealing with boy troubles, or a big test, or family drama, we would declare (it had to be a formal declaration, not just a request or suggestion) a *Dawson's Creek* night.

Then, Scarlett would pull out her ratty copy of the series on DVD, and we'd fall into a world of someone else's (mostly self-imposed) struggles. It was an odd balm for what ailed us, but it worked shockingly well. Plus, any chance to watch Joshua Jackson be a certified hottie was fine by us.

DC nights usually involved plenty of comfort food, too. Often, that meant a bag of stale chips or vending machine Pop-Tarts, since we were rather limited with what we could get late at night on campus. I was glad we'd graduated to half gallons of cookie dough in our own apartment, a brighter and considerably less depressing space than the cinderblock dorm where *DC* nights were born.

Scarlett's right, I decide. *I do need this tonight.*

Between the sheer terror of thinking Esperanza had been hit in a crosswalk and the fact that Thomas didn't even bother to text me today to say he couldn't make it to dinner, I'm having some major Feelings, with a capital F. And then, of course, there's the way my mind keeps skipping back to last night's text conversation with Will and how he apparently is looking forward to seeing me rock my gala dress, or whatever.

"Watching somebody else's melodrama," I say, grabbing two bowls from the cabinet, "sounds like the perfect plan."

. . .

WE'D LEFT off in the middle of season three, which is by any true fan's estimation the best stretch of the entire show. Tonight, we make it all the way to the end of *Stolen Kisses*, the episode where Joey finally harnesses her agency and admits to herself and Pacey that she has those capital-F Feelings for him. Unfortunately, she doesn't share it with anyone else other than Dawson's creepy aunt, who is so committed to the Dawson-Joey-soulmate plot line that it borders on pathological.

"I hate how everyone on this show acts like these two teenagers are predestined soulmates, at the expense of the mental health of everyone involved," I say, holding up my hands to admire the manicure I've finally taken the time to update. I went pale pink this time.

"Dude, I know," Scarlett agrees. "Julie Bowen has no right to guilt-trip Joey for not wanting to date her childhood best friend anymore. And what the hell is with the painting of kid Joey and kid Dawson gazing lovingly into each other's eyes?"

"Right? So gross." My forehead itches, but I don't want to mess up my nail polish. I wipe it awkwardly with the side of my hand.

Scarlett casts me a furtive glance from the end of the couch. "But you know, there's definitely something to be said for exploring feelings when you have them. And not feeling trapped in something just because it's safe."

I shoot her a warning look. "Didn't we already fight about this?"

Her melodic laugh fills the room. "I know. But this was just too perfect an example of life imitating art. I couldn't *not* bring it up."

"I'm sure you couldn't."

Scarlett's green eyes are intense on my face. "Callie."

I feign innocence. "What's up?"

"What are you doing? With Thomas? And Will?"

I feel the heat rush to my cheeks. This is the first time she's mentioned Will to me, other than our argument at the mall the other day. If other people are noticing, then it's too late—I've let my own *Feelings* get away from me.

"I wanted to wait to end things with Thomas until after the book was done," I relent. "It just made sense. Things were so stable for so long. It really felt like the book was what was driving a wedge between us. I hoped maybe...maybe it was all in my head. Maybe things would get better."

She nods. "Maybe. Or maybe this project just brought to light problems that were already there."

I think she's probably right, though it's still hard to wrap my head around it. "Possibly."

She pokes me with an outstretched arm, wearing a mischievous grin. "And what about Will?"

"What about him?"

Scarlett's eyes narrow. "You know exactly what I'm talking about. I sense some major vibes there."

"You sense major vibes from watching me send a text message three days ago?"

"Callie, come on," she says. "You know exactly what I'm talking about. Please don't play dumb."

I inhale sharply. "Fine." I'm not even sure where to begin, but she's sitting there giving me a look like she already knows what I'm going to say, so I just go for it. "It was an accident," I rush. "I tried so hard to ignore it. But I'm...I'm not sure I can anymore."

She's watching me thoughtfully, like a sage older sister who knows what's on my heart and can bring it forth with just a look.

"Things are complicated with Will," I continue, racking my brain for every possible excuse. "He just broke up with someone," I exaggerate, "and I'm not even sure he thinks of me in that way. Plus, I still need to figure out what to do about Thomas. I can't be having these feelings for Will right now."

"Callie, come on." She stands up and walks to the kitchen with our ice cream bowls. "You're obviously into him, and it seems pretty clear he's into you, too. And you know deep down things with Thomas are over."

I start to object, but she shakes her head. "Callie, tell him. Tell them both. It's *not* complicated. You feel what you feel. And I think it would take someone without a romantic bone in their body to not realize Will is feeling the same way. He talks to you every day, he texts you all the time, he invites you out with his friends?" She smiles gently at me. "You know I'm right."

I sink back into the couch, processing what she's said. Scarlett leaves to take a shower, but it takes me quite a while to think everything through.

ten

When I get back from an impromptu jog to clear my head before Saturday's game night with our college friends, I'm surprised to find a tall, spectacled guy leaning over my mixing bowl, reading a recipe out loud to Scarlett. I assume he must be Jonathan.

I also *hope* he is, because, if not, someone has broken into our apartment.

He's cute, I think right away, taking in his curly brown hair and easy smile. Best of all, he seems to be genuinely laughing at Scarlett's jokes, gently resting his arm around her shoulders while she measures out flour, acting like they already *belong* to each other.

My heart twangs a little. I'm happy for her. I really, truly am. But I miss that cozy feeling of belonging to someone.

I introduce myself, grab a shower, and then our friends start to arrive. It's a spirited evening filled with Franzia and Scattergories, and it's just what I need to start feeling like myself again.

By the time the party ends, I'm fairly convinced things are going to be okay. And even though I'm forced to fall asleep Saturday night to the sound of Scarlett and Jonathan loudly exploring each other's erogenous zones in the living room, I'm feeling a lot better.

. . .

WITH THE NEW week comes a renewed sense that I can handle being in Will's presence without losing my shit, so I decide to return to the library to write on Monday.

When I get there, Susan's wrangling her children near the circulation desk.

"Hey-o, Callie!" She grins. "Coming to trivia tonight?"

"Oh," I falter. "Um, maybe?"

Her face falls. "What do you mean, 'maybe'? What if there's a Rodgers and Hammerstein round? Or worse, Rodgers and Hart? We need you there!"

I paste on a smile. "I'm flattered. I just wasn't sure if I was maybe...getting in the way last week."

Susan snorts, looking over to the entryway, where her kids are now waiting for her impatiently. "Oh, you mean how Priya was casting daggers at you all night? Ignore her."

She shifts her tote bag, which is packed to the brim with picture books. "That's more than over, and she needs to move on. Will certainly has."

My heart skips a little at hearing her say that Will has moved on. "I just don't want to make things awkward. And in any case, Will and I aren't...there's nothing going on there. Nothing for her to be jealous of."

I'm hoping that if I say it with conviction, I might believe it, too. "And anyway, I have a boyfriend, remember?" *For now.*

She gives me an incredibly *knowing* glance. "Right," she grins. "Well, whatever is happening," she takes in my glare and quickly corrects, "or *isn't happening* with you and Will, Priya can deal." Her eyes flick to her kids, who are starting to whine loudly. "I should go. I'll see you tonight, okay?"

Resigned to my fate, I nod. She waves and goes to collect her brood.

Just then, there are footsteps behind me. "Did I just hear you and Susan talking about trivia night?"

I turn to face Will. *Of course* he would overhear. Now I can't back out tonight without disappointing both of them.

I steel myself as I take in his eager expression, his eyes just visible over the two humongous boxes he's carrying. My heart is busy flip-flopping away when I realize one of the cartons is balanced rather precariously on top of the other, held in place only by the edge of his hand. "You sure did. Also, can I help you with those?"

He chuckles. "I guess I could call in a favor." He shifts the top box, then steps closer to me so I can grab it from him. My fingers meet his in the process, and I have to remind myself to chill out.

I peek into the open carton. "What are you doing with all this stuff, anyway?" It looks like stacks of old newspapers.

"Someone just donated their late father's periodical collection. There's a lot of local stuff. I have to bring it to the community room and sort things; compare them to our existing collections. We'll keep anything we don't already have in our archives." He walks toward the elevator. "Here, we can bring them upstairs."

"Cool," I reply. "That'll probably be a gold mine for the history students from the university."

"You're not kidding," Will says as we get into the elevator. "One of the professors just assigned his summer historiography class to map the town as it was in 1950. So they've been coming in all week, asking to see census records, newspapers, postcards. They have to figure out who lived where and when and piece things together. Tell their stories. This'll be a huge help with their project."

"Aw, I'm jealous." I poke absently at some of the newspapers in the box I'm carrying. "That sounds like a really fun assignment."

His eyebrows go up in mock surprise. "Wow, I had no idea quite how much of a nerd you are."

"Watch it, Pearson." I shove him playfully with the side of my hip.

He laughs loudly, and it echoes through me, dragging joy from deep within my chest.

We're on the second floor now. I follow Will into the community room, which is sparsely furnished, with just four oak tables and a dingy projector screen. I've been here before for a program, but it's been a while. We set the boxes down on the first table.

He must notice me surveying the room. "This is where your writing class is going to be." He points to the table nearest the projector. "And this is where you're going to be sitting when you get the inspiration for your bestselling novel."

"*Au contraire*," I shake my head. "I'll be sitting in the back, so no one can steal ideas over my shoulder."

He laughs again.

Now I'm blushing, and I don't want him to know. I lower my head over the box I carried up. "Want some help with this stuff?"

He tilts his head quizzically. "Didn't you come here to wax poetic about hedge funds?"

"Well, sure." I pull out a chair. "But this feels like my civic duty. IRA laddering can wait." I flash him a bright grin and start taking out newspapers.

He sits down next to me and begins to empty the other box. "I think we'll have to organize things by category first, and by date within those. I've got a list of our existing collections here," he gestures to a stapled packet of papers. "We can cross-check against it." He lays it down and hands me a pencil from his pocket. "And I should warn you, I'm kind of a difficult boss. Don't let me catch you slacking off."

He's clearly trying so hard to look stern, but his eyes are sparkling, and the corner of his mouth is twitching up like he's about to lose the battle.

I force my lips into a line, struggling not to laugh myself. "Well, *I* should warn *you*, I'm very competitive. I'm going to organize my newspapers faster than you. I'm going to make better piles than you've ever seen. And when I'm done, you're going to be begging me to take your job."

His eyebrows go up, and so does his grin. "Ms. Sheffield, I look forward to working with you."

. . .

WILL and I spend two hours organizing the newspapers, putting them in date order (a task I tell him he's born to do, given his super-advanced library skills), and checking them against the archive holdings list.

As we go, I read snippets of the news aloud to him whenever I find something intriguing, or, more often, hilarious.

"The Samuel Samson family of Second Street is pleased to announce the engagement of their daughter, Sally, to Steven Smith." I stare at the paper in disbelief.

"What?" Will seems equally shocked by the S parade. "You're making that up."

"Nope," I shake my head, pointing to the announcement on the page.

He leans over to see for himself. I can feel his breath on my shoulder. It stirs something in my chest, especially when he doesn't move away immediately. "Now *that* is a masterclass in alliteration," he declares.

I dare to make eye contact, even though it feels dangerous to do so. He's still so close.

But I do it, and I think it startles him, too. His gaze sweeps over my face, and I'm lost. I feel like he's started a fire beneath my skin, and it's engulfing me completely, but it feels so warm and safe that I don't want it to stop.

I catch his eyes lingering on my mouth. It's fleeting, but I know I'm not mistaken.

My breath catches in my throat. "Now who's the writer?" I ask quietly.

I'm surprised to see his face flush. He looks away and clears his throat. "I think that's still you."

Something feels odd about his reaction, but I can't place it. It bothers me, perhaps more than it should, that he seems upset.

"So, how am I doing?" I ask brightly, trying to make him laugh. Anything to lift the weird vibe that's suddenly descended in here.

He pivots to face me again. "Well," he says in mock seriousness, "as employees go, you're a little bossy."

"So snarky," I tut. "I feel like HR should know that you're name-calling someone on their first day."

"There you go again with that attitude," he quips.

I feel the corners of my mouth turn up. "I thought that's what you liked about me."

"Among other things." He's looking at me seriously now, but it no longer feels like this is a game.

I'm not sure whether to issue a clever comeback or give in to the overwhelming urge to reach out and touch him. I settle for sewing a scarlet letter A onto my shirt when I get home.

"Well," I say, breaking his gaze and busying myself with straightening a newspaper pile that's already perfectly flush, "I can't very well give up the attitude. It's my witty nature that makes me such a great writer."

"You are certainly witty," Will says.

"Aw, thanks, Pearson." Without thinking, I reach out and squeeze his arm. It's just the right kind of strong; the sort of solid you can count on, but that doesn't require daily trips to the gym to maintain.

He tenses under my hand, and I immediately realize I shouldn't have touched him. I can't touch him, because I can't control myself around him.

God, I need to break up with Thomas.

My face is blazing now as I rip my hand back. "I'm sorry." I don't know what else to say.

"It's okay." Will turns to face me, but I'm still looking down. "Callie? Hey." He pokes my hand tentatively with his pointer finger.

I force my head to pivot in his direction. He's looking at me expectantly. To my surprise, he doesn't seem upset.

"You don't need to be sorry." His face is earnest again, and I can't handle it. His eyes are so warm, so full. He's drawing me into them, into him, and I'm going to lose myself. I just know it. But I can't stop looking at him, letting myself want him.

I clear my throat. "I should probably go." I need to get out of here.

He blinks slowly, as if clearing himself from a mental fog. "Okay," he nods. "I'll see you tonight?"

"Yeah, absolutely," I say quickly.

"Do you want a ride?" he asks, voice rising like he hopes I'll say yes, mouth stoic like he expects me to say no.

"Um, sure," I answer. "My roommate is meeting us there, so I'll head back with her afterward."

I don't know where the lie comes from, but I rush out with it. I haven't asked Scarlett about going to trivia tonight, but Will had mentioned it last week, and I need a chaperone in a big way. I'll text her as soon as I get back downstairs and tell her I'll buy her dinner if she comes.

"Nice! I can't wait to meet her."

"I'll see you later!" I walk toward the door and wave.

Will shoots me a cheery grin that doesn't set me ablaze, and things feel normal again. *There*, I think to myself. *Everything's okay. I just need some distance. And a buffer.*

I WORK downstairs for the rest of the afternoon. I text Scarlett, and she agrees to come out tonight if I buy her dinner *and* let her bring Jonathan. I hadn't considered that she'd already have plans with him.

But I need a break from melting into Will, and if there's anyone who can turn off my libido, it's Scarlett. And Scarlett would positively *revel* in the knowledge that she fills that role for me.

I text her our team name so the hostess can help her find our table, in case she and Jonathan get there before Will and I do. I also describe Jenna and Priya, who I'm fairly certain will arrive before anyone else, since they both live right down the street from the bar.

I don't know why I bother, honestly; Scarlett is so outgoing, she'd probably have no issue introducing herself to everyone in the place if she weren't sure who she was meeting.

Thanks again, I text her. *I owe you one.*

AT SIX O'CLOCK, I meet up with Will in the lobby and we hit the road. He checks out a book with trivia facts before we leave, and I quiz him the whole way to Rockledge.

"What's the name of the metal tube on the end of shoelaces?"

"The aglet, of course," he says, as if everyone knows this.

I thumb through the book. "Okay, how about this one. What guitarist performed on "Beat It"?"

He thinks for a minute, then replies triumphantly. "Eddie Van Halen!"

I shake my head. "I can't seem to stump you. You're too good at this."

"Keep going through that book. I'm obviously a genius, but there's bound to be something I don't know."

Before I can come up with a clever retort, my phone starts vibrating. "Just a second," I say. I grab it from my pocket and see Thomas is calling. I consider not answering, but I'm feeling pretty guilty for how Will was making me feel earlier, so I decide to take it.

"Hey, Thomas. What's up?" I swear I see Will grip the steering wheel tighter.

"What are you up to tonight?" Thomas asks. "I thought maybe I'd take you to dinner."

I tense up. It's already after six. He's just now calling to see if I want to go out for dinner?

"Oh," I begin, not sure how to let him down easily, and acutely aware that Will is listening. "I'm actually going to trivia in Rockledge. With Scarlett and some friends from the library."

From my left, Will offers quietly, "You can invite him, if you want."

My stomach lurches. I don't really *want* to invite Thomas, but I kind of think I have to.

"Do you want to come? I can text you the address."

"I suppose I could do that," Thomas agrees nonchalantly. "Send me the address and I'll see you there."

We hang up, and the car is silent for a moment.

"Thanks for including him," I finally say.

"Of course." Will looks like he's going to say something else, but he stops himself.

"Should we get back into it?" I ask, turning the page in the trivia book. "I have to find something you don't know before we get to the bar."

"I have faith in you," Will chuckles.

I know you do, I think to myself. *That's part of the problem.*

TRIVIA TONIGHT IS like worlds colliding in the weirdest, messiest way. By the time we arrive, Scarlett has already parked herself on a stool and is talking Jenna's ear off. Jonathan is sitting by her side, hanging on her every word.

This week, Susan's brought her New Releases, as promised, so we can continue Drunk Book Club. Scarlett and Jenna seem very intrigued by the idea of the game, and they want in.

Priya is eyeing us coolly when we do our first shot (the book's main character slept over at her bipolar ex-boyfriend's house, even though he just went off his meds), but then she shifts her attention to something Jax is saying about his job.

While we're trying to find just cause for a second shot (the character running away from her ex-boyfriend's house in the dead of night with a serial killer on the loose is a solid contender), Thomas strolls in. He's still in his work clothes, and he walks over to our table like he owns the place. For all I know, Benderson and his cronies are also venture capitalists; maybe they do own the bar.

"Hey," he says into my ear, slipping me a kiss on the cheek before sitting down on the stool beside me.

"Hi. Thanks for coming." I smile at him, even though I'm feeling all sorts of awkward. And guilty. Mostly guilty, especially when I look up and blush to see Will watching me from across the table.

"What's good here?" Thomas flips through the sparse menu.

"I had a quesadilla last week," I offer. It was pretty good, but I'm not sure that sort of pedestrian food would appeal to my boyfriend. Especially since it was presumably made fresh.

"The burgers are a solid choice." Will reaches his hand out. "I'm Will, by the way. Nice to meet you."

Thomas shakes his hand. "Likewise." He looks around the table. "So, how did you all meet Callie?"

"I already told you," I say quietly. "I met Will and Susan," I gesture to her, and she waves, still caught up in Drunk Book Club with Scarlett and Jenna, "at the library."

"Callie's been regaling us with her masterpiece. Honestly, it's been very exciting to actually have something to do at work." Will's talking to Thomas, but he's still looking at me.

Thomas stares at Will blankly. "Her masterpiece?"

Anger flashes over Will's face for a moment, and then it's gone. "You know, her book."

Thomas laughs. I don't. He looks confused. "Oh," he says to Will. "I thought you were joking."

"I mean, maybe the word 'masterpiece' is a bit of a stretch, given the incredibly *mundane* subject matter," Will says coolly, "But Callie's an amazing writer." He grins at Thomas. "But you know all about that."

My heart is doing somersaults in my chest. *Is Will seriously defending my honor right now?* I look over at Scarlett, desperate to catch her attention. This is the sort of drama she lives for.

I meet Will's gaze, and his smile goes all the way up to his eyes. I can tell he's pleased with himself, because his face then shifts into a smug expression that I've often seen when he's giving me a hard time.

Just then, the waitress comes over to take our orders, offering a welcome distraction from the pissing match that's happening at our table.

Thomas orders the burger. I ask for a quesadilla and a frozen strawberry daiquiri again. Will's face is positively triumphant when I pull a pile of napkins and a straw out of my purse.

THE NIGHT WEARS ON. We win the margaritas, but not the shots. I think that's for the best, though, because Drunk Book Club has gotten beyond lively and probably doesn't need any extra help.

I'm sipping my daiquiri, watching Priya write our music round answers in perfect script, when Susan touches my arm. "So, Will mentioned you're doing that writing class at the library?"

Thomas tenses next to me. I haven't told him yet.

I can feel the heat from Will's eyes across the table.

"Oh," I say quietly, caught in the quicksand of being unable to please everyone at once. "Yep. It seemed like a lot of fun."

Her brows go up, asking a silent question. I gesture toward Thomas with my eyes, hoping she'll catch on. Hoping he won't. She bares her teeth in a line, signaling the faux pas she's just committed.

It's too late, of course. "I didn't realize you'd decided to take the class," Thomas says, looking displeased.

"Oh, you know. It just seemed like a great way to hone the old writing chops." I throw Thomas a lopsided grin, praying goofiness will take the edge off this unbearably awkward situation.

Will wears a look of concern, and maybe something else—something a little like anger, I think.

Before I can change the subject to quite literally *anything else*, Will addresses Thomas. "It's my fault, really. I kept bothering her until she agreed." He assesses Thomas's unenthused face and cracks a smile. "Gotta meet my quotas at work, you know. That's how we get our funding."

No one's laughing, but Scarlett has broken away from shot number four and seems to be listening. "Hey, Thomas," she interjects at about 80 decibels. "How about those stocks, eh?"

He raises his whiskey in salute. "Here's to the bull market!"

She lays a hand on Jonathan's arm and hops off the stool, coming around the table to drape herself between Thomas and me. "I actually had a question about my portfolio," she drawls. "Maybe you can help me."

I slurp down my daiquiri to avoid snickering. It's crystal clear what she's trying to do, but Thomas is either not picking up on it or just loves his work so much he doesn't care.

While she's distracting Thomas with talk of mutual funds, and also possibly with her boobs, which are on full display thanks to her corseted top, I catch Will's eye. "Thank you," I mouth silently.

"Anytime," he whispers across the table, smiling softly at me.

I don't look away, and for a moment, I'm swept up in his eyes; the noise of the bar falling away until all I can hear is my breath; all I can see is how he's looking at me like I'm made of glass and he wants to protect me from shattering.

SCARLETT DROPS Jonathan off at home. He only lives a few minutes outside of town, in a really cute neighborhood with two-car garages and literal picket fences. He's an emotionally available hottie with his own goddamn mailbox. My girl has struck gold.

She knows it, too, and leaves me waiting in the car while they kiss passionately outside his door for 15 minutes.

I check my phone. Two voicemails from Esperanza, one from my mom. I listen to all three, but they're just checking in.

I fire off a text to Susan. *What's next on the list for Drunk Book Club?*

I was thinking Her Majesty's Silent Night, *she replies. Lots of preventable horror story tropes. Very stupid protagonist.*

I'll bring it next week. I make a mental note to find that one at the library.

I open a new message and type Will's name. *Sorry things got so awkward tonight.*

No, I'm sorry. I never meant to create problems between you and Thomas.

I text back before I realize what I'm saying. *I think the problems were already there.*

He doesn't reply immediately. Then he says, *You know I'm here if you need anything.*

Thanks, Will.

I start to put my phone back in my purse, but it buzzes again.

And for what it's worth, I do think your book is going to be a masterpiece. Then: *Not the finance one; that's going to be boring no matter what you do.*

I snort.

He continues: *But you're a great writer, and anyone who makes you feel less than doesn't deserve a place in your life.*

My face heats in the dark. I'm not sure how to respond. He's right. I know he's right. Why am I only just now seeing it? Why have I let myself feel so worthless for so long?

Shaking my head, I push those thoughts from my mind. I need to figure out what to do to move forward.

I stare at the screen of my phone, contemplating the perfect reply. Finally, I type: *You have to say that. You're trying to clinch prime coattail position.*

I'm not worried. No one is immune to my charm.

I laugh out loud. *You've got that right, Pearson.* I'm only half joking.

Are you bringing your manuscript tomorrow for our beta reader session?

I'd sort of hoped he'd forgotten. But the pages are still sitting on top of my desk, and I think maybe I'm ready to face them. *You know it. Bring your red pen.*

See you then, Cal.

My heart is full, and I can't keep the smile from my face. *Night, Will.*

eleven

"Promise you'll be kind?" I push my manuscript across the table to Will.

"When am I anything but?" He grins rakishly.

"Well, when you're turning me in to HR for being too bossy, for one," I joke.

We've taken over the community room again. I have *Her Majesty's Silent Night*, which looks to be the best kind of poorly executed horror novel, at the ready. I'm going to attempt to distract myself with it while Will reads my story.

I'm exceptionally nervous. Both because these pages haven't seen the light of day in years, and because his hair is super tousled today, and I don't know if I can handle it.

"I promise," he holds up a hand as if swearing an oath, "I'll be the epitome of kindness." He whips out a red Bic. "I can't guarantee that my editor pen will be so forgiving, however."

I kick him under the table. "I can't believe you actually brought a red pen."

He smirks. "Really? Violence in the workplace? Now I'm definitely turning you in to HR."

I wrinkle my nose at him and open my book. Over the top of it, I see him absently click the cap of the pen on and off with his thumb. On. Off. On. Off. He settles in and starts to read. The clicking stops.

We sit in silence for a while, occasionally looking up at each other and pretending we haven't. I catch him watching me several times when he thinks I'm immersed in my book. I can always feel the heat from his gaze, no matter how many crazy things Her Majesty is doing.

After a while, he sits back, leaning his elbows casually on the top rail of his chair. His shoulders rise as he stretches, and the rolled cuffs of his shirt shift up along his forearms. I catch a glimpse of his tattoo, which I haven't seen since that night my car broke down. Something stirs in my chest.

He meets my gaze for a moment. "Do you have any idea how good this is?"

Her Majesty just got in the car with a stranger, so it takes me a second to realize he's talking about what *he's* been reading. Not this bad horror novel in my hands, and not the situation we've found ourselves in, alone, once again, in this room.

A flush creeps up my cheeks, heading all the way to my scalp, as it's so wont to do whenever Will's around. "Why couldn't you have been Agent 28?" I ask quietly.

"I'll be Agent 28 for you." Will is surveying my face now, his eyes sweeping over my lips, my reddened cheeks, my eyes that are trying so hard to break away from his, but failing miserably.

I don't know what to say, my heart is so full. He's melting me completely, and I can hardly think as my insides drip away into a puddle of mush. I swallow hard. "I'll allow it."

He blinks a few times, then a smile starts. "Done."

"I'll need you to get me in with a Big Five publisher," I say, slowly regaining the ability to speak. "And I want a sizable advance. At least half a million to start."

He bursts out laughing, then remembers the game, clearing his throat. "Of course, of course. Anything else you require?"

"Hmm." I make a big show of thinking about it. "I'll do book tours, but only if I get a bus."

His eyebrows jump up. "A bus? I think you might be stretching the limits of credulity a bit here, Cal."

"Do you want to be Agent 28 or not?" I cross my arms.

"Okay, fine," he concedes. "I'll get you a bus."

I nod in satisfaction. "That's what I thought."

We smile at each other for a moment. Then, he says, "I do mean it, though. This book is amazing."

I don't know if I seem unconvinced, but he reaches out and touches my hand. "Callie," he says earnestly. "Please believe that."

My eyes fill with tears as I look at him, because he's just so beautiful and wonderful, and he thinks *I'm* wonderful, and I don't know how to handle someone believing in me this much.

I mean, my parents are great, and all, but they're realists. Show up, work hard, and live a simple life; that's what they've always done. They did what they had to do to give me a great childhood, but they weren't big on taking risks. I think that's partly why it's so hard for me to see a future for myself doing something less conventional.

But then here's Will, with no skin in the game, other than whatever's making him sometimes look at me like he wants to touch my face. And he thinks I'm great, and he loves what I write, and goddamn it, I want this.

I want a life for myself where I get paid to write books, where my spirit comes alive when I birth new stories. I want to feel infinite like that.

And I want someone like Will, who is just totally and completely in my corner, along for the ride. Clearly, Thomas isn't going to be that person for me. But I'm going to find someone who is.

Or maybe I've already found him.

"Oh, God, Callie! I'm sorry. I didn't mean to upset you!" Will's out of his chair, his arms going around me, hugging me even though I'm still sitting down. He's at an awkward angle, reaching around my shoulders from the side, and I don't know whether to get up and hug him back or just keep sitting there like an idiot.

I settle for patting his arm like he's the one who's upset. I'm not sure why I can't just do things like a normal person.

"I'm really okay," I say awkwardly, needing out of this hug precisely because of how badly I want to stay in it.

He pulls away and surveys my face. "What's wrong?"

I shake my head, smiling slightly. "Nothing."

His eyebrows wrinkle over his nose. "It was obviously something. I made you cry."

"I'm just," I take a deep breath, "I'm really glad to have met you, Will."

He sits back down in his chair. "I'm really glad to have met you, too."

We're still sitting there, sending bursts of electricity back and forth across the table, when Will's phone rings.

He breaks away, looks down, and his face turns red. "I have to take this," he says, getting up from his chair and walking out of the room.

As he closes the door, I can hear him say, "Hi, Priya. What's up?"

My heart lurches. Thanks to Scarlett, I'd been feeling fairly convinced that the next time I saw Thomas, I'd be having a very uncomfortable conversation with him. Unfortunately, the next time we have plans to get together is on Sunday night at the gala. But I figure this is a discussion that needs to happen in person, and if I've waited this long, another five days won't kill me.

Hearing Will on the phone with Priya, though...some doubt creeps in. Am I just caught up in a crazy crush on an emotionally unavailable, albeit extremely adorable, guy? Am I imagining the scope of my feelings because I'm so lonely with Thomas? Am I imagining the problems with Thomas *because* of these butterflies I keep getting from Will? *Oh, God.* I don't even know what to think anymore.

Will finishes his phone call and comes back in, seeming a little uncomfortable. I try harder to read his aura, to see what kind of call it was, but I can't really tell.

I think if I stay here too much longer, I'm going to go crazy.

"I should probably head out," I tell him.

He looks surprised. "Oh. Okay."

"Well, Scarlett wants my help reading some new chapters she's written." I push in my chair. It's only a half-lie. She *has* been writing, and she *did* say I could read her draft sometime. I don't want to upset Will, but I can't continue to sit here and *feel* and worry and wonder.

"Is everything okay?" Will stands up, too, and closes the distance between us. "I really didn't mean to upset you."

I paste on a smile that I hope is convincing. "Everything's fine," I promise. "Thanks again for your help today."

Damn it. He doesn't look convinced.

"Anytime, Cal. I'll see you tomorrow?"

I nod hurriedly and leave the room before the tears can start.

THAT EVENING, Will texts me while I'm watching *Dawson's Creek* with Scarlett. (I'd declared a much-needed night of someone else's melodrama.)

I have a proposition for you.

Will, that's inappropriate. I smile in the dark.

No, you weirdo. Not that kind of proposition.

I text back: *I know. What's up?*

My sister is coming to visit next weekend. She's begging me to take her to the lake. Childhood nostalgia and whatnot. I'm trying to get a group together to rent a cabin. Maybe play some charades. You know.

My chest feels like it's fizzy, even though I've been trying to push those sorts of thoughts of Will from my mind.

I am really good at charades.

He replies: *I've no doubt.* And then: *Are you in? You can bring Thomas and Scarlett. And Scarlett's new boyfriend.*

I shudder at the thought of bringing Thomas on a group trip with Will. *Who else is going?*

Jax and Jenna, so far, he says. *Susan can't get away for that long without her kids.*

I breathe a sigh of relief. He didn't mention Priya. I would love to go to the lake. I need an escape, and hanging out with Will's friends, plus Scarlett and Jonathan, seems like a good time. And I have a feeling I may need some time away to distract myself after I have The Talk with Thomas this weekend.

I'm in.

His reply comes immediately. *Great! I'll give you the details next week.*

I'll start practicing my charades.

Three words, starts with G, he says.

Green bean casserole? I guess.

Good night, Callie. He adds a winky face.

I laugh loudly enough that Scarlett looks away from the TV.

"Want to go to the lake next weekend? With Jonathan, and Will and his friends?" I ask.

She raises an eyebrow. "I think you've been watching too many shows about teenagers. That sounds like a recipe for major drama." A grin spreads across her face. "I am so in."

I smile back. We sit in comfortable silence, going back to our show.

I text Will again. *Scarlett's in, too. Three words, starts with S.*

See you tomorrow? He replies.

I told you that you're a genius. Good night, Will.

twelve

The day of the gala arrives without a cloud in the sky. My heart is feeling pretty nimbus-y, though. I'm worried about my conversation with Thomas tonight. What I'm going to say, how he's going to react. If I'll be able to go through with it as planned, if I'll do it with grace. If I'll cry.

I know breaking up with him is the right decision. I know it for about a thousand reasons, not the least of which is how I've been feeling when Will's around. But it's more than that. It's about my agency and what I want for my future. It's about being with someone who can be a part of that future without feeling the need to try to control it.

Maybe Will can be that person for me. Maybe not. Time will tell, and I hope to have the opportunity to explore that at some point. But for now, I know with certainty that Thomas can't. Or even if he could, I no longer want him to be.

I live the day like it's happening to someone else, just going through the motions. My head's a blur as I touch up my nails, do my hair.

When I step into my blue dress, I feel nothing.

Thomas picks me up at six and we drive to the university ballroom in relative silence, aside from standard pleasantries. He tells me he likes my dress, but he doesn't acknowledge that he's seen it on me before. I tell him he looks great, which he does. He can certainly rock a tux. But it doesn't mean anything anymore.

Once we get to Briarford, I check us in while Thomas parks his 3 Series. This is not the kind of event where he'd want me to take my Honda. There might be capital-P People to impress.

We're grabbing drinks at the bar when I spot Will. He's talking to Lisa, the head librarian, and a couple of men in suits over by the microphone. His eyes meet mine across the room, and he waves cheerfully, making my heart dance in my chest.

I look around for Priya and finally find her at the hors d'oeuvres table. I'm not at all surprised that she looks beyond stunning in an incredibly backless red gown featuring rhinestones for days. Her hair is swept to one side, her makeup simple but striking. As usual, she doesn't seem particularly happy, though.

I think maybe Priya feels my eyes on her, because she abruptly looks up from a tray of canapés, a deer in headlights. I stiffen, caught in the act, and she wears a look of surprise. Perhaps Will hadn't mentioned that I'd be here. She recovers quickly, though, forcing a pained smile and waving halfheartedly. I do the same. At least we tried.

"Should we go find our seats?" Thomas asks in my ear.

I nod, mouth full of wine.

He guides us over to table 12, cozy against the far wall. I'm happy to discover we'll have a good view of the stage, where Will's going to be presenting.

Thomas unbuttons his jacket and flips the edges to his sides.

"Hey, isn't that your friend?" He gestures to the front of the room.

"Yep, that's Will." I try to force the blood deeper into my face, but I'm pretty sure the blush works its way up my cheeks anyway. "And Priya's over there," I add, pointing to the snacks.

"Wow. That dress isn't at all appropriate," he nods in Priya's direction.

I'm not her biggest fan, but I try to be a girl's girl. I don't love mocking other women's wardrobe choices. And she is objectively gorgeous. "I think she looks nice."

"You look better," Thomas says, making it sound not at all romantic or complimentary, but instead like it's some sort of contest.

I don't know what to say, so I don't respond.

"Anyway, I'm surprised to see them here," he muses, spinning his whiskey glass contemplatively against the table.

"What do you mean?" I take another sip of wine.

"I just wouldn't expect them to shell out for this sort of thing."

My eyes narrow. "Will is volunteering his time. The library co-sponsors the event. Priya's his guest." I almost say *date*, but I can't bring myself to use the word, even if it's the truth.

Thomas inclines his head ever so slightly. "I see."

"Do you have a problem with that?" I ask, unable to temper the acid I feel rising in my throat.

Now it's Thomas's turn to look confused. "Why would I have a problem with that?"

I shake my head. "Never mind."

Is now the time? Should I tell him that this isn't working out, that I want to move on? I'd planned to broach the subject in the car on the way home, but I'm pretty fired up right now. I don't know if I can make it through the night, maintaining this façade.

Just then, the lights dim and a microphone crackles. I see Will adjusting its height, then surveying the crowd with a broad grin. "Good evening. My name is Will Pearson, and, along with the staff at the Greater Linden Library and Briarford University, we're thrilled to welcome you to this year's Chapters for Change gala."

Even at a distance, I can tell he looks good. He's wearing a tux, which I think might have been cut just for him, it fits so well. His hair is fairly tame, at least compared to usual, but it's still adorably ruffled, and I notice the glint of a watch under his shirtsleeve. I don't know why, but a man in a watch always gets me feeling a little hot and bothered.

Will continues his speech. "We're going to kick things off with some words of thanks for our sponsors. Then, we'll move on to announcing the winners of the raffle and the silent auction."

"So he's not just a volunteer, he's an MC," Thomas whispers. "Interesting."

I don't think it's particularly interesting, so I just shrug. And besides, I don't really like his tone.

"Let's see if we win anything in the raffle." He pulls out his tickets and lays them on the table.

I narrow my eyes. Of course he bought tickets for the raffle. He must have done it after he'd parked the car. Like we're aristocrats deigning to open our coffers to the peasants for sport. I try to tell myself that all the money goes to charity, that it's going to help children, benefit programs like the ones Will runs at the library. But my veins are icy, and I desperately want to call him out.

For what, I'm not sure exactly. For being a colossal douche? For acting holier-than-thou? For insinuating that my friends don't belong here? For mocking Priya, whom I don't even like, and for somehow suggesting without words that Will is beneath him?

I'm pretty close to breaking up with him right here, in the middle of the presentation, at this ridiculously appointed gold-napkinned table. God, the cost of renting the place settings alone could have probably funded a whole new wall of children's books.

Why am I here? What am I doing with this person, this emotionless caricature of a human who doesn't understand anything about me? What did I ever see in him? Why did I waste all this time when there was no spark whatsoever?

My chest is tight and I'm seeing stars when I push myself out of my seat, tears pricking the backs of my eyelids. "I need something to eat," I mumble, and I stride off along the back wall toward the appetizers before he can see me cry.

. . .

AS IT TURNS OUT, Thomas doesn't win the raffle, which gives me no small sense of satisfaction. I spend most of the announcements trying to look busy with my hors d'oeuvres so I won't have to talk to him.

When Will is done inviting men in expensive suits up to the stage to thank them for their contributions and the lights come back up, Thomas and I exchange pleasant conversation with the other couples at our table. We're seated with two of his coworkers and their wives, plus a woman who runs a tax agency in town.

My mind wanders as the group talks all things fiscal. Out of the corner of my eye, I see Priya and Will sitting at a table near the DJ. She's leaning in and whispering something in his ear. He looks like he's laughing.

I whip my eyes away. I can't deal with this.

"Come on, let's go talk to Mr. Benderson," Thomas suggests when the conversation at our table hits a lull.

He stands up and begins striding purposefully toward his boss. He doesn't wait for me.

"I'll be right there," I call after him. I need another drink.

I gather my skirt in one hand, an empty champagne flute gripped in the other. I head to the bar and ask for a glass of anything sweet. The bartender passes me a white wine, and I thank him with a nod and a three-dollar tip.

Turning to face the room, I take a deep gulp of my drink and purposely avert my eyes from where Priya has perched her bent arm on the side of Will's chair. She looks happy, and I can't bring myself to glance at Will. I don't want to see him laughing when her lips are that close to his cheek.

Thomas and his boss are over near the silent auction tables, backs to me, chatting with a few men in tuxedos.

When I catch up, they're already deep in conversation. I hear snatches, like "perfect for thought leadership" and "help drive conversions."

Then I hear Thomas's voice cut through the noise of the crowd.

"I've been doing a lot to help her shape it. She's definitely on the right track, and it's going to be a really solid piece of content when we're done. It will definitely be great for marketing to new clients."

My mouth falls open. He couldn't possibly be talking about *my* book, right? *He's* been doing a lot? Other than that one afternoon in his apartment, he hasn't helped me at all.

And what does he mean, when *we're* done? He isn't writing this goddamn book. *I* am.

I have half a mind to march right up to him and call him out in front of his colleagues, but then I remember his boss still owes me a lot of money.

I stuff the anger back down, as deep as it will go, but there's a lot of fury taking up space in my chest, so it doesn't get very far.

I stand there, still as a statue for a moment while I compose myself, before clearing my throat so they'll notice I've walked up behind them.

"Oh, hello, Callie," says Thomas. "I was just telling Mr. Benderson and his friends about your progress with the book."

"So I hear," I reply coolly. Thomas doesn't seem to pick up on my tone.

One of Benderson's ancient colleagues speaks up, sticking out his hand. "Sheldon Crawford. I might like to talk with you also, Ms. Sheffield. I think our firm could benefit from some thought leadership pieces, too. Perhaps a book, or maybe just something we could distribute to shareholders with their quarterlies."

Thomas gives me a triumphant look, which is sprinkled with pride and excitement. He never loves me more than when I'm able to enter his little world and make my mark on it. The book project was ostensibly to help me, sure, but I think he enjoyed it even more because he could finally feel like I was worth it, that I wasn't embarrassing him among those whose opinions he values most.

He's never going to care about me enough until I can be just like him, with his upwardly mobile tendencies, his bizarre fixation on doing everything by the book. His inappropriate professionalism, even when it's his actual life; his stoicism in the face of real feelings. He's never going to be satisfied unless I pretend to be someone I'm not.

I paste on a polite smile and reach out to shake Mr. Crawford's hand. "Callie, please."

He frowns a bit. So does Thomas.

I take a deep breath. "I really appreciate you thinking of me for your project, but I'm actually not going to be taking on any more ghostwriting work for the foreseeable future. As soon as I finish Mr. Benderson's book, I'll be focused on my novel."

The words are out before I even really know what I've said. I'm not sure I'd made a conscious decision to move on from ghostwriting entirely, but it was definitely hovering there, ready to be plucked from the air ever since Will suggested I take the library class. Ever since I pulled my manuscript out of my drawer and realized I could still have more.

Now that it's real, glimmering in front of me, I realize it's what I want. It's what I've wanted all along. I don't have any idea what I'm going to write about, or even what this class is going to entail, but the mere fact that I'll be working towards something that means so much to me makes me feel like my joy is going to spill over.

I look to Thomas out of habit, a silly grin on my face. I'm startled when I see his eyes dark, his face filled with something like shock. My stomach lurches.

"Would you excuse us for a moment?" I ask, grabbing his sleeve and guiding him away from Benderson and company. We walk to the far corner of the ballroom, near where the check-in table is situated. I'm trying to place us enough in the shadows that no one will overhear our conversation. I have a feeling it won't be a great one.

"What," Thomas asks too slowly, too quietly, "was that?"

I take in his perfectly clean-shaven face, twisted with what I can only think to describe as disappointment, or maybe shame. There's anger bubbling beneath the surface, too, hiding in the flush of his cheeks and the narrowing of his piercing blue eyes. Not that he's going to admit it.

"This shouldn't come as a surprise," I begin calmly, then take a deep breath, ready to make him understand. "I don't like ghostwriting, Thomas. It really isn't for me. I want to get back into creative fiction."

He's still just staring at me, so I go on. "Maybe Scarlett can try introducing me to her agent again. Maybe I can get something rolling there." I look at him earnestly, hoping for some remnant of who he used to be, someone who understood me and was the quiet guiding force supporting my desperate striving.

I find none of that in his face. He clears his throat, still too quiet, too small for the emotion I see written all over him. "You just completely humiliated me. And yourself. Do you even care?"

I'm taken aback. "Thomas," I reach for him, but he pulls away. "I'm finishing the Benderson book. It's almost done. They're going to be really pleased with it; you'll see. And then I'm shifting gears. I owe it to myself to make this happen—I've waited years for it, and I'm going to do whatever it takes. Even if it means going back to waitressing at night. I'll do anything to make this happen for myself."

His face is red, and I can tell he's angry. I want to beg him to raise his voice; to let his emotions out. To *feel* something. But he stays so calm it's almost terrifying.

"Callie," he begins slowly, "It just isn't going to work. A lot of people want to be novelists. Most people can't make that dream a reality. And you had a really good thing lined up here—something I worked hard to make happen for you. And then our efforts on this book got you even more opportunities. That was the plan. That's what we've been working toward. I got you on that path, and now you've just thrown it away, and for what?"

I can't help it. I start to cry. Because he doesn't believe in me. Because I don't think I ever really expected him to. Because he's continuing to act like this project was something he handed me rather than something I earned or deserved. And because deep down, he's convinced me to believe it all this time, too.

"You know what?" I raise my chin defiantly, through my tears. My voice is louder now; stronger despite its quaking. "I don't care what you think. I'm going to do it. I don't need you, or anyone else. And if I fail, so what? At least I'll have tried to make something of myself."

Thomas shakes his head. "But you won't. You just won't."

I start to cry again. Out of the corner of my eye, I see Will on the other side of the room, cautiously watching us. He stands up from his chair and walks closer, stopping near the coat rack about ten feet to our left. He tries to make eye contact with me, as if to make sure I'm okay, but I turn away. I don't want him to see me crying.

Maybe that's the signal he needed that I am, in fact, not okay. He walks toward me, closing the distance between us.

"Hi, Cal," he says quietly, stopping just beside me. He takes in my red-rimmed eyes and Thomas's eerily cool composure. He tenses, looking like he wants to punch Thomas in the face. "Everything okay?"

I shake my head, tears still falling. I can't bring myself to speak, because I don't even know what to say.

Thomas looks to Will. "I think we're good here." He angles away, trying to shut Will out of the conversation.

Will's gaze settles on me again. His brown eyes are huge, filled with sympathy and concern. "Really? Because it seems like you've upset Callie."

Thomas turns and glares at Will. "*Callie* upset Callie. She just humiliated herself in front of my boss and several potential clients. And me. But she doesn't seem to care about that, because *you've* encouraged her to subscribe to a deluded pipe dream that she's going to become a novelist."

He turns back to face me, looking directly into my eyes. "Which is never going to happen. If she had that kind of talent or dedication, it would have happened already."

My jaw falls open. I'm staring at him, speechless, trying to process what he's said, what it means.

"Come on, Callie." Will reaches for my arm and tries to pull me toward him. "Let's go. You don't need to listen to this."

"No, hold on," I say, pushing Will's arm away, even though I would give anything to keep touching him. I need to stand my own ground here.

"You've got a lot of nerve, Thomas." I put my hands on my hips and take a step closer. "I don't require your permission, nor do I need your assistance to accomplish this. And believe it or not, I've gotten here on my own, despite your *delusions*." I emphasize the word, mocking his use of it moments ago.

He's just staring at me, breathing heavily, not speaking.

I grow louder, more sure of myself. I'm sure other people can hear me, but I no longer care. "And why can't you ever just be *angry*? It's obvious that you're disappointed in me and think I'm failing you. But you never let your emotions out or pick a fight with me. It's like you're not even human."

He tenses a little at that, like I've struck a nerve. Good.

"Well, I'm not like you," I continue. "I'm angry. In fact, I'm pissed as hell."

He remains unblinking, face devoid of any sort of redeeming emotion. Least of all love.

I take a deep breath, just speaking, not thinking, but still knowing I'm going the right way. This isn't going to wait until we get to the car.

"And another thing," I push my shoulders back, summoning some sort of inner strength that I think might be hiding deep within me. "I'm breaking up with you. This," I wave furiously between us, "isn't working, and I'm done."

Thomas's face is impassive. "Fine," he says, like I've just suggested he exchange a blue shirt for a red one. "I don't think I've really loved you for a long time anyway." The words are cruel, like a twist of a knife. But when I stare at him through glassy eyes, I can't honestly say the same isn't true for me.

Thomas turns to Will. "I hope you're ready to help her pick up the pieces when she fails. It's your fault we're even standing here having this conversation."

If Will was ready to punch Thomas before, I'm certain he's about to now. His eyes flash, and I see his fists clench. I step between them a little, even though I think Thomas would more than deserve it.

"I'm not going anywhere," Will says, stepping closer to me. I can feel his breath on my shoulder.

Thomas looks between us and shakes his head in disgust. Pivoting on his heel wordlessly, he stalks away to the lobby, leaving Will and me standing in silence.

I turn and face Will, unsure of what to say. His breathing is ragged, and I can tell his adrenaline's racing.

I'm not going anywhere.

My mind is blank, and also so very, very full. "Thanks," I manage. Then I cover my eyes and run from the room.

I DON'T KNOW WHY, but as soon as I'm alone outside the ballroom, I burst into tears. I think they're less tears of sadness and more just an expression of frustration; an explosion of the pent-up unhappiness I've harbored for so long.

I didn't make myself look good in front of Jack Benderson and his uppity friends. I definitely didn't wow him. After all this slaving away on his stupid book, I'm sure he won't be recommending me to anyone else who needs a writer. *A ghostwriter*, I correct myself bitterly.

And I didn't wait until the book was done to make a decision about Thomas. I didn't stick to the plan, the ultimatum I had set for myself.

Not like it would have mattered anyway. Even if I'd waited, I think the outcome would have been the same. He and I just don't make sense. Looking back on it from this vantage, I'm not really sure we ever did.

I cry for the lost opportunities, for the years I spent feeling bored or not quite right with Thomas. I cry for the nothing I feel when I look at him. For the very definite *something* I feel when I look at Will, who came here with Priya and who I probably can't have, no matter how badly I want him.

Mostly, I just cry for myself, for knowing I've wasted so much time, and heart, on people and things that ultimately haven't amounted to much.

I'M SITTING on the steps outside the ballroom, head in hands, when I hear quiet footsteps. I look up to see Will walking toward me, his shiny dress shoes echoing against the reflective tile floor.

I make a futile attempt at wiping my eyes, but I know it's obvious I've been crying. Still. "Hey." I manage a small smile.

"I'm so sorry," he says, sitting down next to me. He wraps his arms around me, and I sink my head into his chest. I let out another small sob in spite of my best efforts to keep it together.

He squeezes me tighter. "None of it's true, you know. What he said."

I look up at him then, at his brown eyes that are so genuinely sad for me, and I am overwhelmed by him. By his warmth and his voice and his strong arms telling me everything is going to be okay. I'm overcome by how much I want all of it.

"I know," I answer, reaching up to lay my hand against his chest. "It's just the time." The tears fall again. "I wasted so much time."

He wraps my hand in his and holds it tightly against his chest. I feel like he's pouring his strength deep into my veins, giving me what I need to get through this moment. We sit there together, unmoving, until my tears dry on my skin, stopped in their tracks by the promise of a different future. One that I've given myself permission to control.

I hear the music in the ballroom shift from some sort of upbeat club mix to the beginning of "You and Me" by Tom Petty.

"You don't hear this one every day," he says, rubbing the back of my hand with his thumb.

"Want to dance?" I ask, surprising myself as I stand up, pulling him to follow.

His face flushes, and I think the way it makes my heart swell might be the best thing I've ever felt. "I'd love to," he says, walking down the stairs behind me. He's still holding my hand.

Alone in the lobby, music pouring out through the ballroom doors, we face each other. Without speaking, I meet his gaze. My heart skips a beat. He closes the distance between us, wrapping his arms around me, sinking them against the small of my back. I put my arms around his neck, pulling him tight, burying my face in his shoulder. *This* is the best thing I've ever felt.

I'm not going anywhere.

The music is doing something to me. It's hard to breathe, and I'm hearing the song and somehow it's about us, and I'm suddenly understanding every love story I've ever read that seemed way too cheesy at the time. I'm understanding why it never felt right with Thomas. I'm so grateful it never felt right with him, so grateful for the happy accidents that brought me here, to this empty space with no one but Will, where suddenly my heart doesn't feel so empty anymore.

I feel like I'm having my Pacey and Joey moment. The one where Dawson plans the anti-prom, purportedly in support of Jack, but does it all to try to win Joey over again. And then, in an effort to fix their friend group once and for all, she asks Pacey to dance. And he remembers everything and ruins all other men for millennial women, forever.

That's how I'm feeling right now, dancing with Will. Like he knows it and I know it, and we don't even have to say anything at all. Like he's breathing too fast and I can't catch my breath either, and I feel the heat from his cheek on mine, and I want to lean into him and hold him closer and just give in to these butterflies that are threatening to pound through my chest.

And when I force myself to open my eyes as the song ends, I'm pretty sure that's how Priya is feeling, too. While we were dancing, she suddenly appeared. Now she's standing outside the ballroom, looking pissed out of her mind at what she's seeing, just like Andie McPhee does when she realizes Pacey is in love with someone else.

Not that Will is in love with me. That isn't what this is.

Is it?

Every sensation in my body screaming at me for my unmitigated gall, I pull away slightly. Will seems startled. He stops rubbing my back and looks at me questioningly.

Wordlessly, I nod toward Priya. He follows my gaze.

"I should go talk to her," he says quietly.

I let him go, then see him follow her into the hallway as she turns away with a hurt look on her face. I feel sick.

I can't do this. I can't wait here while he comforts her, not while I can still feel his heartbeat echoing in my chest. I feel the tears coming back. I run for the door. I have to get out of here.

SINCE THOMAS DROVE us to the gala, I have to walk home. It's not far, but it isn't the most comfortable thing in the world in heels.

As I get back to the apartment complex, I feel my phone vibrate inside my clutch.

When I take it out, I see a text from Will. *Where did you go? I really need to talk to you.*

I freeze. I don't know what to say. I can't deal with two breakups in one day. Especially since Will and I were never together in the first place.

I put my phone away and go inside, finding the apartment empty. Scarlett must still be out with her dreamboat. I flip on the light and take off my shoes.

I think I'm all out of tears, but I really wish I weren't. I feel so many things right now, and they're all swirling inside me in a vortex of confusion. I don't know how to get rid of these feelings other than to cry, but I just don't think I can do that anymore.

I flop onto the couch and turn on the TV, trying to distract myself from the issues at hand. I have a bunch of shows taped. I might as well catch up on those.

This is so not the night I thought I'd be having.

Suddenly, right in the middle of my *Jeopardy!* rerun, I hear a knock at the door. I sit up in alarm. It's almost nine, and no one else should be here other than Scarlett, but she has a key.

I grab my phone, just in case I need to call the police, and creep to the door.

I hear a voice as the knocking stops. "Callie. It's Will. Please, I need to talk to you."

My heart just about jumps out of my chest.

I ease the door open, and there he is. His bowtie is stuffed into his pocket, his shirt is unbuttoned, and he looks incredibly sweaty. His hair is completely askew, and he has a totally insane look on his face. Like he ran all the way here.

"Why are you so sweaty?" It just slips out before I can think of something more polite to say.

He's startled, I can tell. He laughs in surprise, then leans on the doorframe next to me. "This suit isn't conducive to an evening jog when it's so humid."

"But your car. You had it at the gala."

He nods. "I let Priya take it home."

My eyes darken. If he's come here to tell me they're back together, I'm going to come apart.

As if sensing my reaction, he reaches out to grab my hand. I jump a little, but I let him keep it.

He shakes his head. "I'm not getting back together with her, Callie."

I slowly raise my eyes to his. He's looking at me so earnestly now that I can hardly stand it.

"Then what about that phone call at the library the other day? And why did you chase after her?" I don't mean to sound so harsh. But I just have to know, because I have to be sure I'm not imagining what's written all over his face. What I felt when we danced to Tom

Petty, when he helped me into the car after that first night at trivia. What I've hoped for every time I've watched him smile at me from across the library, a hope buried deep in my heart, so deep I could barely admit it to myself.

"She called to coordinate our plans for the gala. If it seemed weird, it's because I didn't feel great talking to her in front of you." He gives me a pained look.

My heart leaps about a mile.

"And tonight, I just wanted to make sure she was okay. I still care about her, but it isn't like that for me anymore. We're friends. That's it. I gave her my keys and she drove herself home." He pauses, then tentatively takes a step toward me. "You might notice I also chased after you."

My face heats, and I feel violently fizzy, all through my chest. I don't know what to do with my limbs, my face. He's so warm and so close, and he's still holding my hand.

"You did, didn't you?" I say with more gumption than I feel. A smile starts to creep up my lips. "And why," I ask, poking his sternum accusingly with my free pointer finger, "was that?"

His eyes are huge now, as if he's desperate for something. "Callie," he breathes. He closes the distance between us, putting his arms around me.

Before I realize what's happening, his lips are on mine, so gentle, so soft. My breath is gone, gone, gone as he presses the full length of his body against mine, kissing me like his life depends on it. I'm kissing him back, and I'm lost in a swell of emotions unlike anything I've ever experienced before. Imagine having the best thing you've ever felt superseded twice in one day.

I slide my hand into his hair, and it's softer than I could've imagined. I die a little on the inside when he moans into my lips. I can't believe he's here, that I'm really doing this.

That I'm not ghostwriting my own life anymore.

I can't get enough of his kiss, the warmth of his skin, the feeling of his hair under my fingers. God, I've wanted this so badly. It feels so good to finally let this feeling into the air, to make it real.

Suddenly, I hear an amused cough. It didn't come from Will, and it sure as hell didn't come from me. I open my eyes and see Scarlett standing over his shoulder. I tear my lips away from him.

"Scarlett!" I practically yell, even though she's only two feet away. "You're at the top of the stairs!" Like I'm a sports announcer and I'm letting the entire apartment complex know her exact location in proximity to the door.

She's trying so hard not to laugh, and I shoot her a silent glare. Will's desperately attempting to mash his hair back down, but I've sufficiently mussed it beyond the point of return.

I mentally pat myself on the back. He looks more than a little embarrassed. That, I don't enjoy. I'm not going to apologize for tousling his gorgeous hair, though.

"Hey, Scarlett," Will mumbles. He takes a step back to let her through the door, then reaches out and grabs my hand. I smile like a giddy teenager.

"Hi, Will. Hi, Cal." Scarlett is grinning from ear to ear. "I *so* want to hear how this gala went. I can tell it's going to be one heck of a story."

"Oh," I say weakly. "It definitely is."

She shoulders her purse, pats Will on the head, and skirts past us into the apartment. "Well, I'll leave you to it. Whatever *it* is. Talking, and whatnot. Or whatever you're going to do out here."

She pauses, looking like she's trapped herself in a flow she doesn't know how to get out of. "Have a good night, Will!" She hustles away.

I don't think I've ever heard Scarlett flustered before.

Once she's inside and the door is closed, Will takes a deep breath. "I should go." He looks down at our hands, still intertwined.

I want to cry out, beg him to stay, but he's probably right. What are we going to do, go inside and discuss whatever *this* is with Scarlett in the next room?

Plus, it's been a long day, and I probably should get my emotions in order before I make any decisions. I also just broke up with Thomas, not even three hours ago, and maybe it would be better not to rush into anything. And I have a feeling, if Will stays, I'll be rushing headfirst into *something*, possibly without some of my clothes.

I nod slowly, trying to absorb all the energy from this moment before it's gone. "Okay," I relent. "But you should take my car."

He starts to object, but I open the door and grab my keys from the bowl. I press them into his hand. "Not up for debate," I say. "It's dark, you're sweaty, and there might be feral sorority sisters on the prowl."

He cracks a smile. "Okay. Thanks, Callie." He squeezes my fingers.

I squeeze back. "I'll see you tomorrow at the library?"

He grins, all the way up to his eyes. "I will most definitely see you there." He leans in and kisses me again, so gently it takes my breath away.

I think I sigh audibly, and he chuckles as he turns to go back down the stairs. "Good night, Cal."

"Night, Will."

This time, when he drives away, not only am I still standing outside, but I can still feel his heartbeat echoing against mine, playing a soothing duet in my chest.

I'm not going anywhere.

thirteen

It takes me a while to orient myself to my new reality when I wake up the next morning. You know those times in life when something drastic has happened, like you've broken a bone or, much more drastically, somebody dies, and it just isn't sinking in? Where you start the next day feeling confused, unsure if this thing that's in your head is real or is just part of a really unfortunate dream sequence?

That's what this is like.

When I open my eyes, I'm confused about where I am, for one thing. Somehow, I managed to fall asleep across the end of the couch. I look around and notice a bowl of popcorn kernels and an empty bottle of wine on the coffee table.

Trickles come in, and I start to remember. *Scarlett.* When I came back inside from my rendezvous with Will, Scarlett immediately pounced. She wanted all the juicy details, and she plied me with snacks and Riesling until I'd relayed all the events of the evening. I must have fallen asleep out here.

And then there's the memories of what had happened at the gala. Those hit me in a confusing wave of realization, reminding me that my new reality is very different from the one I woke up to yesterday.

Thomas doesn't love me. And I don't love him. I think I've known at least the second part for quite some time, even before the Benderson book, even before Will. It's just been hard to admit it to myself.

I so enjoyed our quiet consistency, our steady, even-keeled foundation. When everything else was stumbling about on rickety legs around me, it was always so comforting to know he was There, with a capital T. Just There.

But, in being with him, I know I was squashing down a major part of myself, and my dreams. It felt safe, but that was about it. I think I was more in love with what I got from Thomas than I ever was with him.

And then there was the book, which I had finally admitted, out loud, and to other people, wasn't what I wanted to be doing with my life. Ghostwriting, I'd realized last night, wasn't ever going to fill my cup. Standing with the prospect of a lifetime of buried wishes and the melancholy acceptance of *less than* made everything suddenly very clear.

I know it's going to be hard, but I don't want to hide in the shadows of my own potential anymore.

I'm pretty sure, even if I never publish a single book under my own name, ever, I'll be happier writing and trying than squishing myself into a box someone else has made for me. Than being so, so close to what I actually want and never being able to reach out and touch it. I don't want to window shop my own life.

And then there's Will. *Will.* Even sitting here, thinking of him now, I feel a rush of butterflies all through my chest, threatening to burst out of me and fill the entire room with longing. I honestly don't think I've ever felt this way about anyone before.

He's so funny, so smart. He's kind and he works hard. And he takes care of me. *He takes care of me,* even when I don't ask; even before I had any kind of right to need him.

And there's depth there, feelings I never had with Thomas. It's more than just a safe, steady blue sky, no clouds in sight. It's the whole damn sunset, a veritable watercolor palette of *everything*, from those first hints of pink creeping over the horizon to the deep blue of twilight, punctuated by twinkling stars.

I hug my knees, considering my new reality, and a few happy tears roll down my cheeks. I deserve all the colors.

WHEN SCARLETT DROPS me off at the library a few hours later, I go right to circulation. Will's wearing green plaid today, a plain black t-shirt underneath. He's got his nose buried in a book about jazz when I walk in.

"Excuse me," I say, managing to get all the way up to the desk before he notices. His eyes light up over the top of his book when he sees me.

"Can you help me find some books?" I smile in a way that I hope seems flirtatious rather than deranged.

His grin starts slowly, but I think my attempts at being coy hit home. "We have lots of those here. Anything in particular you're looking for?"

"Um," I say, not having thought this far ahead. "Philosophy?"

"Sure, sure," he closes his book. "Let me show you where we keep those. Just a moment." He sticks his head into the staff area and talks with Marian. She comes out to the desk and takes his spot, waving when she sees me. "Right this way." He gestures toward the elevator.

I follow him, staring at the waves on the back of his head, my heart thumping out of my chest. When we get inside, he pushes the button for the second floor and then turns to face me.

"Hi," he says softly.

"Hi," I reply. He's so close now, and it's all I can do not to reach out and throw my arms around him. But he's working, and I need to keep my wits about me.

The elevator dings. We're only going to the second floor. He reaches out and presses the door close button. I feel my breath catch in my chest.

"So, I wanted to apologize for last night," he begins. I think my heart stops. Does he think it was a mistake?

He must catch the shock on my face, because he quickly adds, "Not that I regret it at all, in any way." He smiles at me. "At all."

He reaches out to push a stray strand of hair out of my face. I'm melting, I think. My heart is so full that it's overflowing, pouring out into my chest, so it's hard to hear him when he continues. "But I realize you just broke up with Thomas, and I probably should have respected that you'd need some time to process everything."

I nod, trying to look like there's a shred of logic left in my brain, rather than the complete mush that I think is filling it right now. I probably *should* need that time. I don't feel like I do, though. I so badly want to reach out and touch him. "Will," I begin.

"No, you don't have to say anything," he interrupts. "I don't want to make you rush into anything. We can take our time. I'll be here."

I'm not going anywhere.

I feel like I'm going to cry from how badly I want to hold him right now. But he's right, and he deserves more than feeling like my rebound.

I nod shakily. I'm not going to argue with him. But I have to do things differently this time, with Will. I have to speak my mind. Ask for what I want. "Can you just," I begin, breathing ragged as I tentatively put my hand against his chest, "hold me for a minute?"

"Always," he says, pulling me toward him. He pushes the door close button again and buries his face in my hair. "I'm here for you, Callie," he murmurs.

I wrap my arms around his waist, and we just stand there, hogging the elevator, his heart echoing in my chest like it's showing me the way forward. Even though I'm filled with wanting more, more, more, in this moment, I'm somehow also truly, deeply happy to be exactly where I am.

. . .

GETTING BACK to work on the Benderson book is the ultimate buzzkill after the 24 hours I've had. I set up shop at my usual table, and I struggle in a big way to focus. It's not helping that I can see Will out of the corner of my eye, back in his spot at the front desk.

I just need to push through, to finish this manuscript, and to send it off for review. Then I can more fully close the book on Thomas, figuratively speaking. Plus, my writing class starts next Tuesday, and I don't want to prove Thomas right that I can't do both things at once.

While I'm pondering instead of writing, I feel my phone ring in my pocket. I take a quick look and see that it's my mom. That's weird. She doesn't typically call during the week.

I let it go to voicemail, figuring I can return her call when I head home. My fingers hover over my keyboard, waiting for inspiration to strike. My pocket vibrates again.

My brow wrinkles, but I grab my phone and head for the exit. As I walk by the desk, I hold up a finger to Will to signal I'll be back in a minute.

Once I'm outside, I say hello.

"Callie?" My mom sounds upset, then gives what I can only think to describe as a rueful laugh. "Are you sitting down?" she asks, like this is some sort of movie where people actually can't keep themselves upright when they get bad news.

"No, Mom. I'm not. What's going on?"

"It's Esperanza," she says. "She got hit by a car."

Thank God there's a bench behind me. I sink onto it subconsciously, grateful for its steadying force.

"I'm sorry, what?" I'm not sure I'm hearing her correctly.

"She's okay," Mom says. "Well, mostly. She was walking to pick up her car from the shop."

My heart does a little flip-flop. The car that she was just telling me she was going to get rid of?

"We think the driver was texting," Mom continues. "She hit Esperanza in the crosswalk." Her voice breaks. "The paramedics didn't check her wallet. She's been alone in the hospital since yesterday morning, because they didn't know she had anyone they could call."

I'm struggling to process what I'm hearing. "Is she going to be okay?"

"She broke most of her ribs and fractured her skull. She also broke a femur and her right arm. There's some internal bleeding."

I can't breathe. I don't speak.

"They think she's going to survive." Mom's voice is reassuring, like she needs to convince herself as much as she does me. "They think she's going to be okay."

"What hospital is she at?" I need to get there, now.

"Rockledge Medical Center," Mom replies. "Dad and I are already there."

"I'm on my way," I say through tears. I hang up the phone before she can try to change my mind.

I RUN BACK into the library. "Will," I say, breathless. "I need my car."

"What's going on?" He comes out from behind the desk and puts his hand on my shoulder. "Are you okay?"

I am definitely not okay. "There's been an accident," I reply, sounding like every bad '90s movie where the dad gets hit by a truck and turns into a snowman or something. "It's Esperanza. She's in the hospital. I have to..." My voice breaks and the tears start, but I manage to waver, "I have to go."

Will nods, takes a beat, and then says, "Just a moment." He walks to the staff room, says something to Marian, and then swings his bag down from a hook. "Let's go." He grabs my hand.

I'm bewildered. "You're working."

"I don't think you should be driving right now, nor do I want you to have to do this alone," he says, guiding me out the door. "And, in any case, you were my ride today," he teases.

I smile in spite of myself.

I don't remember much of what happens next, but I know I'm riding in the passenger seat of my car, and Will is driving us toward Rockledge. I can't stop thinking about Esperanza, alone and broken in the hospital. *She's always there for everyone. She deserved to have someone there for her.*

The drive feels both too short and infinite. Before I know it, we're pulling into the parking garage for the emergency room, closing the door, and going to the front desk. "Esperanza Accardi, please," I ask the nurse. She gives directions I don't really hear, pointing toward the elevator.

When the door chimes, Will and I walk inside. This time, he holds my hand. I can't think of anything to say, but he's there. A steadying force. I'm so grateful.

We get to the ICU and step out of the elevator. It hasn't occurred to me that I'm showing up at the hospital with a man my parents have never met, one who is decidedly not Thomas, until just this moment.

As if reading my mind, Will pauses before the doors. "Do you want me to wait out here?" He gestures to the waiting room, a sea of blue chairs and magazine racks; a Schrödinger's box of hope for the families who linger here.

I shake my head. "Please don't." My voice comes out squeakier than I mean for it to. I don't want to do this alone. "Unless you aren't comfortable, I mean."

He wraps his arm around my shoulder and pulls me close. "For you, anything."

I'm not going anywhere.

fourteen

When we find my parents in the intensive care unit, they both wear the same worried expression. My mom raises an eyebrow when she notices Will. My dad, always a stoic, just nods in greeting.

"Hi," I say, coming up to hug them both. "Um, this is my friend Will," I gesture to him, and he sticks out his hand in greeting. First Mom, then Dad, shakes his hand.

"Nice to meet you, Will," Dad says. Mom nods in agreement.

"Likewise," Will agrees, "though other circumstances would have been preferable."

I can't handle any more niceties. I need to see Esperanza, to know that she's going to be okay. "Where is she? How is she?" I ask, craning my neck around my parents to try to get a better view of the corridor of partitioned rooms in the ICU.

They exchange a strained look. "She's okay," says my mom. "She doesn't look like herself, and she's in a lot of pain. But she's awake and sassy." A smile breaks through. "You can go talk to her if you want. Room 342." Mom looks at Will. "They're letting two people in at a time."

I nod. "Shall we?" I grab Will's arm.

"If you want me there, I'm ready," he replies.

"I do. Thank you." I'm steeling myself for whatever this experience might be like, but I'm not sure *I'm* ready. And I know it will be easier if I have someone to lean on.

"Be back soon," I tell my parents. Then Will and I head down the row of cubicles until we find Esperanza's.

I push the curtain aside and almost gasp when I see her. She has a cast on her arm and another on her leg, which is in traction. Her head is wrapped in a bandage, and there are cuts and bruises on every inch of exposed skin. But her eyes are bright, and I can see that *she* is still there, inside her battered body. *Esperanza is still there.*

Choking back tears, I cross the distance to her bedside. "Esperanza," I say, reaching out to gently squeeze her hand.

"C! You came! Oh, I'm so glad to see you." She tries to twist toward me, then abruptly halts, restricted by both casts. Frustration washes over her face.

"Don't worry," I reassure her, grabbing a chair and pulling it to the end of the bed. "I'll sit down here so you can see me without having to move."

Relief floods her countenance. "Thanks, kid."

She inclines her head slightly as if noticing Will for the first time. "This isn't Tom."

I chuckle uncomfortably, not sure how to cut the tension. "No, Esperanza. This is Will. He's a friend of mine from the library, where I've been writing my book." I hope this explanation of what we are to each other is enough for the moment.

"Nice to meet you," says Will gently, waving rather than trying to shake her hand. Always so thoughtful, that one. He pulls a chair up next to me.

"You too, you too." Esperanza looks him up and down. "He looks like Johnny. Don't you think he looks like Johnny?"

I give her a quizzical glance. "Who's Johnny?"

I'm surprised to see her face flush, then fall. "Johnny Giordano. He was a boy who used to come around, calling for me." She looks down at her bandaged self, then adds, "I would have married him if I'd known."

You could have given me a thousand guesses, and I never would have imagined I'd hear Esperanza saying any of what she just shared. For a moment, I'm quiet, trying to process. Then, I ask, "If you'd known what?"

"That he wasn't going to come back." Her eyes are still cast downward.

I'm pretty sure I'm still gaping like a fish. I try to reset my face so as not to seem rude. "Come back from where?"

She looks up and sighs. "He went off to the war. He asked me to wait for him, and I would have. But he left; I don't know why. I really don't. He said he would come talk to me about it before he went away, and I guess he never came. Broke my heart." I see a tear roll down her face. "I never got the chance to tell him I loved him. He never knew." She wipes at her eye with the side of her good arm. "He never knew."

I don't know what to say. I've never heard her mention this before; any of it. The idea of lost love, split across broken timelines, strikes me as perhaps the most profoundly sad thing I've ever heard.

"I'm so sorry," I finally say.

"I have some postcards, pictures," she begins slowly. "At home. In a box on top of the closet. Of Johnny, and of Mama. And my brothers and sisters from when we were growing up. I'd really love to see them again." She wipes her eyes. "Hey, C, do you think you could get them for me?"

I nod quickly. "We'll go get them for you after we leave." I look at Will for confirmation, which he quickly gives with an incline of his head.

Esperanza visibly relaxes, like having these pictures here in her hospital room is going to heal years of grief.

"So tell me something," Will asks. "How's the food here?" He leans forward on his elbows, attention rapt on Esperanza's face.

"Oh, you know," she says with a little laugh. "It's okay." She grimaces a little, then repeats herself as if to convince us it's true. "It's okay. But they brought me this chocolate pudding, and I don't want that. I don't need that kind of thing." She gestures to the tray on her bedside table. "Why don't you take it?" She directs the offer at Will.

I see surprise flash across his face, but he recovers quickly, shooting her a huge grin. "I appreciate that, but I'm not in the mood for hooves right now."

I snort.

Esperanza laughs, too. "Hooves. Hooves, that's funny." She addresses me, "You've got a funny guy, here, C."

I'm glowing, overflowing with warmth for him, for her. For the fact that we all get to be on this planet together, that she's okay, that Will gets to meet this curious human being who broke the mold and makes my heart smile.

I reach out to touch his hand. "You've got that right, Esperanza."

"So tell me something, C. How's work? How's that dining table?" Her eyes are eager for the dish.

"Work's good," I say. "I'm almost done with the finance book I'm writing for Thomas's boss." I string the next words together slowly, dipping my toe in the pond tentatively to test the waters. "I'm going to focus on my fiction writing when I'm done with that. Try again to publish a novel."

It's strange, having these words out there. Her reaction will mean a lot to me, but she's also the first person I've told in the light of day, after the furor of the gala. And she feels like a pretty safe person to test the information on, because Esperanza thinks everything I do is great, justifiably so or not.

"And the dining table is good," I add quickly.

"Well, that's just wonderful!" She hits the bed with her good hand. "You're going to have books! I'm going to read them all. I can't wait, kid. This is great news!"

I can't hold back my grin, or the tears pricking the back of my eyelids. I expected perhaps nothing less, but it means so much that she believes in me.

"I'll set aside some autographed copies just for you," I promise.

"Speaking of Thomas," Esperanza says, ignoring the fact that we really weren't. "Are you all done with him now, then?" She looks pointedly at Will.

My face flushes, but a chuckle rolls out of my chest regardless. "Yeah, unfortunately, that didn't work out."

She nods vigorously. "And Will, this Will," she indicates him with her head. "Is this your new boyfriend?"

My blush deepens, and I stumble over the words that have spilled up into my throat. All that comes out is "Um."

Thank goodness for Will. "Callie and I are still just figuring things out," he jumps in. "But I certainly hope to be her boyfriend in the future." He looks at me and smiles sweetly.

My heart somersaults violently. Oh my God. I think I'm hyperventilating, looking at him now, seeing his grin, filled with affection and focused on me. I try to smile back with some semblance of composure, but I'm pretty sure my face looks like some grotesque combination of embarrassed, enamored, and shocked.

He hides a snicker, so I know my estimation of my face is at least somewhat accurate.

"Aw, well that's sweet," Esperanza saves the situation. "I'm happy for you two, I really am." She jabs an elbow toward Will. "I like him."

"Me too," I agree. "Me too."

TWO HOURS LATER, Will and I unlock the door to Esperanza's apartment and step inside. We're met with a cloud of lavender candles and fresh linen detergent. Esperanza doesn't own a washer, so she cleans most of her clothes by hand in the tub, hanging them afterward on an ancient wooden drying rack. Her building does have laundry facilities, but she never wants to spend the money if she doesn't have to.

We kick off our shoes by the mat. Will looks around, taking in roughly 30 statues of the Virgin Mary and countless mismatched frames filled with family photos that sit on every available surface.

"I'm famous," I say, indicating the kitchen wall, where Esperanza's taped up a letter I sent her several years back. I'd drawn a Christmas tree at the bottom, and, while I'm no artist, she seemed to really like it.

"Wow." He stands, arms behind his back, assessing the letter like it's hanging in the Louvre. "Excellent use of color and form."

I snort and shove him teasingly with my hip. "You're silly."

He pushes back. "You're silly."

On impulse, I reach out and wrap him in a hug, squeezing tightly, like I can squash all of my gratitude into his chest so he can carry it with him and know how much I care.

He hugs me back, then kisses the top of my head. "I absolutely love Esperanza," he says into my hair.

"You and me both," I agree. I pull away, grabbing his hand. "Thank you so much for being here with me today."

He shrugs his shoulders, rolling the praise away. "It's no big deal."

"No, actually, it's a very big deal. I really, really appreciate it."

He smiles at me, eyes as full as my heart feels. "Anything for you, Cal."

I need to step away, or I'm going to be all over him here, which feels inappropriate in about a thousand ways.

Clearing my throat, I pull him out of the kitchen. "Let's go find the photos she asked for."

He nods, and we head toward the bedroom. I flip on the light and see the closet over on the right. It's a walk-in, which is a surprise given the relative lack of other amenities in her apartment. She has somewhere in the realm of 15 articles of clothing hanging up, and only a few pairs of shoes on the floor.

I spot the box on the top shelf, brown with the words "Photos and Scrapbooks" scrawled on the side. "Can you help me get this?" I ask Will.

He reaches up to grab the box, which slides down in a cloud of dust. He coughs, fanning the air around his face to clear it.

"I guess she doesn't look at these very often," he remarks.

"Evidently." I try to brush the remaining dust away, accidentally urging it toward my shirt in the process. "I think I'll leave this for her to open," I say. "But I should probably clean it."

I walk to the kitchen and dampen a paper towel, then head over to Will, who's brought the box to the entryway. I swipe the dust off the surface of the box, then wash my hands.

"Ready to head out?" I ask.

He nods, picking up the box in one arm and pulling open the door with the other. "After you."

As the door slams shut behind us, I have a fleeting thought, one that I try to push away but find I can't. I wonder when I'll next be here, if Esperanza will be able to come home. Will she have to stay in the hospital for months? Go to rehab? End up in assisted living? Is this the end of her life as she knew it?

We never really know, I think to myself, *when things are going to profoundly change.*

WHEN WILL and I bring the box of photos to Esperanza at the hospital, my grandmother, Josephine, is just getting there to see her. "We already had a chance to visit," I explain. "Maybe you can just bring Esperanza this box?" I gesture to the carton in Will's arms.

"Sure," my grandmother agrees. "What's in it?"

My eyes skip to the huge words on the side of the box, wondering how she managed to miss them, but I just say, "Oh, some photos she wanted. Of your family from back in the day. And some of Johnny Giordano."

Josephine's eyes darken, and I see all kinds of emotion flash across her face. "She shouldn't be looking at those."

I tilt my head. "I don't understand."

My grandmother sighs. "Johnny was no good for her. And it isn't going to help Esperanza get better if she spends all her time looking at pictures of him, thinking about what went wrong."

"What do you mean, he was no good for her?" My eyebrows scrunch together.

"He came from nothing. His father worked down at the brickyard. Johnny was going to do the same thing, until he got drafted. He wasn't going to make a good living. It would barely be enough to get by." She appraises my face, looking for some sign that I understand.

I'm not sure I do. "But *our* family came from nothing," I say slowly.

She nods. "But my father was a painter. He started a business. He provided for us."

"Your father was an abusive alcoholic," I say quietly.

Her eyes flash, and she starts gesticulating wildly, a sure sign that the Italian in her is coming out to play. "Johnny was no good," she says again. "He kept her out late. God knows what they were doing. And he'd come around, smelling like beer. It wasn't right." She shakes her head. "It just wasn't right."

"But she loved him."

Josephine scoffs. "Love isn't enough, you know. It wouldn't have been enough for Esperanza. She's too naive, too simple. She never would have been able to make enough money on her own to support herself, much less a family, if he got her pregnant."

Will is frozen there, hefting the box onto one hip, watching the exchange unfold with raised brows.

My grandmother continues. "Frank was different. Solid, dependable. When he came around and asked about her, we knew he was a better option. Inherited his father's store. Good, honest guy. If there'd been no Frank, maybe things would've been different. But when

Esperanza told me Johnny was leaving for the war, that he asked her to wait for him? I knew we needed to do the right thing."

My stomach twists in knots. *We?* "The right thing?" *What the hell does she mean, the right thing?*

Josephine looks older now, her eyes tired and distant as she takes a deep breath. "Johnny came by to see her before he shipped out. I got to him before he could talk to her." She crosses her arms.

No no no, my mind cries. The wheels are turning, and I think I see where this is going. I don't want it to go there. I can't hear this.

"I told him she was with Frank, that they were going to get married. He didn't like it, wanted to talk to her. But I said she wasn't home, and he left, and…I just never told her."

My mouth hangs open. I'm struggling to process what she's told me. Esperanza had a real shot at happiness, all those years ago. And Johnny *had* come back, but my grandmother sent him away, thinking she knew better what Esperanza needed. And then Esperanza had gone on to marry Frank, and she'd been miserable, and they'd gotten divorced, leaving her without the kids she'd wanted, without a stable income, without a home.

"How…how could you do that?" My voice comes out in a whisper. "She loved him. She thinks he never came back for her. She's lived with that heartbreak, all these years." My chin wavers, but I try to hold back the tears. "And it wasn't even true."

Josephine's eyes are wet, too, but she maintains an impassive expression. "Sometimes love isn't enough," she repeats.

I shake my head, ready to say more, but Will grabs my arm.

"Come on," he says quietly to me. "Let's go give this box to Esperanza."

I nod, tears starting to fall with force now. We don't even say goodbye to my grandmother as we walk away.

WHEN WE GET to Esperanza's room, she's asleep. I let the curtain fall closed behind me and take a few tentative steps closer to her bed. I watch her chest rise and fall, wondering what she's dreaming about, whose face fills her mind.

I look at Will and motion with my head to the bedside table. He nods and crosses the room, then sets the box down next to her forgotten lunch tray.

"Thank you," I mouth.

"Of course," he whispers.

We turn around and head out, leaving Esperanza to rest.

fifteen

After my grandmother revealed that she was the antagonist in the story of Esperanza's life, the one responsible for preventing a happy ending, I fall down a rabbit hole of what-ifs. Of questioning things I'd thought were a given, like who Josephine was, and what I knew of Esperanza.

Was she truly so silly and childlike at heart, almost edging on a caricature at times, or was it a defense mechanism to deal with the loneliness that encroached anytime she let her guard down? What might have happened if Josephine hadn't come to the door that day? Could Esperanza have built a life for herself with Johnny, away from her family's meddling, that yielded the happiness she deserved?

I can barely focus on the Benderson book, my thoughts swirling like a vortex of wondering and grief for Esperanza's lost opportunities. It also isn't helping that I've moved from my usual table at the library to the one next to the circulation desk, so I can be closer to Will.

I haven't gotten much done the last few days.

But August is looming, and I need to press on. I want to be done with this project so I can shift my focus to my writing class, to querying agents. To Esperanza. And to Will.

I haven't quite figured out yet how to tell Esperanza what I've learned, or if I should tell her at all. I haven't even mentioned it to my parents, because I'm not sure how they'll receive the information. I don't think I can handle the vilification of any other beloved family members right now if they don't react with pure, unadulterated rage.

My brain is also mush whenever I interact with Will, whose every action makes me fall even further into the abyss that is wanting him. At trivia this week, I struggled to even remember the name of my favorite Rolling Stones song ("Beast of Burden") because I was so caught up feeling the heat of our knees touching under the table.

It doesn't help that his hair is very messy today, and I can't stop thinking about running my fingers through it.

Needless to say, there's a lot that's distracting me from my writing.

"Callie." Will is leaning on the edge of his desk, eyes twinkling.

I snap out of my trance. "Yes, Will?"

He grins. "I just noticed that you were looking over there," he gestures to the far wall, "and it seems like your computer is over here." He points to my table.

"You caught me." I close the laptop abruptly. "I can't focus on this. Not with everything else that's going on."

Will's mouth forms a line as he nods. God, I want to kiss him so badly.

"I understand," he says. "What can I do?"

"You don't need to do anything." I tap my pointer finger against my lips, pondering. "Except keep standing there, looking adorable."

He vogues for a moment, then leans his chin in his hands. "I'm not sure I have a choice."

I'm beaming now, swept away by his charm, with no desire to escape the floodwaters. "You're cute."

"Callie!" he says in mock surprise. "I am *working*. It's totally inappropriate to come on to public servants while they're on duty."

I roll my eyes at him. "I think I'm going to head out." He looks a little crestfallen, so I add, "I can't focus at all, so I might go for a walk.

Clear my head a little." I shoulder my laptop bag and slide the computer in. "Want to come over tonight? We could watch a movie or something."

My question has the desired effect. Will grins. "I very much do," he accepts. "Seven o'clock?"

"See you then." I squeeze his hand, then force myself to let go and head for the door.

I FINISH MY WALK, which does absolutely nothing to clear my head, but I'm feeling pretty good by the time I get home. There must be some endorphin action happening under the surface. I peel off my pink yoga pants and sink onto the couch in just an oversized t-shirt.

Flipping open my phone, I decide to check in on Esperanza. I dial her room at the hospital.

"Hello!" she answers, with her usual brash surprise.

"Hey, Esperanza. It's Callie. Just calling to see how you're feeling."

"Not bad, kid. Not bad. One of my bandages is coming off today. And they're going to let me hobble around with crutches soon."

Given how she'd looked last week, I'm pretty impressed that she's almost ready to take a stroll, regardless of what accessories she might need to accomplish it. "That's wonderful! I'm so glad to hear it."

I play with the fringe on the blanket that's wedged under my thigh. "Hey, did you get that box of photos?" I want to make sure my grandmother didn't take it while Esperanza was asleep.

"Oh, yes, I did, C. I thank you. I've been looking at them. It's been really nice to see. He really does look like Johnny, your Will."

My Will. My heart smiles at the words. "I'd love to see the pictures sometime." I quickly add, "If you'd want to share them."

"Oh, of course." She's excited now. "I'll tell you about them. Yep, I'll tell you all the stories."

"Perfect. I'll be there to visit you later this week, okay? We can look at the pictures then."

I hear a grin in her voice. "I love you, kid. I'll see you then!"

"Love you, too. Keep feeling better, okay?" I remind her.

"I will, I will," she says, hanging up.

I'M CLEANING THE APARTMENT, listening to music, when Scarlett gets home.

"Wow, are we having a health department inspection?" she asks, surveying the assortment of cleaning solutions and rags I have strewn everywhere.

"I invited Will over to watch a movie tonight," I explain. "But given what I'm finding in some of these corners, we probably should be cleaning more often anyway."

She shoots me a knowing glance over the top of her pink Ray-Bans, then tosses them and her wristlet onto the table. "You're cleaning for him? Somebody's in deep."

I throw a rag at her. "Don't worry, that one was clean," I promise, as she attempts to jump away.

She laughs like a carillon, both melodic and extremely loud. "Well, I'll make myself scarce later, okay?"

I start to protest, tell her she doesn't have to.

But she shakes her head, shutting me down. "Nope, I'm going out. I'll go over to Jonathan's. You and Will need time," she insists. "Time without the specter of Thomas hovering behind you, time outside of a hospital, and definitely time away from the library. Just, time. To figure things out."

She's right. I know she's right. "Thanks, Scarlett."

"Anytime," she shrugs. "I'm going to make a smoothie, but then I'll help you straighten up for a bit before I head out."

. . .

WE CLEAN in relative silence for a while, working in different rooms of the apartment. My phone is blasting classic rock from the kitchen, and Scarlett sings along loudly whenever she knows the words, but it's quiet enough in some corners that my thoughts start to drift.

Now that I know, for today, at least, Esperanza is okay, I allow my daydreams to cascade into a waterfall of Will. Of how badly I want to be around him, all the time. Of how he makes me feel. Of how I want this era of butterflies and heart flips and flushes up to my scalp to linger forever.

I feel older than I ever have, finally unwrapping the wisdom of the ages; learning what people actually mean when they say they're falling in love. I hesitate to use the word, even in my head, but I know that it's there.

Somehow, I'm also feeling younger again, like I've been hit with my very first crush. Like I'm still in that adorably naïve teenage phase when you think that falling in love is going to be some sort of date night montage. Twirling pasta under twinkle lights in an outdoor café; hide-and-seek in a bookstore; chasing each other around a laser tag arena. That sort of thing.

Doing something covertly coquettish like accidentally-on-purpose brushing hands while at the movies, or leaning in to smear paint from your paintball pellets over their nose, then sinking to the ground in a sea of passionate kisses. Doing all of these things while Third Eye Blind's "Never Let You Go" plays in the background. You know.

Most of those, admittedly very specific, dating clichés aren't happening right now, with Will. (Although our hands have brushed a number of times, and my stomach has gone into a series of hysterical somersaults immediately afterward.)

But the *feelings* that accompany those teenaged fantasies? That heady sensation, the fizziness that spreads through my chest and nearly convinces me that, if I just ran really fast with my arms outstretched, I could fly? Even, sometimes, the Third Eye Blind guitar riffs in my mind?

Yeah, that's happening. In a big way. And when it does, it's consuming my every thought. He, quite literally, takes my breath away.

And I don't think this has ever happened to me before. Certainly not with Thomas. I think back over the other guys I've dated, or even been interested in, before that. Even when I was 13, and had what I thought was the biggest crush in the world on Sam Collins, the goofy redheaded cellist who lived next door, I don't think my heart ever sang movie montage songs whenever he was in my periphery.

I love every second of this. And I'm also terrified. *What does this mean*, I keep asking myself. I'm falling, down, down, down, so hard and fast, and I'm not sure I'll be able to extricate myself from this pit if something goes wrong.

I shake my head, trying to banish the thoughts. *Just focus on today*, I admonish myself. Today, things are great, and Will's coming over, and we're going to have a wonderful time. And for today, that's all I can control.

sixteen

Will knocks on the door at seven o'clock on the dot. Even though I've been cleaning and primping all afternoon, I still feel like the apartment (and my hair) aren't quite ready for his arrival.

"You just saw him a few hours ago," Scarlett kept reminding me before she scurried away to Jonathan's.

"It's different now," I'd insisted.

Because now, for the first time, he's coming over to my apartment, both of us fully expecting a date-like evening. There won't be stale relationships or past loves to taint the encounter; no spilled daiquiris or thoughts of work or family trauma to unpack. Just Will and I, alone, ready to actually explore this living, breathing thing that we have between us.

I steal one last glance in the mirror as I rush to answer the door. "Damn it," I mutter to myself, furiously trying to smooth down my brown waves. They immediately bounce back to their original height. I decide they're probably a lost cause.

I take a deep breath and pause in the entryway, trying to regain my composure, then I open the door.

Seeing Will standing there, his navy blue T-shirt hugging his pectorals, his chocolate brown eyes sparkling, makes me go a little weak in the knees.

"Hi," he says, smiling at me like my hair isn't springing recklessly away from my scalp at every turn, like my dress isn't wrinkled beyond measure from my anxious sweating and last-minute freakish cleaning. Like I'm someone who is making his heart wildly palpitate the same way he does mine.

"Hi," I mumble shyly. I'm too busy visually devouring him to remember social convention, so it takes a moment for me to invite him inside.

"Come on in," I say finally, reaching for his hand and pulling him into the apartment. The entryway is cramped, and I've basically just forced him to join me in a four-by-four box.

He tentatively reaches for my other hand, then rubs his thumbs tenderly over the backs of my wrists, circling around and around until I can't even remember my last name. I'm utterly lost, in his eyes, in his smile, just aimlessly waiting for directions like I've never had a romantic relationship before, much less a visitor.

"We should probably try to make it a little farther inside," I manage after a minute.

He hasn't taken his eyes off my face. "You're probably right."

My insides are a swirling mess, an out-of-control cyclone of heat and want and longing. I nod again, as if agreeing with my own idea that we should actually enter my living space, rather than continue to linger in its apertures.

Eventually, we succeed in making it down the hallway. "I'll give you the grand tour," I offer, still holding his hand.

"I definitely want the *grand* tour," he says earnestly. "Anything that's basic or introductory-level just won't do."

"Just so you know, it's customary to tip your tour guide," I smirk, feigning a deep commitment to this bit we're engaged in. Anything to cut the tension that's thrumming through the air, making it hard to hear, to think, to breathe.

"I give great tips," he promises.

"You mean like telling me what to do all the time?" I tease, leaning into his chest.

"Like that, yes." His arm goes around my shoulders. "Or like me forewarning you I'm not sure I can make it through the night without kissing you."

I'm taken aback, because it both seems completely natural that he'd be kissing me tonight, given how all of this *feels*, but also like maybe he wouldn't be, since he's trying to be a gentleman and give me space during my time of unprecedented emotional turmoil.

In either case, I didn't really expect him to call attention to how urgently our bodies seem to be crying out for each other. At least, not so quickly after arriving here.

I try to shake it off and stop overthinking what he said, since it could only be construed as a positive thing.

Back to the bit about tipping, I remind myself. "Wow," I quip. "That forewarning is a great heads-up, and the kiss, the perfect form of compensation. A tip that works on two levels."

I pull back, take his forearms in my hands, and pretend to appraise him. My stomach somersaults around like it's an entire children's gymnastics class. His arms are perfectly sculpted, so warm and powerful beneath my fingers. My eyes catch on his tattoo again, and I have an overwhelming urge to touch it. "Yes, I think a kiss will do just fine."

He snorts. "Sounds like I'd really be twisting your arm."

"Oh, you've no idea how much." I shoot him my most flirtatious smile. "Now, on with the tour."

I gesture to the left. "Here's the kitchen, and this, as you'll see, is the dining nook, featuring the best little table you've ever seen."

He nods fervently. "I see why Esperanza was so set on giving this to you guys." Sliding into one of the chairs, he makes a big show of getting comfortable, then pantomimes eating a meal. "Yep, it's a great table."

I sweep past him. "And this is the living room, complete with an ill-advised all-white couch and 42-inch television."

"They're both fine specimens," he says, pretending to assess the space.

"And then back here," I indicate the hallway beyond the living room, "are the bathroom and bedrooms."

He meanders slowly to the edge of the bathroom door, and I hope he's noticing how clean everything looks. I'd literally scoured the tiles with a toothbrush for the entire duration of my Offspring playlist, but I feel like I can't tell him how rare it is for things to look so immaculate without potentially grossing him out.

He casts a glance toward the bedrooms. Scarlett's is loud, filled with hot pink, bright orange, and teal. She has a glitzy beaded curtain hanging in front of the closet and an incredibly furry magenta shag rug shaped like a bear skin lying across the floor. Her desk is a mess, and there are clothes strewn everywhere. I guess she didn't manage to make it in here to clean earlier.

Will stops in front of my door, taking in the pale purple comforter, subdued pink throw pillows, and relative lack of stuff. My manuscript is back in its place of honor on my desk, laptop powered down beside it. My messenger bag is hanging on the back of my chair, but otherwise, everything is pretty much put away. I hadn't needed to straighten up in my room a whole lot before Will came over. I'm actually a bit of a minimalist, especially compared to my eclectic roommate.

"So this one's yours, right?" He gestures.

My mouth curls up on one side. "How did you know?" I take a step closer to him, revel in the warmth emanating from his eyes.

He shrugs. "It looks like you." Taking four steps backward toward Scarlett's space and craning his neck to peer through the doorway again, he nods definitively. "And this most definitely looks like Scarlett."

"Well, you've passed the first test," I joke, wrapping my arms around his waist and pulling him toward me. "Knowing the difference between me and my roommate."

"That's a huge relief. I've been studying for weeks, but I didn't know what to expect from the exam." Will surveys me, his mouth quirking up into a gentle smile. "I would hate to disappoint you by failing so soon."

I'm swimming in his eyes like they're a vat of hot chocolate. I want to drink all of him in, forever. "I'm not concerned you're going to fail. I don't see that happening."

His lips skim over my cheek, making just enough contact that the butterflies in my stomach start to emerge from their cocoons. "Well, that's a relief."

I reach out to play with his hair, letting his glossy locks dance around my fingers. Under, over, and under again. Our eyes meet, and I'm almost swept away.

Will clears his throat, but his voice still comes out thick. "Geez, this is some tour."

A breathy chuckle escapes my throat. "If you liked it so far, you're in for a real treat."

His brows go up. Way up. "Is that so?"

I blush. I hadn't meant for that to sound quite so provocative, but here we are. "Well, I know how to throw a mean movie night," I backpedal.

I offer him my hand, and he laces his fingers through mine. "Shall we head to the cinema?" I ask.

"You have a cinema here? This is quite the apartment."

"Oh yes. We're really capital-F Fancy." I gesture to the living room, neater than it's ever been before, the muted yellow throw pillows perfectly fluffed against the white microfiber couch.

"Looks like a great place to watch a movie," he says, surveying the space. "Do you get to stay, or do you have to go give a tour to some other guy?"

"Oh, no. I'm here for the duration."

"Excellent." He squeezes my hand, sending a rush of heat up my forearm. Feigning innocence, he continues, "I don't know if this is appropriate given the quasi-professional nature of our relationship, but I think you're pretty cute. You know, as tour guides go."

I jab him with my elbow. "As tour guides go? Not just in general?"

"That too," he assures me, a twinkle in his eyes.

"So," I say, gesturing to the shelves behind the couch. "We have quite a selection of DVDs, ranging from the obnoxiously artsy to the cloyingly cliché. You can choose the evening's first film, since you're my guest."

Will follows me to the shelves and stops just behind me. He drapes his arms over my shoulders, leaning his chin into the crook of my neck, sending my heart racing. He shimmies closer, his firm lines coming to rest against my curves, his warm breath against my cheek. "Hmm. What am I in the mood for?"

My stomach lurches. I know what *I'm* in the mood for, and it sure as hell isn't watching a movie. Maybe I should try to cool things down. Things like my libido.

I gesture to the shelf, indicating some of the less-sexy movies in our collection. "Perhaps something with explosions? We have *Die Hard*."

I feel him nod against my shoulder. "Christmas in July. I like where your head's at, Sheffield."

I'm barely breathing now, and my voice comes out raspier than I'd hoped it would. "*Die Hard* it is." I grab the case clumsily, almost dropping it on the floor, then rush to the DVD player to get things set up.

When I join Will on the couch a moment later, I put a few inches between us, just to be safe. Out of the corner of my eye, I see him sliding his hand up and down his thigh, like he's also filled with nervous energy he doesn't know what to do with. Like he's considering using that hand to reach out and touch my leg, but he's trying to resist.

The air between us feels thick, heavy with anticipation and want. We're stealing glances at each other, trying to gauge the other's exact position on the couch, calculating how to shift our bodies from asymptotes to tangents.

Once, I look over and catch his eyes running down my arm, to my hand, to the knee that it's sitting on. He blushes and drags his gaze guiltily back to the TV. Thirty seconds later, I find a way to shift in my spot so my leg is nearer to his. I can feel the heat radiating off him, and even though we're not touching at all, there are sparks everywhere we're close. *I could die from this*, I think.

It isn't until John McClane is getting off his flight that I remember I haven't offered Will anything to eat or drink. I jump up like a spider is crawling on my head, my thigh springing away from his. "Oh! We have snacks."

He looks startled, which is understandable given how insane I'm acting.

Hurrying to the kitchen, I inquire over my shoulder, "What can I get you to drink? We have water, seltzer, wine. Orange juice, apple juice, cranberry juice. All the juices. Coke?"

"Um, water's good," Will says, still seeming surprised at my sudden departure.

"Perfect!" I'm too chipper, my nerves getting the better of me. After all that waiting and wanting, he's here, and he wants to be with me. All I'd have to do is reach out and touch him, and I'm not sure we'd be able to stop the floodgates. And honestly, the excitement is pretty hard to take.

I grab two highball glasses from the cabinet and fill them with water from the tap. Balancing them between my arm and my chest, I snag some Junior Mints and a bag of chips from the counter, then head back to the couch.

"Cheers," I offer, handing one of the waters to Will and gently clinking my glass against it. "Snack?" I gesture to the chips and candy I've tossed onto the coffee table.

"Maybe in a minute," he says, reaching for my hand and guiding me back to the spot beside him. "Come sit down."

I sink onto the cushion and face him.

"Is everything okay? Here, with this?" He gestures between us.

My eyebrows scrunch. "Of course it is."

His chest fills deeply, like he'd been holding his breath. "Okay, good. Because you seemed..."

"Nervous?" I suggest wryly.

He nods, running his thumb along my forearm, gaze sweeping my face.

"I really am. I don't know why." I shake my head, eyes downcast. "I'm sorry. It's not you. I mean, I think it *is* you."

He starts, and I rush to explain further, "I just mean, I think it's because of how much I like you."

I see a smile creep across his face.

I grin back. "I really, really like you, Will."

"Oh, do you now?" he teases, brushing a stray wave out of my face and tucking it behind my ear.

Eyes full, heart aching with how deeply I *feel* everything about him, I nod wordlessly, emphatically.

"And I," he says, moving his fingers against my cheek, "really, really, *really* like you, too." He lingers on my face, stroking my skin, sending swirls of warmth everywhere he touches. His hand moves to caress my jaw as he leans in and brushes my lips with his.

My breath catches in my throat as I part my lips, kissing him back tentatively at first, then with more urgency. His tongue slides into my mouth, and I moan a little, opening more fully for him, returning the gesture. I'm all heat and breathlessness and butterflies as I throw my arms around his neck and pull him closer to me.

Our kisses grow in intensity, my hands on the back of his head, running through his hair, stroking his neck. He's still at an angle, but he's leaning into me, gently shifting my body into the plush cushion at my back. His fingers are on my face, running along my arms, then lacing through mine and bracing our hands against the back of the couch.

His breath is ragged when we break apart for air. "Oh my God," he says, shifting my hips to drag me closer to him. "You have no idea how long I've wanted this."

"You haven't even known me that long, in the grand scheme of things," I counter, plying his neck with kisses.

His dark lashes lift, and he looks directly into my eyes. My chest feels like it's going to explode from the intensity of the connection. "Sometimes you just know."

Oh my God. Oh my God. Is he saying what I think he's saying?

I sit up on my knees and move to straddle his thighs, pushing him back into the couch, and catch his face in my hands, kissing him deeply. He's all hard, strong, lines against me, and I feel like I'm losing all awareness of who I am.

His hands go around my back, pulling me into his chest, rolling my hips against him. I can't control the sound that escapes my lips, and he catches it in his mouth, whispering back my name.

I'm on another plane entirely now, my emotions heightened like never before. I'm drowning, in his eyes and in his kisses, which is why I've never been more startled in my life as when his phone starts ringing in his hip pocket.

We both pull away abruptly, acting like we've never heard a ringtone before. "Sorry," he breathes, going back to caressing my collarbone with his lips.

Then it rings again. Trying to catch my breath, I gesture to his pocket. "Do you need to answer that?"

He looks reluctant to stop, but he shifts to reach for the phone. "I guess I can just see who it is."

His face falls when he checks the caller ID. "It's my sister," he says. "I should take this."

I hurry out of his lap as he absently runs a hand through his hair, which I've utterly destroyed in my passionate explorations. "I'm so sorry," he says. "I'll be right back."

I shake my head rapidly. "No, no, it's okay. You can take it in my room, if you want."

He nods and strides quickly away. "Hello?" His voice fades down the hall.

I take a deep breath, smoothing my hair and adjusting the straps of my dress. I can hear snippets of Will's baritone bouncing around the doorway from my room, but I don't catch much.

I busy myself with straightening the pillows, then go to the kitchen to top off our water glasses. I don't want to actively eavesdrop on his conversation.

"You shouldn't have done that," I hear him say suddenly, loudly.

Shouldn't have done what? Molly's supposed to be here this weekend for our lake trip. Whatever this conversation is, it must be pretty important if it needs to happen tonight.

"I can't just do that," Will says. He sounds pissed.

I hear more mumbling, bits and pieces. I grab a bottle of white zin and two glasses, trying to find something, anything to do so I don't overhear something I'm not supposed to.

"Fine. I'll see you this weekend." Will strides out of my room, shaking his head.

"Everything okay?" I pop the cork out of the wine and pour some for each of us.

He sighs deeply. "Yeah, it'll be okay. Sisters, you know? Always trying to meddle." He laughs uncomfortably, like he's forcing himself to release the tension prematurely.

I think about Josephine, and how she shaped Esperanza's story with a bitter mix of pure intentions and haughty judgment. I incline my head. "Well, though I don't have a sister, I've seen what havoc they can wreak."

I hold up one of the wine glasses, a silent question, and Will nods, taking it gratefully. "To sisters," he says, saluting my glass with his own.

"To sisters." I take a sip, sinking onto the couch with one knee bent beneath me.

Will's free hand finds my thigh and starts to absently move back and forth, sending sparks through me all over again. "I'm really sorry about the...interruption."

Just then, Bruce Willis issues a string of profanities.

Will and I exchange a look of surprise. I'd forgotten the movie was even playing, and it seems like maybe he did, too. A giggle escapes my throat. I mean, I've seen *Die Hard* before, and I'm not shy about a well-placed curse word. But in this moment, the swearing cuts through the tension and somehow strikes me as beyond hilarious.

Now he's laughing, too, and we're leaning into one another, mirth streaming from our eyes. I don't even know that the situation should be this funny, but here we are.

"Ah," I say, finally catching my breath, my head on his shoulder. "What an evening."

He presses a kiss to the top of my head. "Merry Christmas in July, Cal."

We clink glasses again. I curl into him, my arm wrapped around his waist, my head sliding down against his chest. I can feel his heart beating on my cheek. "God, I love this," I breathe.

"You and me both," Will says, squeezing me tighter.

I lift my hand and move toward his arm, tentatively reaching my pointer finger out to stroke his tattoo. "This," I say, noticing his heart picks up its pace, "has been of great interest to me for quite some time."

"Oh, you like that?" Will asks, in what I can only think to describe as a voice dripping with want.

"Very much so." I bring his arm to my mouth and kiss his tattoo, an understated black line drawing of a typewriter. The paper behind its ribbon reads "*Per aspera ad astra.*"

"To be honest," I drag my lips along his skin, "I never really thought I was a tattoo person." I pull my gaze back to his and whisper, "But this is incredibly hot."

I feel him tense up against me. "Is that so?" His voice is gravelly.

"Mhmm." I absently trace the lines on his skin, enjoying the effect I'm having on him. "Can you tell me about it?"

His hand tightens on my thigh. "My tattoo?"

I nod against his beating heart.

"Well, I also didn't think I was much of a tattoo person," he said. "But then life happened, and it just felt like maybe sometimes, I needed a reminder. Of who I was, what I'd overcome." Something like grief is reflected in his eyes.

"Through hardship, to the stars," I whisper, kissing his forearm again.

His eyes fill with warmth and surprise. "You speak Latin?"

"Only a little bit." I shake my head, lips still flush to his skin. "But I've always liked this phrase."

"You're really amazing, you know that?" He gathers me tighter against him.

"Best tour guide you've ever had?" I raise an eyebrow.

"Oh, absolutely. I'm giving you five stars for sure." Will leans down and kisses me deeply. "Okay, fine," he reconsiders. "Six stars."

I smile against his mouth. "What about my tip?"

Then he's laughing, and kissing me again, and pulling me against his chest, and we're just curled up together on the couch, radiating love back to the universe.

"That'll work," I say, and we stay there together, intertwined, to the sounds of explosions and breaking glass on TV and Will's heartbeat in my ear until we both fall asleep.

seventeen

Light is streaming through the curtains when I finally stir. It takes me a second to realize where I am. Memories from last night start to creep in. My eyes rove over the empty bottle of wine and the screensaver looping cheerfully on the television. How did we manage to fall asleep here on the couch? All night?

I shift slightly and notice Will's arm is draped over my waist, my head in his lap. He's leaning on his right side against the arm of the couch, an elbow tucked under his ear. I don't want to jostle him too much and risk waking him, but I'm concerned he's going to be late to work. Or, judging by how bright the room is, it's possible that ship has sailed.

At some point in the night, it looks like he's pulled the blanket from the back of the couch over us. God, this is comfortable. His tattoo is right next to my face, and I have an overwhelming urge to kiss it. It probably wouldn't be the worst way in the world for him to wake up.

And I do think it has to be at least nine o'clock, given the light levels in the living room. And how much my stomach is growling. The library opens at ten, I remember with a sigh. I should wake Will and offer him some breakfast.

I pull my lips along his arm, giving in to my urge to toy with the typewriter there. He starts to stir, making adorable sleepy noises. As his eyes flutter open, he says, "Oh, shit."

"Good morning to you, too," I greet him, planting one more kiss on his arm. "When do you have to be at work?" I sit up and stretch.

He checks his watch, which has left an indent on his cheek. "It's 9:06. I have to be there by 9:45."

Not so late, then. But almost. I attempt to flatten my hair, which I'm pretty sure is looking quite disheveled after spending the night in Will's lap. "Do you want some breakfast real quick before you go?" I try not to get my hopes up, because I really don't want him to go, even though I know it wouldn't be personal if he did.

He starts to shake his head, and I'm afraid he's about to say no, but he stops himself. "Sure, that would be nice." He surveys my face and flashes a grin. "I wouldn't want to disappoint you by leaving."

"You think awfully highly of yourself, huh?" I press a kiss to his cheek and stand up, heading for the kitchen.

He follows, taking a moment to neatly fold the blanket and drape it over the back of the couch. "I mean, you did let me spend the night, and we haven't even gone on a date yet. Some would suggest that makes you easy."

I gasp in mock offense and flick a stream of water at him from the sink, where I've been filling the coffee pot. "I can assure you, I'm a woman of upstanding morals."

His eyes are twinkling as he wipes his face dry, then crosses to me and puts his arms around my waist. "Of that I have no doubt."

My heart. We're doing that dance now, the one with eye contact that yearns, where the air hums with electricity between us. His gaze drops to my mouth, then flicks back up to my eyes.

My breath flutters out a little, and I manage to ask, "Would you like some coffee?"

He nods, still staring at my face. "Mmhmm."

Before I consciously realize I'm doing it, I'm lifting my chin to his and kissing him deeply, as if I can channel all the feelings that are swirling in my chest directly into his via mouth-to-mouth. He's kissing me back like he's feeling the same way, and I'm falling, falling, falling.

After a minute, I force myself to stop. "You have to go to work," I say, pulling my face away ever so slightly.

"Maybe I'm sick today?" He smiles mischievously.

I survey his face, place the back of my palm against his forehead. "You do feel a little warm," I joke, feigning concern.

"Okay, you've convinced me. I'm sick." He leans in and kisses me again, tightening his grip around my waist, pressing all of him into all of me in a way that takes my breath away.

"I would so love it if we could spend the day here," I say begrudgingly, breaking away from a kiss that felt like it was heading somewhere much more erotic, "but you should go to work. And I need to write. I'm trying to finish the finance book by next Tuesday, so the clock is ticking."

He gives me puppy dog eyes, and I'm pretty close to telling him he never has to leave, but he sighs and runs a hand through his hair. "You're right. I should go to work. And you should write. And I don't think you're going to be able to focus here, where there's no Marian to keep me in line."

I put one hand on his chest and kiss the spot where his heart is beating beneath. "No, you're definitely way too adorable for me to get anything done if we aren't in public."

I step away, even though my brain is screaming at me to stay put, and I start making coffee. "I'll come work at the library later, though. I don't know if I can go all day without seeing you."

He grins at me. "I *am* way too adorable."

"And modest, too," I tease, rummaging in the freezer. I strike gold with a package of bagels. "Want one?"

Will nods. "Sure. Thank you. It's not every day that a gorgeous woman cooks me breakfast."

"I should hope not. I'd have to be very jealous if that were the case." I throw two bagels into the toaster oven and turn back to face him. "And these are premium freezer bagels, which are basically the pinnacle of dating breakfasts."

I blush when I realize what I've said. "Not that we're dating," I add quickly. It's probably too soon to assume anything about what he's looking for.

Will quirks an eyebrow up and sweeps his gaze over my face. "Are we not?"

I blush even deeper. "I don't know," I mumble. *Yes, I want to scream. Please say we are.* I manage to compose myself. "I guess I don't want to rush into anything."

A hurt look flashes across his face, so I hurriedly add, "Because I don't want to make you feel like you're a rebound." I take his hand. "That isn't what this is to me. At all."

A smile starts in one corner of his mouth. "I mean, you're making me a frozen bagel, the pinnacle of dating breakfasts. I don't feel cheap at all."

We both laugh, and the toaster dings. I plate the bagels and grab some condiments, passing them to Will to bring to the table. I snag the coffee and pour it into mugs before joining him. "As well you shouldn't. Only the best for you, Will."

He slides into the chair across from me and squeezes my knee under the table. "This is the best breakfast I've had in a long time."

My blush goes all the way to my scalp this time. I watch him put cream cheese on his bagel (*a solid choice; I can't be with a man who doesn't like cream cheese*) over the top of my coffee mug. I don't know why, exactly, but he looks like he belongs here. And I realize I'm more than okay with that.

AFTER WILL HEADS out to go to work, I hop into the shower. I'm so lost in my thoughts that I don't even hear my phone ring.

When I get back to my room, I see that I have three voicemails. Naturally, they're all from Esperanza's line at the hospital.

"Callie!" The first one begins. "I wanted to let you know I'm up and about today. I know you said you were going to visit. They keep bringing me cookies, and I don't need that stuff. I've got them in a pile by the bed. When you come, I'm going to give them to you. You can have them with your boyfriend. With your Will. I'll see you later, kid!"

I smile, wondering how hospital cookies taste.

The second message is brief. "Hi, it's me again, kid. Esperanza. I realized I didn't actually tell you it was me the first time. So I just called you up to let you know who it was. I'll see you soon!"

I hit play on the third voicemail while I get dressed. I pick a purple sundress with white and yellow daisies. I love this one because it has a flowy, ruffled skirt. I'm feeling light and airy today, thanks to Will, so this dress seems like the perfect choice.

"Hey, C!" the third message begins. "Don't let me forget when you come tonight to show you pictures of Johnny. I found one where he looks so handsome. Thank you, thank you for bringing them to me. You've got a good head on your shoulder, kid. I'm lucky to have you in my life. Thank you."

My eyes are hot, threatening to spill tears down my freshly washed face. *I'm the lucky one,* I feel like saying. But I don't want to bother Esperanza right now. I know she's been doing physical therapy in the mornings, and I'm going to visit later anyway.

I replay the last message while I finish getting dressed and start on my hair. Only on the second listen do I catch the singular "shoulder" turn of phrase, which makes me chuckle. Esperanza is a character unlike any other.

AT THE LIBRARY THIS AFTERNOON, I'm torn between staring at Will and earnestly trying to finish this stupid book once and for all. While I technically have two weeks from next

Tuesday to wrap up, I really want to meet my self-imposed deadline, just to prove to myself that I can. A little part of me knows I also want to prove Thomas wrong, whether he ever knows about it or not. I *can* do this well and in a timely fashion, even with other distractions.

There's also this weekend's lake trip keeping me from the task at hand. I've opened a second document on my laptop and am making a to-do list so I don't forget to pack anything or prepare the apartment for our absence. It's rare that both Scarlett and I are away for more than one night, and I want to be sure we don't forget to take the garbage out or water Scarlett's monstera.

Thinking about the lake is also distracting in that I'm not sure what to expect. Will's sister is going to be there, and I'm perhaps unreasonably nervous to meet her. I desperately want to make a good first impression. I also desperately want to be left alone in a cabin with her brother, but I don't necessarily want that to be apparent. So I'm a little stressed out about how to straddle that line.

Scarlett and Jonathan, I'm pretty sure, will get very drunk and act ridiculous, then be all over each other and disappear to do God knows what in their room. Jax and Jenna will probably get into a shouting match about soccer or something and head to bed early so they can wake up for a lakeside jog at daybreak. I'm guessing that might leave Will and me alone with Molly, who will be an unwitting third wheel.

My brain keeps jumping to how wonderful it felt to wake up with Will this morning. How warm and safe and content I was, and how badly I want that to be a regular occurrence. How afraid I am to mess this up, to cheapen it by rushing things. How badly I hope it happens again this weekend at the lake.

I'm so lucky to have found Will, who makes me feel alive in every conceivable way. Not everyone is so fortunate. I think about Esperanza, who maybe found that love in Johnny, once upon a time, and then lost it due to a cruel twist of fate. I so wish she could see him again.

It dawns on me all of a sudden. Maybe she *could* see him again.

For all we know, Johnny is alive and well somewhere, pining over her, too. The wheels are spinning faster now, and I open a Google tab and hurriedly start typing in his name.

Apparently, there was a baseball player by the same name in Chicago back in the '70s, and most of what I find is related to him. Once I sift through his Wikipedia page, several retrospective ESPN articles, and about a hundred fan sites, I get to the paid phone book listings and "Do they have a criminal record" websites for the 242 people in the U.S. named Johnny Giordano. I click on several, but one tries to tell me my laptop's been infected with a virus, and the others all want my credit card information.

Still, I press on, Googling every combination of Johnny's name and last known location that I can think of. I even try looking up military units that were deployed out of Rockledge in the '50s in hopes of finding some sort of news article about awards for valor. Hoping I don't find any obituaries about brave servicemen lost on the battlefield.

I spend about 45 minutes chasing down leads, but ultimately, I come up short. How am I going to find Johnny?

Then, in another rush of enlightenment, it hits me. I jump out of my chair in excitement, rushing over to the New Releases shelf where Will is resetting a display.

"I have the best idea ever!" I think I surprise him, because several books slip out of his hand before he turns around.

"Sorry about that." I stoop to help him pick up what he dropped.

"Not a problem. If someone is going to mess up my display, I'd prefer it be you." He grins at me and reaches out a finger to stroke the inside of my palm, covertly so no one else can see.

A little shiver of pleasure runs through me. I swallow down the rising desire to kiss him passionately right here in the middle of the library, in full view of Lisa, who is manning the circ desk while he deals with the New Releases.

I clear my throat. "So, I was thinking about how lucky I am to have found you," I notice his cheeks go pink, "and how not everyone gets that lucky."

He thinks for a moment and then nods. "I agree; we should start an organization to help everyone find their Will Pearson. It's what's best for humanity, really."

I crack a smile and playfully hit his arm. "No, weirdo. I was thinking about Esperanza. And about Johnny." Taking a deep breath, I continue. "What if we could find him? And bring him to see her?"

"I love the way you think," Will says softly. "How would you find him, though? Google?"

I shake my head. "I think I've already exhausted that option. I didn't find anything." I take a deep breath. "I was hoping maybe you could help me. I want to do some research in special collections."

Both of Will's eyebrows go up. "That would be quite the undertaking. We have tens of thousands of documents up there. And we don't even know where he lives."

"That's true, but we know he used to live near Rockledge. That's where Esperanza grew up. And you have the *Rockledge Gazette* in special collections. I think it might work."

"It's definitely worth a try." He glances at his watch, which I'm thrilled to see he's still wearing. I'd let it slip to him on Monday night that I really like how it looks on him, and I guess it made an impression. "I'm going on my lunch break in 15 minutes. If you want, I can meet you in the archives then."

My eyebrows wrinkle over my nose. "But what about your lunch?"

Will's eyes sparkle at me, and I almost fall into them. "This cute girl I know made me a really amazing breakfast, and it was pretty filling. I think I'm good for now."

"Thanks, Will." I smile softly and squeeze his arm. "I'll meet you up there in a few minutes, then."

. . .

I'M elbows deep in newspapers by the time Will joins me in special collections.

"I've been telling Lisa for ages we need to start digitizing these," he says, closing the door behind him and sitting beside me. Before I have a chance to respond, he turns my chin toward him and kisses me deeply, parting my lips with his tongue. The room starts spinning, and I struggle to enforce good library behavior as I kiss him back.

After a minute, he breaks away, out of breath as he presses a kiss to my cheek. "Sorry. I've been waiting all day to do that."

I smile wryly. "We've already done that today."

"Well, it's been too long, and I needed more." He grins and kisses me again.

In spite of myself, I start to imagine what other things we could do here, with no one else around. The archives room is fairly secluded, with rows and rows of shelves and several tables, all tucked away in the corner by the third-floor elevator. My thoughts jump from a breathless make-out session between the stacks to some more serious encounters against the back wall before I manage to wrest control back and remember why we're here.

"Anyway," Will says, pulling away again. "I'm distracting you from your project."

"So very much." He has no idea the extent to which his presence is a distraction, but I'm not about to send him away.

"Sorry," he shrugs, not sounding very sorry at all. "So how can I help?"

"Well, this is the pile of papers I've already checked," I point to my left. "I'm just scanning headlines and obituaries right now, and anything that mentions the Korean War. I'm pretty sure that's when Johnny would've served."

Will nods. "Okay. Give me half your pile. I'll start on those."

I hand him some newspapers and squeeze his hand. "Thank you for doing this." Running my thumb over his wrist, I add quietly, "It really means a lot to me."

He lifts my hand to his lips and kisses it, like I'm some sort of visiting royalty. "I know it does. I'm here for the duration."

"Or at least until your lunch break is over," I tease.

"That too," he grins.

I think my heart is going to explode from happiness at this point, but I want to focus on the task at hand. I so want to head to the hospital later with Johnny's contact information in hand. If I can find something, anything that points to where he used to live, I'll drive to Rockledge, talk to neighbors. Make phone calls. Seeing Esperanza's smile when I tell her I've found him would, I think, actually make my heart burst open.

THREE HOURS LATER, we've made it through the bulk of the *Rockledge Gazettes* from the 1950s and 1960s. Will hung out and helped for a half hour, but then he had to go back to work.

I'm feeling more than a little discouraged when I pack everything back up and sign myself out of special collections. I really had expected to find something.

"Anything?" Will shoots me a hopeful look when I walk past him on my way out.

"Nope." I try not to look as disappointed as I feel. "I'll try again next week."

"I can help you more then, on my break or after work."

A smile grows as I take in his rumpled hair and his warm eyes, so eager to do the right thing. "That sounds great. Thank you."

He grins back. "Anything for you, Cal."

I'm not going anywhere. I shiver at how deeply I'm feeling him right now.

"I have to head out now if I'm going to get to the hospital before visiting hours are over," I say apologetically. I'm apologizing both to him and to myself, because I really don't want to leave. "And then I need to go home and get ready for our weekend." I flash him a huge grin. "Any snack requests for the drive?"

Scarlett, Jonathan, Will, Molly, and I will be heading up to the lake together in Jonathan's RAV4. Jenna and Jax are coming separately.

"Hmm. Junior Mints? Cheez-Its?"

I raise an eyebrow. "Cheddar jack, or regular?"

"Cheddar jack, obviously."

I nod as if assessing him. "I knew you were the perfect man."

Will snickers. "Lack of Cheez-It compatibility would definitely be a big problem."

"Well, I'm glad we don't have anything to worry about there," I say. "I'll see you bright and early tomorrow morning, okay?"

His smile is so warm it makes my insides melt. "See you then. Thanks again for breakfast." He pauses and lowers his voice. "And thanks for last night. I love waking up next to you."

My heart is somersaulting around in my chest, but I manage to return his smile. "I love that, too."

MY VISIT with Esperanza is fairly uneventful. She shows me pictures of Johnny, as promised, and he is indeed quite handsome. I think I see why she says he reminds her of Will, too. In the first picture she shows me, I see that Johnny is tall, dark, and thoughtful, with straight black hair that sweeps across his brow when he inclines his head to offer a slight smile. Even though his mouth barely ticks up, his eyes are warm, positively overflowing with love.

"Who took this photo?" I ask.

"Oh, that was me. Yep. I took that picture." Esperanza's eyes are misty. "He took me to the cinema, and then we walked around town. This picture is from in front of the soda shoppe. We went inside and got a chocolate milkshake after the picture we saw."

"One shake, two straws?" I ask with a grin.

She nods in the affirmative. "It was good, that milkshake. I'll never forget it. And then he walked me home, and he gave me his letter jacket. It was chilly that day. But he told me to keep it."

She touches the photo as if she can reach back into the past. "Josephine wasn't too pleased when she saw that. She and some of my other sisters didn't want me to go steady with him. Because his father worked in the brickyard, you know? It wasn't a great living. But I knew he was a real gentleman. After that day, there was never anyone else for me."

I swallow the lump that's risen in my throat. "How long after this did he have to leave for the service?"

"It was about eight months later. He graduated from high school in June. I didn't manage to do that myself, but Johnny didn't care. I was off working, grabbing news stories off the wire at the *Rockledge Gazette*. Hey, C, did you know I was the one who pulled the story about Kennedy's assassination?"

She's told me this plenty of times, but I pretend it's novel. "Wow, Esperanza. That's amazing!"

She nods repeatedly. "Yep. Yep, that was me. But of course, that was well after Johnny. That wasn't until the '60s."

"And Johnny left in the '50s, right?" I'm desperately trying to steer her back on track. I want to learn as much as I can about Johnny without letting her know why. I may need more background if there's any hope of finding him.

"Yep, that's right. '52, I think it was. And he asked me to wait for him. And I would have. I was going to tell him yes. But then he never came back." Her eyes dart over the photos, reliving the memories they contain.

"I'm so sorry," I tell her. "I wish there was something I could do."

"Well, that's okay, C. It's just life, you know. I had my chance, and I married Frank, and that was fine. He was a good man. I just couldn't make it work, you know? I never loved him like I loved Johnny."

I nod. I'm bursting to tell her what I'm trying to do, that there might still be a chance. But I can't. I can't let her know, because to dangle hope and then snatch it away would be needlessly cruel.

"Hey, C. Can you help me? I want to get up and go for a walk.

Grab those crutches over there," she gestures to the end of her bed. "Help me get out of here."

I oblige, helping her get situated, swing her legs over the side of the bed, and hoist her up to hold the crutches. "Ready?" I ask.

She nods vigorously. "I can't wait to get out of this bed. I can't wait to go home."

"Soon," I promise, patting her arm and steadying her as she stands. "Soon."

eighteen

The doorbell rings right at eight the next morning. "That's them!" Scarlett shouts.

I throw the last of my clothes into a duffel bag and join her in the hallway. "Did you water the plant?" I ask.

"I sure did." She digs in her purse for her sunglasses, which she perches stylishly on top of her head.

I ignore the uncomfortable feeling of not having time to check "water plant" off the list on my computer. I make a mental note to do it when I get back on Monday, even though it's unnecessary. It'll just make me feel better.

Scarlett grabs her pink suitcase and matching tote and cracks open the door. "Coming!" she yells, a queen readying her public.

We awkwardly bump down the stairs with our luggage toward Jonathan's SUV, which is running in the space closest to our apartment. He and Will both get out to help us with our bags.

"Morning, babe," Jonathan says, taking Scarlett's suitcase from her hand and plying her with an uncomfortable amount of PDA.

Will and I exchange an amused glance as he reaches for my duffel.

"Hey," he says quietly, sending me a secretive smile.

He continues to have quite the effect on my heart, which starts racing on sight. "Hey," I whisper back, feeling suddenly shy now that our relationship is out in the open in front of Scarlett and Jonathan. Granted, they don't seem to be paying us any attention whatsoever.

I sneak a quick glance into the SUV. Molly is sitting behind Jonathan's seat, bent over her cell phone. I don't know what Will has told her about us, and I don't want to spoil anything by giving him a full-on tonsil exam like Scarlett's doing with her paramour.

Will must sense my hesitation, because he pulls me into a quick hug, then kisses me gently on the lips. As he pulls away, he whispers in my ear, "I'll say hello in more detail later."

A shivery thrill shoots up my spine, sending warmth to all my extremities. I'm looking forward to whatever his detailed hello will entail.

We load into the car, Jonathan tossing bags into the trunk, and Will holding the door open for Scarlett, up front, and then for me, behind her. "Do you want me to take the middle?" Will asks.

"I don't mind it," I offer, hopping in. I slide next to Molly, whose jet-black waves look just like her brother's. "Hi," I stick my hand out to shake hers. "I'm Callie."

Her eyes twinkle just like Will's, too. "It's so nice to meet you. Will has told me so many good things."

I turn to face Will, who is buckling up next to me. "*Only* the good things, I hope?"

He flashes an evil grin. "I can't breach sibling confidence by answering that question."

I shove him playfully with my hip. "You're ridiculous."

He laughs loudly, then catches my hand against the buckle of his seat belt. "And you're the best."

He doesn't let go of my hand.

"So, Molly," I shift my attention away from how badly I'm longing to sink into Will's chest like I did on the couch on Thursday night. "What brings you back to our neck of the woods?"

Something like concern flashes across her face, but she recovers quickly. I think I feel Will tense up beside me, too. *What's that about,* I wonder.

"Just in town to see Will and chase some nostalgia," she says nonchalantly. "I haven't been to the lake since we were kids. I love it up there. I'm so glad you all agreed to come!" She grins. "Most of my friends are in San Diego now, except Margo in Rockledge. But she's busy until Monday, and I didn't have anyone else to ask."

"I was so glad you invited us," I say in earnest. I'm looking forward to making new memories on Lake Manacqua. Ones that don't involve Thomas. I'm also pretty excited about the whole weekend-in-a-cabin-with-Will thing.

I'm not totally sure what the sleeping arrangements will be this weekend, but I know the cabin has four bedrooms. In deference to Molly, Jenna, and Jax, who are unattached, it could be fair to do two rooms of each girls and guys, but we could also split things other ways. Like Scarlett and Jonathan, Molly and Jenna, Jax, Will and me. Or Scarlett and Jonathan, Molly and Will, Jax, and Jenna and me. I'm hoping to get another chance to fall asleep next to Will, but I don't want to make things awkward.

In no universe do I imagine Scarlett and Jonathan will agree to *not* share a room.

"Anyone want snacks?" I pull two boxes of Junior Mints and the cheddar jack Cheez-Its Will requested out of my purse.

"Me!" Scarlett reaches back from the front seat. I put one of the containers of candy in her hand.

"Cheez-Its, please," says Molly.

"I'll share with you," Will adds.

"Is everyone okay with me being the DJ?" Scarlett asks, plugging her phone into Jonathan's AUX cable without waiting for a response. She puts her playlist on shuffle.

The first song, no joke, is "Nightswimming."

"I'll cover your ears," I offer, cupping Will's face in my hands.

"Oh, Will's always hated this song," Molly pipes up in between mouthfuls of crackers. "Ever since Dad broke my REM CD on the kitchen floor in a fit of rage."

My head whips to see Will's face. He's staring straight ahead, like he doesn't know whether to yell at Molly or burst into tears. It wouldn't surprise me if he were imagining ice cream behind his eyes like I do.

"Sorry, broseph," Molly reaches across my lap to tap Will's arm. "I guess I shouldn't have said anything."

Will shakes his head. "No, it's okay. I mean, it's the truth, right?"

"I had no idea." I squeeze his hand, wanting to remind him that I'm here.

He shrugs it off. "Our dad is a jerk, plain and simple. I'm glad we don't have to deal with him anymore."

"Here's to ridding ourselves of parental burdens! Here's to REM!" Jonathan yells, raising one hand in the air like he's giving a toast. I wish he would just focus on driving.

"Here, here!" Scarlett shouts, thrusting her Junior Mints upward with such force that several are lost to the floor mats.

THE REST of the drive is uneventful. Scarlett dominates most of the conversation, and I make polite attempts to get to know Molly. Will is pretty quiet, but he never lets go of my hand.

When we get to the lake, it's time for lunch. "Shall we pick up the keys to the cabin and get grilling?" Jonathan asks.

"Sounds good to me." Molly rubs her stomach. "I'm starving."

"Scarlett and I can go get the keys from the registration office," offers Jonathan. They rush away, being very obvious about groping one another as they do so.

I shake my head. "I'm so glad those two found each other."

Pulling a cooler out of the trunk, Will nods. "It must be isolating, to be so very dramatic, and so very horny."

I snicker. "Oh, I'm sure." I take a handle of the cooler and help him bring it over to the outdoor grill near our cabin.

"I'm going to take a dip in the lake," Molly announces from behind us.

Will furrows his brow. "We don't even have the key to the cabin yet. Where are you going to change?"

Molly shrugs. "I've got my bathing suit under my clothes." She pulls a halter strap from under her shirt and waves it in the air at him. "See you in a bit!" She jogs off down the beach.

"And then there were two." I close the distance between Will and me, wrapping my arms around his waist and burying my face against his sternum. This. This is where I want to spend the rest of my life.

"Mmm," he says, his voice vibrating in his chest and making my cheek hum. "What should we do now?" He peers down at me with a mischievous look.

"I can think of a few things," I reply, searching his face for understanding.

He weaves his fingers through my belt loops and drags my hips into him, so all our negative space melds together and I can't tell where I end and he begins.

I move my hands around his neck and tip my chin up to look at him. His eyes are intent on me, shrouded in wanting in a way that makes me wish we were alone on this trip.

His hands migrate to the backs of my thighs, stroking and teasing upward along the edge of my denim cutoffs.

I'm pretty sure he understands what I was suggesting.

"I wish we had the key to the cabin," I whisper, kissing his neck as his fingers continue to roam up my shorts.

"I asked Molly to bunk with Jenna tonight so we can get our own room," he murmurs back, lips about to collide with mine.

Lava erupts through me, starting in my chest and trickling down to my stomach, down to the wetness that's pooling between my thighs. "Oh really?" I ask coyly. "Did you think you were going to get lucky, or something?"

Will breaks away and looks at me seriously. "I'm not going to pressure you to do anything you don't want to do." He runs his hand through my hair, coming to rest on the back of my head. "I just like waking up next to you."

I'm blushing, and then I'm wrapping him in the tightest hug imaginable. I don't know how I came to deserve this, this wonderful human who supports me and makes me feel so, so much. He's hilarious and sweet and an absolute genius; he turns me on in every conceivable way, and yet I'm also perfectly content just to sit by his side and let life happen all around me. God. He's so perfect.

"I like that, too." I breathe into his skin.

We just stand and hold each other for a minute, and we're only interrupted by a loud jingling sound.

"Hello, lovebirds." Scarlett brandishes the keys to the cabin on the tip of her pointer finger. "We're back. Sorry to interrupt."

I pull away from Will and straighten my shorts, which are a bit askew thanks to his meandering. "I'll bring in our bags," I mumble, grabbing them off the ground and taking strides toward the cabin that are too big, too awkward. Like I'm a teenager who just got caught making out with her boyfriend when her parents got home early.

"I'll help you with the burgers," I hear Jonathan offer to Will.

Scarlett follows me into the cabin. "Oh my GOD, Callie," she squeals, shutting the door behind me. "This is really happening! I am so happy for you. Will is HOT. And he's funny. He's seriously perfect for you."

I agree with her, but I try to play it cool. "I do really like him," I admit calmly. Peering around the corner of the cabin's soaring great room, I gesture to the bedrooms. "Which one do you and Jonathan want?"

Scarlett surveys the options and selects the only room with a TV. "You and Will should take the room all the way at the end," she points. "We'll put Molly and Jenna in here, next to us. Then Jax. That way, Molly won't have to listen to her brother having sex all night."

"Scarlett!" I throw a sofa pillow at her as hard as I can. "Will and I are not having sex."

She waggles a finger at me and grins. "Not yet."

I roll my eyes. "Whatever; it's not like anyone's going to be able to hear anything over the noise of you and Jonathan going at it, anyway." I'm not trying to be a bitch, but every time Jonathan spends the night, they are LOUD.

Scarlett reaches into her toiletry bag and throws a strip of condoms at me. "Just in case," she says. "Go put those in your room."

I glare at her, but I stick the condoms in my pocket and walk down the hallway. The room at the end is L-shaped, with a large window overlooking the lake on one side. Another window, complete with a deep cushioned seat, graces the other wall.

The bed, set under the window looking out to the lake, seems to be a queen, and it's made with pale blue sheets decorated with red and white canoe paddles. On top of the four oversized pillows, a bolster embroidered with the words "Lake Life" is taunting me with its kitsch.

There's a white wicker dresser opposite the bed and two matching nightstands flanking it. I toss the condoms into the top drawer of one of the nightstands and head back out to the great room to grab my duffel and Will's backpack. *Leave it to a man to pack an entire weekend's worth of stuff in a backpack*, I muse as I bring the bags down the hall.

I unpack my duffel into the dresser, putting Will's backpack on top. I don't feel right rooting through his things, but I make sure to leave him two of the drawers.

"Lunch is ready!" Jonathan yells a few minutes later, poking his head in from the front porch. "And Jenna and Jax just got here."

"Coming!" Scarlett shouts back. We troop outside to join the others.

THE AFTERNOON FLIES BY. Molly comes back from her swim, and it's clear she and Jenna have already met, which makes me feel a lot better about forcing them into sharing a room. Jax, Scarlett, and Jonathan spend over an hour playing a rousing game of poker. I lose track of the number of times Scarlett suggests they make it strip poker.

Will and I sit together at the picnic table, sipping hard lemonades and chatting sometimes with both groups, and sometimes just with each other. The drink is only 5 percent alcohol, but I start to feel tipsy after three-quarters of the bottle. When Jax offers me a second, I pass. Even in my addled state, I remember that alcohol and swimming don't mix, and I'm eager to go cool off in the lake.

I finally convince everyone to take a dip. We head inside to change, taking turns in bedrooms and the bathroom, then race to the lake, getting instant relief from the humidity in the cool waves.

We float around and talk until the sun starts to set, then go back to the beach. I run inside and throw a sundress over my bathing suit. It's growing chillier with the waning light, but the sun still dapples some warmth down to our vantage by the water.

Jax grills up some chicken and veggie kebabs, and we eat and drink and talk for hours, wrapped in blankets on the sand. Scarlett does a hilarious impersonation of her mother, and I laugh until I cry. Jenna tells us about a guy she's seeing who will only wear gray socks, because he thinks they're essential for his football team to win. Jax encourages her to go easy on Gray Socks Guy, and he tells us about his lucky game day shirt.

Molly regales us with tales of her life as an ER nurse, and I feel more grateful than ever to be self-employed and get to work from anywhere. Particularly the anywhere where people aren't. Will teases her and says that if it's so bad, she should move home. She gives him a pointed look, and they both fall silent.

I suggest a game of charades to break the tension, and because Will had promised one when he floated the idea of a lake weekend. It's so easy, being with them. I'm so glad I met Will, and that he brought me into his world. I think this weekend is just what I needed to take my mind off everything happening at home, in my real life—

the book, Esperanza's accident, my grandmother's betrayal, my breakup with Thomas, my vocational woes.

With every second that I sit here, surrounded by the sound of the lake lapping against the shore, my heart starts to heal and feel just a little bit more whole. I think Lake Manacqua and I might have a good future together after all.

nineteen

The moon is full, its glow doing a delicate dance with the waves on the lake. Will and I are the last ones on the beach, everyone else having turned in for the night. As they all stood and stretched, one by one, offering reasons for needing to head back to the cabin, Will and I lingered, never straying from an unspoken commitment to buy ourselves some precious moments alone.

The humidity of the afternoon stubbornly hangs over the water, like a cloying perfume you can't quite clear from your nostrils. There's a calming breeze whispering across the beach, though, which cools my skin as it sings me its lullaby.

I tip my head back, eyes closed, trying to absorb this feeling, the sense that this is one of those moments I'll always refer back to when trying to define what constitutes a perfect day.

Will's been sitting with one arm slung over his bent knees, drawing absently in the sand next to our beach blanket. Suddenly, he tips toward me, a smile starting. "You know what I think?"

He's so close now, his breath on my cheek. I feel the heat start to rise in my chest. Enamored by his eyes, glittering in the moonlight, I can barely form a response. "What's that?" I ask, hardly managing a whisper.

"I think," he reaches for my hand, "it's time I reconsider my feelings about night swimming."

I wrinkle my nose at him. "The activity, or the REM song?"

His smile comes easily, flowing like lava. "Both."

I let him pull me to my feet. Our hands fall away as he peels off his t-shirt, which is clinging defiantly to his skin in the humidity.

I try not to stare as his bare chest comes into view, but I fail miserably. He's surprisingly tanned, given how many hours he spends working toward a vitamin D deficiency under the library's fluorescents.

His tattoo is on full display, its words of optimism like a homing beacon for my heart.

I grab the straps of my sundress, slipping them off my shoulders and letting the whole thing flutter to the ground. I try not to notice Will's gaze as it sweeps me up and down, taking in my pink bikini and the swaths of bare skin it neglects.

We wade into the water, and it hits me like a block of ice.

"Jesus!" I cry out, pain receptors on high alert as I stride further away from the shore. It's the middle of summer, and I can barely breathe for the stranglehold the moisture has on the air. It felt great, floating around in here earlier. Now, even though the sun's down, I can't believe the lake is so cold.

A glance over at Will's distressed expression suggests he's having similar thoughts, though he seems to be hiding it better than I am.

I'm up to my stomach now, and I wince every time a wave ripples past, chilling the skin along my belly button. I crouch so my shoulders go beneath the water's surface. Maybe this will help me stay warm. Or at least *warmer*.

Will glides through the water to where I've stopped. I'm jealous of the shadows that get to hang on his face, here in the encroaching darkness.

"It really is freezing in here," he says, letting out an involuntary shiver.

"Do you want to duck under the water? Maybe that will help."

He nods. "It might." He takes a deep breath and propels himself beneath the surface, emerging a moment later with a gravelly chuckle. "Or maybe not. That wasn't the best."

I reach out to rub his shoulders vigorously, up and down, like I can convince the warmth of the air to reinvade his body. "Sorry," I offer, distracted by the water sluicing off his hair, down his neck, to his chest and beyond. Each droplet glistens as it rolls down his tanned skin, making me wish I could be one of them.

Eyes wide on me in the moonlight, Will hovers within arm's reach. "You don't need to be sorry," he says.

"But it was my misguided idea that you submerge yourself," I protest.

"That's true," he acknowledges, putting his arms around my hips and pulling me into him. Before I can react, he reaches under my knees and picks me up, fireman style, so all of me is outside the water. I gasp in surprise at the sudden breeze on my chilled skin.

He leans in and whispers in my ear, "I guess I'll have to dunk you."

"You would never—" I begin, but then he does. He tosses me gently into the air, but it still sends me soaring a few feet away from him, and I fall into the water with a huge splash.

Shaking droplets from my hair, I emerge with a vendetta. "Will Pearson!" I fix him with my most withering stare. "I am so going to get you for that."

His eyes glint mischievously. "I was hoping you'd say that."

I pull my arms back as hard as I can and hurl a wall of water his way. He ducks and sends one right back.

"You fiend!" I scream. I lunge at him, planning the perfect storm of splashes, but he grabs me mid-jump and pulls me to his chest.

"I don't think so," he admonishes.

"I've never lost a splash battle before, and I'm not about to give up my title." I pout, sending a tiny splash between us.

He chuckles. "I'm sorry, but I can't concede defeat, no matter how good you look in that bathing suit."

Heat rushes up my cheeks. He always knows what to say to set me on fire.

He drags my hips closer, hands coming to rest on the small of my back. My breath is coming in rapid bursts now. Our eyes meet, and I feel like a thousand fireflies have just come to life in front of my irises.

Tentatively, I reach out and touch his chest. Even in the frigid lake, he feels warm; solid and safe. I swirl my fingers around on his skin, illuminating every inch of him like he's the canvas on which I'll paint my masterpiece.

My hand continues its journey down his taut stomach, drinking in the feeling of his reactions, countless little movements and twitches as he comes alive to my touch. He pushes back against my hand in protest when I pull away to explore somewhere new, his breathing growing more and more ragged with my descent. His skin sends little jolts of electricity through me, and I can't stop moving my hands across every inch of his torso, finally pausing just north of his black swim trunks.

"Callie." His voice comes out jagged.

I can't take it anymore. I'm falling into him, lips crushing his, my tongue sliding into his mouth. My hands are in his hair, on his chest, moving furiously like if only I can get enough, the desire inside me will be satisfied. But I won't ever be satisfied. Nothing is enough where Will is concerned.

He's kissing me back just as passionately, hands on my back, pulling me into him until we are one, a glowing orb sending light back out into the universe.

Now his hands are roaming too, casting tendrils of heat along my arms, my back, my midriff. He tentatively slides his fingers along, then under, the strap of my bathing suit top, continuing until he's circled my entire torso, grazing the underside of my breasts. A groan slips past my lips.

"Is this okay?" he asks.

"So very much," I reply hastily.

He resumes his exploration of my chest, slipping under my top with his palm, thrumming my nipple with his thumb, and making my whole world lurch. I'm falling fast now, seeing stars, swirling downward until I can barely remember where I am. I lean toward him, arching into his touch. I want more, more, more; I need it. I've waited so long for this. For him.

"Damn it, Callie," he whispers into my mouth.

Emboldened by the effect I seem to be having on him, I roam lower on his chest, rubbing his sides up and down with both hands, tipping them inward and running my thumbs along his hip bones. I dip them teasingly under the waistband of his bathing suit, meeting the firm skin of his upper thighs, and I can feel him harden against me. My heart goes into a triplet of palpitations. *Oh, God.*

We're a mess of limbs, hands, mouths, coming closer and sliding apart, the tension between us like a magnet, always teasing us back together. I can't stop wanting him, this, his body, his heart. This is more than lust, though I've never been this turned on in my life.

Will is kind, and strong, and so fucking smart. He takes care of people. He makes me laugh. He lifts my soul. And in this perfect series of moments, mine cries out to his, vibrating with the words I haven't dared to let myself acknowledge: *I love you I love you I love you.*

The situation has reached a fever pitch at this point, but I'm not sure how much farther we can take it here, in the lake. It's both too shallow (we could be seen) and too deep (we might actually drown) to do more. Plus, the water is freezing, and I'm a little concerned about losing feeling in my extremities.

He must be thinking the same thing, because he slowly pulls his lips away, kisses me on the cheek, and wraps his arm around my shoulders, pulling me firmly against his chest. "I love this," he breathes.

"I love this even more," I agree, body still humming with energy as I swirl my fingers through his hair.

"Always so competitive," he laughs against my forehead, running his hands along my back in strong, sweeping movements.

"I just can't afford to lose, where you're concerned," I say, partly to be coy, and partly because it's the God's-honest truth.

We stand there for a few minutes, our hearts beating into each other's chests. We're steeping in the beauty of the moment as it surrounds us, making something new from what we've both poured out into the water tonight.

"We can't do this here," he finally gives voice to my thoughts.

I nod against him, face still nestled in his chest. "I know."

"But I'm not letting you off the hook," he jokes, in a way that's both lighthearted and incredibly sultry.

My blood stirs at his words, but I manage to keep it together. I tip my head up to look at him. "Do you mean to tell me you missed the chance to turn that into a fishing joke? While we're actually standing in a lake?"

He's smiling down at me now, making me feel like I could float here forever, under the moon, buoyed by his joy. "I might be just a little bit distracted."

"Huh," I say, running my finger down his cheek, his neck, his chest, stopping short of anything more. "I can't imagine why that would be."

He shoots me a mock scowl. "You're a terrible flirt."

"I think I'm fairly excellent, actually," I tease.

"You certainly are." He gathers me to him again, squeezing both arms around me, pressing a kiss to the top of my hair.

We stand there again, unmoving, for what feels both like an eternity and a fleeting moment, reveling in the feeling of finally being free, free to hold each other, free to live these feelings out loud.

Eventually, the water gets too cold to bear, and we begrudgingly trail our way back up the sand, holding hands and wearing our hearts on our nonexistent sleeves.

Will wraps me in our blanket, and I shudder into its warmth. I raise my right arm and put it around his shoulders, too, welcoming him to come underneath. We huddle together then, braced against the night air, much cooler now than when we'd made our first foray into the water.

"So," I grin wryly, "what's the verdict on REM?"

He nods slowly, considering. "I think I've rewritten those neural pathways. This was more than enough to convince me."

I grin. "And the night swimming itself?"

He kisses my cheek. "That was never in question."

"This lake is freezing. I feel like it should have been at least a little bit of a question."

A chuckle rises from his chest. "This is true. But spending time with you? Like this?" He pulls me closer for emphasis. "No question whatsoever."

My heart is overflowing into my ribs, and I'm pretty sure I'm going to melt into a puddle at his feet, right here on the beach. I've never felt like this before; didn't even know it was possible to feel like this.

It doesn't have to be just safety, comfort, stability. It can also be fireworks, butterflies, passion. I deserve all of those things. I need them. And with Will, I have them.

I close my eyes, trying to breathe in the energy of this moment, make sure I don't lose it to the breeze.

With his arm tight around me, his breath on my ear, his heartbeat still reverberating in my chest, I hear the wind's refrain, sending truth into my veins. My mind is humming with the same words, over and over and over again. I force them down, even though they're fighting back. It's too soon; I don't want to risk anything that's happening between us.

He presses another kiss to my cheek, and the words battle their way out of my chest, up my throat. I manage to choke them back, but I know I won't be able to keep them at bay much longer. And I'm not sure that I want to.

I love you I love you I love you.

twenty

Will and I finally stumble numbly back into the cabin just after midnight, still wearing our bathing suits. I'd thrown my dress over mine, and Will had put his Rush t-shirt back on, but they aren't nearly enough in the chill night air. Our beach blanket is nearly soaked through, too. My body is crying out for warmth.

The lights are off in Jenna and Molly's room, and I see the glow of the television peeking out from under the next door, Scarlett's high-pitched squeal soaring over the intro to *The Office*. I can't decide if she's laughing at the cold open or if she and Jonathan are engaged in some sort of intimate encounter. Jax has the lights blaring into the hall, but he's sprawled out on the bed, snoring loudly.

Will pulls his door closed as we walk by. "Guess we tuckered them out," he says in a low voice.

"I guess so. Who'd have thought we'd be the life of the party?"

He chuckles and puts his arm around my shoulders, pulling me in. "You're always the most exciting person in the room."

"Aw, thanks. Likewise." I plant a kiss on his cheek. We stop in the doorway of the last bedroom in the hallway.

"Are you sure this is okay?" Will gestures to the room, the bed. I know exactly what he's really asking.

"I mean, we already spent the night together," I quip, but I feel nervous. That was an accident, and this feels like it could turn into something. Like it probably will. And my body is definitely ready for that, but I just want to be sure it's not too soon—so soon that Will wonders if I'm using him to work out frustration from my breakup. Even if that feels like it was already a lifetime ago.

"You know what I mean," he says, turning to face me. "Like I said before, we can just sleep. It's really okay."

The air hums with tension for a moment. I shake my head. "I don't want to go to bed yet." My eyes flick to his, a silent question.

He gathers me to his chest, dragging my hips to his. "Not tired?"

"Nope," I murmur, slipping my hands under the edge of his t-shirt, rubbing his chest and feeling my insides dip.

Our eyes hold congress, making my heart flutter, and I know we both understand where things are headed.

He nods slowly, gaze flicking to my parted lips. Wordlessly, he lifts my chin and sweeps his mouth along mine. His kiss is firm and warm and filled with longing. Our tongues tangle as we step slowly toward the bed.

He eases me back gently onto the canoed coverlet, then bends down to slide my dress up over my thighs. His hands skim my belly, my breasts as he lifts it off me, revealing my pink bikini top beneath. "You have no idea how badly I've wanted this," he breathes.

I quirk my lips as I lie there, looking up at him. "Oh yeah?"

He raises an eyebrow. "Yeah."

I grab his waist and pull him down onto me. "Come show me."

We're kissing wildly then, my hands tearing off his shirt, his skirting under the halter tie at my neck to slip the knot free. Impatiently, he pulls my bikini top down, revealing my bare breasts. A small moan escapes my throat when he takes me in his mouth, the warmth of his tongue encircling my nipple.

"Oh my God," I breathe. I run my fingers through his hair as he works his magic.

I eagerly pull his shirt off, revealing his taut stomach and warm chest. I run my hands hungrily over every inch of exposed skin, still wanting more, more, more. Frustrated by every scrap of fabric between us, I rip my bathing suit top off and throw it to the side.

His hands explore, slowly, gently. Every touch sends fire through my veins and warmth pooling lower. Will tentatively drops his hand under my bikini bottoms, and a small moan escapes my lips.

"Do you like that?" he asks, dipping a finger into the wetness between my thighs.

I can't manage to respond in words, so I just moan again and grab for his shorts, hoping to return the favor. I roam across his front, and he presses back into me, begging for contact. I give him what he needs, and he's rock hard against my hand. *Oh my God.* Slipping my fingers inside the leg of his bathing suit, I find him warm and hard and waiting for me.

"Oh my God, Callie." His eyes flutter closed.

I decide that this is enough foreplay, especially considering we've been doing nothing but turning each other on with no release for weeks now. "Scarlett gave me an embarrassing number of condoms," I offer, gesturing to the nightstand. "Unless you have some."

His face turns beet red. "I do," he admits. "Not that I was expecting anything."

I shake my head. "Don't worry about it." I nudge the drawer open and gesture with my elbow. "Here, just use these."

He grabs one and opens it, and I help him slide it on, fingers closing around him as I do. He groans a little, so I keep going, rubbing up and down the length of him.

"You sure you want to do this?" He steps back, and my fingers slip off him as he seeks reassurance in my face.

"Very sure," I add, reaching for him, begging him to come back. I slide my bikini bottoms off and toss them onto the ground. "Your turn." My voice comes out gravelly.

He lets his swim trunks fall to the floor, and I try not to stare. Then, he knocks my knees apart and positions himself between my thighs. I need him so badly now that I let out a much louder gasp than I intend when he finally pushes in.

I'm not even sure I'm breathing, not even sure I have to anymore. We're coming together and drawing apart, touching each other in a frenzy of need. I try to stay as quiet as possible so our friends, and especially his sister, don't overhear us, but I'm pretty sure some of the noises escaping my throat would be audible from well outside the cabin.

"You're perfect," Will breathes into my neck, showering me with kisses. "Damn it, Callie. You're perfect."

Hearing him say this almost undoes me completely, but I manage to clear my head enough to respond. "What a time to tell me that, Will." I grin wickedly. "A girl could almost think you might have an ulterior motive in this scenario."

"Ask me in a few minutes," he says, brown eyes melting me from the inside out. "And I'll tell you again."

"No need to rush it," I joke. "Take your time. We'll have plenty of opportunities for talking later."

He grins, then covers my mouth with his and goes back to making me feel like I'm about to explode from pleasure.

And then, at last, I do. I can't control myself anymore, and my heart is on fire, and so is my body. I arch up to meet him, and he slams into me, finding his release at the same time. I cling to him and ride the waves cascading through me until I'm lying, listless and glowing, in his arms.

We're silent for several minutes, basking in what's just happened as we lie side by side. He gently rubs his fingers up and down my hip while I stroke his chest with the back of my hand.

Then, he props himself on one arm and leans toward me, brushing hair from my forehead, gazing into my eyes. "I'm not sure if you heard earlier, but I said you're perfect."

I feel a shiver go through my entire body, and I'm not sure how to respond. "I can assure you, I'm not," I manage.

Will kisses my cheek and lays his head on my shoulder. "You are to me."

I lace my fingers through his. "Somehow, I know exactly what you mean." I squeeze his hand. "Also, you're adorable."

"No, you're adorable," he teases, poking me with an accusing pointer finger.

"Along similar lines," I begin tentatively, drawing circles on his skin with my free hand, "I really enjoyed that."

He feigns innocence, both eyebrows rising. "Enjoyed what?"

"You're the worst, Will." I move to tickle him, but he beats me to it, rolling over and pinning me beneath him, tickling me until I'm laughing so hard I can't catch my breath.

"Okay, okay, I give up! You're the best!" Tears are streaming out of my eyes.

Will looks down at me with amusement. "That's what I thought." He leans down and kisses me gently.

It's in that moment that I realize we're both still naked, and I'm suddenly aroused all over again. When I wrap my arms around him and pull him down to me, I discover I'm not the only one.

twenty-one

I wake up the next morning tucked into Will's chest under the canoe comforter. He's still asleep, his breathing soft and even, with one arm draped over my side. His dark waves are unruly on the mountain of pillows, his tattoo stark against his bare skin.

I smile in the darkness, reveling in the comfort of this moment, remembering with a blush the activities of the night before. As he starts to stir, I press a kiss to his shoulder.

"Good morning," I whisper as his eyelids flutter open.

"Morning," he says with a sleepy smile, tightening his arm around my waist.

We cuddle together for a few minutes, then I hear Scarlett yelling from the hallway.

"Time for breakfast! There are yummy, yummy pancakes! Please be sure you're dressed before you leave your room!"

I roll my eyes. "I imagine that's directed at us."

"Mmhmm." Will leans in and kisses me deeply. "But what if I don't want you to get dressed?"

I snort. "Then I guess we won't get pancakes."

"I think I'm okay with that." He moves on to caressing my neck with his lips, sweeping his hand along my bare breasts under the blankets.

Suddenly, there's a loud pounding on the door. "Callie! Will! Time to put your clothes back on!"

"She's relentless," Will groans, rolling away from me.

"We could ignore her," I muse, stroking his chest.

"Yeah, but will she stop?"

I shake my head. "She definitely won't."

"I think that's enough to kill the mood for me, unfortunately," he says, unfolding himself from the bed and reaching for a pair of shorts.

I lay there and stare at him while he gets dressed, memorizing every line of his body.

"What?" he asks.

A smile creeps past my lips. "Just enjoying you."

"You didn't do enough of that last night?" he jokes, reaching out a hand to pull me from bed.

"I'm not sure I ever will," I say honestly, standing up and wrapping my arms around his neck, pushing my body into him.

"Callie," he tenses against me. "I need you to put some clothes on if you're going to hug me. I don't trust myself right now."

I laugh and touch him in a very sensitive area, lightly, teasingly. He lets out a little moan.

I can't help but smirk, enjoying taunting him perhaps more than I should. "You mean all this," I gesture up and down my body, "is too much for you?"

"You couldn't possibly be too much for me," he says, kissing my cheek. "But I'm very distracted from the idea of eating pancakes right now."

Scarlett cracks the door open, and we both jump about a mile.

"Ah!" she screams, shielding her eyes when she realizes I'm naked. "I'm so sorry. I was just checking on you. It was so quiet in here last night, I wanted to make sure you got back safely from the beach." She's obviously lying, since just moments ago she'd commanded us to get dressed.

Will snorts. "You were *not* quiet last night," he mumbles into my ear.

"Scarlett rarely hears anyone but herself, regardless of the scenario," I joke in a whisper.

"Okay, you guys, I can hear you right *now*." Scarlett puts one hand on her hip, still covering her eyes with the other. "Whatever, just come out and have breakfast."

"We'll be right there," I promise.

She closes the door and stomps away in mock petulance.

"We'll have to revisit this later," I say, kissing Will on the cheek and tearing myself away before I can give in to the urge to touch him further.

"I'm on board with that plan," he replies.

WE FINISH the pancakes and sit around the kitchen table talking for over an hour before Jenna decides we should head outside to enjoy the nature we came here for.

"I'm going to get the kayaks ready," she says. She'd brought two on her roof rack, and there were three more in the lean-to off the side of the house.

"I'll help you!" Scarlett volunteers, heading out the door with Jenna. Jonathan follows along like he's her shadow.

"Callie, you and Jax go, too. Enjoy the sunshine. Will and I can clean up the breakfast stuff," Molly offers.

"You sure?" I ask, taking in the colossal mess Scarlett made while cooking.

Molly shrugs. "I dragged you all out here, so I feel like I should be on dish duty."

"Then why do I have to clean, too?" Will jokes, poking her in the shoulder.

"Because you're my big brother and that's your job." Molly sticks her tongue out at him, then they both get up and start clearing dishes.

"Okay, we'll meet you outside," I say, striding to the door. Jax is right behind me.

The kayaks are laid out on the ground, the two Jenna brought looking an awful lot better than the ones that came with the cabin.

"I think we'll need to hose these off," she says, pointing to the dried leaves and spider webs on the dingier trio.

Jax nods. "I'll turn the water on. It's around back." He jogs away for a moment, then returns, dragging what might be the world's oldest hose.

"Move out of the way," he instructs Scarlett, who is busy making out with Jonathan right next to one of the kayaks, her back to us.

She must not hear him, because she neither stops embarrassing the good name of her Catholic high school nor moves away from the kayak.

"What do you think?" Jax asks me, nodding toward the hose in his hand and then at Scarlett's turned back.

My mind flashes to the interruption before breakfast. "Oh, absolutely yes."

Jax turns the hose on her, and Scarlett yelps as the stream of water hits her back. She whirls around, lunging out of the path of the hose.

"I am *so* going to get you for that," she runs at Jax, tackling him to the ground and attempting to wrestle the hose away.

"This will end well!" Jonathan observes in amusement, taking a step away from the melee.

"Yeah, I'm not in the mood to get soaked right now," I say, lunging backwards as Scarlett waves the hose around madly. "I'm going to run inside for a minute and get her a towel."

I pop open the door to the cabin and head toward the hallway. I'm pretty sure Scarlett brought several extra towels. I'll look for them in her suitcase.

Molly's voice summons my attention, bringing me to a halt in the shadow of the hallway just short of the kitchen. "I really wish you would come with me."

There's a pause, then Will clears his throat. "This just isn't a good time, Mol."

"Because of Callie?"

"Yes, that's a big part of it."

Dishes clink, then Molly asks, "And what else?"

"Work, you know? My job. My apartment. My whole life is here."

I hear the water turn off. "There are great libraries in San Diego, you know." *San Diego? Does she want him to move?* My breath catches in my throat.

He doesn't reply, so Molly continues. "I didn't think working at the library was really your dream career, anyway." She pauses, then goes in for the kill. "I thought you wanted to be more than that."

Will's voice is bitter now. "I don't need to listen to this from you. You know why I'm there. You know what I gave up. Hell, Molly, you're half the reason I gave it up in the first place."

I have no idea what he's talking about, but I desperately want to. I hold my breath, hoping I can overhear more of this conversation without being noticed.

"Real nice, Will. Blame me for something that wasn't my fault. You're more like him than you realize."

There's a vicious pause, and I can feel the air around me chill from 20 feet away.

Will's voice is like ice. "You know what, I'm done having this conversation. I love you, Molly, but I'm not going to uproot my life. I'm just not." His footsteps head toward the kitchen door, and I duck further down the hallway.

I hear Molly cross to him, her voice going lower, almost pleading. "Please, Will. Just think about it, okay? I really want us to be a family again."

There's a pause, then he speaks. "Okay. I'll think about it."

"Really?" she squeals.

"Yes," Will says. "But I don't want to talk about it anymore right now."

I hurl myself through the doorway of Scarlett's room just as Will leaves the kitchen. I hear him cross the great room, and then the front door opens and closes. Molly's still clinking dishes in the kitchen, so I grab Scarlett an extra towel and sneak back outside.

Molly wants Will to go with her. To San Diego. *Forever?* My heart stills in my chest. God, I hope not. We're just figuring out this thing between us, and it's the most amazing ride of my life so far. I don't want it to end.

But the way he paused when she begged for them to be a family again, and then said he'd think about it, has me reeling. I love that he wants to take care of his little sister. It's so consistent with who he is as a person, and his instinct to protect the people he loves is part of the reason I fell so hard, so fast, for him. But I can't fathom losing him.

It has all just felt so perfect. Maybe even too perfect. And if it comes down to me or Molly, I know he's going to choose her. He'd *have* to. It's who he is, and I can't honestly say I wouldn't want him to. I mean, he has to. *Right?*

Whatever we've started, maybe it's too intense to burn this bright for long anyway. I may not be a real novelist yet, but I know the tropes. I know how this sort of romance ends. Circumstances always drive them apart.

Maybe, like in this case, it's family. Maybe the male love interest has to take care of his ailing mother or his wayward sister. Maybe he can't leave home, even though he desperately wants to follow the main character wherever she goes.

Maybe the heroine, desperate to clinch her dreams, has to choose the big city over her small-town love. They cry, they pine. They agree it's for the best if they break up and part as friends. She goes off and does her own thing, and she's wildly successful, of course.

Someday, he sees her in the audience at his jazz bar and they exchange *furtive* glances, like, *we both know we'll always love each other, but I'm here with my husband and you're playing the piano and now I'm too famous for you.*

Okay, so that's just the plot of *La La Land*. But I think it kind of applies here, because I've come too far to give up on myself again. No matter how I feel about Will, I *can't*. If he follows Molly to San Diego, assuming that's what she's talking about, I can't go with them.

I've already put someone else's idea of how I should live my life on a pedestal for far too long. I can't do that again. No matter how badly Will's messy hair makes me want to barricade myself in his apartment, to rearrange my world like it's merely his living room furniture, to push and pull and perfect every corner so the Feng Shui is perfect and I can stay there forever.

I have to choose myself this time.

I don't see myself living in a university town forever. At some point, I'll probably move, either back home or to a bigger city within driving distance of family, where I can be closer to some sort of career. Whatever that might look like.

Especially when my parents get older and need my help, I'm not going to leave them alone. And Will has his own family stuff to deal with. I can't follow him to San Diego. *Right?*

No. No matter how much I long to wrap myself in a fleece blanket on his couch and settle in to savor him like the best book I've ever read. No matter how much his eyes reflect everything I'm thinking, everything I'm feeling. I still have to choose myself.

I just wish I didn't have to.

I shake away my thoughts. We still have another lake day, and it had promised to be a glorious one, before this unpleasant dose of reality hit. Maybe there's a chance it still can be.

Plus, there's the promise of another night in the canoe bedroom with Will and whatever else that brings.

I need to be able to function. I can't spend the afternoon considering all potential trajectories of our relationship, good, bad, and in-between. I have to be here, be present.

And anyway, as I'm learning, more and more every day, life can profoundly change at any given moment. There's no reason to think too far ahead. Who knows what's coming next?

. . .

THE REST of the day passes uneventfully, and I do my best to forget what I overheard earlier. We paddle around in the kayaks for a while, with Jax and Will following along on flamingo floats. We return to shore for lunch, hot dogs this time.

There's more charades, more hard lemonade and beer. We finish the Junior Mints while playing bocce ball, then Will and I settle in on a beach blanket with books, sharing the last of the cheddar jack Cheez-Its.

Scarlett and Jonathan have retreated to the cabin for some alone time, which, frankly, is a relief. Hopefully, they can get some *urges* out of their systems and return to the group ready to showcase a more tolerable level of PDA.

Molly and Jenna decide to go for a jog, and Jax falls asleep again, face down on the picnic table.

"I feel like he should get checked for sleep apnea." I tilt my head at Jax from our vantage on the blanket.

"Oh, he definitely has it," Will agrees. "I've known him for years, and he's always snoring, and always tired, no matter how much he sleeps."

"That's no good." I replace my bookmark and roll onto my side. "Hey," I say, putting a hand on Will's arm.

He lays his book on the ground and turns to face me, too. "Hey," he smiles, leaning in to kiss me softly.

"Can I ask you a question?" I regret it the moment the words are out, but what I overheard this morning has been weighing on me heavily, despite all the hard work I'm doing internally to forget it. I don't think I'm going to be able to distract myself until I bring it up.

His eyebrows scrunch over his nose. "Anything," he assures me. "What is it?"

I trace absent circles on his arm, looking down. "Earlier, I...heard something. About you possibly going to San Diego?" My eyes lift to his, and I see a flash of sadness there.

"Ah." He clears his throat.

"I'm really sorry," I rush. "I wasn't trying to eavesdrop. Well, not at first. But I was there, and you and Molly were talking, and I couldn't help but overhear. And then I couldn't walk away, not knowing. Not knowing if you were...leaving."

He grabs my hand. "I don't want to leave." His eyes are earnest, and I want to believe him. So badly.

"But what about Molly?" I ask softly.

He shakes his head. "I don't know. I have to figure out what to do." He runs his fingers through his hair. "That's why she called me when I was at your apartment. She bought a plane ticket for me. For next week, when she goes home. She wants me to come with her, visit her neighborhood. I think she's hoping I'm going to fall in love with it and then decide to move there."

"And are you going?" I don't bother to pose my question gracefully.

"I'm not planning on it." He shakes his head, as if convincing himself. "I mean, what's the point?"

I shrug. "I don't know."

He assesses my face. "Do you want me to stay?"

I try not to get lost in his eyes. "Of course I do. Not even a question." I suck in a breath. "But I can't make that decision for you. You need to choose for yourself what's right for you."

He nods slowly, then leans in and presses his lips to mine. I savor every taste of him, even more so now that I know I could lose him.

"I think being with you is what's right for me," he whispers.

I'm not going anywhere.

And then something takes root, bubbling up from my core. The words from last night roll up into my throat again, spilling onto my tongue, stopped there by a last-second survival instinct. My heart is overcome with the urge to scream them out, to shout them from the top of a mountain. But I can't let them out into the ether until I'm sure. Until I know that they're safe, that Will is ready to say them back.

As per usual, I have no poker face.

Will looks concerned. "Are you okay? You look upset. And you're shaking a little."

I nod, looking away. I guess I can't keep this a secret after all. "I'm fine. It's just that there's something I really wanted to tell you, but I'm afraid."

"Now, come on, Callie," he says, tucking a lock of my hair behind my ear. "I promise I'm not that scary."

I chuckle. "Okay." I take a deep breath, surveying his freckles, the way his mouth is still tipped up into a smile. The way he's looking at me like he never wants to leave. The way *I* never want to leave.

I clear my throat, nervous in spite of everything. "I just wanted to tell you. I needed you to know that I love you."

His eyes soften, and he breaks out into a huge grin. "I love you, too," he says, without hesitation, like it's the most natural thing in the world. Like he was already thinking it and was happy to be able to let it out, also.

I throw my arms around his chest and squeeze. "I love you so much."

"I love *you* so much." He presses a kiss to my forehead. "More, even."

I giggle. "This isn't a contest, Pearson."

"Ah, but where you're concerned?" He runs gentle strokes down my back. "All I do is win."

twenty-two

The rest of the afternoon goes way too quickly. We stay out of the water once the sun sinks below the horizon; we learned last night that it's just too cold. But we spend lots of time on the beach, reading and playing Trivial Pursuit.

Jax, who it turns out is an excellent cook, makes us grilled chicken fajitas for dinner, and they're delightful. We all roast marshmallows and sip wine under the stars, laughing and joking and enjoying each other well into the night.

When Will and I finally head inside, I need a shower to rid myself of the smoky campfire smell. I consider asking him to join me, but I don't want to assume anything. I really like where things are right now, and I'd rather see what transpires organically.

He's reading on the window seat when I get back to our room.

"*Dracula?*" I ask.

He holds it up. "You got it."

I consider him playfully. "Are you a vampire?"

He bares his teeth. "Guilty!"

"Uh oh. I need to find some garlic to wield." I sit down next to him, momentarily forgetting I'm still in just a towel. I hope he doesn't notice the flush creeping up my cheeks. I wasn't intending to be so forward.

"Don't worry," Will says, closing his book. "I like you too much to scare you off with vampire behavior. With you, I'll retain my human form and proclivities."

"That's a relief." I put my head on his shoulder.

He leans forward and pretends to bite my neck.

"Hey now!" I jerk away, laughing. "I was promised quarter from your vampire-ness!"

He laughs and pulls me back to him. "Okay, okay. No more biting." He leans in and kisses me deeply, so deeply my stomach drops. His eyes twinkle mischievously when he shifts back and says, "Unless it's the fun kind."

I raise an eyebrow. "Will Pearson! And here I was, thinking you were a gentleman."

"Where you're concerned," he grins at me, "I am both very much a gentleman, and also very much not."

A laugh escapes my lips despite my efforts to stick to the bit. "And which part of you is here in the room with us right now?"

He surveys me seriously. "Which part do you want to be here right now?"

I tentatively run my hand across his chest, then raise my gaze to his. "Maybe the second one."

Our eyes hold for a moment until a silent agreement is reached. He pulls my head toward his, gently kissing me as his hands slide under my towel. I arch toward him, needing more of his touch against my warm skin.

"I don't even care if you're actually a vampire," I say into his ear between kisses.

He laughs and pretends to bite my neck again. "That's good, because now you're one, too."

"Ahhh!" I pretend to scream and launch myself backward, losing most of my towel in the process. Will's eyes sweep over me, slowly, teasingly, making me long for his hands to follow the same path.

He puts his book on the floor, then stands up and peels off his shirt. Then everything else. My breath catches in my throat.

"I'm going to need you to come down here now," I say quietly.

He lowers himself to the window seat, and I shimmy over to make room for him. I raise my lips to his. "Thanks," I breathe into him.

He intertwines our fingers, and then I'm lost, to him, his soulful eyes, the hard lines of his body. We're a mess of caresses and soft moans and wanting and joy.

Will pulls me to places I've never been before. He brings my heart to another level and ignites something in my body I've never felt before, either. God, I love him. And being with him here, like this? Sex with Will is like the perfect combination of love and lust and chemistry. He makes me feel alive in every conceivable way.

We're both pretty caught up in the moment, and I'm a little worried we're going to roll off the window seat. I tell him as much.

He sits up, and I park myself in his lap, straddling his thighs. "I want this," I murmur into his chest. "I want this forever."

He smirks. "I'm flattered you find me this attractive."

I snicker. "What's not to like?" I touch him everywhere, showing him the everything there is to like. I love teasing him, but I'm not giving him what he wants. Yet.

His hands continue to rove, enticing me to come closer. When his mouth joins the game and closes around my breast, I decide I've had enough. I guide him into me, and he groans in pleasure.

"I can assure you," he breathes with much effort, "the feeling's mutual. About all of that."

We're moving together now, so in sync, and I feel like I'm going to explode from the weight of it all. From how good it feels to be both here in my body, in this moment, and to be in my head, knowing what's growing between us in the light of day. This is the real thing.

I can picture my whole life with him. I see us, together, cuddling in my apartment while we read books from the library. Me working on my laptop while he cooks breakfast in the kitchen. Meeting him for lunch at the library. Waking up on Christmas morning and having slow, passionate sex, then baking cinnamon rolls, then hosting my parents and Molly for dinner in our dining room. I can see our future together stretching before my eyes like it's real. Like it could be.

My mind can barely handle the excitement, and apparently, my body can't, either. I lose myself completely in the feeling of him inside me, and it sends me over the edge. He follows closely behind, and I sink down weakly, panting, against his chest.

We're silent for a few minutes as we catch our breath. Then, I run my fingers thoughtfully through his hair. "I didn't just mean the sex, you know. When I said I want this forever," I whisper in his ear.

He nods against my cheek. "I know. Neither did I."

WE HEAD out bright and early on Monday morning, because Will is working a closing shift and needs to get back to Linden by noon. My body is crying out for more time under warm blankets with him; more moments away from real life. More time to figure out *us*, without any interference.

But we aren't going to get that, at least right now. On the way home, we're dropping Molly off at the train station. She's heading up to Rockledge to spend the week with Margo, her friend from high school. Will offered to drive her, but she said she wants to be free to head back whenever she feels like it without bothering him for a ride.

Scarlett is planning to go home with Jonathan after they bring Will to work and me to the apartment. Jonathan took the day off today, and they have some exciting afternoon planned that I'm sure involves plenty of nudity, but which they also claim will feature a picnic and a scavenger hunt.

Regardless, at least after Will gets out of work tonight, it'll be just the two of us again.

This morning, while we were lying together in bed, holding hands and savoring our escapism, he'd asked me if I wanted to come over tonight after he leaves the library. Because he was working until close, he wouldn't be able to go to trivia.

"You can go without me," he'd said.

"That's okay," I'd replied, snuggling into him. "I'd rather come see you when you're done working."

I haven't been to Will's apartment yet, and I'm really excited to see it and get to know him on a deeper level. I'm sure my mother would say I've already gotten to know him on a deeper level, and that I've given away the milk for free, or whatever.

But it's different. And I want to be part of his life in every way, including the knowing-what-his-apartment-looks-like way. So even though we're leaving the lake, I'm really looking forward to tonight.

The ride home is fairly quiet. I think everyone's a little tired from our lakeside romp. Molly throws on her Beats and leans against the window with her eyes closed. Scarlett plays the soundtrack to *Rent*, but she doesn't even sing along, so I assume she's exhausted.

In the backseat, Will pulls me into him, and I rest my head on his shoulder, my hand on his thigh. I think I drift off at points, but at others, I just revel in the silence and enjoy how it feels to be close to him.

Something's changed over the weekend, and it's not just because of the more physical developments of our relationship. I think it's also because our feelings are finally out in the open, and we've both admitted to them, that we're now more comfortable, more confident together.

The chase is always a thrilling part of a romance, but I'm really enjoying being able to kiss Will whenever I want. Being able to tell him I love him. Hearing him say it back. I'm swirling with all sorts of warm, squishy feelings, and I can't wait for more.

When we get to the library, Will gives me a huge kiss that makes *Scarlett*, of all people, look up from her phone and say, "*Geez.*"

"Oh, please. Like we haven't seen way worse from you two," I point between her and Jonathan. She sticks her tongue out at me.

"I'll see you tonight," Will says, grabbing his backpack from his feet and kissing me again.

"See you tonight," I reply, unable to wipe the goofy grin from my face, even as I watch him walk toward the library. Especially when he turns around to wave before going inside.

I notice Scarlett's eyebrows go up in the passenger mirror. "You've got it bad," she teases.

"What can I say? I'm a woman in love."

Scarlett whirls to face me. "Love, huh? Wow, there must have been something in that lake water."

I scowl at her.

"Or was the sex just that good?" She laughs out loud at her own joke.

"It has nothing to do with that," I reply, looking down at my phone.

I love you, I text Will.

"Oh really?" she asks dubiously.

My phone dings. *I love you, too.*

"I mean, it certainly didn't hurt," I answer.

WHEN I GET HOME, I throw all my clothes right in the washer. There's about a pound of sand in the bottom of my bag, so I put that in, too. I hope it will all drain away. I push the "extra spin" button for good measure. Last year, when I got back from Aruba with Thomas, I had to repeatedly scrub the machine by hand to get all of the sand out.

Once the laundry is going, I make a quick grilled cheese and crack open my laptop. Tomorrow is D-day for my book, and I really want to finish the last section and read everything over today. Then, I'll have tomorrow to give it a final edit and email it to Mr. Benderson. I'm sure he'll have some tweaks, but I'll have everything in two weeks ahead of the actual deadline. That ought to count for something.

Then I can shift my focus to my writing class, which also starts tomorrow night. It feels like cosmic timing.

I throw on a classical playlist, which always helps me focus on mundane topics like *this* drudgery, and my fingers start to fly across the keyboard. It only takes me an hour and a half to knock out the last chapter of the book. I honestly expected it to require at least twice that long, so I'm pretty pleased with myself.

I hop up to switch the laundry when I hear my phone ringing.

"Hello?" I flip open the washer and start tossing bathing suits and shorts into the dryer. They feel miraculously sand-free.

"Callie! It's Esperanza!"

"Oh, hi!" I feel guilty. I should have called her sooner to check in. "How are you feeling?"

"Oh, good. Good, kid. Thank you. I'm actually going to be taking a walk today. I thought maybe you'd want to come by and walk with me."

I toss in a dryer sheet. "Walking, huh? With or without crutches?"

She laughs. "No, still with the crutches. But my physical therapist says maybe I could just use one from now on."

"That's amazing! I'm so glad to hear it." I glance down at the time on my phone screen. 2:02 pm. If I leave soon, I'll be able to visit Esperanza *and* get back in plenty of time for my evening with Will. "I can come visit you this afternoon, if you want. Is anyone else there with you now?"

"No, no. Nope. Your grandmother Josephine was here earlier, but she had to head out. She's babysitting Melanie's kids today."

That's no surprise. My mother's sister is a divorced corporate lawyer and often needs help with her four kids, all of whom are under the age of ten.

"Okay. I have a couple of things to finish up at home, but I can probably head out by four, okay? Then I can visit with you for a couple of hours."

"Oh, yes, please do! I can't wait to see you."

I grin, even though she's not here. Because I can't wait to see her either. "Me too, Esperanza. See you soon!"

We hang up, and I finish with the laundry. It should be done in the same amount of time it takes me to do a quick read-through of the

Benderson book. Cosmic timing, once again. The universe really seems to be lining up for me today.

I hurry back to my desk and gulp down what remains of my sandwich, then dive into deep focus as I review the manuscript. Things are sounding a lot better than I expected.

I'm so excited: to see Esperanza, to help her walk again. To get back into my Johnny research at the library and hopefully reunite him with Esperanza. To be done with this godforsaken book, to start my writing class tomorrow. To see Will's apartment tonight, to get a chance at a life with him. I don't think I've felt this good in a very, very long time.

twenty-three

I'm so efficient with my editing that I find time to sign up for a free trial of a genealogy account before I head to the hospital. I try several fruitless searches for Johnny, but I resolve to give it another go tomorrow.

When I get to Rockledge, Esperanza is in great spirits. She's actually leaning on her crutches, with the help of an orderly, when I arrive.

"Hi, C!" She waves at me, momentarily forgetting she needs to keep her hands on her crutches to stay upright. The orderly grabs her elbow before disaster strikes.

"Wow, you look great!" I cross the room to hug her. "You're going to be going home in no time."

She nods excitedly. "I know, I know! I can't wait to get back to my little apartment." Esperanza shoots me a grin. "Want to walk with me?"

I return her joyful expression. "So very much! Let's go."

We stroll up and down the hallway of the hospital for almost thirty minutes, me holding her arm and making sure she doesn't wobble. After a while, she says she wants to go back to her room and rest.

There's a dinner tray waiting for her when we arrive, so she digs into some pasta while I fill her in on what's new with me.

Well, not *everything* that's new with me. I'm not sure she'd appreciate the stories about Will and me at the lake, so I leave those out.

The evening flies by, and I realize I should let her get some rest. Will had told me he gets out of work at eight, but that he has to close up. He'd asked me to swing by his apartment a little after 8:30.

That works out perfectly, really, because visiting hours at the hospital wrap up at seven. If I leave then, I'll have time to head home, shower, and change before going to Will's.

"I think I should head out," I tell Esperanza apologetically just before seven o'clock. She's been yawning anyway. "You seem tired, and visiting hours are ending." I look down guiltily. "And I'm going to meet a friend."

Her eyes grow bright. "Is it your Will?"

That makes me smile. "You always know what's up, Esperanza."

She laughs. "Well, I don't know about that." She shifts uncomfortably in bed. "My stomach doesn't feel so great. Can you call the nurse? I need help getting to the bathroom."

I ring for the nurse and busy myself with straightening up around the room while we wait. When ten minutes pass and no one on staff comes by, I push the call button again. Esperanza is looking increasingly distressed.

"I'm going to go find someone, okay?" I touch her arm. "I'll be right back."

What I find is the charge nurse playing on her phone at the desk, and it takes a lot of self-restraint not to unleash a string of profanities.

Instead, I take a deep breath. "Esperanza Accardi needs help getting to the bathroom. She's feeling sick. We've been pushing the call button. Can someone come quickly?"

The nurse, whose name tag reads "Monica," flicks her blonde ponytail over her shoulder in annoyance. "Sure, I'll send someone." She looks back down at her game of Candy Crush.

I give her my best withering stare. "Can't *you* help her? It's been almost 15 minutes."

She returns my icy expression. "I'm the charge nurse. I'm supposed to coordinate care."

"Surely you also know how to provide it?" I ask in the sweetest tone I can muster, given the circumstances.

She throws her phone onto the desk. "I'll be right there." I think I hear her mutter a curse word or two at my back as we walk away.

When we get back to Esperanza a minute later, she's doubled over on the bed.

I rush to her. "Are you okay?"

She shakes her head, waves me off. "I'm okay, C. It's just my stomach. I'll be fine once I get to the toilet."

I step out of the way so Monica can lift Esperanza from bed and guide her to the bathroom.

"You should head out, C," Esperanza calls over her shoulder. "You need to get to your Will. I'll be fine here."

"I don't mind waiting." I don't fully trust the nurse to do her job at this point.

"No, no," Esperanza stops in the bathroom doorway. "You take off. I'll call you tomorrow."

I hesitate. "Are you sure?"

Monica looks like she's going to gouge out her own eyes.

Esperanza nods deeply, vigorously. I'm afraid she's going to knock herself over, unsteady as she is right now. "Get out of here! I'll talk to you tomorrow."

I can sense that she's starting to get upset because I'm not listening to her, so I grab my purse. "All right. I'll talk to you tomorrow."

Now she smiles. "Love you, kid."

"I love you, too." I point toward the bathroom in command. "Now go feel better."

She nods and mumbles, "I know, I know," as she hobbles away with Nurse Ratched.

. . .

I CONSIDER CALLING my mom on the way home from the hospital to tell her about the issue with the nurse and let her know that Esperanza might have caught a stomach bug. But I know Mom's been struggling with the stress of Esperanza's hospitalization. She's had to assume a lot of responsibility, too, because Esperanza's sisters don't really understand what's going on.

I'll let her have a relaxing evening, I tell myself, *and I'll call her tomorrow.*

When I get back to the apartment, Scarlett is still out. She and Jonathan are either having the world's longest picnic or she's planning to spend the night at his house again. I toss my purse on the floor and grab some Clorox wipes. Every time I get back from the hospital, I feel better if I clean my bag and my keys.

Then, I peel off my yoga pants and t-shirt and hop in the shower. I try to channel meditation strategies, imagining the stress of the hospital dissipating with the steam. I'm desperate to get back into this morning's headspace before I go see Will.

I dress quickly, throwing on a white V-neck and jean shorts. I decide to let my hair air dry, but I put on some foundation and mascara before I head out.

By the time I pull up alongside Will's Camry, my waves have set and my hair is mostly dry. Mentally, I'm feeling substantially better, thanks to the reset the shower provided me. I also blasted Tom Petty on the way over, because it reminds me of the night Will kissed me for the first time.

Will's apartment complex has outside entrances like mine and Scarlett's, and, aside from a black plastic chair next to the door, his small porch is bare. I don't think I expected some sort of floral wreath, but seeing the chair reminds me that I actually know very little about Will, from his decorating style to his deep, dark secrets. If he even has any.

I'm a little nervous when I knock on the door. That fades quickly when Will pulls it open and wraps me in a huge hug.

"I missed you," he murmurs into my hair.

"You just saw me this morning," I tease.

His mouth quirks up. "Regardless, I still missed you."

I swim through his hot cocoa eyes. "I missed you, too."

"Come inside," Will says, pulling me by the hand and closing the door behind us. "How was your afternoon?"

"Not great, honestly." I shake my head. "Well, it was. And then it wasn't. I can tell you about it later."

"Whenever you're ready to talk about it, I'm your willing audience." Will gestures to the hardwood expanse before us. "In the meantime, welcome to my apartment."

"Wow," I say, eyes roving over a whole lot of nothing. "You're either a very clean minimalist, or you're about to move and you didn't tell me."

He chuckles. "I don't have a whole lot of stuff. In fact, I think the suitcases Molly left in the guest room have more clothing in them than I own."

"Now that, I believe."

"I actually got home a little late tonight, because I stopped to grab some of that mint cookie ice cream you like." His eyes are sparkling.

My heart melts. I'd mentioned the ice cream to him in passing a few days ago. The fact that he remembered, and then thought to get some for me, was quite possibly the sweetest thing any guy has ever done for me.

I can't decide if that's pathetic, given the duration of my relationship with Thomas. I guess that it is, but that it in no way diminishes how nice it was of Will to go out of his way to make me happy like this.

"That's so sweet of you," I say, kissing his cheek.

"I'll get you ice cream any day of the week." He grins boyishly. "Especially if you're willing to share."

"Well, of course." I sweep my arm outward in a mock bow. "Your wish is my command."

He chuckles. "I'll have to keep that in mind for...other scenarios."

I stick my tongue out at him. "*So* not what I meant, but okay."

"I can work with 'okay,'" he jokes. "Anyway, because I got home late, I was just in the middle of cleaning up a mess Molly left in my bathroom when you got here. Apparently, it's been there since before we went to the lake, which is unfortunate. Do you mind if I go finish real quick?"

I jump away in mock disgust. "Do you mean to tell me that you've been touching me with gross bathroom hands?" I assume he's kidding. I hope so, anyway.

"Only the best for you," Will jokes. Noting my legitimately disgusted expression, he clarifies, "Molly dropped powdered foundation all over the sink. It's not *that* kind of mess."

"Well, that's a relief." I would've been heartbroken, after all this, to discover that Will is some sort of unhygienic slob.

"I'll be right back. Make yourself at home." He surveys the apartment as if seeing it for the first time. "Probably the best place to do that is on the living room couch, honestly. Most of my furniture is pretty uncomfortable. The best Ikea has to offer, which, admittedly, isn't all that good."

I snort. "I'm sure I'll be fine."

He heads down the hallway, and I walk slowly into the living room, surveying the black Ikea coffee table and well-worn microfiber couch. A television remote and an empty water glass sit astride Will's copy of *Dracula*, which a red bookmark with the library's contact information tells me he's about halfway through. I hadn't gotten a great look at his progress yesterday when I interrupted his reading session in my towel.

The couch wears a blue fleece throw blanket like an afterthought, but it's otherwise devoid of accessories.

Next to the TV looms a large bookshelf that matches the coffee table. It isn't overstuffed by any means, but Will has filled all the available space, carefully alphabetizing his substantial collection. I smile to myself, because of course he has.

I run my fingers along the spines of the books, trying to absorb both their stories and the essence of *him* from this exhibition of who he is, deep down. *"You can tell so much about a person from what's on their bookshelf,"* Scarlett always says.

As I work my way along the shelves, I tease out books that are new to me and read their back covers, gingerly replacing them when I'm done. Much of Will's collection includes novels I've read, but I make a mental note to ask to borrow the ones I haven't. I want to breathe in as much of who he is as I can.

I laugh when I see he has several quintessential man books right in a row: *1984*, *Animal Farm*, and a gorgeous leather-bound edition of *The Collected Works of Edgar Allen Poe*, punctuated only by George Orwell's *Why I Write*, which is a bit unexpected. Next to the Poe doorstop, a small black paperback catches my eye. Thin white letters reveal a fraught title, *Fault Lines*. And then I see the byline. William S. Pearson.

My jaw drops. Tentatively, I reach for the book, slipping it out of place.

I flip it over to read the back cover.

In this stunning debut novel, author William S. Pearson explores the cataclysmic implosion of a family. What can go wrong, and who is to blame, when a house is no longer a home? Pearson's powerful prose is topped only by the emotional depth of this semi-autobiographical story that will leave you reconsidering what it means to express unconditional love.

I'm pretty sure my jaw is still on the floor. Will is a *published author*? *Will* is a published author?

And he never told me?

Not once, in all these weeks of getting to know each other, of him encouraging my own writing dreams, of telling me he loved me, had he thought it might be important to mention that he's already accomplished the biggest thing I hoped I someday could?

Did he not want to make me feel bad? Does he hate his book? Did he get into an accident and have a profound case of amnesia?

I'm not mad, exactly, but I'm struggling to process how this makes me feel.

As my mind is swirling there in front of the bookcase, Will comes back from the bathroom. I don't turn around, but I can feel his eyes boring into my back, taking in what I'm holding in my hand.

"Ah," he finally breaks the silence. "So I see you've found my book."

I turn slowly to face him. I'm hoping my confusion is still etched on my expression so I don't have to ask the question, since I'm not sure how to do so without seeming accusatory.

Will clears his throat. "I, um." He looks down. "I don't really like to talk about it. I'm sorry I didn't tell you."

Okay, I appreciate his apology. But I'm still confused.

I finally speak. "I don't understand. You've been helping me with my writing for weeks, and you never thought to mention that you're a *published author*? And we're..." I trail off, not sure how to define what we are, because we haven't yet, but that's a question for another time. "You told me you love me," I couch tentatively. "I'd like to think you feel...safe with me."

Will's eyes cloud, and he looks decidedly uncomfortable. He walks to the couch and sits, then pats the spot next to him with a questioning gaze.

I feel wary, somehow, but I join him. "You don't have to tell me," I say, suddenly hyperaware that I've pushed him when he specifically said he didn't like to talk about it.

"Cal," he leans over and gently kisses the top of my head. My heart stirs, awakening at his touch. "It's okay. I think I want to." He nods into my hair, as if making up his own mind. "I think you should know."

There's silence for a few moments as he sits back up. He seems to be willing himself to speak. Finally, he begins. "Things in my house weren't great when I was a kid. My dad is...well, he's not the best,"

Will says softly. "He's got a mindset from an older generation, that he's the provider, that kids should be seen and not heard; all that sort of thing." He pauses, toying with the corner of the fleece blanket. "Sometimes, he'd lose his temper. In a big way. He'd yell at my mom. He'd berate Molly and me to the point that she wouldn't even come out of her room when he was home."

My eyes fill with tears, watching his do the same. He swallows. "He never hit us, or anything. But it always felt like he wanted to, you know?"

I think my heart breaks for him in that moment. I nod, even though I *don't* really know, because my parents never treated me that way, ever. I want to reach out to comfort him, but I feel paralyzed by the story he's relaying.

"I always tried to put myself in the middle of things, to stop him from screaming at my mom or Molly. Sometimes it worked, but he would turn his anger on me. When I was a kid, we sometimes had fun together; he'd play baseball with me in the yard or take me to the movies. But any semblance of that went out the window when I started standing up to him. It killed me to lose him, because I still wanted him to be my dad. But I did it anyway."

I can't help it. I take his hand in mine and squeeze hard.

He squeezes back, still looking down at the blanket. "When I started college, it was like a breath of fresh air. Finally, I could just *be*, without always waiting for the other shoe to drop. But I was still haunted by the things that had happened when I was at home; the things I knew were still happening while I wasn't there to try to stop them."

He takes a deep breath. "I became friends with Priya my junior year. She encouraged me to go see a therapist, just to have someone to talk to. I didn't want to at first, but she was so insistent, and I knew she was just trying to help. So I went."

He looks up at me and thoughtfully tucks a strand of hair behind my ear. "The therapist listened, to all of it, and it was such a relief to get everything off my chest. He suggested it might help me to start journaling to get my feelings out on a regular basis. I gave that a try for a while, but what ended up coming out was something else."

I nod slowly, realization hitting. "Your novel."

He smiles ruefully. "My novel."

I'm still holding it in one hand, and he reaches out to absently trace the letters on the cover.

"And it was great, for a while," he says. "It felt amazing to use these horrific experiences and turn them into something good. I was taking this writing seminar, and I showed the manuscript to my professor." He meets my gaze. "She's the one who's teaching your writing class, actually."

"Oh, wow," I say.

Will inclines his head and continues. "I've always been a big reader, and I kind of pictured myself as the dark, brooding, coffeehouse writer type. I felt like maybe I'd finally found my *thing*."

I laugh a little at the idea of Will being a brooding coffeehouse writer. He smiles, too, which makes my heart feel lighter.

"My professor loved the story. Like, really, really loved it. She had a friend who was an agent. She set up a meeting, and one thing led to another, and the agent had a friend at a small press, and…well, you see what happened." He indicates the book in my hand.

"But that's amazing, Will," I finally speak. "Why keep this a secret? And why not keep writing?"

He looks down again, like the weight of his past is pushing his spirit into the ground. "Because it destroyed my family," he says, so quietly I can barely hear him. "Because it made everything worse. It made my dad worse. He said I was airing the family's dirty laundry, that I'd humiliated him at work, that the neighbors wouldn't even talk to him anymore. My mom, who almost never shared her opinions, told me I was no longer welcome in their house. And I think that hurt more than anything he ever did."

He's managed to utterly shock me twice in one day. My eyes fill with tears again, for him, for what he's endured, all while he was only trying to heal. He was just a kid.

"Will," I breathe, putting my arms around him. I bury my lips against his shoulder, kissing him gently, like I can heal him with my flood of sympathy. "I'm so sorry."

He wraps his arms up over mine, hugging me closer to him. His voice breaks. "One night, Molly called me, crying, saying he was screaming at her and wouldn't stop. He'd found a copy of my book in her dresser and was telling her she wasn't his daughter anymore; that she should just leave and never come back. She was terrified, hiding in the bathroom to get away. It was my fault."

Tears are streaming down his face. "I had to get her out. I told her to pack a bag, and I drove home immediately. I brought her here. I slept in a sleeping bag on the floor for the last two weeks of the semester so she could have my bed. I failed all my finals. And then when summer break hit, I dropped out. Got an apartment. I'd already been working at the library on the weekends, but they said I could go full-time."

He lets go of my arm, wipes his eyes, and turns to face me. "Without my parents' help, I couldn't afford to go to school. I didn't want to take out loans I'd be saddled with for the rest of my life, and even if I did, Molly couldn't keep sleeping in my dorm. She was only 16 then. I needed a place to live, a place where she could stay until she was old enough to be on her own. So I worked, and she finished high school here. Graduated a year early, even; she's so smart." There's intense pride on his face now, mingling with the reawakening of years of trauma.

My chest aches at what he's been through; what he's done. I don't have words, so I sit, willing the overwhelming ache I'm feeling to wrap him in warmth; to give him solace of some kind.

"I helped Molly apply to college. She got nearly a full ride, so we were able to swing it without help from my parents." He inhales deeply, coming to the end of the marathon. "She graduated last year. Moved to San Diego for nursing, as you know." Blinking the tears back, he finishes. "She needed to get as far away from here as possible. But I think she still misses it. The place itself, maybe, or just having people who feel like home. That's why she's so desperate for me to follow her."

We sit in silence for a moment. That moment stretches into several. I reach for him again, and he leans his head on my shoulder. His breathing is ragged, and I feel his damp cheek against my neck. I want to be his steadying force. I'm so grateful I can give that to him, after all he's given to me.

"Anyway, it's been fine," he breaks the silence. "I stuck around town, and I worked at the library while my friends finished up senior year and graduated. I would go to work, then see Jax, Jenna, and Priya in the evenings." He smiles ruefully. "Susan would join whenever she was free, though things were pretty touch-and-go there for a while, what with the three kids and all."

Will starts drawing aimless circles on the back of my hand. "Priya and I started dating after a while, and that was a nice distraction, too. Until it wasn't. I stopped feeling it long before I was able to end things, which I think only made the ending harder for both of us. I cared about her too much, as a friend, from all those years when she was there for me, with the book, with my family. I just didn't want to hurt her."

My stomach lurches. "I've certainly been there."

He inclines his head and takes a deep breath. "I'm okay with my life. I love working at the library. Books are my safe place, you know?"

I nod. "I very much do."

He shoots me a small smile. "And I feel like I'm making a difference, too. It's so rewarding, helping people, especially kids. I love running children's programs. But every once in a while, when no one else is around, I sneak up to the fiction stacks and find my book. And I pull it off the shelf and I just...want. I want something else. I want more."

"You can have it, you know. If you want it." I rub his back in what I hope is a reassuring motion.

He shakes his head. "I'm not so sure that I can."

"I can help you," I promise. "I'll do whatever you need."

His eyes are full, then. Of sorrow. Of longing. Of something that looks a lot like love. "I know you will." He wraps me tightly in his arms and presses his lips to the top of my hair. "Thank you, Cal."

We sit there, locked together, for what feels like an eternity. I try to will his pain away, coax it to seep into my veins instead. Maybe pain works through osmosis like water, and it will move toward my skin, an area of lower concentration. Maybe I can take this away for him, even if just for a little while.

I'm not sure if it works, but after a while, I feel some of his tension dissipate.

Will finally breaks the silence. "I love you, you know."

"You know, I didn't?" I grin sarcastically.

"You're silly," he says, gathering me closer. "But I'm here for it."

I snuggle into his chest. "I love you, too."

Neither of us speaks, but it's as if we have, and we stay there curled up in our grief until we both fall asleep. It's too heavy a feeling for either of us to be alone with right now.

twenty-four

I wake up on Will's couch, a strange energy humming through me. I'm warm, I feel safe, and I'm filled with love when I see Will's messy hair in my periphery as I open my eyes. The air still hangs with the sadness of last night, though, and I curl in a little tighter to send him more strength.

On top of all that, today is my self-imposed manuscript deadline. August 1st. The day I can be free of the Benderson book once and for all.

I'm basically done. I'd finished up with my edits when I worked at home yesterday afternoon, but I want to take some extra time to read everything over again today to make sure I didn't miss anything.

After all, as much as I'm ready to be done with ghostwriting, I'm not eager to make a name for myself as the queen of typographical errors.

And, because today is apparently the most important day of my life, it's also the first session of my writing class. I haven't even had time to be nervous, much less excited, because I've been so busy focusing on Esperanza, and Will, and the ghostwriting I've been hurrying to finish.

From my vantage in Will's lap, I can just make out the time on his watch. Shortly after eight o'clock. We have plenty of time. I exhale a little, relief from a stress point I didn't know I had.

Will has to work today, and I don't want to be in the habit of making him late. Or even the reason he always has to rush. I wonder when we'll be at the point of just purposely staying over at each other's apartments so we can go to bed at a reasonable hour. Maybe we can even do crazy things like actually brush our teeth and get ready for bed.

I do love falling asleep on the couch with him. But at some point, I need to talk to him and confirm that he wants to be a couple. That we're more than just two people who say "I love you" and have (admittedly mind-blowing) sex. That we're an "us" I can bring home to meet my family. Granted, he already met them. But *that* kind of us, anyway.

Once we have "the talk," I think it'll be easier to suggest we actually have on-purpose sleepovers.

"Hey," he says, stirring and pulling me back against him. "We really have to stop spending the night on couches." It's like he's reading my mind.

"As long as I'm spending it with you, I think I'll be satisfied." I kiss his chest.

"Along those lines, actually. Would you want to stay over again tonight? For real?"

"Will Pearson, are you propositioning me?" I pretend to gasp. "A lady can't accept such offers without losing her veil of propriety."

"Oh, please," he rolls over and pulls me on top of him. "I've seen you without any of your clothes. At all. Twice." His eyes glint up at me mischievously.

I almost fall into them. "And?"

He smirks. "*And?* While I wouldn't say no to that being a regular occurrence, I would also like to see you more. Possibly wake up next to you when we've both actually put on pajamas before falling asleep."

"You say that now," I toy with his hair, "Because you've never seen what I wear to bed."

"Horrible Victorian nightgowns?" he asks, rubbing a hand up and down my back.

I wrinkle my nose and nod. "Yep. Tons of scratchy lace. Floor-length, gross brown flowers, the whole nine."

He considers my face, then dips his gaze to my lips. "For you, I'll brave the terror of frumpy bedwear."

Then he leans in and kisses me, slipping his tongue against mine. My breath catches in my throat, and I return the gesture fervently. I could definitely get used to this.

"Wow," I say, as his mouth moves to my neck. "You certainly know how to start the day off on a high note."

"You haven't seen anything yet," he promises.

WHEN WILL and I finally stumble out of his living room at 9:15, he offers me breakfast. I happily accept, and he shows up my frozen bagels in a big way. He cooks us omelets with actual chopped vegetables, toasts the end of a baguette, and even bothers to peel some oranges.

"Wow," I say, leaning backward on the kitchen counter in Will's Tom Petty shirt. "If the wake-up call wasn't enough to convince me to spend the night more, I think this breakfast would be."

"Hey, I have to pull out all the stops for you, Cal," he says, deftly flipping the omelet without dropping it.

What kind of culinary wizard can do that, I wonder, watching his hands on the spatula, his wrists as he moves the skillet back and forth on the burner. God, I want to touch him.

I sip the coffee he hands me and shake myself out of my trance. "And why do you have to impress me, exactly?"

He shrugs. "They just hired a new guy at the library. His name's Mike. He has messy hair, too, and I know how you are about sloppy book nerds. I don't want you to lose interest."

I toss my head back and laugh. "I can assure you, you've got me hooked. I'm not going anywhere." It feels good to be able to throw that line back at him.

He smiles softly, offering me a plate with a picture-perfect omelet. "Good. Shall we eat?"

I nod and follow him to the counter stools along the kitchen's half-wall.

"I don't have an awesome table like you do," he apologizes.

"That's okay. I like the stools. They feel very urban chic."

"Well, you know me. I'm always hip to the trends." He puts his hand on my knee under the counter.

"Hey," I hedge, swallowing a bite of food. "I just wanted to make sure you were okay. Because of what we talked about last night."

He blinks twice before responding, then nods slowly. "I'm okay. Thank you."

"I'm here if you ever need to talk." I cover his hand with mine and squeeze. "That's part of this, too, you know. It's not just about my smoking hot bod."

He snorts. "You're funny. And yes, I know."

He's gone back to his omelet, but I have another thought eating away at me, and I don't think I can keep it in. "Also," I start quietly, "what if you tried writing again?"

The color drains out of his face. "I can't."

My eyebrows knit together. "I don't understand. You're the one always encouraging me to follow my dreams and whatnot. Why can't you?"

He turns to face me. "Please, can we not do this?"

I take in his pained expression and want to hug him, to soothe away whatever is causing him this distress. "Okay, we don't have to do this. I just want to help."

"Look," he exhales deeply. "I get enough of this from Molly. I don't need it from you, too."

I'm taken aback by the bite in his tone. "Okay, sorry," I reply, purposely adding a bit of depth to the words so he realizes I'm offended.

"Molly barely even visits me, you know? I'm lucky she came this summer. I mean, Jesus. She moved to the opposite side of the country as soon as she could. I think if there weren't an ocean in the way, she'd keep going." He pushes food around on his plate. "I can't risk driving her away further."

"But doesn't she want you to write?" I try to sound conversational so the information keeps flowing.

His eyes flash. "She says she does, but ultimately, it's in pursuit of *her* goals. She pushes me to do more because she wants me to quit my job here and follow her. If I'm working as a writer, all of a sudden, she thinks I can just live anywhere. But if I started writing again and *didn't* move to San Diego, I think she'd be beyond pissed."

I lay my fork down on the counter. "Okay, but that isn't your problem. Molly doesn't have the right to dictate how you live your life."

"You don't have siblings, Callie. You don't understand." Will stands up and grabs my empty plate. "Not to mention, your parents actually want what's best for you. I don't have that."

"My parents love me," I admit, "but they don't always encourage my choices. Especially when those decisions are risky or don't seem financially sound."

He spins around, and I realize his face is red. "It isn't the same, okay? Can we please stop?" His breathing is ragged as he stares at me, unblinking. "I already asked you to stop."

I sit in stunned silence, blinking back tears. How did we get here, from shameless flirting and sensual touching to him putting up this wall between us? My voice shakes as I push back from the counter. "I...I'm sorry, okay?"

He shakes his head and looks down. "No, *I'm* sorry. I just...I can't do this. I can't write again. I can't reopen those wounds. And I don't want to talk about it anymore."

I nod. "I understand. Sorry for pushing you."

"It's okay." But his eyes are still lowered, and it doesn't seem okay. At all.

"I should probably go, so you can get ready for work." I grab my clothes from the couch and slip his t-shirt off over my head. I brave a quick glance to see if his eyes have followed my path to nudity, but he's busying himself with the dishes. I don't know why, but his apparent lack of interest in my naked body makes me want to cry even more.

I quickly get dressed and pick up my purse. "Do you still want to get together tonight?"

He nods quickly and crosses to me. "Absolutely. Call me when you're done with your writing class." He wraps me in a tight hug.

I melt into him and lose a few wayward tears. I wipe them with the back of my hand before I pull away. "I'll see you later, then. Bye, Will."

Before he can say anything else, I'm out the door.

I DECIDE to work at home today. It doesn't escape my attention that I first met Will at the library, which I ran to when I was working on the Benderson book and wanted to avoid Thomas. Now, as I'm about to submit the manuscript, I'm staying away from the library in an effort to get space from Will.

Our words were cordial by the time I left his apartment, but my insides were still a bit of a mess. Things didn't *feel* okay, even if we were pretending they were. I didn't like the tone he took with me when I suggested he try writing again, or how angry he got when I pushed him, ever so slightly.

I snort when I think about the irony here—I hated Thomas's too-calm demeanor, his inability to exhibit any real emotion, and yet I'm now put off by someone wearing their heart on their sleeve.

But it's not my fault that Will had a traumatic home life. I feel for him. I want to wrap his heart in my arms and never let go. I want to take away his pain. But I can't undo what happened to him. And he shouldn't be taking his frustration out on me.

How was I to know that Molly is always on him to pick up the authorship mantle again? And how could I ever have guessed that she had ulterior motives for that?

Also, isn't it a little hypocritical, really? Will repeatedly nudged me back to writing, building me up, and making me feel like not only am I *good* at this, but that I owe it to myself to keep trying. To stop living on someone else's terms.

So why shouldn't he take his own advice?

I try to banish these thoughts from my mind so I can focus on my final read-through. It's not the easiest thing I've ever done, but I manage to push through my edits by the time Scarlett gets home at four o'clock.

"Are you ready to witness history?" I ask her.

She drops her purse on the table. "Ooh, what am I going to witness?"

"First of all," I tease, "your purse does *not* go there."

She sticks her tongue out at me and moves her bag to the hook in the entryway.

"Thanks," I call after her. "Anyway, I'm all done with my read-through of the Benderson book. And now I'm about to hit send, thus ridding myself of this horrific project forever. Well, until they send back edits."

"Ahh!" She shrieks and runs back to the dining room to lean over my shoulder. "Let me see!"

I gesture dramatically to the file on my desktop. "Behold, Benderson_Finance_Book_8-1-17_Final."

She clasps her hands to her heart. "Aw, it's precious. What a perfect little ghostwritten baby."

"You're so weird." I drag the file into the email I've drafted. "Ready?"

She puts her hand on my arm. "Beyond ready. Do it!"

I hit send. Six months of work whooshes away into the ether.

I sort of expected a wall of relief to crash over me in this moment, but I generally feel the same as I did thirty seconds ago.

"So, how does it feel?"

When I turn to face Scarlett, her eyes are expectant.

I shrug. "Good, I guess."

Her eyes narrow. "You guess? You've been waiting for this moment for half a year. And now you're free to move on to other, more creative endeavors."

Lowering the lid to my laptop, I nod. "I know. You're right. I think maybe it's just a lot right now. Thomas, Will, Esperanza. The book, the career change. Resurrecting my failed manuscript. The writing class." I push back my chair. "It's like a swirling vortex of feelings in there." I point to my head.

She puts her arm around me compassionately. "I understand. It'll get easier."

I know she's right. But at the moment, it doesn't really feel like it.

twenty-five

I make a burrito bowl and then head over to the library for the first night of writing class. Will has already left for the day, and my heart pangs sadly when I walk by the circulation desk and see only Lisa standing there.

Class is being held in the community room. It's hard not to think about the romantic encounters Will and I have had inside these four walls. *Stop it, Callie.* I try to remember why I'm here. I owe it to myself to be fully present tonight.

Just as I promised Will that day we sorted the 1950s newspapers, I grab a seat in back. Not that I actually think anyone's going to steal my work, but I feel more comfortable existing in the periphery. Of any given situation, really.

I pull a notebook, pen, and my laptop out of my bag and arrange, then rearrange them, on the table in front of me. No one else is here yet, and I'm filled with nervous energy.

The door swishes open behind me, and I'm surprised to see Susan walk past me to a desk in the front row.

"Susan?" I guess she didn't notice me when she went by.

"Oh my God, Callie! Hi!" She returns to the back row and plops down beside me. "Sorry, I didn't even see you there."

"I had no idea you were taking this class," I say while she unpacks her bag. Looks like she's not even bothering with a laptop, just pen and paper.

"Yeah, you and me both." Susan's mouth tips up. "I've been looking for something to get me out of the house periodically. Trivia's great, but I can't do anything else that costs money. Doug and I just took a deep dive into our budget, and the trajectory did *not* look good, let me tell you."

"Ugh, I'm sorry." I'm not really sure what else to say.

"Yeah, well, that's what having three kids will do to you," she pipes cheerfully. "Anyway, Will mentioned the class, and I thought it might be fun. Just for something to do. And who knows, maybe if I'm good enough, I can get some teaching credits in the English department next semester. God knows they don't have enough Physics labs to keep me busy. The extra money would be nice." She artfully draws the date at the top of her paper like a teenaged girl. "Anyway, enough about me. What's new with you?"

I think I inadvertently raise my eyebrows, but it's just because I have no idea where to even begin. I haven't seen Susan since the last time I went to trivia.

A lifetime has passed since then.

"Well, I submitted the finance book today," I start.

"Oh my God, Callie! That's amazing! Congratulations!" Susan squeezes my shoulder. "You must be feeling so relieved right now."

Smiling politely, I move my pen to the other side of my notebook. "Yeah, it's nice to be done. They confirmed receipt but haven't sent edits yet. I'm assuming those are coming at some point."

"Well, if they send edits, hopefully they're minimal." She draws a scrolly line under the date.

"Absolutely. And hopefully my ex has nothing to do with the editing process." As soon as I've said it, I realize the idea of possibly having to deal with Thomas again has been weighing on me. I doubt he'd get involved, but one last opportunity to show me he's disappointed might be too much for him to pass up.

Susan snorts. "Will would kick his ass if he bothered you."

"I'm sure he would." I start to relocate my pen again, then decide to write the date on my paper, too.

"So, how are you and Will?" Susan lowers her voice as three other people enter the room. Two look to be college-aged, and I'm guessing one is the teacher, because she goes directly to the projector and doesn't sit down.

"Good," I say, because I think we are. If she'd asked me a few days ago, I would have responded with an emphatic "Great!" But I'm not so sure anymore.

"I'm glad to hear it. He's a really special guy, you know? I'm happy you two were able to work something out."

"Thanks, Susan. That means a lot."

Just then, the woman at the front of the room dims the lights and turns on the projector.

I survey the class, which still consists just of Susan, myself, and the two blondes near the teacher. "I guess this is it, then?"

Susan shrugs. "Free library classes don't always have the uptake you'd expect."

"Will's going to be pissed. He worked so hard to sell this," I joke.

She grins. "I think that was just for you."

I'm pretty sure I already knew that.

The teacher, a curly-haired brunette in her late thirties, clears her throat. "Hi, everyone. My name is Lilly Sobelle, and I'm going to be your instructor for Creative Writing. Thank you so much for coming!"

There's an awkward smattering of applause from the two girls up front. Susan and I exchange amused glances, then join in.

Lilly smiles, then continues. "As you might know, I teach at Briarford University." Her eyes survey the group. "Two of you were in my freshman seminar this past year, I believe," she gestures to the younger girls, "and I know Susan from the faculty lounge." Her eyes come to rest on me. "I don't believe we've met."

"Hi, I'm Callie Sheffield." I wave hello, like I've never introduced myself in a classroom setting before.

"Oh, Callie! Will Pearson mentioned you."

I stare blankly. He did? When was he talking to Lilly? Wasn't she his advisor, back when he was in college, like half a decade ago?

"Oh, well, that was nice of him," I stumble over my words like an idiot. God, I need to stop talking.

Lilly sends me a kind look, acting like nothing I've said is at all out of the ordinary. She steps around in front of the projector and leans back against the table. "So, the first thing we're going to do tonight is talk about our goals for our writing," she explains. "Since there are only four of you, I'd really like to cater to what you're each here for."

Will was right. I can tell already she's an excellent teacher.

We go around the room and share what we're hoping to learn. The girls in front, who introduce themselves to me and Susan as Kara and Sam, say they'd like to work on dialogue and plot structure, respectively. Susan explains she's a novice and is hoping to acquire a new hobby. Then it's my turn.

"I used to write," I begin. "I'd like to get back into it. I'm not really sure what to write about, though. Or even if I have what it takes. So I guess I'm interested in focusing on ideation, and how to know if those ideas are worth pursuing."

Lilly nods. "Thanks, everyone, for sharing. This was really helpful." She clicks a few buttons on her keyboard and pulls up a document titled "Setting the Scene."

"For our first exercise, I'd like you to imagine the place you feel most at home. It might actually be your house, or it could be somewhere else. Your office, a park. It might even be a person—being in their presence."

I pick up my pen and write "Setting the Scene" under the date.

"Remember," Lilly continues. "Great writing pulls the reader into a specific place. But you don't need to describe the backdrop. The scene is a living, breathing environment that's shaped by the characters and their feelings. You can use their emotions to help set the scene. You can also pull from their surroundings to showcase emotions and personality traits."

Susan is already writing, pen scratching along the page.

My mind is racing, but I'm drawing a blank. Fortunately, Lilly keeps talking, buying me precious time to think.

"Please write a one-page scene in the place that makes you feel most at home. Include at least three sensory details, and find a way to convey the emotional undercurrent of the scene. But don't directly tell us how the character feels. Show us. If she's tense, maybe it's hard for her to breathe. If she feels hopeful, maybe the room seems bright or large." She takes a swig from her water bottle. "Any questions?"

No one says anything.

"No problem," Lilly adds. "I'm here if you need anything."

I stare down at my paper. It stares back, taunting me with its paucity of words.

Where do I feel safe? Where do I feel at home?

Suddenly, it hits me.

I begin to write.

The dining room table was covered in dings and scratches, call-backs to days gone by. Sarah ran her fingers over the deepest gouge, pulling memories from its trenches like long-lost time capsules.

This is where she ate cinnamon rolls on Christmas morning, back when life was sweet. It's where her parents told her they were splitting up, when everything started to fall apart. It's where Jack sat, hair askew, looking utterly adorable the night of their first date, before the ground beneath their feet grew shakier. And it's where Sarah had tea with Agnes the day before their worldly planes diverged forever.

It's only when "worldly" and "planes" start to run together that I realize I'm crying a little. I try to blot my tears off the page, then rub my hands on my jeans to dry them off. This is both easier and harder than I thought.

. . .

THE REST of class sails by, and I end up filling a page and a half describing Sarah's safe place. I can't decide if this is a story I want to continue or if it was merely the catharsis I needed today, but I'm fine with either.

"Great work today, everyone," Lilly says. "I'm going to run downstairs and photocopy your stories. I'll take them with me to look over between now and when we next meet. You can take your originals." She walks between us, collecting our work. "On Thursday, we'll start with a new exercise, and I'll rotate through one-on-one meetings with each of you to go over my feedback."

"Thank you," we mumble en masse as she runs out the door with our papers.

"That was great!" Susan jumps out of her chair. "I think this is going to be my new hobby."

I laugh. "I'm glad! You deserve a break from the kids. Even better if it's spent doing something you like."

"See, you get me," she grins, wrapping me in a hug. "See you Thursday, okay?"

"Bye," I wave, gathering my things. I didn't even use my laptop. Maybe I'll just leave that at home next time.

I head downstairs slowly to meet Lilly and reclaim my story. My head is bent over my phone in the elevator, trying to think of what to say to Will.

I finally settle on, *I'm all set. Did you want me to come over?*

My fingers drum nervously on the side of my messenger bag as I await his reply.

I've managed to grab my story from Lilly and get out to my car before my phone registers his text.

Yeah, for sure. See you soon.

Nothing wrong with that response, certainly, but it does lack a bit of the witty banter I've come to expect from him.

Whatever, I tell myself as I turn out of the library parking lot onto the dark side street beyond it. *We had one fight. Things will be better tonight.*

. . .

AND FOR THE MOST PART, they are. Will greets me with a huge, lingering hug, which seems to be saying both "I missed you" and "I'm sorry."

"I thought we could have some of that ice cream I bought you," he says over his shoulder as we head to the living room. "You never got any last night."

"I'm more than on board with that plan," I grin.

So we eat generous helpings of mint cookie crumble and watch *Jeopardy!*, cuddled on his couch. I fill him in on submitting the Benderson book and the writing class, and he regales me with tales of the shipment of books that came in today, all printed upside down. We're laughing and touching, and things are feeling a lot better.

But when I fall asleep in his arms tonight, I'm left with the lingering feeling that we aren't quite back to where we were before our earlier conversation. I'm hoping we can get there soon.

twenty-six

I head home from Will's early this morning, because Scarlett and I have a leftover quiche that needs to be eaten. She and Jonathan made it a few mornings ago when he stayed over, but they decided to double the batch for some reason. I'm growing weary of eggs, but I don't want to waste food.

Plus, Will wants to get to work before the library opens so he can explain the shipment of misprints to Lisa before setting up a program he's running in the children's room.

After I clean up from breakfast, I'm uncomfortably full. The quiche was delicious, but I probably should have stopped at one piece.

I prop myself up in bed with my laptop on my knees, gingerly avoiding my stomach. I'm feeling like I perhaps ate all the quiche in Linden when my phone starts buzzing.

It's Mom. I check the time—only 9:30. I can't imagine why she's calling.

Awkwardly shoving the phone between my shoulder and my ear while trying not to drop my teetering MacBook, I answer the call.

"What's up?" I ask unceremoniously.

It's quiet on the other end for a moment. I'm about to ask if she's still there when I hear her sniff. *Is she crying?*

"Mom, is everything okay?"

She sniffs again, then clears her throat. "Esperanza has taken a turn."

My laptop falls off my knees. "What do you mean, she's 'taken a turn?'"

"She had a stroke."

The words echo through the silence. My brain isn't computing. I just saw her. She was fine. How could she have had a stroke?

Unable to formulate coherent thoughts, I say just that. "I was with her yesterday. She was fine. More than fine, actually. She was up and about, walking around the hospital. Talking, laughing. I don't understand."

Even though I can't see Mom, I can tell she's shaking her head. "I don't know, Callie. They don't really know what happened. The doctor said her blood pressure went really high last night, and before they could do anything, she'd had a stroke."

Now I'm angry. "Before they could do anything? They should have done something immediately."

"I know." Mom's voice is quiet. "It sounds like some time passed. They wanted to give her something to help with her blood pressure, but it had to be approved by the doctor. I guess it took too long."

I have a sinking feeling as a sudden realization hits me. "Her stomach was upset yesterday. She kept asking for the bathroom, but it took the nurse forever to come help her. I wonder if that's connected at all."

There's silence on the other end for a moment. "I don't know," my mom finally says. "I have no clue what caused it."

My thoughts are a tornado inside my head. Could I have prevented this? If I'd stayed, could I have pushed the doctors to evaluate Esperanza? Maybe she just needed antibiotics.

I lean my head in my hands. *Oh my God. This is all my fault.*

"Okay," I say through the tears that are now stinging the backs of my eyelids. "So what do we do now? What needs to happen? Rehab? I can call around, try to see where there are openings."

"Callie," my mom says gently. "She's in a coma."

In that moment, my world grinds to a cruel, screeching halt. I'm ugly crying, tears pouring down my face. I cover the mouthpiece of my phone, trying to maintain some semblance of dignity. I'm pretty sure I'm not the only one sobbing.

Mom breaks the silence, and I can tell from the waver in her voice that her emotions are indeed getting the better of her, too. "I don't know how to do this. I'm sorry. The doctor who called me earlier didn't have good news." She swallows hard. "They...they don't know if she's going to wake up."

I'm gasping for air now; I don't think I can form words. I will myself to breathe deeply, trying desperately to still my chest and return a steady stream of oxygen to my lungs. I channel everything I've ever learned about breath control from doing yoga videos with Scarlett and finally manage a shaky, "O....o....okay."

"Dad and I are going to the hospital now," Mom continues. "She's back in the ICU. It's probably better if you don't come right away. They're limiting visitors. And Esperanza isn't alert anyway."

"I have to see her."

"I know, sweetheart. Let us get there first. We'll get more details and figure out what the next steps are. Your great-aunt Maria is the health care proxy, so she's heading over, too."

Health care proxy. So they're already considering the possibility that she's not going to wake up. That *decisions* will have to be made.

"She was fine, yesterday, Mom." I'm practically pleading now, even though she's not the person I need to convince. "She just needs time. They can't take her off life support yet. Her body just needs time to heal."

"It isn't up to me, Callie." Mom's voice is quiet. "But I'm going to do everything I can."

I nod through my tears, which are falling with renewed vigor at the thought of Esperanza, alone in the hospital, teetering on the edge of this world and the next. Not ready to leave, but her fate totally out of her hands. Out of my hands.

Only up to Maria, whose entire life has frankly been a series of extremely bad decisions. Drugs, abusive husband, neglected kids. Hell, she was probably part of the plot to drive Johnny away, way back when.

Johnny. It hits me like a ton of bricks. I haven't found him yet. Esperanza can't slip away. She has to be okay, because I still need to find Johnny. So she can see him again.

I can feel bile rising in my throat. "Maria shouldn't be in charge of this. She couldn't understand medical information if it was explained to her by Elmo."

"Callie," Mom warns. I don't understand why she's bothering to uphold any semblance of tact. I know she agrees with me. "I'm heading to Rockledge now. I'm going to do what I can."

"Okay, fine. I'll let you go." I hang up abruptly, exploding in sobs that rattle my chest as I throw the phone onto my bed. I need to let her get to the hospital, before something happens that we can't fix.

AS SOON AS I hang up from my mom, I text Will through my tears. *Are you at work yet?*

He replies immediately. *Yeah, but it's fine. What's up?*

I quickly dial him, and he picks up on the first ring.

"Cal? You okay?" His voice drips with concern. I've never called him at work like this before.

I take a shaky breath. "Not really. Esperanza had a stroke."

"What? How is that possible?" He's basically yelling, which is what I feel like doing right now, too.

"She's in a coma." I swallow hard. "And they don't know if she's going to wake up."

There's silence on the line as he processes. "I don't understand," he says finally. "She was fine when you saw her yesterday. What happened?"

"I don't know. Her blood pressure was high, but they couldn't get her medicine in time, or something? And then she went into a coma before they could do anything? And her sister, who is a complete idiot and has a history of horrible decisions, is going to get to decide if she lives or dies."

I'm breathless, and my tears have been momentarily replaced by fury. I'm angry with the doctors, who should have done more. I'm angry with Esperanza, for letting Maria be in charge of important decisions. The most important decision.

And I'm angry with the universe, for holding Esperanza out like a carrot and constantly taunting us with losing her. First, at the diner, when we thought she'd gotten hit by a car, then in the nightmare-come-to-life of her accident, when she actually was. And now this.

"If she hadn't had her accident, she easily could have lived to 95. Or more. She was in perfect health." My breath is coming hard and fast now, and I'm practically shouting. It's like I'm trying to convince him of something. I know this isn't doing any good. But I'm just so angry.

"Anything can happen to anyone at any time," he says gently.

I know he's right, but I don't need to hear it today. "Well, it shouldn't have happened to her now. This isn't her fault. And it could have been prevented if people had been paying more attention." I bite back.

"You're right," he agrees, even softer. "It shouldn't have happened. And it definitely could have been avoided."

I'm fighting the tears again and failing. "I'm sorry," I wail, immediately realizing I've gone too far with him. "I'm just really upset."

"Please don't apologize. I actually, honestly, understand." His words are like a hug. I want to be with him, here, now. I need an actual hug from Will to take away some of this pain.

He must be thinking the same thing. "Do you want me to come over?"

I shake my head even though he can't see me. "No, it's okay. You're working."

"You're more important. I can be there in ten minutes."

I picture his earnest expression, and my heart melts. He's so good. I don't know what I did to deserve Will.

"I love you," I tell him, squeezing every ounce of my emotions into the words. "Thank you, truly, so so much. But you have the children's program today. I can't let you miss that."

Normally, I love thinking of him reading to kids. Right now, though, it's not quite enough to lift my spirits. Not all the way.

"Once I'm able to compose myself, maybe I'll come query some agents from my usual table at the library. I think I'll need the distraction."

"I love you more," he says, a smile creeping into his voice. "I'll be back downstairs by 11. When you get here, come to the desk and ask me for help finding a book. Then, we can go hide somewhere, and I'll give you the biggest hug you've ever had."

Now I'm actually smiling. "Thanks, Will."

"Anything for you, Callie. I'll see you soon."

When I hang up the phone, I'm feeling both better and worse. Worse, because telling Will has made this more real, somehow. Better because his support is absorbing some of the pain.

I shut my laptop and walk it to my desk, shaking my head as if to rid myself of my emotions. I need to get out of here. I'll get dressed and head to the library, work on my story for class. Send out some queries for my old manuscript. I busy myself with finding an outfit as I build a mental to-do list. Keeping my brain occupied will definitely help.

I NEEDED MORE time than I thought to be mentally ready to leave the apartment. But two hours later, I'm dressed, concealer smeared over my puffy undereye circles, and headed toward the library. My appearance is vaguely approaching normal, and I'm ready to tackle the day and take my mind off what's happening in Rockledge.

"I need help finding a book," I say to Will when I walk in, just like he told me to.

He assesses me with a look of concern. Maybe my makeup job isn't as good as I'd thought. He pastes on a smile, which I think is solely for my benefit. "I know just the one. Come with me."

I let him lead me to the elevator. I have less oomph in me than I'd hoped. I couldn't even come up with which book I was looking for. Not like it matters, really. There's no one here, and I'm not sure Marian's hearing is good enough to dial in to our conversation.

When the elevator doors close, Will pulls me into his chest. His lips go to my hair, and his arms wrap around me tighter than I would've thought possible. "I'm so sorry," he whispers.

I feel tears starting at the corners of my eyes. I don't want to cry again, here in the library. I need to be strong, and I have too much to do. I *need* to have too much to do if I'm going to get through this.

I don't speak, so Will asks, "Are you planning to go to the hospital today?"

"My mom said not to go yet," I manage, taking a shaky breath and willing ice cream behind my eyes, "but I think I'll probably go crazy if I don't try. I'm hoping once she and my dad get more information, they'll be able to calm things down and keep people from making any rash decisions. Maybe once it's a little more stable, I can head over."

I hate that what I'm really saying is "if unqualified people don't decide to take Esperanza off life support." I hate that I can't bring myself to just say it. I hate that we're in this situation in the first place. On so many levels, this could have been prevented. Should have been prevented.

"Do you want me to go with you?"

I shake my head. "I really appreciate it, but no, it's okay. I feel like things could get weird this time. And possibly ugly. And besides," I look up at him with a wry smile, "Esperanza's not even going to know that you're there."

He tries to return my expression, but it doesn't reach his eyes. "I'll do whatever you want. Weird and ugly don't bother me."

I kiss the center of his chest where his heart has been beating against mine. "I know. Thank you. I'll let you know if I need you there. And maybe I can come by your place afterward?"

"Please do," he says, returning my kiss on top of my head. "And don't hesitate to call me if you want me at the hospital."

"Thank you." It's all I can think to say.

"I mean it, Callie." His voice is tender against my hair. "It's okay to need people."

THE REST of the afternoon at the library is a blur. I let Will get back to work and sit near his desk, alternately staring at my laptop screen and gazing off into space. I manage to query two agents with my completed novel, but my Sarah story from class is not moving along as quickly as I'd like. I have a jumble of disjointed notes in a Word document, but no overarching idea has grabbed me. Nothing feels right. And I'm not sure, given how my heart is doing at the moment, that I'm going to be able to remedy that anytime soon.

At 4:30, I get a text from my mom saying that they've been in with Esperanza and she's still unresponsive. No one else is at the hospital, and they're going to hang tight for a while.

I'll come by tonight after work, I reply.

There's nothing for you to do here, Callie, Mom replies.

I need to see her.

DESPITE MOM'S fervent efforts to keep me at home and Will's repeated offers to accompany me, I wrap up at 5:45 and head to the hospital alone. Driving is a bit of a whirlwind, and when I pull into the parking garage, I realize I don't remember how I got there. *Maybe I should have let Will come with me*, I muse as I lock up the car.

I meet my parents in the ICU waiting room. They nod in greeting, their faces both somber and exhausted.

"There's a nurse doing her vitals right now," Dad explains. "If you want to go see her after that, you can."

"Thanks."

"The doctor came to talk to us a bit ago, after I texted you," Mom adds. "They did some tests and learned she has an infection. It's a Gram-negative rod bacterium. Like *E. coli*, or similar. It's most likely what caused the stroke."

I stare blankly, thinking in monotone, like I'm as dead inside as I feel. I already know the answer to my next question. It isn't even really a question, but I feel like I have to voice it. "And how did she get an infection?"

Mom's eyes are heavy on mine. "She had to have gotten it here."

"Right. Because Esperanza has been in the hospital for too long to have brought something in from outside. So, once again, someone else has made a mistake that could prove catastrophic for her."

No one replies, so I rattle along with my rage. "She's not a cat, you know. We're already at life six or seven, and she's not a fucking cat. One of these times, someone else's mistake is going to kill her."

My dad clears his throat a little uncomfortably. "People might be able to hear you."

My voice rises. "I don't care. They're the ones who potentially killed someone who shouldn't have even been here in the first place."

Mom's eyes fill with tears. "I know."

"None of this should have happened," I finish, suddenly out of steam. I'm trying not to look at my parents, not Dad's stoic, distant sadness. Not my mom's loosening resolve. I can't cry here.

"I'm going to ask if she's ready for visitors," I say quietly, heading to the nurse's desk before anyone can stop me.

They tell me she is. As it turns out, I'm the one who isn't ready.

WHEN I ENTER Esperanza's room, wearing a surgical mask and a yellow paper bodysuit the desk attendant said was to prevent the spread of additional bacteria, I'm not quite sure what to expect.

What I certainly didn't anticipate was seeing Esperanza looking so normal, so much like she had yesterday. Her gray hair is softly flopped off her forehead and onto her pillow, but otherwise, she could just be sleeping.

I'm not loving the monitors beeping all around me, or the fact that she's intubated. But hopefully with a few days to recover, she'll be waking back up, and then she won't need to be on life support anymore.

Taking a tentative step forward, I consider whether it's okay to talk to her. If it's too weird, since she can't reply.

"Hi, Esperanza," I say into the void.

Soulless beeping greets me in return.

"So, I heard about your stroke," I try again. "I'm really sorry that happened." My eyes well up. "I wish I had stayed longer yesterday. I wish I had made them give you antibiotics. You probably had an infection. Well, that's what they're saying, anyway. But maybe some medicine would have helped?"

I look down at her, air forced into her lungs over and over again by machines. My wavering chin is wet beneath the mask as the tears fall freely. I guess it doesn't have a very tight seal.

"I don't know," I continue. "I'm just sorry I couldn't prevent this from happening to you." I reach out to touch her hand. Her whole body moves in that moment, and she starts shaking her head back and forth, like she's trying to break free from the tubes and cords restraining her.

I jump back for a moment, because her moving of her own volition really wasn't on my bingo card for the evening.

"Esperanza?" I ask hopefully. *Does this mean she's okay?*

She moves more, shaking her head back and forth wildly at the sound of my voice.

"Can you hear me?" Optimism is rising in my chest now, filling me faster than logic can stamp it back down. Surely the doctors have already done plenty of tests of her brain activity. But it feels like she's reacting to what I'm saying. *Something* is happening.

I pull out my phone and navigate to a recent voicemail she left me. "I'm going to play something for you, okay?" I press start and hold the speaker near her ear.

The memory of her voice haunts every corner of the room. *"Hey, C! Don't let me forget when you come tonight to show you pictures of Johnny. I found one where he looks so handsome. Thank you, thank you for bringing them to me. You've got a good head on your shoulder, kid. I'm lucky to have you in my life. Thank you."*

Fat tears are rolling down my cheeks as I watch Esperanza reacting to hearing her own voice. It looks like she's trying to open her mouth. To talk to me.

"Oh my God," I breathe. I have to get someone. "I'll be right back, okay?" I squeeze her hand and sprint into the hallway.

I'm looking for a nurse, any nurse. I see a woman in blue scrubs leaving a room several curtains down.

"Excuse me! Excuse me!" I'm breathless when I catch her. "I think a coma patient is waking up. I need a nurse or a doctor right away."

The nurse, whose name tag reads "Kimberly," gives me a skeptical glance. "I highly doubt it, but let's go check it out."

I glare at her. "Trust me."

I storm back to Esperanza's room, not even looking over my shoulder to see if Kimberly's following. I can hear her clogs clomping over the tiles behind me.

"Watch," I say, pointing to Esperanza. Then, loudly: "Esperanza, I'm back."

Esperanza starts moving again. I give what I hope is an "I told you so" glance to Kimberly, but I'm not sure what's conveyed over the top of my surgical mask.

Kimberly's gaze softens, and she shakes her head. "It could mean something. But it also might not."

Hands shaking, I pull out my phone and play the voicemail again. Esperanza starts moving her head, vigorously shaking herself back and forth.

"See?" I point at the bed desperately. "She can hear me. She recognizes her own voice. She's still there." I'm basically pleading now. I need Kimberly, or someone, to acknowledge what I'm seeing. Then they can stop Maria from making an irreversible decision.

Kimberly smiles gently. "That does seem promising. But we've done a lot of tests, and there hasn't been much brain wave activity that would indicate recovery is possible. So far, anyway."

I'm about to protest when she continues.

"But, look. I'll call the doctor and tell them what we're seeing here." She gives me a quizzical look. "Who are you to the patient?"

"I'm her great-niece. But she's..." I'm not even sure how to qualify our relationship, to explain that this is not some distant relative I only see on holidays. "She's incredibly special to me," I manage.

Kimberly reaches out to touch my arm. "Look, I'm sorry I doubted you at first. Everyone wants their loved one to get better, you know?"

I nod. "Of course."

Her gaze shifts back to the bed, to Esperanza now resting peacefully again. "It's just so rare that they do, once they're in this state."

I don't respond right away. I don't know what to say, what she's trying to tell me. Hadn't she seen the movement, the reaction? Does she mean most people don't come back from this, but maybe Esperanza can? God, I hope so.

Kimberly clears her throat. "Okay, I'm going to call the doctor and update him on what's going on. Why don't you head out? Go get yourself a shower and a hot meal. We'll call her health care proxy in the morning with an update. You can check in with them and figure out next steps."

Next steps. The words send terror through my core. The only next steps should be continued testing, more recovery time. Esperanza has been alive for 84 years. What's a few more days to see if her body can heal? Why does a decision need to be made so quickly?

I nod, but I feel like this is happening to someone else. I leave the room wordlessly, peeling off my mask and bodysuit outside the door and shoving them in a trash can. I don't bother going back to find my parents to tell them I'm headed out. I can't bring myself to describe what I've seen, to relay what the nurse said about next steps.

I don't remember leaving the hospital or driving home. I don't remember taking a shower or falling onto my bed in just a towel. I don't even remember sobbing myself to sleep.

twenty-seven

The light sends shards of glass through my eyes the next morning. I shift in bed, trying to parse memories to figure out why I'm here. I was supposed to go to Will's. *Will.* My fingers fly to my nightstand and grab my cell phone. It's about to die, thanks to being left off its charger all night.

I see I have two missed calls and a voicemail from Will. There are also several increasingly concerned text messages that started in the realm of "Did you still want to come over" and ended with a definite note of panic, with him wondering where I was and why I wasn't answering.

Voicemails. Suddenly, the chaos of the last two days comes flooding back. The fight with Will. The hospital visit. The writing class. Esperanza in a room full of machines, trying with every fiber of her being to come back to us.

I close my eyes and sink weakly back onto my pillow. My head is pounding, my eyes feel like they're going to splinter into pieces, and I am about 100 percent certain I can't face whatever today is going to bring.

After several minutes of lying in bed despondently, it occurs to me that I should call my mother and update her on what happened last night at the hospital. At least if she's aware, she might be able to help nudge things in the right direction.

She answers on the first ring. "Callie, thank God. You just disappeared last night. Is everything okay?"

"I'm sorry," I say, regretting leaving without telling my parents what had happened. "Things in there were pretty tough. I just had to get away."

"I understand."

"But," I add, "something happened that I need to tell you about."

"Oh?" Mom asks.

"I'm pretty sure Esperanza can hear us," I say, trying to keep my voice level.

Hope edges into Mom's voice. "What do you mean, she can hear us?"

I take a deep breath, thoughts racing. I need to speak slowly and explain carefully so she understands. So she can intervene. It might actually be a matter of life or death.

"So, when I was talking to her, she was moving her entire body, like she could hear me. I played her a voicemail that she left me a couple of weeks back, and I'm certain she recognized her own voice. She moved her head back and forth like she was trying to break free of the ventilator." I pause, playing with the fringe on my blanket. "I'm sure she wanted to talk to me."

My mom is quiet for a moment. "Did you tell anyone else?"

"I found a nurse; her name is Kimberly. I showed her what I was seeing. She said it might mean something and that it might not, but that she'd tell the doctor so they could repeat some tests and try to figure out the situation."

"Callie, this is huge," Mom says.

"I know. I feel like this could be enough to convince Maria to keep her on life support long enough to let her heal."

"Well, I'm certainly going to try to make that happen." My

mother is suddenly businesslike. "I'm going to call your grandmother now. Then I'll touch base with Maria."

"Please let me know what they say, okay?" I can't sit here and wait, not knowing.

"I will. I'll talk to you soon."

"Thank you. Talk to you soon." I hug my knees and rock back and forth, afloat on the rough seas of my emotions. Fear, anger, hope. Incredible sorrow. Worry. It's killing me not knowing what might happen.

About the only thing I do know is that I can't really help.

Tentatively, I flick open the last text message from Will. *Callie, please call or text me. I'm getting really worried.*

I draw my lips into a line. I hadn't meant to worry him. I'd been so overcome last night that I'd totally forgotten to reach out and let him know I couldn't come over.

Hey, Will. I am so, so sorry I didn't get back to you last night. Things at the hospital were really emotional, and when I got home, everything was a bit of a blur. I completely forgot I was supposed to come by.

I leave the text unsent for a moment, considering. Does this sound like a cop-out? Especially in light of what had happened at Will's apartment at breakfast on Tuesday? I shake my head, attempting to clear my worry. He'll understand. I let the message swish away.

His reply comes seconds later. *I know. I actually texted Scarlett when I didn't hear back from you. She said you were asleep.*

Of course. I hadn't even seen my roommate last night. She must have come home after I'd gone to bed. But of course, Will would reach out to her and make sure I was okay.

I re-read his message. He didn't actually say "Don't worry about it; it's okay." *Is he mad at me?*

I decide candor is probably a smart move, all things considered. I text back, *Are you upset with me?*

A few minutes pass, so I get up and start to get dressed. Sneaking a look at myself in the mirror, I note gaunt eyes and incredibly frizzy hair. I look about as awful as I feel.

I hear my phone buzz on the bedspread while I'm stepping into my shorts.

No, I'm not mad. I was pretty worried, though. Then: *I do wish you'd let me come with you. I want to be there for you.*

I swallow hard. *I want that, too.*

Will texts again. *Want to try again tonight? Or should we go to the hospital instead?*

I smile in spite of how numb my face feels from all the sobbing I've been doing. I love his use of "we," his decision that he's a part of this now. I decide to stop fighting his help. I probably *can* do this alone, but I no longer wish to.

I have writing class tonight, but I'll come over after that. I think I'll hang around the apartment today and try to catch up on life. I'll plan to go to the hospital tomorrow.

I can practically see his eyes light up as he sends his response. *Can't wait to see you, Cal. Let me know if anything changes.*

I think my eyes are brighter now, too. *Will do. Have a good day.*

You too. I love you, he texts.

I breathe a sigh of relief I didn't even know I was holding in. *I love you, too.*

THE DAY PASSES QUICKLY. I query a few agents and spend a substantial amount of time staring at a blinking cursor on my laptop screen, desperately trying to think of something, anything to write. I consider working some more on the Sarah story I'd started in Tuesday's class, but it feels a little heavy, given current events.

Eventually, I switch gears. I need to feel like I've accomplished *something* today, so I decide to do some laundry and vacuum the apartment.

"Do you want to go out?" Scarlett offers when she sees me cleaning.

"Nah, it's okay. I'm just going to get some stuff done at home."

She fixes me with a knowing look. "You can't focus on your writing, so you're trying to distract yourself. Why not distract yourself at the mall?"

I return her expression. "Because that went so well last time."

"Ha!" she chortles. "Fine! But I'm more than willing to give up on approving these edits anytime. Just say the word."

"Seems a little self-serving, no?" Smirking, I start the vacuum.

I can hear her laughing over the sound of the motor.

WRITING class is off to a decent start, but I'm still struggling to focus. When Lilly calls me over to do a one-on-one, I will my brain to come back to the community room so I don't humiliate myself.

"So, how's your week going?" Lilly casually crosses her ankles to the side.

I shrug noncommittally. "It's okay."

She clearly sees right through my deception, but she paints on a bright smile. "Well, that's great to hear. And you know what else is great?"

I shake my head.

"Your story," she says slowly, like perhaps I'm as slow as I currently feel.

I flush. "Oh. Right. Well, thank you so much."

Lilly cocks an eyebrow at me. "Is everything okay?"

"Um, well. Not really," I admit, burning my gaze through the table in front of me. "I'm dealing with some family stuff this week. A sick relative. And some work things." *And relationship drama*, I add internally.

She nods knowingly. "To be honest, I think some of that came through in your story." When my face blanches in mild shock, she continues quickly. "But that's totally okay. The best writing comes from our most poignant emotions."

What she says tugs on something in my mind, and the words tumble out before I can censor them. "Speaking of that, I'm curious about Will Pearson's book."

Now it's her turn to look surprised. "What about it?"

I roll my pen on the desk in front of me. Back and forth. Back. Forth. Back. "We've been seeing each other," I incline my head, unsure if this is the right way to begin, "and I saw the book at his apartment. He hadn't mentioned it to me previously, almost like he was trying to hide it? Anyway, when we've discussed it in the time since, it's seemed like he has some deep-seated trauma surrounding writing in general. Possibly because of how his first book was received."

Lilly's mouth dips downward. "It's really a shame, everything that happened with his family. Both before and after the book."

"I agree. And I hate that it's making him feel like he isn't allowed to try again." I pause, wondering how open I can be. Will had mentioned me to Lilly ahead of this class. How often do they talk? Might she repeat any of this conversation to him when she sees him next?

Lilly's gaze is still kindly intent on my face, so I decide to forge ahead. In my normal state of mind, I probably would have been more reticent. But today, all bets are off.

"He wants more," I say in a rush. "He's made that clear. But he feels like he can't have it, and it breaks my heart."

She leans toward me across the table. "Will is extremely talented. He could easily make a living as an indie author." Her expression is earnest, just like his. I see why he likes her so much. "His first book had an incredible reception by everyone outside of his family. Reviewers loved it; his agent and publisher snapped it up on sight." She sighs. "But he has to want it. He has to be ready."

I hang my head, suddenly ashamed I've breached his confidence. "Of course, you're right. I just wish I could help."

Lilly lays her hand on my arm. "Hey, Callie, the fact that you even care enough to mention this to me? That means you'll be there to help whenever Will's ready. He's a lucky guy."

I'm pretty sure my cheeks turn a deep scarlet. "I appreciate that," I say, standing my pen upright and drawing aimless circles on the blank page before me. "But to be honest, I think I'm the lucky one."

"You two make a good pair," Lilly replies. "Tell Will to give me a call sometime," she grins conspiratorially. "I'll work on him a little bit for you."

"That sounds amazing," I chuckle.

"Now, let's talk about your story." She's suddenly businesslike. "Listen, I'm not going to sugarcoat it. You've got some incredible talent yourself. The raw emotion in this piece really pulled me into Sarah's world, and it left me wanting more. A lot more."

I think my jaw is on the floor. "Wow, that's great to hear."

Lilly turns the paper over and consults her notes. "Now, I did have a few suggestions for some edits. But truly, Callie, this is far beyond what I'd expect from a new writer."

I swallow hard. "Well, to be honest, I'm not really new. At this, that is."

She raises a brow. "Oh?"

"I actually wrote a novel," I explain. "A few years back. But I queried several agents and there weren't any bites."

Her eyes light up. I can tell this is where she gets her energy—connecting people with their dreams. "And then what?"

"And then nothing. I just finished a ghostwriting project for a financial advisory firm. But I haven't found a home for the novel yet." I don't bother mentioning all of the time I spent waitressing, because I suspect a writing instructor would say that's too much of a segue from the real plot.

"Would you be interested in talking to Will's agent?" Her mouth turns up a bit on one side.

My heart's pounding so hard now, I think it might race straight out of my chest. "What...what do you mean?"

"Will's agent, Jess," she says with a smile, "is my best friend from childhood. I funnel all kinds of writers her way. To be honest, I give myself credit for basically launching her career." She pretends to crown herself.

I laugh, but inside I'm reeling. Introduce me to her friend, Will's agent? Give my novel another chance? The idea is thrilling, yes, but I'm also not sure if I can take another rejection. At least, not right now, with everything else that's going on.

"That's really kind of you," I say. "Can I think about it?"

Lilly grins. "Take all the time you need. Feel free to bring your manuscript to class anytime, and I'll hand-deliver it for you. I meet up with Jess every week for coffee."

Even without the swirling vortex of chaos that's decimating my life right now, I'm not sure how I can send my novel to Will's agent, via Will's college professor. It would be like stealing his path to success, which *he* deserves to follow. And for whatever reason, he feels he can't right now. I'm not sure if I can usurp that. I don't know what that might do to our relationship.

"Anyway," Lilly says. "Let's get back to your story."

WHEN I HEAD to Will's apartment after class, he's in the middle of a phone call. He mouths "Sorry" to me and waves me inside, leaning the phone against his shoulder as he embraces me loosely.

"So you'll be back tomorrow?" he asks.

I hear a voice on the other end that sounds a lot like Molly's.

"Okay, I'll pick you up at the train station in the morning." There's a long pause while Molly rattles on, then Will sighs deeply. "We already talked about this."

I raise an eyebrow. Is she still trying to get him to go to San Diego?

"Look, I can't discuss this now," he says, taking two seltzers from the fridge and handing me one. "I'll see you tomorrow." He rolls his eyes and mouths "Sorry" to me again. "Okay. Have a good night."

Will hangs up the phone. "Sorry, a third time. That was Molly."

I survey his face, desperately seeking a hint of information about their conversation. "She's coming home tomorrow?

He takes a swig of his drink. "Yep. First thing. Then her plane leaves in the evening."

The air hangs heavy with a question, but I don't want to ask it. We settle onto the couch, and Will drapes his arm around my shoulders. It feels warm and safe, and in an instant, some of my worry starts to dissipate.

"So, how was class?" he asks.

I kiss his forearm where it rests next to my cheek. "It was good," I begin slowly. "I actually talked to Lilly about you."

He tenses beside me but plays it cool, sipping slowly from his seltzer. "Oh yeah?"

"Yeah, you know. Just about how cute you are."

Will smirks. "Since Lilly is my ex-college professor and your current teacher, that sounds like a highly inappropriate topic of conversation."

Should I bother explaining? Will it lead to another fight? *I shouldn't avoid this*, I think to myself. I can't tiptoe around him like I did with Thomas. We need to be able to talk about the big stuff.

Taking a deep breath, I go for it. "She really liked my story. She offered that I could run my novel by her friend. Your agent. Jess."

He grins, but there's something hollow in his expression. "That's amazing, Callie! I'm so happy for you!"

I survey him for a moment, sitting there, trying with every fiber of his being to be excited on my behalf. He's so good. I know he wants more for himself. How much would it undo him if I found a way to get it for myself, stole his path to success? If I left him behind?

"Look, Will." I turn and face him on the couch, taking his hand in mine. "I don't want to fight with you. But Lilly and I both think you're incredibly talented. And that I'm not the only one who should be talking to Jess."

He blinks twice, then looks down. "Callie."

"I'm not trying to upset you," I rush. "I know you need to feel ready first. But whenever you are, I'm here. Lilly's here. You deserve more, Will. And we'll help you get it."

If he looked angry the other day, now he just seems depressed beyond measure as he shakes his head. "It's not going to happen, okay?"

"But why not?" I'm basically pleading now. Because if *Will*, the strongest person I know, can't reopen old wounds to chase his potential, how can *I* possibly be strong enough to risk rejection again? Because if *he* won't go back down that road for himself, how can *I* shove him out of the way and make it my own? Because, even if I did, what unspoken jealousy and regret would simmer between us forever?

"Cal, please stop." He pulls his hand away.

"Fine. You're not ready yet." I shake my head. "It's okay."

"Don't you get it?" The air is thick as his face reddens. "I don't want this. *You* want it. You want it so badly that you assume I want the same thing." He breathes deeply. "I love you, Callie. But we aren't the same person. And just because we're together now doesn't mean I can change for you."

His words knock the wind from my chest. I shake my head. "I'm not asking you to change."

"But don't you see? That's actually exactly what you're doing." He stands up and walks to the kitchen.

I feel fury boiling in my chest, and I'm not sure I can tamp it out. Everything is wrong, and I'm powerless to stop it. I couldn't put the brakes on this train even if I wanted to.

"Don't you get it?" I yell then, my voice louder than I expected. "You're letting fear dictate your future."

He starts to shake his head in protest, but I yell louder. "You made me implode my entire life, all on the basis of chasing my dreams. *You* encouraged me to do that. And you're no better than I was. You're telling me to do things you won't even do for yourself."

I can't read his expression as we face off over the half wall. The fact that his eyes are empty terrifies me more than anything else.

"Maybe I'm not the guy you thought I was," he finally says.

My eyes fill with tears. "Yeah, maybe you're not."

Before I can stop myself, I grab my purse and storm toward the door, slamming it shut behind me.

twenty-eight

Will's empty expression haunts my nightmares. I toss and turn all night, waking up in a cold sweat just before the Will in my dream tells me he doesn't love me anymore.

The day doesn't improve much when my mother calls, first thing in the morning.

"Callie." Her voice is wiry. "I spoke with your grandmother."

My heart leaps into my throat. "And?" I'm not sure I'm ready for the "and."

Mom sounds like she hasn't slept. "Updates from the hospital aren't great. They've repeated the testing, thanks to your insistence. But they haven't found any evidence that Esperanza's recovering."

The air whooshes out of the room. "But she can hear us."

I can picture my mother shaking her head. "I don't know, Callie. They're saying there's no brain activity."

"She can hear me!" I'm almost yelling, begging the universe to acknowledge me. "I know she can!"

"I believe you," Mom whispers. "But Maria isn't planning to let things go much longer."

Panic rises in my throat. "What do you mean?"

"They're not going to keep her on life support indefinitely. Maria says it's not what Esperanza would want. She says it's *ungodly*."

The globus sensation in my esophagus makes me gag. "None of them know enough to understand the science behind any of this, much less what some sort of benevolent God might or might not want."

I assume my mom is silent because I'm edging on insulting her Catholic upbringing, but I decide to keep talking. "Look, this can't happen. We can't lose her." My voice breaks. "I'm going to call Maria. I'll try to explain."

"That isn't going to do any good, Callie." Mom's voice is gentle, with a hint of the desperation I feel.

"Well, then, I'll call Grandma and ask her to talk to Maria." My mind is racing, desperate for a plan. "We have to stop this. It's only been a few days, and Esperanza deserves more of a shot. You know that."

Mom's voice wobbles. "I know that."

"Okay then," I say. "I'll talk to you later."

THE FIRST CALL I make is to Maria. I've probably only spoken to her on the phone once before, and it was almost certainly a time when I was looking for Esperanza at her house. Breathing in all of the courage from the room, I dial.

It goes straight to voicemail.

At the beep, I give it my all. "Hi, Maria. It's Callie. Josephine's granddaughter. Listen, I want to talk to you about Esperanza. It's pretty urgent, actually. I wanted you to know that she can hear us. She's still there, and we need to give her a chance to heal. She may get better. Please, please call me." I leave her my number.

I try Josephine next. She answers on the first ring.

"Hello?" Her voice is scratchy.

There's no time for niceties, so I go right in for the kill.

"Grandma, it's Callie. I need you to talk to Maria. You need to ask her to give Esperanza more time."

I can tell she's been crying, is still trying to work through the tears. "She turned her phone off," she says. "She won't talk to me."

"Then go to her house." I grit my teeth. "Or I'll go to her house. She needs to listen."

I hear her sobs in the background, like she's attempting to cover the phone and failing.

"I don't think I've ever asked you for anything," I plead. "I am begging you to intercede here."

Josephine clears her throat. "I'll go over there right now."

WAITING IS EXCRUCIATING. I pace around the apartment, aimlessly picking things up and forgetting what I'm trying to do with them. I call my mom every 30 minutes, asking if she has any updates. "I'll let you know when I hear something," she promises during our sixth conversation.

I need to do something productive, or I'm going to lose my mind. I grab my laptop and log back into the ancestry site. If I can't appeal to my family's logical sensibilities, maybe I can convince them to bow to the gods of romance. Maybe if I can find Johnny, they'll let Esperanza hang on a little longer, even if it's just to give them a chance to say goodbye. Even if she never wakes up, at least *he* can say goodbye. I think they owe him that much, after what they did. After how they ruined two lives.

I type his name, his last known location. I try every possible iteration, every conceivable misspelling. Scrolling through endless results, each one less relevant to the real Johnny than the last, I feel my chest tighten until I think my lungs are going to shatter.

"No," I yell to no one with each door that slams in my face. "No, no, no!" I throw my mouse across the room, watch it smash open against the wall. "Damn it!" I scream.

Thick sobs shake me now. We're going to lose her. I can't help her, and she will go to her grave with a love unrealized. Even the idea of her going to her grave at all crushes my chest like a vice. I can't lose her. Not like this.

We were so close. So fucking close, with so many unreal near-misses. Like Esperanza's life was actually a work of fiction, and the author was trying to overdo it with foreshadowing. It almost seems fake, like we've been walking the pages of a very depressing novel. And now here we are, in the third act, and it's going to end exactly how the author's been teasing it would all along.

I can't do this. Blindly, barely thinking, I race for the door, grabbing my keys and my purse. I don't even head for my car. I just break into a run.

My feet pound the pavement, slamming to the rhythm of my broken heart. "Not today," I hear them say as they reverberate against the road. "Not today."

When I get to Will's apartment, I pound on the door. "Will!" I call breathlessly. "Please, open the door."

The air around me is silent as I catch my breath. There are no footsteps inside.

I check the time on my phone. He and Molly should have been back from the train station by now. And her plane wasn't scheduled to leave until dinner time. They should be here. She'd need to get her things.

I dial his number and listen as the phone rings once, twice, three times. Voicemail.

"Will?" I hope I sound less insane than I feel. "Please, I need your help. I know you're upset with me. But I need you." My voice starts to shake as the tears reappear with a vengeance. "They're going to take Esperanza off life support. I'm trying desperately to find Johnny before it's too late. But I can't."

I hold the phone away from my face to blunt the sound of my sobs. "She deserves to see him one last time. Even if that's all they get, she deserves to be with him at the end. I have to do this for her." I wipe my eyes with the back of my arm. "Please call me."

When I hang up, I just stand there on Will's porch, staring at his door, tears still streaming down my face. I have no idea what to do, how to fix this. I've failed Will, I've failed myself. I've failed Esperanza. I can't fix any of it. It's too late.

I don't even know where I'm going when I turn around and walk away.

THE REST of the day goes by in a blur. I can't go to the hospital, because I'm not even sure I'm coherent enough to drive, and I don't want to be there if the worst should happen. I try my mom again in the evening, but she's still heard nothing.

I decide to call my grandmother.

"Well? How did it go?" I ask coolly.

"She wouldn't discuss it, Callie," her voice is heavy. "Maria says this is what God would want. What Esperanza would want. I told her what you said, about how she can hear you. But Maria said it's cruel to keep someone alive on a machine."

I'm dead inside. "So that's it, then?"

Josephine's voice is so quiet I can barely make it out. "I don't know what else to do."

I throw the phone down, hard, against the couch. I can hear my grandmother still talking from the speaker, but I hit the "end call" button and sink into the cushions, closing my eyes in defeat.

Will never called me back. I guess I've ruined what we had. I've pushed him away to the point of no return if he doesn't even want to help me find Johnny.

And I can't save Esperanza. I can't even give her one last gift, the love she deserved to have her whole life.

Time swirls around me, an eddying darkness that rips my heart from my chest. I have no idea where or when or even who I am. The room's all out of oxygen, and I don't care, because none is reaching my lungs anyway. My sobs have wrecked me beyond the point of repair.

At some point, I slip away into the void.

twenty-nine

I dream that Esperanza's calling. "Hey, C! It's me! I just wanted to say thanks for the walk. It felt good to get up and move around."

Dream-me chuckles. "It was my pleasure."

I imagine that I can hear the smile in her voice. "You're a great kid, you know."

I start to cry, and I can't tell if it's just in my dream or if it's in real life, too. "I wanted to save you," I wail.

"Hey, it's not your job to save me," she says. "You did so much. You did all you could."

"But Johnny. I wanted to find him. You deserved to be happy. You deserved...so much more than all of this."

"I had everything I needed," dream-Esperanza says. "Yep, I had it all. Don't worry about me, C."

I'm sobbing now, and I can feel it slipping away, feel her slipping away. The pixels of the dream are sparkling in front of me, like dust that's about to blow off in the wind. "Please stay with me," I beg through gasps for air.

"I love you, kid." I can barely hear her now.

"I love you, too," I whisper.

And then she's gone.

My eyelids snap open. The room is pitch black. I'm still fully dressed, sitting up on the couch. The apartment is silent. Scarlett must be out.

Taking a deep breath, I summon all the energy left in my body and stumble to my room, collapsing onto the bed. I'm pretty sure it's just moments later that I fall asleep.

I'M STARTING to dread the dawn. It seems like the morning light is a harbinger for more chaos, more endings. Today is no exception.

I flick an eyelid open when I hear my phone buzzing on my nightstand. I somehow had the presence of mind to plug it into its charger before I passed out last night. Almost immediately, I come to wish I hadn't.

"Hello?" I pick up the call from my mom.

"Callie." Her voice is totally devoid of emotion.

My heart can't take it. It aims for wry humor, because that's the only way I can make it through this conversation. "I don't really love that you're calling me right now."

She's silent.

"Tell me." I squeeze my eyes shut.

She takes a deep breath. "Esperanza passed in the night."

I don't open my eyes. If I scrunch them tightly enough, it will trap the tears inside. "I think I knew that as soon as I answered the phone," I say quietly.

She's definitely crying now. "I'm so sorry, Callie."

"You have nothing to apologize for." I remember that this loss, so raw and real, is hers, too. Maybe even more hers than mine. "I'm sorry, too." My voice breaks. "I'm sorry we couldn't save her."

"It wasn't your job to save her," says my mom, sounding so much like the dream version of Esperanza that I wonder if maybe she isn't really gone, but rather hovering here, whispering words into my mother's ear.

"But I wanted to."

There are only sniffling sounds for a moment as we both attempt to adjust to this new reality. "It happened last night," Mom finally manages. "She hung on for seven hours after they took her off life support. She breathed on her own almost all night without help."

The anger starts to creep back in. "If her body was strong enough for that, surely she could have recovered if given more time."

"Perhaps," Mom offers. I know she's not openly agreeing with me merely as a kindness, because the minute someone else validates my feelings, I'm going to burn up in rage.

My mind is a blur of fury and grief and distress. I'm not sure how long we sit there wordlessly, but she finally speaks again. "I should go," she says apologetically. "I need to help your grandmother with the arrangements."

Arrangements. The word shakes me to my core again. This is really happening.

I nod, even though she can't see me. "And will Maria be helping with that?"

"No," Mom bites out. "No, she won't."

I DON'T GET out of bed all morning. Eventually, Scarlett comes home from Jonathan's and finds me crumpled like a shell of myself around my pillow.

"Callie!" She runs to my side, puts her arm over my shoulder. "What happened?"

A ragged sob shakes out of my chest. "She's gone," I wail. "Esperanza's gone."

Her face fills with shock, then she wraps me in her arms and squeezes me tightly. "Oh my God, Callie. I'm so sorry. I'm so, so sorry."

I let my walls down and collapse into her. We cry together until I can't breathe, until I'm pretty sure I'm too dehydrated to summon another tear.

"I'm going to make us some tea," Scarlett says eventually. Then, surveying my face, she asks, "Did you call Will?"

I shake my head, eyes downcast. "No."

"He would be here for you in a heartbeat, you know." Scarlett fixes her ponytail and surveys me thoughtfully. "Can I call him for you?"

I shrug. "You can do whatever you want. I called him yesterday, and he didn't respond. I think things there might be over."

Scarlett's brows furrow tightly. "That seems unlikely. In fact," she says with a knowing glance I despise whenever I see it, "I can almost guarantee that isn't the case."

Now she's pissing me off. "I can't deal with that today, okay?"

She crosses her arms. "Fine. I'm going to get the tea. But I'm not letting you sabotage your relationship with Will. He makes you so happy, Callie." She tosses my phone onto the bed, where it hits my leg. "Maybe you should try him again."

She heads to the kitchen, leaving me alone to have a staring contest with the black screen of my cell phone. She's right. He does make me happy. But I think I've ruined everything, and it may already be too late.

SCARLETT DROPS THE WILL TALK, and I channel the other Scarlett (O'Hara), deciding to worry about him tomorrow. Scarlett takes great care of me, urging me into a hot shower, cooking us spaghetti and meatballs for dinner, putting in season three of *Dawson's Creek* while I stare off into space.

While we're watching Joey not ask Pacey to stay, I feel my phone vibrate. I look down to see a text from Susan.

Want to come over tomorrow to work on our stories for class?

I smile faintly. *I would love to, but my great-aunt just passed away, and I think I'm going to be laid up for a few days.*

Oh my God, Callie, she texts back immediately. *I'm so sorry to hear that. I know how close you guys were. Can I do anything?*

I consider asking her to convince Will to call me back, but I think better of it. *No, thank you. But I appreciate the offer.*

Let me know if anything changes, she says. *And text me when you get information about the service.*

"Everything okay?" Scarlett asks, glancing up from her popcorn and noticing I'm on my phone.

I nod quickly. "It was just Susan. She wants to come to the service."

"That's nice of her." She holds out the popcorn bowl. "Want some?"

"Nah, I'm okay." I watch Pacey tell Joey it was always up to her whether he sailed away on *True Love*. Will's face flashes before my eyes.

My heart feels sick. "I actually think I'm going to head to bed. It's been a long day."

"Okay, sweetheart," she waves. "I'm here if you need me."

THE DOORBELL RINGS when I'm finishing my coffee the next morning.

"Callie!" Scarlett yells from the entryway. "It's for you."

Puzzled, I finger-comb my hair and wrap my arms around my braless chest. I'm still in my pajamas, but I guess it *is* almost eleven o'clock. Late enough for unannounced guests to be socially acceptable.

I see Susan's blonde ponytail peeking up over Scarlett's shoulder. I relax a little. "Hi, Susan." I apply a grin with joy I don't feel, but I'm glad she's here, and I don't want to offend her.

"Morning. Here you go." She hands a box of doughnuts past Scarlett, who skips away to finish her Pilates workout.

My fingers close around the container. "You didn't have to do that."

Susan shrugs. "It's not a big deal. I thought maybe you could use some comfort food today."

A little bit of warmth returns to my chest. "Thank you," I say, feeling really, truly grateful. "Want to come in and have one?"

"I'd love to," Susan replies apologetically, "but Doug and the kids are in the van. We're headed to the playground." She grins. "I'd need more than just doughnuts to prepare for that."

I chuckle. "Like a road beer?"

She snorts. "Yeah, something like that." Her grin fades. "Hey, have you talked to Will recently?"

My eyes widen at her question. "Um, recently, yes. But not for a couple of days."

She studies my expression. "You need to call him, okay?"

I shake my head. "He went to San Diego. I think it's clear that he's moved on from me. From this." I wave my arms wildly in the air. "I might have...I might've messed things up with Will. I pushed him away."

Below us, Doug honks. Susan looks over her shoulder. "I have to go." She scratches her nose. "But look, I care about you both too much to stay quiet. You need to call Will. It isn't what you think."

"Okay," I say quietly.

She doesn't seem convinced by my noncommittal reply. "Please," she adds quietly.

I nod and try to sound earnest. "Okay." Gesturing to the parking lot, I remind her that Doug is waiting. "You should head out. Thank you again."

"Anytime, friend," she says over her shoulder as she bounds down the stairs. "See you soon."

As I watch her leave, I consider her words. It's not what I think? It's not that Will is upset because I pushed him too far? It isn't that he went with Molly to San Diego? He's probably there right now, enjoying the life Molly's built in the California sun, wanting it for himself, too.

I sigh deeply, imagining what I could have had. What I almost had.

I try to shake it off. This is on him. He's the one who owes me a phone call. He could've put a stop to this schism any time he wanted to.

I feel like I'm going to break down. If I lose myself to this sorrow, on top of everything else, I'm not sure I'll have anything left.

I can't deal with this today.

A FEW HOURS LATER, Mom calls to let me know that the funeral has been set for Tuesday.

"Would you like to be involved?" she wonders.

"Involved how?"

She pauses. "We need someone to deliver the eulogy."

The air leaves my lungs. "I don't think so."

"No pressure," she says. "We just thought of you because you're such a beautiful writer."

I consider her horribly transparent attempt at flattery. Could I really stand in front of a room full of people who are missing Esperanza and read a love letter aloud to her? Could I really do it while my insides are this raw, while I feel like my heart is beating somewhere else, far outside my chest?

I think about how I couldn't save her. How I didn't find Johnny. How I couldn't hack it as a writer. How I drove Will away. How I fail at everything I start. Everything that matters.

I don't want to fail anymore.

For Esperanza, I think I can do this. I think I have to try.

"Okay," I say quietly.

thirty

I don't know how I manage to get to Tuesday. Everything I do after Esperanza dies feels like moving through frigid ocean water, but not like when you're splashing about on the shore. No, it's more like when a violent wave knocks you off balance, shoving you under, and you're desperately trying to break through the surface to fill your hungry lungs with air.

I can barely function.

Scarlett picks up the slack at home, doing my laundry and keeping me fed. Susan texts me multiple times, sending me everything from funny cat videos to words of support.

I don't hear from Will at all.

I'd spent all day Monday working on notes for the eulogy. Nothing felt good enough. I couldn't decide if I should make my speech intimate and personal or more generic. The more superficial it was, the easier reading it might be. If I stood there and dissociated, I figured, I might be able to pretend that all of this was happening to someone else.

. . .

DANIELLE SMYTH

I'M a shell of my former self when I get to the funeral home. I don't really remember putting on my black cocktail dress, something I'd bought for a theme party in college and hadn't imagined I'd be wearing for this sort of event.

Jonathan picks up Scarlett and me at the apartment so we don't have to drive. I don't think I could find the funeral home or even recall how to start my car right now, so the gesture is greatly appreciated.

Josephine had decided not to bother with calling hours, so we're only doing a short service here and then heading to the cemetery. Then, there's some sort of luncheon back at my mom's cousin's house, a few minutes away. I'm not sure what kind of emotional state I'll be in by then, so I might have to pass.

We pile into the cramped lobby while waiting for the doors to the service space to open. My elbow is smashed into Scarlett's side, a closeness that's only acceptable because she's my best friend. And because I need the reminder that I'm not alone.

There are already at least 45 people here, and probably only room for 30. If that. I'm not surprised, really. Esperanza meant so much to so many people.

A gangly funeral home employee who looks like he belongs at a haunted hayride comes in just before 11:30 to open the doors. My whole body tenses as I see the casket come into view. It's baby blue and chrome, like some kind of hot rod from the 1950s. My mom had told me they picked the cheapest one, because Esperanza's estate was only worth about $1,500 and an antique television.

As the crowd starts to filter out of the waiting area, creating sight lines into the funeral room, I catch a glimpse of Esperanza's hands, folded across her chest.

I can't go in there.

Scarlett must sense my trepidation, because she reaches out to rub my back. "I'm here," she says. "I've got you, Callie."

Tears pool in my eyes as I nod. "Thanks."

I'm not sure if that's going to be enough.

. . .

WE TAKE our seats alongside my parents in the front row. Scarlett and Jonathan send me sympathetic looks as I repeatedly run my thumb over the folds in my notecards, passing back and forth across the creases until I'm pretty sure I could start a fire from the friction.

Mom squeezes my hand. "You're going to be okay." She casts her eyes downward. "We all are."

The minister ascends the podium, and a hush falls over the crowd.

"We're gathered here today to celebrate the life of Esperanza Accardi," he says, flipping his Bible open to a ribboned page. "Let us pray."

Everyone bows their heads, so I follow suit. But I don't pray. I slip into the abyss of my mind, letting the darkness settle in every crevice. I'm sobbing inside, but that's the price I pay for outward stoicism. So I can keep it together, get through today. Maybe someday, get through to the other side of this grief.

I'm swept away so completely I don't even hear the minister announce it's time for the eulogy. Scarlett gently taps my knee.

"It's time," she whispers.

My heart dashes away, scurrying about my chest like it's never beat steadily before. I see the room spinning, feel a cold panic wash over me.

I can't do this.

But I have to do this.

I owe her this much.

I rise on shaky knees and walk to the podium, nervously creasing my notecards within an inch of their life. I'm pretty sure I'm hyperventilating, pretty sure I'm going to faint from lack of oxygen and hit my head on the stairs. Not sure I'll ever see life beyond this room.

I smooth the cards in front of me and adjust the microphone, looking out over those assembled. Scarlett is already dabbing at her eyes, but she manages to smile at me encouragingly. Beside her, Jonathan pats her back. I notice Susan, Jenna, and Jax huddled together inside a clump of old Italian relatives. Even the fact that my friends came to support me doesn't bring me back into my body.

I stare blankly at the crowd, their expectant faces watching me implode before them. I'm going to shrivel up and die here, I think.

And then, in the back row, I see Will.

I jump in such surprise that my notecards drop to the floor.

He's wearing his gala suit and a black tie, rumpled hair gleaming in the harsh lights of this even harsher space. His gaze is intent on me, and his brows go up when we make eye contact. Then he nods, sending me strength from across the room.

I absorb every bit of it and feel my resolve start to grow. I nod back.

I can do this.

I'm trembling, but I know there's power in just getting started. One step at a time, I tell myself. I pick up the cards from the floor and smooth out the wrinkles. And I begin.

"There's such a fine line between life and death. Death is an abyss one can fall into immediately and suddenly, or slowly and with plenty of forewarning. Either way, our last moments are always final. Once we cross to the other side of that line, there's no coming back."

My voice is shaky, like I'm just coming into it for the first time. But it grows stronger as I continue, my heart still pounding, my mind going to another place, well outside of my body. My strength coming from across the room, where I can feel Will sending me all of his. And maybe some of it emanating from a place deep inside my chest, where it had been hiding all along.

"It hasn't sunk in yet that Esperanza is gone. I still feel like I can reach out and touch the tangibility of her existence." I swallow hard. "But there are no gradations in death. She's gone. In the same way someone who left this plane millennia ago is gone. She's as far away now as she'll ever be."

I hear a few sobs in the audience, which makes my eyes instantly fill with tears. I dab them quickly with a tissue and power on.

"I'm so grateful for all of the time I got to spend with her. I'm glad she was such a part of my life that my whole family, regardless of whether they were also hers, got to know her. She visited my mom's parents. She visited my dad's parents. She loved to talk about basketball with my roommate, and sometimes she even brought us furniture."

Scarlett cracks a smile, which I return over the top of the lectern.

"Most of my friends and coworkers knew of Esperanza or had even met her. She attended every party, every graduation, every funeral, every wedding. She was persistently early and always came bearing gifts (usually things someone had given her that she thought we could use) or doughnuts (usually strawberry frosted).

"She would get the mail upon arriving at your house, and honk loudly and repeatedly when she departed. She'd call when she got home to say thank you and to let us know that she had arrived safely. She'd call the next day to say thank you. She called everyone, all the time, and always asked how they were doing and what was new.

"She remembered every birthday and every phone number. Every single one. On your birthday, she was the first to call in the morning, and immediately after wishing you well, she would remind everyone else in the family that it was your special day to ensure that they also called. She brought people together and fought with everything she had to keep them that way.

"She loved to walk. She was tough and strong, and everyone who met her refused to believe she was 84. She had the innocence of a child, but she was very smart in so many ways. I think we all underestimated her at times.

"When I was in college, Esperanza became my pen pal and my confidante. She wrote to me every week, at least once, whether I had time to reply or not. I have every letter she ever sent me, and I know she kept many of mine. One was even hanging on the wall in her kitchen, because she liked how I had doodled a Christmas tree on the bottom.

"Esperanza's 'little apartment,' as she called it, was full of things like that. She had many, many photographs, given to her by near- and far-flung branches of her large family. Everyone loved her.

"Many of us mean a lot to a variety of people in different ways. I'm pretty sure Esperanza meant the same thing to everyone she met. She was everyone's fun, eccentric, generous friend.

"Once when I was 12 or so, Esperanza was babysitting my cousins and me. I sort of had the sense that, being the oldest, I was really the one in charge, and she was there as a just-in-case."

I hear a few chuckles from the crowd and see my cousin Clare grinning. I manage a smile back. "When we went to bed that night, she walked up and down the hall yelling, 'I love you! God bless you! Goodnight, beautiful children!'"

I look up from the podium and gaze around the room at all the love Esperanza's collected. I see it reflected in every face.

I dab my eyes again. "I've never forgotten that moment. And I know I never will."

My eyes sweep the crowd, drawing from their energy to power through the rest. "She loved us all so much," I continue, "and I know I'll always miss her. But I'm just so grateful she was in my life. And I know all of you feel the same way, because that's what Esperanza was for all of us. She was our person."

I see nods, then a smattering of polite applause. I take a step backward, as if my soul has just settled back into my body. It had definitely gone somewhere else while I'd been delivering the eulogy.

As I walk down the stairs and head back to my seat, I lock eyes with Will. He gives me a gentle smile, and my frigid heart starts to melt. In that one expression, he's saying so many things. I hope I have the chance to say them back someday.

But now isn't the time.

· · ·

AFTER THE SERVICE, there's a clump of congregants in the lobby again. The pallbearers are readying the casket, so we're all standing idly by until the procession departs.

I'm chatting with my cousin, Clare, whom I haven't seen in about five years.

"I loved your eulogy, Callie. It reminded me of so many good times with Esperanza." Her eyes twinkle. "I still laugh about that sleepover you mentioned. Remember how we hid her slippers?"

I laugh, then wonder if it was too loud, because several decrepit dowagers turn around and glare.

"I think maybe *you* hid her slippers," I tease. Clare has always been one for behavior that pushes the limits of social acceptability.

Just then, I feel someone touch my shoulder.

I know without turning around that it's Will.

"I'm going to go find my mom," Clare says, looking between Will and me with great interest. "I'd love to meet your friend later, Callie." She lowers her eyelashes in what I can only think to call a flirtatious manner. It feels supremely out of place here.

I guess she hasn't changed much.

"Callie," Will says, stepping closer and turning to face me.

My cheeks flush when I lay eyes on him, even though I'm trying with all my might to banish the memories.

"Will. Thank you so much for coming." I try to sound gracious, but I'm struggling to maintain my composure, and I fear I might have come across a little deranged.

"Your speech was beyond beautiful," he offers, eyes wide like he means it.

I couldn't have done it without you, I want to say. *Seeing you saved me up there,* my heart wants to shout. Instead, I incline my head slightly. "That's really sweet of you."

We stand in silence for a moment, the air between us humming with sorrow and longing and regret.

He clears his throat. "I was always going to be here, you know. No matter what happened with us. I'm always going to be here for you, Callie." He looks deep into my eyes, and I feel myself falling. I quickly shut that door. Now is not the time. If that time ever comes again.

I nod curtly, working so hard to resist the gravity summoning me toward him. "I know." Because I did. *"I'm not going anywhere,"* he'd said.

Except when he had, several days ago, when I needed him most.

I cast my eyes over his shoulder, spying Maria shuffling out of the ceremony space. I make a mental note to keep tabs on her so I can be sure to avoid her completely.

"How are you doing?" Will searches my soul from two feet away.

"I've been better," I say, feeling the tears about to start. "How was San Diego?"

Will furrows his brow. "What do you mean?"

Now it's my turn to look confused. "San Diego. You went with Molly."

He's shaking his head, and I'm not understanding why. "I wasn't in San Diego."

"Then where the hell were you?" I erupt.

He opens his mouth as if to speak, but I barrel over him. "You were gone. She died, and I needed you. And you weren't here." The tears are streaming down my face now, my hands balled up into fists. I want to run away, to go anywhere he isn't.

"Callie," Will says, trying so hard to meet my gaze even as I look absolutely anywhere else. "I told you I wasn't going to San Diego. Why would I lie to you?"

"I don't have any fucking clue." I'm almost yelling now. Thank God most of the guests have trickled outside to their cars. "Why did you do any of what you did?"

He shakes his head like I'm misunderstanding something important. "I wasn't in San Diego, okay? I was in Pittsburgh."

I feel like we're having two different conversations. I throw up my hands. "You know what, I can't do this right now. I'd love to hear more about why you ran away to another city and ignored my desperate plea for help for multiple days. But we'll have to talk about it later. I just...I can't."

Before he has a chance to respond, I turn on my heel and run in the opposite direction.

WILL DOESN'T COME to the cemetery. I move in a blur, mumbling a psalm, tossing a yellow rose onto the casket. Making small talk with extraneous relatives, then running in the other direction when I notice Maria's daughter is already driving Esperanza's car.

I need a distraction, so I tell Scarlett I'm going with my parents to the luncheon. She and Jonathan decide to head to the grocery store to restock our pantry.

My mom's cousin got deli platters and some cold salads and laid them out on folding tables in her garage. I'm making a plate, letting everyone else swirl around me, when my grandmother walks over.

"Your eulogy was perfect," she says. "You did Esperanza justice. She would have loved it."

I don't know what to say, so I just stand there holding a serving spoon filled with pasta salad over my dish.

"I realize I haven't been a very good grandmother." Her eyes fill with tears. "I know I've made mistakes. But I tried to fix this one." Her voice breaks, and she looks directly at me, face streaming with sorrow. "I tried to fix it. I'm so sorry."

I blink once, then twice. I'm floored by her words, and I don't know how to respond.

Then, it's like a familiar voice is whispering in my ear. "It wasn't your job to save her," Esperanza's words spill forth from my tongue.

Josephine tips her head, considering, then nods deeply, as if coming to agree with what I've said. Her features relax, and my heart lifts. I've comforted her.

And that's when I know. Esperanza's still here. She's all around us, sweeping through the breeze to heal our hearts and teach us how to live without her.

She'll be there in the extra moments I pause before speaking in anger. The forgiveness I share before I'm ready, if it means taking away someone else's pain. The selfless actions I take without a thought as I try to live my life out loud.

The memories when I run my fingers over the scratches on my dining room table.

She was the best of all of us. And from now on, she'll be the best part of those who are left to love her.

"You've got a great heart, Callie," Josephine says, spearing two rolls of turkey onto a slice of bread. "That's what I told your friend when he came by the other day, too."

I stare at her blankly, balancing my plate in my hands. "What friend?"

"The boy from the hospital," she says, dolloping potato salad next to the lunch meat. "William."

Will.

My heart just about stops. "What do you mean, when he came by the other day?"

Josephine surveys my face but finds no shred of comprehension. "He came by to ask me about Johnny. Wanted his address and everything." She looks down. "I'm not proud to tell you, I did have it. He'd written to Esperanza a few times after she moved out and married Frank. I was still living at home. I kept the letters all these years." She shakes her head as if disgusted with herself. "I don't know why. I don't know what I thought I was going to do with them. But Esperanza was married; she got out. She escaped what we dealt with growing up. She'd made her peace with it. I thought it was better if she didn't know. Why revisit the past?"

My jaw must be on the floor. It must be through the foundation of this garage we're standing in, burrowing all the way into the dirt beneath.

I start slowly, incredulously. "Will came to your house?"

My grandmother nods. "He did. I gave him the letters, if you want to see them." She goes back to the catering trays, adding green salad to her dish.

I can't keep up. This isn't making sense. When did Will go to her house? How did he even know where she lived? Why was he looking for Johnny?

My breath catches in my throat when it suddenly hits me. *Because I asked him to.*

I'd called him, desperate, begging for help. Needing to find Johnny so Esperanza could say goodbye. Hoping against hope they'd get more time. That this nightmare would stop, that they could have their happy ending. Wanting to give her *something, anything,* to feel like she left this world clinging to even one shred of what she put into it.

Will had dropped everything to go to my grandparents' house and demand Johnny's address? And then what?

Oh my God. He'd said he'd been in Pittsburgh. What was in Pittsburgh? *Who* was in Pittsburgh?

I swallow hard, dropping my plate on the table. "I have to go," I mumble abruptly. And then I break into a run.

thirty-one

I run until I feel like my legs are going to fall off, and then I run some more. The luncheon was less than a mile from the funeral home, which was a five-minute drive from my apartment. And that's only ten minutes on foot from Will's, which is where I'm going.

By the time I get there, my lungs are living on borrowed oxygen. I draw in deep, gasping breaths, imploring the atmosphere to give me more air. I clatter onto the chair on the front step, desperately trying to recover.

The door swings open.

"Callie?" Will looks puzzled by all the commotion. He's still wearing his dress shirt and pants, but his tie and jacket are gone. He runs a hand through his hair in confusion. "What are you doing here? And what was that noise?"

I take in his befuddled expression, and it strikes me that his eyes look puffier than usual. *Has he been crying?*

"I needed," I gasp, "to see you."

"Why are you so sweaty? Did you run here, or something?" He manages a small smile, parroting my line from the night of the gala.

I stand up, and my legs instantly regret it. But I need to be closer to him. Need to know if it's true.

"Did you go to my grandmother's house? Were you looking for Johnny?" I ask bluntly.

He blinks once. "Of course I did. Yes."

"But why?" I search his face for the answer, even though I already know.

"Because you needed me and I wanted to help you." He reaches for my hand tentatively, as if asking permission. God, after how I treated him after the funeral, he probably thinks I hate him. No wonder he looks upset.

I let him keep my hand, squeezing his fingers in mine.

Buoyed by my positive reaction, he takes a deep breath, looking directly into my eyes. "And because I love you."

I'm still catching my breath, but I'm pretty sure I'd be lost for words anyway.

"And because," he says, rubbing his fingers across the back of my wrist in a way that makes my heart melt, "I can't imagine being at the end of my life and not having spent it with you. And I wanted to make sure that didn't happen to someone else."

My eyes are wide, trying to process everything he's saying. He loves me. *Still*, in spite of everything, he loves me and wants to be with me. Not just now, but forever. To the point that he'd fight my battles for me, pick up the mantle of my quest when I couldn't do it on my own. Even after what I'd said to him, how I'd pushed him away and triggered him. He was still fighting for me.

"Why didn't you tell me?" I finally ask. "Why didn't you call me back?"

Will looks down in regret. "When you called, I was dropping Molly off at the airport. She and I got into another fight about San Diego, and she booked an earlier flight out on Friday." He swallows hard. "I listened to your voicemail when I got back to the car, and then I went straight to your grandmother's house." At my confused expression, he adds, "Scarlett got me the address from your room."

Of course she did. And *that's* why she guaranteed things weren't over, I realize. She'd heard from Will. She knew what he was doing. But why didn't she tell me? Why didn't *he* tell me?

Like he's reading my mind, Will shakes his head. "I didn't want to call you until I had answers. I didn't want to tease you with the possibility in case things didn't work out. But I'm sorry if I made you think..." He glances down at our hands. "Well, all kinds of bad things. That we were over because of what happened last week."

"It's okay," I whisper.

Will manages a small smile. "Anyway, after I got what I needed from Josephine, I went back to the airport. Exchanged the ticket from Molly for a flight to Pittsburgh. Got on a plane."

What he's saying is hitting me now, confirming what I suspected when I left the luncheon. "You found him," I say, mesmerized by what he's done for me, by how it feels to hold his hand. To have this chance again.

I'm not letting go this time.

Will nods in confirmation. "I found him." His eyes cloud with regret. "And he wanted to come back with me. To see her." He wipes a tear from his cheek. "I was with him on Saturday, and it was amazing. But then I got a call from Susan. She told me what had happened. That it was too late." He's openly crying now, tears carving paths down his face at breakneck pace. "I was too late. And I couldn't bring myself to call you and tell you I failed."

I start to speak, to tell him it's okay, but he cuts me off.

"I'm just so sorry, Callie. I'm so sorry I couldn't fix this."

"It wasn't your job to fix this," I say softly, feeling Esperanza in every word. "But I love you so much for trying." I close the distance between us, wrapping my arms around his shoulders, burying my face in his chest. "I love you so much regardless of any of that."

"I love you, too." His voice breaks against my hair.

We stand there, letting our energy hum together, recharging what powers this thing between us. What I'd thought we'd lost.

"I'm really sorry," I say finally. "For pushing you about your writing."

Will shakes his head. "Don't be. I know you were just trying to help."

I look up at his face, still marred by the tears he shed for me. "I just want you to be happy."

The corners of his eyes crinkle, and he inclines his head. "You know, I think I am."

Now I grin back. "Oh yeah?"

"Yeah." He leans down and kisses me, and everything washes over me all at once. Love, and relief, and the gratitude that I have this person in my corner. I wasn't sure I'd ever get to be with him again, like this. God, I'd missed him.

When we break apart, he strokes my cheek slowly. "And honestly, I know that you're right."

This wasn't what I was expecting. "What do you mean?"

"I do want more. And I think maybe writing will be part of that for me." He clears his throat. "But I may need some help to get there. I thought about it a lot this weekend, and I think I need to go back to therapy to work through some of what I've been feeling."

I nod slowly. "That could be helpful. But please don't do it just because you think it's what I want."

"No," Will shakes his head, "I think I need to do it regardless. I'm not sure where it will lead. I did enjoy writing my book, and I'd love to do more someday. But I need to deal with some of the trauma first."

I put my hand on his chest, feeling his heart beating beneath it. "I'm glad you're going to get help if you think you need it."

"I also had another thought, one that's been tugging at my mind for a while." His eyes are bright, suddenly alive with excitement. "I'm going to go back to Briarford to finish up my degree. But I want to change my major."

I definitely didn't anticipate this, either, but now that he's said it, it makes perfect sense. "What are you going to study this time?"

His smile is huge now. "Library science. I think I'd like to work toward a director position someday. And I really love what I do."

I match his joy. "That's an absolutely amazing idea. Watch out, Lisa."

He wrinkles his face in mock sorrow. "Poor Lisa."

We both laugh.

As we fall silent, and the only input to my brain is the feeling of his warm chest under my hand, I realize I need something else. Something I'd been too scared to ask for last time. Something I'm too scared *not* to ask for now.

"Just to verify," I hedge, "because I don't want to repeat the mistakes of the past. Both our mistakes and those of others." I think of Esperanza and Johnny. "Can I be really lame for a minute and ask you to define our relationship? Before misunderstanding or poor communication wreaks havoc again?"

Will looks like he's going to laugh, but he swallows it back. "Have I not been clear enough about my intentions, Ms. Sheffield?"

I stick my tongue out at him. "You know what I mean."

He drags me against him, wrapping his arms around me tighter than I thought possible. "I love you. And I want to be with you, now, and as long as you'll let me."

He grins down at me. "And if I'm being honest, I've already planned out the speech I'm going to give at your celebratory party when you win the Pulitzer, and that may be a ways down the road. So I'm hoping to be in this for the long haul."

"You wrote a speech for my Pulitzer party?" I tease.

He nods in mock solemnity. "And it's really good."

I kiss his cheek. "I love you. And I want all of that with you, too."

"Well, now that we've settled that," Will says, looking me up and down. "Would you like to come inside and have some water? Or possibly a shower?"

I wrinkle my nose at him. "Do I look that sweaty?"

"I mean, it's not the *least* athletic you've ever looked." He pushes the door open with a wry smile. "Shall we?"

"I am actually really thirsty," I say, and I follow him inside.

. . .

SEVERAL HOURS GO BY. I drink about a gallon of water, then I take Will up on his offer of a shower. It might be the best shower I've ever had, both because I'm so sweaty from my run, and because I discover the source of his amazing ocean scent is actually his shower gel, which I am now using.

After I'm all cleaned up, I get dressed in Will's Rush t-shirt and a pair of pajama pants he left out for me. They're comically large against my waist, but they're incredibly soft, and I love that they're his.

After I run his brush hastily through my hair, I join Will on the couch.

"Hey," he says quietly, inviting me into him with an arm around my shoulder.

"Hey," I murmur, sinking into his warmth.

"I like your outfit."

I laugh. "Why, thank you. It's from the Pearson Collection."

What a weird day. The panic, the desperation, the sorrow from this morning still swirl through my chest, now mingling with the cozy comfort of this moment.

"So what was he like?" I ask finally. "Johnny?"

Will pulls me closer. "I can see why she loved him." He idly traces a maze on my right shoulder. "Johnny lives with his daughter in a suburb of Pittsburgh. He's tall, and quiet, and when he talks to you, you get the sense that he's suffered some major trauma, but he never seems ungrateful, you know?"

"Oddly, I think I know exactly what you mean," I murmur. "He sounds like Esperanza to me."

"I thought the same," Will agrees. "He was definitely really surprised to see me at first. But when I explained why I was there, he was totally on board with going to see Esperanza." Will exhales sharply. "I wish he'd had the chance."

"I can't believe you did this for me." I turn to face him. "And I'm so grateful you tried to help her." Fat tears roll down my cheeks. "Esperanza would have been, too."

Will wipes the tears from my face. "I'd do it again in a heartbeat. And if you want, I'll take you back there. Johnny said we're welcome anytime."

I don't even have to think about it. "I want to meet him."

He smiles gently. "I thought you might."

thirty-two

Three weeks later, I'm holding Will's hand, waiting anxiously outside a red brick house in a quaint Pittsburgh neighborhood. I hear footsteps inside, then a tall brunette in leggings and a Carnegie Mellon soccer t-shirt comes to the door.

"Hi," she smiles warmly. "I'm Carolyn, Johnny's daughter. You must be Callie." She sticks out her hand, and I shake it. Her blue eyes are friendly.

"It's so nice to meet you," I say. "Thank you so much for having us."

"Come on in," Carolyn offers, gesturing with one arm. "Dad's just in the family room."

The house smells like apple pie. I smile at the notion that Johnny, at least, ended up with some small part of the American dream.

Carolyn shows us to a well-appointed family room, with a matching gray sofa and armchairs across from a large television. Countless portraits of smiling faces line the walls, beckoning to halcyon days of the past.

Johnny is sitting in one armchair, a newspaper in his lap. He's long and lithe, and when he looks up to greet us, I see he shares his daughter's kind blue eyes.

"You must be Callie." He stands on surprisingly steady feet and crosses the room to shake my hand. "Thank you for coming to see me."

"Honestly, the pleasure is mine." I can't quite believe I'm here.

"Please, have a seat." Carolyn indicates the sofa. "Do you or Will want something to drink?"

"Some water would be wonderful," Will grins. "The airplane air was pretty dry."

"Isn't that always the way?" Johnny grimaces.

"Do you like to travel?" I ask, needing to know everything. About him, about what Esperanza's life could have been like.

He shrugs. "I did, once upon a time. Even after I got back from the service, I still liked to see the sights. Especially National Parks. We took a lot of road trips when Carolyn was young, my wife and I."

My eyes flick up in surprise. Of course, I knew he'd been married. Will had explained that Johnny's marriage had ended when Carolyn was 12, and he raised his daughter on his own after that.

"That sounds really nice," I say.

Johnny inclines his head, and I sense he's revisiting the past. "It was."

Then his eyes sparkle, and I suddenly see why Esperanza had said he reminded her of Will. They have the same aura.

"But I'm not sure you came here to talk about Carolyn. Or my ex-wife." He chuckles, adding, "And I'm not sure that's really what I invited you here to talk about, either."

He's right, of course. "You want to hear about Esperanza," I say with a smile. It isn't really a question.

I watch Johnny's eyes water, but he manages to keep them from overflowing. "I never stopped loving her. Still haven't." His eyelids close, lost in memories. "If I'd known she felt the same way…" He shakes himself out of a trance. "Well, anyway. Life happens. I've had a good one. It brought me Carolyn." He smiles at his daughter as she returns with two waters and plops down in the other armchair.

"Good catch, Dad," she jokes.

We all chuckle. Will is looking at me encouragingly, giving me space to start the conversation we're all here for.

"People think of life like this book that has to have a happy ending, right?" I finally say. "But I don't think it really works like that. It's more just a series of moments, some happy-ending-like in their own right. But it's not like one story all propelling itself toward a joyful conclusion."

I take a sip of my water, considering. "It seems to me that some love stories are like that, too. And just because they don't happen at the end of *your* story, doesn't mean they're not the fairy tale they felt like at the time."

A tear spills over Johnny's cheek. "Can you tell me about her?"

And so I tell him Esperanza's story.

THE WEEKS that follow our trip to Pittsburgh are a bit of a blur. I hear back from Benderson Partners, and they have only minimal edits to my book. I knock those out in a few days, and they pay me promptly.

I don't have to deal with Thomas at all.

Molly calls Will and apologizes for their fight about San Diego. She tells him she's interviewing for a job at Rockledge Medical Center. God knows they could use some decent nurses. Will seems greatly cheered by the apology, and by the prospect of his sister living within driving distance again.

I pour myself into my writing class, spending most of my time outside of sessions trying to goad a story to life. I don't know if it's the grief I'm struggling to work through, or the simultaneous distraction of being head-over-heels in love with Will, but I'm not having any luck with writing.

One Thursday night, Lilly calls me over to her table while the others are working through a prompt.

"I met with Jess yesterday," she says, the corner of her mouth ticking up in betrayal of her obvious attempt to bury the lede.

"And?" I ask, trying to calm the lava now gurgling up in my chest. After our trip to Pittsburgh, I'd finally decided that I was ready to share my manuscript with Lilly and her agent best friend.

"She really loves your novel." Lilly lets the grin spring free, all the way up to her eyes.

There goes the lava. "Oh my God, really?"

She nods deeply. "Yep. You should be getting a call from Jess this week, but she desperately wants to rep you. Don't tell her I told you," she tacks on conspiratorially.

"Cross my heart," I say, drawing an X on my chest. "Lilly, thank you so much. I don't even know what to say."

She shakes her head. "Honestly, I didn't do anything. Just set your pages down in front of someone with good taste. And now," she hits the table for emphasis, "the hard work begins. Jess will have a much easier time selling your novel to a publisher if you have another one ready to go. Or at least something you're working on. So let's talk about that."

I pinch my lips together. "I've been trying. I don't really have anything."

She sits back in her chair, crossing her arms. "Seems to me you've been through an awful lot lately. Maybe you just need a bit of a mental break."

"Could be," I shrug. "But my other novel was born out of an intense period in my life, too. I'm a little ashamed to admit it, but I think I thrive on conflict."

Lilly snorts. "No question about it, you're a writer at heart."

I pretend to bow. "It's an honor to join your ranks."

"So then I wonder," she says slowly, "what emotions are pulling most heavily on your heart right now? A lot of times, those will guide you to the story you need to tell."

Nodding slowly, I consider her words. I think perhaps *every* emotion is grabbing for my attention at the moment. The gumption I found when I pushed Thomas away. The confidence Will helped me discover to pursue writing the way I wanted to. Falling in love with

Will, becoming so enamored by his eyes, his body, his heart. The passion and lust and longing; the desperate desire to help him find what's missing for him, too.

And then there was grieving Esperanza, grieving all the things that could have changed to prevent her death. Sadness for her and Johnny, that they didn't get a chance to explore the love they'd found. Anger at those who took it away from them; guilt that I get to have the opportunity they'd lost.

And then it hits me. "I know which story I need to tell."

thirty-three

I'm sitting at the dining room table, furiously typing on my laptop, when the doorbell rings. I hop up and run to answer it.

Will. Seeing him makes my heart do a little flip-flop. "Hey, you," I grin, wrapping him in a hug.

"Hi there," he replies, turning to kiss my cheek. "I don't want to interrupt you; I know you said you were writing today. I just came over to bring you something."

I pull back and notice he's carrying two cups and a folder. "You brought me two coffees? Or is it this file of paperwork that you felt would make my day?"

He smirks. "No, silly. I brought you *one* coffee. And the paperwork is for me." His eyes light up as he brandishes the folder. "Application for Briarford's Library Science program."

"Oh my God, I'm so excited for you!" I lunge to hug him again and slosh some of the coffee against his arm. "Oops. Sorry about that." Awkwardly wiping his skin with my bare hand, I gesture toward the apartment. "Maybe you should come inside? I'll get you a napkin."

"I actually really didn't want to distract you. I know you're writing," he repeats, but he follows me inside when I grab his hand.

"Sure, sure," I tease. "Then why did you bring yourself a coffee? I feel like you were just begging for an invitation to stay." I thrust a napkin at him, almost knocking into the coffee a second time.

"I mean, a man can dream," he jokes. "I'm just going to set these drinks down here," he indicates the table, "before you spill them again." He sets the cups down gingerly, making a big show of avoiding me completely.

"You're ridiculous," I tell him, throwing my hands around his shoulders. "And I love you so much."

He feigns offense. "I'm a little sad, but you're cute, so I'll let it go." He leans down and kisses me deeply, sending butterflies racing all through my chest. "And I love you, too."

I'm starting to feel like I'd rather continue to explore Will than work on my story when he breaks away, gently kissing my forehead. Thank God one of us has restraint.

"So what's all this?" He gestures to my laptop, my notebook, and the dingy cardboard box sitting atop the table. He reaches into the box, then pulls his hand away. "Oh. These are Esperanza's photos."

I nod in confirmation. "They are indeed."

Will raises an eyebrow. "I'm intrigued. What're you working on?"

"I'm taking on one last ghostwriting project," I reply with a small smile. "Well, it's actually more like *ghost* writing, two words."

"I don't understand." He looks confused.

"I think," I say slowly, "that there's someone else's story that's begging to be told. And they aren't around to tell it."

Realization hits, and he starts to nod. "Esperanza."

"At first, I was totally lost on what to write next," I explain. "And I was struggling in a big way with the injustice of what happened to Esperanza and Johnny. Especially with their broken timelines. It was killing me to think that she missed the opportunity to know what it's like."

"What what's like?" Will strokes my hand, looking into my face so tenderly that I feel like he can read my soul.

"Love," I say, meeting his gaze. "Love lived out loud." He smiles at me softly, and I take a deep breath. "They were so close to having it, but it was ripped away from them. And even though they both went on to lead full lives, they never forgot each other. What they could have had."

I take a deep breath. "And that feels like the greatest tragedy in the world to me. What they lost, and how close they came to finding it again, at the end." Tears roll out, and I let them fall.

"But I'm a writer," I continue, voice shaking. "And I can write any story I want."

"You sure can," Will murmurs.

"And at first, I thought, whatever I write is just a story. It isn't real. But then I thought about what books mean. To those of us who write them. To those of us who read them. To you, who get to share them with the next generation. To Lilly, whose entire *raison d'être* is helping bring stories to life."

I feel like I'm rambling, but his eyes are still intent on my face, so I press on. "When any of us is gone, what's left, anyway? Just our stories. So who's to say that *this* story is any less real than the life someone actually lived?" I look down at a photo of Esperanza, smiling for the camera. "I want to tell the story that should have been."

The story that should have been. I can see it like a film reel; black and white scenes playing out in the darkness. Johnny and Esperanza, laughing at the movies. A heartfelt engagement on her front porch. Welcoming their first baby. Cooking dinner in their cramped kitchen. Fighting, mostly about the small things. Making up, realizing they have all the big things. Decorating a Christmas tree. Playing at the beach with their kids. Growing up, growing old. Doing it all together. The images get faster and faster as I imagine the life they could have had, if...if.

I shake my head, clearing the ghosts from my mind. "So anyway, that's what I'm doing," I say. "I'm going to ghost write their love story. The story that should have been."

I can't change the past. But I can honor two people who deserved so much more. I can make sure that, at least somewhere, in some universe, they get the ending they deserve."

Will is quiet for a moment, then he says softly, "That's beautiful. That's so beautiful, Callie."

I blush, taking his outstretched hand. "Thank you. But it isn't me who made it beautiful. It's her." I wipe a tear from my eye. "I just hope I can do justice to her story."

Will pulls me tightly to his chest. "You will," he says, kissing the top of my head. "You will."

thirty-four

The rain stopped almost as soon as it started. Esperanza peeked through the floral curtains and saw the angry green sky giving way to a pale pink sunset, beams of light breaking through the darkness. She let the fabric fall closed. Johnny should have been here by now.

She strode angrily toward the kitchen, her face a mask of indifference. He was leaving tomorrow, shipping out to fight in the war. He'd said he would come see her to get her answer. She'd thought she meant more to him than a broken promise.

If he doesn't come, it's not your fault, she told herself. You don't control him. You don't control what he does.

Esperanza reached to poke at the strands of fresh linguini her mother had left drying on the table. Still too wet to put away. She wiped her hands on her skirt, looking aimlessly around the room for any sort of distraction. Anything to take her mind off the heart that was breaking deep within her chest.

Just then, she heard the doorbell ring. Straightening up in surprise, she crossed the room, getting to the entryway at the same time as her sister, Josephine. "I'll get it," she said.

Josephine nodded and went back up the stairs.

Esperanza smoothed her hair nervously and pulled open the door. Her heart fluttered wildly when she saw him standing there.

"Johnny," she whispered.

His expression was stoic as always, but his blue eyes were bright as they swept over her face. "I'm sorry I'm late," he said. "I got caught in the rainstorm. I had to duck under the awning at Smith's to avoid getting drenched." He looked down at his clothes. "Not that it helped too much."

Esperanza cracked a smile. "No, no, I'd say that it didn't."

"Anyway," Johnny cleared his throat. "I'm here now. And I think we have some unfinished business."

Esperanza's blood felt like lava. When they'd sat together at the soda fountain last week, he'd asked her if she'd wait for him. He was shipping out, but he wanted to marry her when he got back.

And she hadn't been sure, at first. The question felt like it came out of nowhere, because they'd only been seeing each other since April.

But in another way, it felt like the most natural thing in the world. Time with Johnny passed so quickly; flowed away like it had never been there in the first place. In a life filled with challenges, he made everything feel easy. And he made her feel alive in a way she wasn't sure she could live without.

And with him here, now, staring at her with such an earnest expression, like she was the most important thing in his universe, she no longer remembered why she'd said she needed time to think it over.

"Of course I'll wait for you," she said, reaching out to touch his hand. "Of course I will. I'd wait for you even if you didn't ask, to be honest." Esperanza looked up and met his gaze. "My heart is always going to belong to you."

Johnny's eyes melted then, as he looked down at her with so much affection. "I love you, you know."

She grinned. "I know that."

He reached into his pocket. Her heart caught in her throat as she saw him pull out a small blue box.

"I got you this," he said, handing it to her. "I hope you like it."

Esperanza popped open the box with shaking hands. Inside, lying on a bed of crushed velvet, she found a delicate gold band with a perfect, sparkling stone at its center. Tears pricked the back of her eyelids as she slid it out and put it on her finger.

"What are you saying, then?" she asked, not quite believing this was really happening.

His eyes sparkled brighter than the diamond. "I thought that much was obvious."

Esperanza smirked. "I'm going to need you to say it."

Johnny dropped to one knee and held out an arm dramatically. "Esperanza, would you do me the honor of being my wife?"

"Of course I'll marry you," she said. "In every single lifetime."

author's note

I started *Ghost Writing* years ago and couldn't bring myself to finish. It was too real, too raw to peel back the layers of my past and relive the events that are reflected and fictionalized here. But one day, I realized I was ready, and then the words just poured out like they'd been waiting on my heart all along.

Writing this book was honestly one of the easiest and most satisfying things I've ever done. I think that's largely because the real Esperanza lived so fully, and her story felt so important, that all of the other elements of the book coalesced around her as I was writing. It was truly an otherworldly experience—it felt like the words wrote themselves.

There really was an Esperanza, though that wasn't her actual name. Just like in the book, she was my great-aunt. She was really more like a surrogate grandmother when I was a child, and she became a rather unlikely friend when I grew up.

But she was somehow always there—showing up for dance recitals, parties, and softball games; the first to arrive at every gathering; waiting for you at the airport hours before your plane took off or landed, just to say hi. If it were your birthday, she would call you first

AUTHOR'S NOTE

thing in the morning with good wishes. She never (and I mean never) forgot. And she didn't just do this for me; she did it for all of her siblings, all of their kids, and all of THEIR kids—probably 50 or more people who felt like she was THEIR Esperanza.

Eccentric in ways both silly and simple, and generous beyond words, she was filled with a childlike innocence despite her fascinating, oftentimes dark lived experiences. The real Esperanza was somehow critically important to the lives of everyone in her circuit, from neighbors to countless extraneous relatives to friends from church. She even saved the lives of two different people through completely selfless acts of bravery that I think most of us would be too afraid to risk.

Everywhere I've gone in life, she was there. My friends from college knew all about her, because she wrote to me once a week. My husband's colleagues met her at least once when she showed up while he was working, just to say hello.

She was hilarious, perhaps occasionally unintentionally so, but she just lived so fully and freely as herself that she was a joy to be around. For most of the time we had together, she was retired, but my older relatives tell me she was always this way, even when she was a young woman.

The real Esperanza grew up with a wonderfully loving mother who died young, and an abusive father she never forgave. These circumstances shaped every facet of who she became. She came of age during World War Two and learned quickly to stick up for and take care of herself.

One of the most memorable experiences of my life was when she was the subject of a detailed oral history project I completed for my undergraduate degree. It was enlightening (and at times shocking) to see the 1940s, and my family's past, through her eyes.

I don't think I fully appreciated how much she meant to everyone around her until she died. Even at an incredibly youthful 84 years old, she still did everything on her own. I think we somehow actually expected her to live forever.

AUTHOR'S NOTE

At 83, she decided that I should have her dining table, so she carried it down the stairs from her second-floor apartment by herself, put it and its four chairs into her car on her own, and drove it to my house. Like the fictional Esperanza, she walked everywhere—truly, everywhere—and she seemed easily 15 years younger than she was.

That all came screeching to a halt, though, when she was hit by a distracted driver while out on one of her daily walks. Despite countless injuries, she survived the impact. Of course she did, we all thought. She truly seemed invincible.

She was recovering in the hospital, and things seemed like maybe they were going to be okay, but then she contracted an infection and went into a coma. Much of what happened next frames the story of our fictionalized Esperanza, so I won't go into it here. But that period when our larger-than-life friend was hovering between life and death was one of the hardest of my life.

Ultimately, the decision to let her hang on a little longer wasn't up to me, and someone else decided it was time. I'm not sure I'll ever get over that. We're coming up on a decade without her light in the world, which somehow feels like both 100 years and a week. Grief is funny like that.

It wasn't until after she died that I learned about Johnny (also not his real name). The rest of this story is fictionalized, with Callie and Will springing up from figments of my imagination to scaffold the story I desperately needed to tell.

I don't really know anything about Johnny or how he and Esperanza met. In real life, he was killed in action during the Korean War. And I do know, not long before she died, she told someone that he was the love of her life. The tragedy that they were separated by broken timelines never sat right with me.

I know it isn't real. But maybe somehow, in some otherworldly way, this story, Callie's story, will allow Esperanza and Johnny to be together. I can't change the past, but at least here, in these pages, this selfless person who brought so much joy to everyone around her can finally have her happy ending, too.

AUTHOR'S NOTE

I hope that by sharing this, she will live on and touch the lives of even more people. It matters, because she was so unique. I want the world to know someone like her was here.

Thank you so much for being a part of the journey.

Danielle Smyth

about the author

Danielle Smyth has dreamed of being a writer since childhood, and seeing that dream realized is the ultimate happy ending. When she's not writing, Danielle runs a small business. Her favorite days are spent traveling, eating tacos, and reading with her family.

Made in the USA
Middletown, DE
20 October 2025